A
LEGIONNAIRE'S GUIDE
TO
LOVE AND PEACE

A

LEGIONNAIRE'S GUIDE

TO

LOVE AND PEACE

A Novel

EMILY SKRUTSKIE

DEL REY

NEW YORK

Del Rey

An imprint of Random House
A division of Penguin Random House LLC
1745 Broadway, New York, NY 10019
randomhousebooks.com
penguinrandomhouse.com

A Del Rey Trade Paperback Original

ISBN 978-0-593-97407-0
Ebook ISBN 978-0-593-97421-6

Printed in the United States of America on acid-free paper

1st Printing

BOOK TEAM: Production editor: Cindy Berman • Managing editor: Paul Gilbert •
Production manager: Nathalie Mairena • Copy editor: Laurie McGee

Title page illustrations:
Sarah Skrutskie (figures); ricorico/iStock.com (banners);
jozefmicic/AdobeStock (path)

Book design by Alexis Flynn

The authorized representative in the EU for product safety and compliance is
Penguin Random House Ireland, Morrison Chambers, 32 Nassau Street, Dublin
D02 YH68, Ireland, https://eu-contact.penguin.ie.

For Mariano, because I didn't think I had this kind of
love story in me before

A
LEGIONNAIRE'S GUIDE
TO
LOVE AND PEACE

CHAPTER 1

DEATH WOULD COME FOR KATRIEN TODAY, BUT NOT UNTIL THE sun rose.

The eerie quiet of the war camp doubled the noise of every furtive step she took as she hurried down the rows of tents. Her height and bulk had never made her one for sneaking, but she gave it her best shot, keeping her head low and her senses battle-wary. The soldiers had been told last night that command's mercy had granted them a full extra hour before the dawn horns would sound, but it hardly mattered for Kat, who like many of her brethren had not slept a wink.

The misty haze that preluded the sun's rising was tinged with the scent of brimstone. It would only get worse in the light.

If questioned, she could probably fumble some excuse for her stealth. Most of the troops were nursing well-earned hangovers from last night, others dozing off a marathon run at the camp's Silk Row. Really, there was only one person she couldn't afford to be seen by, but as long as she took the right path, she'd make it back to her decade's tent unscathed.

Just as that thought was settling, a sharp voice snapped, "Katrien!"

Kat sprang to attention, whirling to find her centurion, Mira Morgenstern, staring after her with bruised blue eyes that suggested, though rank divided them, they were equal in sleeplessness.

"You should be resting," Mira said. There was a startling lack of reprimand in her voice. Kat had been well-trained never to expect sympathy from her, and she didn't know what to do with it, especially not on this fraught morning. Before the relief could settle, Mira's eyes narrowed. "What are you doing out on this end of the camp?"

Kat reeled for an answer—a lie—between her sleeplessness and the shot of pure adrenaline that was her commanding officer catching her. Over Mira's shoulder, she spotted a looming tent crowned with a latticed pattern of feathers and latched onto it like a lifeline. "I was praying," Kat offered, nodding to the chapel and patting the golden token that hung from a chain around her neck.

On any other morning, the charade would be transparent. In the three years Kat had served under Mira, her centurion had never once caught her seeking out the hosts—not for guidance, not for luck, not even for comfort. If Kat had any interest in the heavens' favor, the Aurean token she wore would be properly cultivated and brimming with angelic power. Instead, it was nothing more than an ornament, the second place people looked after her size had drawn their eye.

But who could blame her for seeking out the hosts on a morning like this one? If she was lucky, if the good life she'd lived was fitting in their eyes, she'd be welcomed into their fold later today, along with every other soldier in the vicinity. Just beyond the horizon lay the Mouth of Hell and the Demon Lord's foul citadel, and command had declared the full force of the seven assembled legions would be marching on it with no quarter. Nothing less would do when the High King of Hell was on the verge of alchemizing antigold and rendering himself immune to Aurean power. He would be unstoppable—though at the moment, with his scores of demonic generals, thousands of underlings fresh from the Mouth, and tens of thousands of thrall soldiers resurrected to fight in his name, Kat already wasn't optimistic about their chances. Even less so about her own personal odds of surviving the day on the front lines.

Though now that she thought about it, if she really wanted to get in good with the angels before they shook her hand, telling lies to her commanding officer wasn't tipping the scales in the right direction.

And then there was the matter of how she'd *actually* spent last night.

For a moment, Mira held her gaze with icy stillness, and Kat was certain she'd been sniffed out. But maybe the hosts were on her side after all, because after a beat, her centurion gave her a terse, approving nod. "Finally decided to take my advice?"

It took a heroic effort to keep her expression from souring. Mira wore ten Aurean tokens, each of them cultivated not just by her own effort but by generations of Morgensterns before her. They'd been placed in her hands with inherent power that Kat could never hope to match, and Mira knew nothing of the effort it would take to start fresh from a single piece.

At least, that had always been Kat's excuse, but it rang hollow even as she tried to muster the willpower to spit it out. Maybe she should have put more work into trying to draw her token's power. Maybe if she had, she'd have a fighting chance on the battlefield today.

"If I could somehow cultivate overnight, that would be incredible," Kat said instead, with as much diplomacy as she could manage. "But I figured it couldn't hurt to ask the hosts for mercy."

Mira's lips pursed sympathetically. She took a step toward Kat, lifting one hand to set it firmly on her shoulder. Kat fought the urge to bolt before her centurion got close enough to notice that Kat smelled less like incense, the mark of a long night spent in quiet contemplation in the chapel tent, and more like—

"Katrien," Mira said solemnly. "You're one of the finest soldiers I've ever had under my command. Even if you never reached your potential as an Aurean, I'm proud to have fought by your side. And if the worst comes to pass today, I'm sure the hosts will bless and protect you. I was just heading to the chapel myself to begin attuning for the day ahead," Mira added, glancing back over her shoulder at the tent.

Kat followed her gaze and immediately wished that the Mouth of Hell could get it over with and swallow her right away.

"Emory?" Mira called.

You weren't supposed to come this way, Kat wanted to mouth at him, but instead she wrestled her face into what she hoped read as pleasant surprise as the man stiffened and fumbled a gesture that landed somewhere between a wave and a salute. His hair was cut short enough that it barely looked rumpled, and the bags under his eyes were in-fashion enough not to stand out, if Kat and Mira were anything to go by. All things that could be explained by a night of restless tossing and turning, and *not* the fact that the last Kat had seen of him was barely ten minutes ago, and he'd been gloriously naked.

"Centurion," Emory said. "Kat," he added and tugged noticeably on his collar.

Nothing for it. Kat wasn't even going to make it to the battlefield today. She could practically feel Mira's confusion teetering toward suspicion through the hand her centurion still had anchored on her shoulder. "What are you doing on this end of the camp?" Kat asked, trying to make "*I thought we agreed you'd go* left" ring through in her tone.

But she couldn't keep herself from grinning. It was breathtakingly unfair, the way the world felt bright and full of romance on the day she was going to leave it.

Emory seemed to be fighting not to grin back, scuffing at the stubble on his cheek as if trying to smooth his features into obedience. "Ah well, the horns are still a ways away. I wanted to put a word in with the hosts before that," he said, hitching his thumb at the chapel tent.

Maybe Kat should have prayed for real. Holy intervention might be the only way the two of them got out of this unscathed. Mira's brow was furrowed, no doubt chewing over the two of them producing the exact same excuse for the exact same question. "I told him last night," Kat blurted. "The chapel closer to the officer tents is bound to be less crowded this morning."

In all likelihood, it was true. Aurean officers went to the chapel for quiet contemplation as they attuned their token arrays for the battle ahead. The infantry, on the other hand, could only pray, and there were more of them. The chapel tent closest to her decade was probably stuffed to bursting all night long. Everyone had been desperate for comfort last night—whether it be from the hosts, a bottle, or a warm body.

She couldn't be thinking of warm bodies right now. Not when Mira was looking between the two of them appraisingly. "This," she said after a long, breathless moment of deliberation, "is why the two of you are the hinge of your decade. Possibly the best hinge pair in the century. You can't train this kind of synchronicity. The fate of Telrus relies on soldiers like you two."

Hosts above, their centurion sounded like she might burst into tears at the mere thought. "There's only so much a coordinated battle pair can do—" Kat tried to interrupt, but Mira cut her off with a flick of her hand.

"Listen to me, Katrien. This is what's going to keep the two of you alive today. I shouldn't be saying this, but . . ." She glanced from side to side, then dropped her voice low. "As long as you stay focused, as long as you hold your line together like you always have, you'll last until . . ."

It was strange, the way she trailed off then. Kat had never

known Mira to be anything other than ruthless and practical, and if anyone was going to be blunt about their inevitable demise, it was her. So her next words couldn't be something along the lines of *until you meet an awful, bloody end at the hands of Hell's legions.*

And if that wasn't the case, what did their centurion know that the two of them didn't?

Emory's head had tilted to an angle she knew well, and Kat was certain he'd caught the same strange implication in Mira's silence. "Of course we'll give it our all," he said, meeting Kat's gaze.

On any other morning, she'd make a face behind Mira's back or saunter over and poke him in the ribs for sucking up to command. But the weight of his eyes on her took her back to mere hours ago, to staring into the bonfire shoulder to shoulder as around them the camp filled with the sounds of soldiers choosing their final indulgences. She'd been imagining herself burning on the tip of a demon general's flaming sword, buried under a pile of thralls, no spear in her hand, no shield at her back, and she'd let the craving for a *real* sensation to counter it push her inch by inch until she'd breached the distance between them with barely more than a brush of her arm against his.

Emory's warm brown eyes had snapped to hers immediately, full of that same clarity that was turning everyone around them into drunken fools, horny fools, or some combination of the two, and he'd said, "Let's get out of here"—less with certainty, more like a dam had suddenly crumbled all at once and he was lost in the flood.

If the way he looked at her now was anything to go by, the waters were still raging—and it was only in the burgeoning light graying the horizon that Kat understood what a monumentally *stupid* thing the two of them had done. Mira was right. Battle discipline held the century together. Order was everything in the legions of Telrus, and its fulcrum in the decade was the hinge pair—the battle partners who led from the core of the formation. Fraternization that threatened that discipline and focus was a grave offense, a disciplinary scar on your record that would follow you the rest of your days, precisely because it disrupted that synchrony they trained so desperately to achieve.

Emory was the shield to her spear, and together they made up the beating heart of the Third Century's first decade. For three years, they'd fought side by side, developing the perfect focus necessary to hold their line together at the fore. His unwavering discipline had kept her alive for three years, and so it was inevitable, really, that in the desperate scramble for a distraction in the face of a certain end, he'd been the first thing she'd turned to.

But if that end was less certain, then maybe they were doomed for other reasons—especially if Kat couldn't look him in the eye without an obvious heat rising in her cheeks, one the waning night was doing less and less to hide.

Maybe Emory had the right idea.

Maybe she'd have been better off spending the night praying to the hosts.

"Well, don't let me keep you from—" Kat tapped her token twice, then nodded to the chapel tent. She tried to tell herself it was for the best, the way Emory's face fell slightly as she turned her back and began to hustle toward the infantry section of the camp. It was in the hosts' hands now, and Kat only dared to ask for one thing more—if they could somehow do her a favor from beyond the Seal of Heaven and keep Mira in quiet contemplation long enough that their centurion never returned to her own tent.

There were few places for privacy in a war camp, especially in the infantry, where decades were quartered together ten to a tent. But the officers had been summoned to a high command meeting around midnight, leaving their section eerily empty and their luxurious individual tents an opportunity too good to pass up.

They'd broken Mira's cot.

By Kat's best estimates, she still had an hour until the horns sounded. It would be plenty of time to find a cold bucket of water and stick her entire head in—and maybe then she'd finally be ready to meet whatever fate the hosts had in store.

CHAPTER 2

THE NOISE WAS ASTOUNDING. NO MATTER HOW MANY BATTLES Kat weathered, she always forgot how senselessly loud everything got in the thick of it. The battlefield was awash in the screams of thralls hurling themselves artlessly against the century ranks, and the shrill peal of Mira's whistle barely cut through the clatter and squelch of bodies and weaponry colliding. Kat hefted her spear as the fore of their formation dropped back through the lines, leaving nothing but Emory between her and the slavering hordes.

She laid a hand on his shoulder, as she had hundreds of times over the past three years on the front. He bent low under the weight of his shield, sweat already trickling from beneath his helm. A droplet traced down the join of his shoulder, over the bruised impression of teeth.

She was back in her centurion's tent, no armor but her skin, laughing helplessly in the tangled remains of the cot their combined weight had collapsed.

"Kat," Emory murmured.

No, he muttered.

No, he *shouted*. Kat's grip on her spear tightened, and she barely got one foot back to brace before the next wave of thralls was upon them. She hadn't aimed—hadn't been thinking straight enough to sight her target—and she caught the thrall by the shoulder, the point of her spear lodging in sinew as it let out a horrific wail.

She'd never be used to this part either. To looking into a human face that had been stolen and twisted for the Demon Lord's foul purposes, into eyes that had gone glassy with their final rest, lodged in a body that still walked, animated by a scrap of demon flesh welded to the back of its neck. Driven now by its cruel lord's hunger for conquest, that body would throw itself ravenously against the legions of Telrus, doing everything in its reanimated power to drag new converts to the Demon Lord's cause from the ranks of the living until its vital functions had been, as they put it in training, "sufficiently destroyed."

A spear in the shoulder wouldn't do it. The thrall shoved hard into the blow, doing its damnedest to burn the shaft through Kat's palms. She tightened her grip and heaved, wrenching another scream from its throat.

All the battlefield's noise was awful, but this was the worst of it. Thralls could feel pain, but it never slowed them. They weren't really the enemy, only unfortunate corpses, and so Kat could never keep her sympathy at bay when she made them wail, even if they were relentlessly trying to kill her through all that writhing and screaming. The best she could do for them was gifting the poor things a quick, clean ending.

Usually she was better at it than this. With the first thrall caught on her spearpoint, there was nothing to stop the next one from slipping past and driving itself hard against Emory's shield. He met it with a grunt, his footing sure and steady as he deadened its momentum, shoved, and bludgeoned its neck with his shortsword. The slice bit deep enough that the thrall's entire body jerked, loosing another warbling howl at the indignity of losing its motor functions. Its head wobbled uncertainly, and Emory threw it back with another shove as Kat bore hard into the base of her spear and put the thrall she'd stuck on its ass.

It tried to get up, but another scrambled over it, their limbs catching in a haphazard tangle. Kat saw her opening. She yanked back her spear, lined her blow up with the fresh thrall's chest, and drove it home with everything she had. The sturdy iron tip plunged through ribs, through meat, through organs so vital none of Hell's magic could convince the dead to wake without them. Kat tugged, the thrall coming with her, and Emory stepped forward, punching ahead with his shield to clear the body from her spear.

Before Kat had been drafted, she'd imagined battle the way it sounded in stories. Heroes fighting valiantly back-to-back, blades whirling in dazzling forms that pushed the limits of each combatant's skill. The ugly reality was this: Battle was a machine, one Telrus had perfected over the long years since the Mouth opened and the Demon Lord's conquest spilled into their plane. The thralls were a mindless horde, and the only way to win against their overwhelming numbers was unbreakable order.

There was no elegance. You waited for the whistle. You moved with your decade rank, five soldiers across and five rows deep, one half of the century on either side of your centurion. You waited for her whistle. You took up your spear and thrust it into flesh until the whistle said you could stop.

And you hoped against all hope that you'd last until that call.

If there was any heroism on the lines, it was in the cooperation between battle partners. The shield, the spear, the work they did in tandem. Kat and Emory had survived three years honing their craft in the effort to beat back Hell's invasion that culminated in this long slog to the Mouth, but today was Telrus's last stand—the last chance they had to defeat the Demon Lord before he alchemized the end of Aurean power. Their odds were clear. Until their time was up, they'd continue to fight, continue to lead their line forward. Two pairs of battle partners on either side of them, five shields locked together in a line that advanced with every step Emory took, five spears that worked in a rhythm to match Kat's.

The only glory they could hope for was in the perfect, determined silence that hung between them.

But fatigue was inevitable. Spears began to dip. Shields began to shudder in their bearers' grips. On her left, Kat caught the flash of Sawyer's bared teeth. On her right, Ziva took her next squalling thrall with a bitter shout of her own. Exhaustion was sinking its claws in Kat, no matter how hard she rallied against it.

For all the fear and anxiety of being at the fore of the ranks, the relief of Mira's whistle was always paired with a pang of disappointment. Kat wanted to do *more*, to prove she could fight harder. Her spear had just gone clean through a thrall's guts when the shrill blast came, and the next pair behind her crowded at her back as she tried to jerk her weapon free from the poor corpse trying to pull its way down her shaft.

"Break, my count!" Emory shouted over the clamor, ramming the pommel of his sword four times into the back of his shield to mark it off, but he hesitated when Carrick and Elise dropped back on either side of him.

He wasn't supposed to hesitate. He'd never hesitated before.

"*Go,*" Kat grunted.

He caught her gaze, stricken, but she only ducked her head, dropping her bulk to her knees as the spearbearer behind her lunged forward and took the thrall through the eye. Kat hauled back, her spear coming free soaked with foul-smelling bile, and with Emory's shield tucked behind her, they rushed from the battle line and down the other four ranks to the rear of the century.

Under the clamor of battle, the back rank was a chorus of lungs wheezing like bellows. Some soldiers dropped to their knees for a brief respite, and the century's aides ran up and down the line, swiping already-filthy cloths over their gore-spattered weapons and offering sips from waterskins that carried a lukewarm, frothy brew laced with salt and stimulants. It was a moment to appreciate the mechanism of the Telrusian legions—a moment that could only happen because for a few brief minutes, they could do nothing but watch the machinery chew forward.

Kat tipped her head back, her spear's butt driven into the ground like an elder's cane as she bore her weight into it. She'd lost count of how many turnovers they'd been through today. The only markers that gave her a vague sense of the battle's progress were the red-ribboned flags that towered over the legions, each marking another hundred yards of ground gained.

There were far too few of them. The Mouth ahead seemed no closer than it had been this morning. Under the glare of the afternoon sun, its brimstone scent choked the air, making it even more of a fight for Kat to get her breath back. The Mouth's malevolent glow had a tendency to draw the eye, the pulse of flowing magma hypnotic even from this distance. It wasn't just magma. Kat barely understood the high science, but she knew it was forged by some interplanar magic that held the Mouth of Hell open and loosed its evil upon her world. Looking upon it felt like looking a predator in the eye. Like looking away would be your next mistake—and the last you ever made.

But the Mouth was trifling against the citadel that loomed beyond its gullet. The Demon Lord had built a shrine to his malice over the rift, a towering obsidian palace that reflected the Mouth's writhing glow. The High King of Hell was fortified within it, watching his armies make way for his evil as he inched closer and closer to alchemizing the end of Aurean magic and his own invincibility. From the reports—from the scouts who survived getting close enough—he was on the verge of succeeding.

It was for that reason Telrus had mustered seven legions and battled to his doorstep. The mire of this fight was the end result of decades spent pushing back against the invasion and six months pressing this ruthless offensive, but from where Kat sat, the distance between here and the citadel might as well have spanned to the moon overhead. There'd been a tacit understanding when the high command had distributed their marching orders. Today, there would be no retreat. Their job was to gain that ground, no matter the cost, until they couldn't anymore. To do everything in their power to beat back Hell itself—and when they had nothing left to give, to die.

Whistle. Another rank fell back, and the decade shuffled dutifully forward. With their breath recovered, their awareness could finally expand to include the rest of their rank—and as the hinge of the decade, it was up to Kat and Emory to make sure everyone was ready for their next turn at the fore. Already, Emory had his head bent close to Carrick's, the two shieldbearers shouting into each other's ears over the clash ahead.

Kat took stock of her panting spear line, catching Sawyer's eye at her right. "Problem?" she asked, eying his battle partner.

"Took a bad hit, and his shoulder's acting up again," Sawyer replied.

Kat hissed through her teeth. Carrick's old injury predated her time with the century, but at least that meant she knew how to handle it. "I'll back you up next turn. Let's try to keep them off his shield as much as possible."

"Giselle too?" Sawyer asked, glancing to his right, where the youngest and newest member of their decade was glaring at the fore of the lines with her whole body wound tight and her spear white-knuckled in her grip.

"What's your count, Giselle?" Kat hollered.

"Eighteen," Giselle replied, unblinking. As usual, battle had transformed her into a flighty ball of teenaged rage. They all suspected she was a runaway of some sort, a wisp of a blonde who'd thrown herself into the war on a mission of revenge she'd never deigned to fill the rest of them in on. As with all fresh recruits, she

wasn't particularly good at it—*eighteen, only eighteen?*—but she more
than made up for it with sheer tenacity that Kat, as a draftee,
scarcely understood.

Emory's attention wrenched away from Carrick. "Remember
what I told you. Stick them once, well."

Giselle gave him a coltish huff, but Kat wagered she'd be picking up the pace on their next rotation. Emory had taken the kid
under his wing the second she'd been assigned to their decade,
and she'd gone from barely knowing which end of the spear was
which to working in functional tandem with Gage, her big lug of
a shieldbearer. Emory had kept her alive—even if today it'd all
prove to be for naught.

"Let's let Giselle focus on getting that number up," Kat told
Sawyer with a firm hand on his shoulder. "You and I are more
than enough to get Carrick some space."

Whistle. Kat stepped back from Sawyer to let the next set of
battle partners pass through the ranks. The motion rocked her
into Emory's side, and he steadied her with a gentle hand at her
hip. "Easy," he murmured, close enough to send a thrill skittering
over her skin.

Here in the tight press of the midcentury, there was no choice
but to cozy up with your battle partner. Here was where they
leaned on each other, heads bent close to counter the relentless
noise. It was a place for prayers to the angelic hosts, for little luck
rituals, for anything you could grasp that would carry you through
your next turn at the fore.

"Strawberry rhubarb pie," Emory muttered in her ear.

Kat grinned. "High season, start of summer, when the berries
roll right off in your hands?"

"There was a patch down the road from the orphanage. They
always thought it was the raccoons sneaking in there at dusk to
lighten their harvest," he replied, boyish mischief sparkling in his
eyes. "But I couldn't take too many, because Miss Ophelia said
they'd raise the prices too high for her if their yield started to dip,

and if I wanted that pie, I couldn't exactly slip the berries for it into her stores one by one."

Kat could picture it with painful clarity, the wide-eyed, round-faced boy peering hopefully into the kitchen as the orphanage matron pushed her latest masterpiece into the oven. "Has to be Miss Ophelia's?"

Emory shrugged. "Haven't had a better one since, but on a day like today, I'm not picky. I'd kill for a slice from the baker in the next town on the road out of Hell, even if they can't make a crust worth a damn."

Kat leaned into him. "The point of the exercise is to dream big."

He chuckled. "Fine. *Miss Ophelia's* strawberry rhubarb pie. Though I'm gonna have to troop to the far end of the continent to get it. Your turn."

Kat tapped her chin. "Bread, fresh from the oven."

"Just *bread*?"

"There's no such thing as *just bread*. Especially not when it's so fresh it steams when you tear it in half."

"You can't tell me to dream big and then pick *bread*, Kat. Not today."

"Fresh from the oven, though—"

"Bread."

Emory was doing that thing that drove her absolutely out of her skull, the thing where he tried like hell to maintain a serious, stoic face when she could see the laughter he'd bottled steaming out of his ears. The press of the ranks, the clatter of gear, the stench of death—all of it came second to the way he looked at her with that suppressed humor sparkling in his eyes. She tugged his chinstrap, dropping his helm forward.

Focus. They needed to focus. They needed to make it one more turn if Emory was going to eat his matron's strawberry rhubarb pie again, if Kat was going to have another chance to savor the simple pleasure of fresh bread. The mere thought of those delights was one of the easiest ways to convince yourself the fore was worth surviving—and through the long years at the front, the two of them had never drawn a blank when dreaming of the food they'd have on the other side of this war.

Whistle. A nervous silence fell over their decade as they stepped up, now separated from the fore by only one line of battle pairs. Their breathing was starting to accelerate as one. Emory moved back into position ahead of her, his shield loose at his side until the moment he needed to heft it.

"This morning," Kat whispered, and Emory tensed. "I thought we agreed that I'd take the south path out of the officer section, you'd take the north."

This wasn't the time. She could get this answer later. But with every turn at the fore, *later* was getting more and more impossible. Fatigue was setting in. And Kat couldn't take not knowing.

"You went to the chapel instead," she said, bending close enough that she could feel the heat off his neck. "How come?"

Emory turned back just enough that she could see the edge of his smile. "Had to put a word in with the hosts. Needed to say thank you."

And before Kat could spin him around and demand to know what *that meant,* the whistle blew once more. The rank ahead broke back, Emory took a steady step forward, and Kat moved in tandem, her spear coming up to maintain the distance he needed to lock his shield into the decade's line.

The ugly monotony of battle took over, but between the thralls in her own way and the extra help she was lending to Sawyer, Kat's focus was hopelessly scattered. She needed something better than fresh bread, something to fix her mind on that would keep her hungry for a future that was looking bleaker by the minute.

But every time she asked herself what she craved, she couldn't help circling back to that morning. To the feeling of Emory beneath her. To the way he'd laughed when he didn't have to put on a show as the hinge shield and the way she'd wished she could hear him laugh like that—*make* him laugh like that—at least once more before the end.

Yearning wasn't doing her attention any favors. Kat barely registered the change in the wind. The brimstone scent that crept stronger and stronger into the dust they kicked up. The shadow that loomed from beyond the choke of the thralls.

"*Shock knight!*" a voice howled over the fray.

The icy fear that gripped her had little equal on the battlefield. Across the line, spearbearers dropped to one knee behind their shieldbearers as the second-rank shields lunged forward to lock in place above them. Kat ducked low, keeping her spear braced as she angled it through the gap next to Emory's head.

When the demon hit the line, it felt like the world had ended. The force of it rattled through the entire decade at once—shattering, thundering, grinding them into the dirt. Kat dug her weight into Emory's back, doing her best to keep him upright against the towering lieutenant of Hell's ghastly strength. Through the gap in the shields, she could only make out pale, leathery skin, swelling muscle, and the flash of iron-tipped horns.

"Push, my count! One, two, three—" Emory's shout vibrated through her, every shieldbearer in the fore joining in a wordless chorus as they shoved in unison and threw the demon on its heels.

From the heart of the century, the whistle shrieked—not the sharp blast of a rank changeover, but a long scream that could only mean one thing.

In the desperate seconds before the shock knight recovered its footing, the ranks parted clean down their middle.

And from their heart, Mira charged.

The centurion hit the demon like a ballista bolt, knocking all nine feet of it back on its thrashing tail as it howled in outrage and swiped at her with a claw-tipped hand. Mira caught the hit with a crack across the buckler strapped to her left arm, and before it could swing again, she leaped into the sky—five yards, easily— and held her sword aloft.

It caught the murderous red glow of the Mouth and turned a molten, angelic, radiant gold.

An Aurean going full tilt was a spectacle, and Kat could never tear her eyes away. Around her neck, Mira's ten tokens gleamed— some for speed and power, some for the radiance that blazed from her sword, and one in particular that lightened her mass, letting her move like a firework when the occasion arose. Since her time in the chapel this morning, she'd clearly maintained perfect attunement, chaining the power of all ten together to multiply the effect of each tenfold. If that focus slipped, even for a minute, it would take the centurion at least a half an hour to put it back together again. She was a miracle to watch in battle, and as the ranks re-formed, Kat could barely keep her eyes on the point of her spear as the decade braced to catch any thrall who slipped past the brawl playing out ahead of their line.

Mira came down hard on the demon, her sword searing deep into the meat of its ashen red shoulder. It howled, tossing its head, and its horns caught the side of her torso, crunching against the gleaming, battered plate armor she wore. The hit sent her rolling right to the feet of the century, her golden blond battle braids spilling from her helmet as she spat dirt and sprang to her feet.

The shock knight was a smart one. It knew not to give her a second to breathe.

Mira tried to brace, to catch the oncoming blow and counter it with every ounce of strength she'd cultivated into her tokens. To her credit, she managed to snag the horns aimed at her throat and root her feet before they closed the distance. But the demon's momentum was relentless, and though she dug deep ruts into the already-churned earth, it shunted her back.

Back into the fore.

The ranks split for Mira again, but not on purpose. The fore dissolved into a messy tangle of limbs struggling to get out of the way, that famous Telrusian war discipline blown back like a bough in a storm. Somewhere in the jumble, Mira's glowing sword flashed again, plunging into demon flesh. All thoughts of food left Kat's mind entirely at the stench.

The demon twisted, and no amount of host-granted lightness could deaden the wrecking ball Mira made in her heavy armor as her foe smashed her through the ranks of her soldiers. Kat lost her footing. Lost her spear. Nearly lost her wits as something cracked her hard across her helm.

"Re-form," Mira snapped. "Get back in line, you fucking—"

Kat hauled to her knees. The chaos in her periphery felt far too distant. The line. Where was the line?

There. Two full yards from where she'd landed.

Which was another two yards from where her spear had ended up.

Which was barely any distance at all from the feet of the nearest thralls.

Kat's fist closed around the Light of Angels token swinging from her neck, the sun sigil grinding into the roughened calluses on her palm. She was an Aurean in name only. She'd never learned to channel angelic power through the token she wore, and even if she had, its light alone was never going to save her.

She held it anyway. She was about to die, and she wanted her mom, and this was the closest she was going to get.

"Kat!"

The shout split through her haze, as Emory's voice always tended to. Her head snapped up to find a thrall bearing down on her. Her other fist sealed around nothing but air. Fists would have to do, then. She held them up, squaring to the lunging thrall.

Kat was expecting it to knock the wind out of her, but instead the thing that took her breath away was the soldier who threw himself between her and the mindless, slavering husk. Emory hit the thrall in a full-body tackle, his shield knocking it back a yard as he brought his shortsword up to catch the next one approaching in the gut. Kat's brain found its foothold in the sight.

He'd broken the line. He'd come for her. The absolute *fool*.

She couldn't let it be for nothing.

Kat dove for her spear, coming up in a roll as she swept it in a wide arc that snapped the first ankle it found and sent the attached thrall toppling into its fellows. Behind her, the decade was shouting their heads off, a wall of tumultuous noise that totaled to *Get your ass back in line*. They needed their hinge. She wasn't equipped to take on a horde solo.

But she wasn't solo. Kat's back found Emory's, and her muscle memory locked in. They'd drilled this before a thousand times. Telrusian tactics on the smallest scale imaginable. A century of two. Shield and spear in perfect harmony. And yet, it wasn't that perfect harmony, that dream of battle, that Kat was thinking of as she flew into motion, desperately plunging her spear into whatever flesh would take it. It was the messy tangle of last night, the imperfect joy of it, the way she'd thought, *If this is the end of everything I fought for, at least we had this*.

"The devil-loving *fuck* do you two think you're doing?" Mira's ragged voice howled from somewhere above them. Kat didn't dare look up. Any spare glance now was just asking for a thrall to spring into her lapse in focus.

She probably should have. It would have helped her notice the shock knight had set its sights on easier prey than an Aurean.

The demon plowed into them, turning them from toy soldiers to rag dolls in the blink of an eye. Kat's brain lagged again, the pain and terror struggling to catch up to her until the moment she tried to draw her next breath and found she couldn't—not with the shock knight's weight bearing down on her. Something twitched beneath her back. It was probably Emory.

This, then, was how it must end. The shock knight rearing back off them, its horrifically huge fist cocked back for the blow that would finish it. The thralls crowding in at the edge of her periphery, hungry glints in their eyes. Her centurion closing at Aurean-fast speed and still too slow. Her decade watching in terror. Her battle partner stirring feebly, unable to do anything but accept the death he'd volunteered for when he enlisted.

Kat hadn't signed up for this, hadn't chosen this death, but she could choose how she met it. She fought to keep her eyes open.

So she didn't miss a single second of the meteor streaking overhead.

The light scored across her vision so blindingly that for a moment she was certain this was it, this was death, this was the hosts welcoming her with open arms and golden radiance. But her body was still in an unconscionable amount of pain, and no blow was coming down to put her out of her misery.

The shock knight's face was tipped skyward, its mouth hanging open. The thralls cowered, covering their eyes.

The demon came unstuck. Kat braced for the blow, but instead it shoved off them, doing her shattered ribs no favors, and broke into a sprint like a startled deer bolting, tearing through thralls as it cut a line clean across the battlefield in the direction of the citadel.

Whatever the shock knight thought it could accomplish, it was already too late. The meteor struck the citadel with little fanfare. From this distance, it was difficult to tell, but it seemed to have vanished into one of the looming arches that crowned the highest tower—the ones from which the High King of Hell was sometimes spotted watching over his minions' foul work.

The noise of battle fell away. Every living soul held its breath.

The next burst of light put the meteor to shame. In a blink, it had washed the battlefield in golden glory and vanished just as quickly, spilling from every crevice of the citadel and intensified by every obsidian facet of it. In its wake, Kat swore she could hear the toll of angelic bells.

Then every thrall on the field slumped like a puppet with its strings cut.

The noise came back all at once, a confused warble working its way toward a roar from the ranks as some wondered what had just happened, some voiced a justified suspicion, and others skipped right ahead to screaming in triumph. Kat rolled sideways, regretting it instantly, and found Mira toeing one of the thralls, then prodding her sword deep into its flesh in a way Kat found distasteful. But live thralls never passed up an opportunity to scream over every little injury.

This one was grave-silent.

Beneath the jumble of the Telrusian confusion, a shudder built like the rumble of a stampede. Even though it felt like a knife was twisting in her side, Kat shoved herself upright, her pain-glazed vision snaring on the distant lip of the Mouth. Either she was hallucinating—not impossible—or it was *moving*.

Her eyes latched onto the pinprick of the shock knight that had just beat the ever-loving shit out of her. Every demon on the field sprinted for the Mouth. A tidal wave of bodies flowed out of the citadel proper, demons pouring from every opening like ants whose colony had just been flooded. They flung themselves into the Mouth, plunging down its interplanar throat without a second of hesitation.

And the Mouth was getting smaller. As its shoreline receded, the citadel foundation that sat atop it began to crumble away. The whole structure lurched like a drunk, then bent like a drunk trying to tie his boots, then gave a final inebriated heave and lost its constitution entirely as it toppled into the Mouth.

Just before it crossed the rim, five sparks of light rocketed from the part that had formerly been its precipice, arcing high over the chaos beneath them. One rose above the rest with a showy little flourish of a starburst, timed impeccably with the moment the Mouth sealed, its murderous, molten glow fading to a cool, stony basalt.

Kat was in an outrageous amount of pain. Reality bled fuzzy at the edges. But she could have sworn—though distance made it somewhat difficult to tell, and the legions' confused noise wasn't helping—that the rising star, blazing over the battlefield, shouted something that sounded suspiciously close to "You're welcome!"

CHAPTER 3

A THOUSAND YEARS AGO, WHEN THE HOSTS KNEW THEY COULD no longer remain on the material plane, they forged hundreds of thousands of tokens imbued with angelic power as a gift to humanity. Some granted the bearer strength, others agility, others great feats of mental acuity. In this moment, Kat owed the hosts many prayers of thanks that at the Forging, they saw fit to create healing tokens.

What would have been months of recovery time was cut down to the span of an afternoon under a well-cultivated healer, and the Telrusian legions had drafted every single one of them they could muster over the course of the campaign. But a single Health of Angels token stamped with healing power was one thing. Deadening the pain that was part of the process was another kind of token entirely—and a Balm of Angels token wasn't necessary to wear the striped red sash of the legions' healers. Some were fortunate enough to have both tokens in their lineage. Of those, a handful could attune to both at once, their attentions cultivated into a potent mix of relief and restoration.

Kat had not scored one of those lucky few. The only comfort she had to offset the pain was a strip of leather lodged between her teeth as she sat on a bench in the med tent with a healer running one hand over her back, the other clutching their token. Kat's body had racked up its fair share of scarring over her time at the front, and she'd had the misfortune of having her bones reset a few times before, but never so many at once. She'd asked the healer not to tell her the total. She knew it was worse counting down.

It was also worse when your entire decade was packed in the med tent with you, but that couldn't be avoided. It was more efficient—always the bottom line when it came to orders from the high command—to have all non-dire injuries seen to in a batch, and so Kat was seated side by side with the rest of the spear line, gritting through the pain as Sawyer leaned over her to wave his hand and get Brandt's attention.

"You gonna tell the nice doctor how you hurt your head?" Sawyer simpered.

Brandt huffed. "I'm gonna tell Mira, is who I'm gonna tell. That asshole in the second decade needs to get written up. She's had it out for me for a *year*."

"He knocked his skull on a spear during a changeover," Sawyer explained to the healer with a barely restrained grin. On the bench across from them, Carrick snorted.

Kat knew she should probably be trying to keep her spears in line, but then she'd have to roll the bones on whether she could manage spitting out the leather strap, making her point, and getting it back in before she cracked a tooth.

Brandt's battle partner could have helped, but Javi was pointedly ignoring his spearbearer's bluster. As usual, he had his nose buried in a battered book that looked to be held together by nothing but valiant stitching and a whole lot of hope as another healer ran a diagnostic hand up and down his shield arm. Kat tuned out Sawyer's razzing, trying to pick out the title. It was easier than looking to Javi's left, where Emory was bent double under the ministrations of yet another healer who hadn't lucked into a token that could absorb the incredible amount of pain it'd take to set him to rights. He, too, had leather in his teeth.

He whimpered around it, and Kat swore the temperature in the tent ticked up a couple degrees.

"So what I heard," Carrick muttered to Elise, the other shield-bearer barely bothering to lean in, "is that the whole thing was a setup. Even if the Demon Lord was close to alchemizing antigold, marching on the citadel made no sense. We never could have taken it—we were meat under a pestle. Or . . . metaphor, metaphor—"

"Bait," Giselle piped up from the far end of the spear bench.

Carrick pointed to her. "Bait. Because the real strategy all along was to send in those Aureans."

"Those weren't Aureans," Brandt interjected.

"You got hit in the head, what do you know?" Sawyer sniped, and Kat yelped around her gag as Brandt knocked into her trying to take a swipe at him. Fortunately Brandt's injuries did more to subdue him than any of the healers could, and he dropped back to the bench clutching his forehead.

"Easy," Ziva said, elbowing Sawyer from his other side. "If they were Aureans, how come we've never seen anything like them before? You'd think high command would use assets like that if they had them."

"They were gold. They were glowing," Sawyer countered, counting on his fingers. "They were just doing it a lot brighter than anyone we've ever seen. 'Sides, what else would they be?"

"The hosts themselves," Giselle's battle partner, Gage, offered from the end of the shield line. It sounded outrageous in their low, tremulous voice, but the kind of outrageous that felt just shy of right. Who but the hosts themselves could kill the Demon Lord and crumble the Mouth of Hell? Maybe the Seal of Heaven had finally broken after a thousand years, and divine mercy once again shone on Telrus. Maybe they'd entered the promised age at last—one where Aurean might was no longer the only thing capable of standing against the forces of evil.

"Wasn't the hosts." On the shieldbearers' bench, Elise bent forward over her knees, glancing conspiratorially up and down the lines. "Night before last, I wanted to know what the centurions were up to, so I snuck into that secret meeting. And then the even more secret meeting the high command called after *that*."

"Bullshit," Brandt blurted, but Kat caught Ziva's eye across Sawyer's midsection. The two of them had compared notes on the morning before the battle—Kat because she felt she might burst if she didn't tell Ziva about her whirlwind night with Emory and Ziva to lament because her battle partner hadn't come back last night, which almost certainly meant she'd scored with the gorgeous cook the two of them had spent the entire campaign fighting over. But if Elise had been skulking around the centurions instead—

"They've been holding out on us," Elise said. "Waiting until we were close enough to strike without missing. *That's* why we were pushing for the citadel. It was never supposed to be a suicide run. What I think I heard—*think*," she couched, "is that we were clearing a path for a team of heroes to make a surprise attack. And one of those heroes is a hundred-token Aurean."

"*Bullshit*," Brandt echoed even more vehemently and immediately flinched.

"Impossible," Carrick agreed.

Javi's book snapped shut. "It's feasible," he declared.

"Oh, *feasible*," Carrick muttered, waggling his eyebrows at Sawyer.

"It would take an incredible mind to wield a hundred tokens at once. Even with each piece cultivated individually, it must take half a day to attune them all together, but I don't see why one couldn't, given enough time."

"You ever read about anything like that?" Ziva asked, nodding to the book in Javi's lap.

"In one book—"

"Novel or history?" Carrick interrupted.

". . . Novel," Javi muttered, deflating. "If you want *history,* the great Magnus Lythos holds the record at seventy-two, which he only achieved at the age of sixty, and that was a hundred years ago."

"Right, yes, how could we forget?" Brandt groaned with his head between his knees.

"Could you all stop being assholes?" Elise asked. "Nothing but a hundred-token Aurean was going to take out the Demon Lord."

"Then why even bother with infantry?" Giselle muttered. A hefty silence settled over the tent, quiet enough that Kat could hear the healer currently wrestling her ribs back into place breathe a faint sigh of relief.

Kat loosened her jaw, letting the leather drop gracelessly into her lap. "Because we can't leave it all to the Aureans," she gritted out. "Like you said, Javi, we've never seen anything past seventy-two in our lifetimes—and even Magnus Lythos probably couldn't have gotten the job done. So we all had to do our part to keep the forces of evil at bay, even if all we could do was stick a spear in some thralls and pray the demons never broke our line. Many of you chose to be here. Some of us didn't. But we showed up. We did our part. And look at us!"

She caught the eyes of each and every soldier in her decade. Most were staring at her as if she'd sprouted a second head.

"We marched to the edge of the Mouth. We faced the legions of Hell at their doorstep, and we held fast. We . . ."

The next words wouldn't come. Kat's throat closed tight

around the possibility of stating something that was by all counts true but still impossible to believe. *We lived. We survived to the war's end.*

Worse, her gaze settled on Emory, on the way he'd leaned slightly forward while she was talking, the way he seemed to be begging her to go on. Because if the war was truly, *truly* finished, well.

There had been no conversation yet—not about what they'd shared, and not about what had changed between the choice they made at the fireside and the moment they now faced, where the future was suddenly full of possibilities. Possibilities Kat had *entertained,* certainly, as a thought experiment, as a natural consequence of being joined at the hip to a handsome young soldier for the past three years, but not ones she'd considered with any seriousness.

Now they sat in the aftermath of their indiscretion, paying for it bone by mended bone. No other member of their unit had been beaten as badly as the two of them. They'd failed their decade as its hinges, and true to every warning about fraternization they'd ever been preached, it had nearly cost them their lives.

"You were victorious," a new voice announced.

Every spine in the tent straightened, some with more success than others. Kat, for her part, instantly wished she hadn't dropped her gag as she learned the healer's hands were nowhere near completing their work. But in the presence of a centurion—and in the presence of Mira Morgenstern in particular—you couldn't afford to slouch.

"At ease," Mira said, but it had the weight of a dare, and none of them had the temerity to test its bounds. She stood at the entrance to the med tent, her posture prim and perfect with her hands folded neatly behind her back, accentuating the ten golden tokens that lay in a single rank across her chest, hung on chains that wove with the spill of her glossy, flaxen hair.

They never saw her with it down from its battle braids. It was yet another reminder of the aftermath they lived in, uncontestable proof that the world had shifted.

"Katrien is right," Mira continued. "The infantry may not have had the glory of winning this war, but you had the honor of fighting it, and were it not for our efforts, there wouldn't have been an opening for the finishing blow in the first place. As to the nature of that blow, as Elise has so helpfully informed you, securing herself latrine duty for the next three weeks—"

Elise sucked a breath through her teeth.

"—it was indeed the work of Aureans who have been training for this moment their entire lives. There will be a briefing for the century later this evening, but I can see it might not be soon enough, given the amount of misinformation certain elements in this decade tend to spread."

Her imperious gaze landed pointedly on Sawyer before crossing to the shieldbearers and making sure Carrick knew she had him in her sights as well.

"Of far more immediate concern to you sorry fuckers . . ." Mira said, and a twinge rattled through Kat. Mira's tone only dropped from that haughty, overeducated high-speak to the scuzz of common infantry for two reasons. The first was that she was mid-battle and ready to kill.

The second—

"We have a disciplinary matter to settle."

Pain had obliterated enough of Kat's common sense that she opened her mouth to confess right then and there. *Yes, I broke regulation and had a consensual encounter with my battle partner and fellow hinge. Yes, in your cot.* She could add, *In my defense, we were both sure we'd die yesterday,* but she doubted it'd buy her any sympathy.

Mira's focus, however, was still centered on the shieldbearers' bench. "We are all very lucky to be alive, but none more so than Emory here. And because I was out fighting ahead of the lines at the time, I had the great fucking misfortune of watching him violate a precept I believe I've drilled into you all more times than I can count. Anyone care to share what it was? *Other than you,*" Mira added as Emory tried to dislodge his gag.

"He broke rank," Giselle piped up from the opposite bench, and Emory frowned at the protégée he'd trained perhaps a bit too well.

Mira gave her a stiff nod that was, in her language, the equivalent of gushing praise and a pat on the head. "The line was intact—a fucking miracle after that shock knight got right into it. Your only job when something like that happens is to make sure that shield wall is rock-solid for the next hit. You're the hinge shield of this decade, Emory. If their order gets disrupted, it's your sacred duty to guide them back to it. And instead, you threw yourself out ahead of the rest of the century. Spit that thing out and tell me why."

Emory's gaze found Kat's as he pulled the leather strap from between his teeth. It felt fraught, felt *obvious* in plain sight of their decade and their centurion, but Kat couldn't tear herself away. "I'm only half of the hinge," he said roughly. "My battle partner had been knocked out ahead of the century. I saw an opening to cover her so she could get back in line."

Kat had never heard him deliver a wrong answer so confidently before. She wondered if the healer noticed the kick in her pulse as dread began to dampen her palms.

"What you did," Mira said, a lethal edge in her tone, "was choose the life of a single soldier over a hundred. The century lives and dies by that line, and you thought it was worth punching a hole in it to protect one person."

Emory's breath caught—whether from physical pain or from the shame of Mira's reprimand, Kat wasn't sure. Unlike most of their unit, Emory was an enlisted man. He'd spent his entire adult life in the service of the Telrusian army, signed on for twenty years where most of them would serve only five. Up until recently, his record had been completely unblemished. And Kat had helped him break that streak.

"It was my fault," she blurted. "I should have gotten back in line faster. He never should have felt like he needed to defend me in the first place." Her memories of the moment were a tumult of panic in the wake of the shock knight's blow, but surely there was something she could have done. Surely Mira would understand.

But Mira was pursing her lips, shaking her head, and looking at her with terrifying fondness. "You're wrong about the first part, but the second bit is right. Emory moved on the assumption you couldn't defend yourself, but you're a single-token Aurean and a seasoned warrior with three years of service under your belt. Why he felt the need to come to your aid—"

Kat tried to school her features into perfect blankness that only got more difficult as Mira's brow furrowed in uncertainty. She looked like she was right on the edge of figuring out why she'd needed to requisition a new cot last night.

But before Kat could take another haphazard stab at deflecting suspicion, Mira seemed to arrive at an entirely different conclusion, if the diabolical grin she flashed was anything to go by. Her attention snapped to the healer at Emory's back. "Make sure he's in top shape. Ahead of the briefing tonight, I'd like to put on a demonstration bout for the troops. One that should put to rest any notions that Katrien needs defending. Emory, you'll duel her. Spear to sword."

Jeers and claps echoed up and down the benches as the decade realized the spectacle they were in for. Kat and Emory locked eyes again.

A slight smile tugged the corner of his lips. She'd be in so much trouble if she mirrored it.

"Put him on his back, Kat," Mira added before sweeping out of the tent—and thank the hosts for that, because Kat was momentarily gripped by the urge to blurt that she already had.

CHAPTER 4

IN THE HOURS THAT PRECEDED THE ASSEMBLY, KAT FOUND HERSELF seized by an absurd hope. The war had been long enough, hadn't it? Weren't they all sick of fighting by now? Mira's briefing was mandatory, but the demonstration bout was scheduled as a prelude. Surely the rest of the century would rather have the free time than be forced to watch something so base and violent and, frankly speaking, unnecessary.

She should have known better. The beaten dirt patch ahead of the Third Century's command tent was clotted with more than a hundred people—easily close to two hundred, by Kat's war-honed estimation—which meant that not only had every rank turned up early for the briefing, but other soldiers from the greater legion had gotten wind of what was about to happen and decided to pack in.

"I should have let that shock knight finish the job," Kat groaned.

At her elbow, Ziva smirked. "Don't act like you're not going to have fun with this."

"I'm not," Kat whined, only half lying. She agreed with Mira's assessment. Emory had made a staggering mistake, one he should have been far above as the decade's hinge shield. But though Kat's pride demanded she show him just how stupid it had been to come after her, it was waging outright war with the part of her that craved another bite of him. To humiliate him badly enough for the lesson to stick was to threaten her own prospects.

Ziva seemed to find it all invigorating. "What's the worst that could happen?" she asked with a shrug and a grin that told Kat she knew exactly how out of hand this could get.

"Maybe if I knock him down fast . . ." Kat muttered, but she knew that was just wishful thinking. Mira wanted a spectacle— a teachable moment for the whole century. Kat would have to take Emory out of commission entirely to earn them an early reprieve, and the healers could only fix so much.

Also, as she knew from dueling him many a time before, Emory wouldn't go down easy.

She risked a glance across the circle that had been chalked in the dirt to mark the bounds. Emory stood on the far side, turning the wooden training sword he'd been issued over and over in his hands as Carrick shook him by the shoulder, muttering in his ear. He looked relaxed, almost contemplative, but Kat knew better. The motion was the tell—his desperate attempt to adjust to the unfamiliar weight of the waster before that sword became his sole defense. He knew what was coming, and he knew his dignity—as a soldier, and especially as a hinge shield—was on the line.

He caught her eye, and even from this distance, Kat could see the smile he was fighting to keep down.

It's not funny, she wanted to shout, but maybe it was. A bit. Maybe that's why this whole thing felt surreal. Just days ago, she couldn't fathom finding joy in fighting ever again. That desperation to use her body for something else, something far less brutal, had gotten them into their little predicament in the first place.

And now here she was, a war at her back, unable to deny the part of her itching to step into that ring.

A sharp whistle rang out over the assembled crowd, and every eye snapped to the wooden platform that stood at the front of the command tent, where Mira towered resplendent in her officer's kit. Kat suppressed a frown at the sight of her centurion so polished. She hadn't seen Mira dressed up like this in years, and nothing about this occasion warranted it. She wore an intricate ceremonial chestpiece—not the battered one that saw battle— and her pauldrons had been polished to a shine that matched her ten tokens, which she wore on display instead of safely tucked beneath her shirt.

"Third Century!" Mira called over the crowd, and roughly half the assembled soldiers thumped their chests in acknowledgment. "And guests," she added, drawing some good-natured cheers from the interlopers. "We're leading off today's excitement with a little demonstration. A reminder that though we may have downed the High King of Hell and sent his foul servants back to the heart of the abyss, that's no reason for our fighting prowess to lose its legendary edge."

Ziva and Kat exchanged a long-suffering look. Trust Mira to make a bout like this sound like duty, rather than performance.

"Our duel today will be fought spear to sword. Our combatants hail from the first decade among our ranks. Our sword, Emory!"

On the far side of the ring, he hoisted his weapon, drawing a wave of frothy shouts and applause from the crowd.

"And our spear, Katrien!"

Kat lifted her sturdy wooden spear, and the noise doubled.

It was hard not to let it go to her head. She knew part of it was simple logic. In a duel between spear and sword with no shield in the mix, spear was always the favorite, and people liked sure bets. Most of these soldiers barely knew her beyond the token that hung from her neck—a rarity among infantry—and the fact that she towered over most of them.

But maybe some of them remembered the training bouts where she'd put on a good show or her turns on the front where she'd led her decade in thralls dispatched. Maybe she had a smidge of a reputation to maintain as her decade's hinge spear. It couldn't hurt to build some credit with her comrades, especially not in this moment where she risked very little.

She just wished it didn't have to come at the expense of Emory's dignity.

"Combatants, take your places," Mira announced.

Kat bent low enough for Ziva to knock her knuckles against the leather helmet that protected her skull. "Don't get too carried away," Ziva warned with a knowing look.

Kat fought back a grin as she stepped up to the edge of the ring. She levered down the point of her spear, bracing one hand against the heel. The tip was blunted, but it didn't do anything to calm the shudder of nerves that nearly overtook her as she trained it on her opponent. They were both clad in padded practice armor, but they'd weathered enough bruises and fractures in training to know how much good that did against a properly aimed blow.

Emory squared to her, both hands firm on his sword grip. He looked off-balance without a shield to even him out. Vulnerable, even. With a shield in his hand, she'd be hard-pressed to keep him off her.

Without one, he was going to have the fight of his life trying to get past her reach.

"Ready!" Mira shouted, then blasted once on her whistle.

Emory was the one with something to prove here. He was the one who lunged before Kat had a chance to step forward off the boundary line. The crowd roared as he swung hard, shunting the tip of her spear aside, but she planted her feet and countered his strength, the length of her weapon giving her the leverage she needed to make it easy. He was forced to dance back before the dull spearhead could catch him in the gut, but he didn't have time to reset his stance before Kat was springing forward.

She caught him square in the chest.

The whistle screeched, the soldiers jeered in approval, and under the cascade of noise, Kat mouthed *Sorry*.

Emory grimaced, but there was a dangerous, playful spark in his eyes, one that promised to get back at her one way or another.

"Again," Mira called, and again the whistle sounded.

Kat took the initiative this time, her spear held low as she sprang at him. Emory blocked with a fluidity she fully expected. For the three years they'd been partnered, they'd trained these movements over and over, sparring, honing, dragging each other through exercise after exercise, all in the name of coming back alive, and they *had*. The absence of that weight now made the fight feel surreal. With the stakes removed, it was more of a dance than anything. A dance with two hundred pairs of eyes watching their every move.

Watching as Emory tried to step in through the deflection and move up into her space. The sudden surge of noise from the crowd nearly drowned out Kat's instinct as Emory plunged down her shaft, his sword cocked back. Too close to block. Too close to do anything but—

Kat ducked her head and threw herself forward. The headbutt caught him right on the rim of his own protective helm, and it took everything in her power for Kat to keep her feet as the force of their collision rattled through her brain. Emory wasn't so lucky. The impact knocked him down to one knee, and before he could get his wits about him, she had her spear pulled around to square the tip over his heart.

His surprised grunt was swallowed by the crowd's eruption. Mira's whistle barely surfaced over the noise.

Kat blinked. She'd been trying to catch him off guard, but she hadn't expected to succeed so spectacularly. Had getting in close thrown him off that much? In penance, Kat bent, offering a hand, and Emory let her pull him back to his feet. "Sorry's not gonna cut it for this one, huh?" she muttered in his ear.

"I might have seen the hosts for a second," he replied, dazed but still smiling. Kat clapped him on the back, and he knocked his shoulder into hers. "Think she's had enough, or—"

"Again," Mira barked.

They exchanged a rueful look. Kat had a sneaking suspicion one of them would have to break a bone to get the centurion to call it—as well as a far more certain sense that Emory wasn't learning a damn thing from this. As they retreated to opposite sides of the chalk circle once more, she racked her brain for *something* that would convince Mira this farce didn't need to go on any longer, but the crowd's shouts and heckling made it nigh impossible to think.

Unless . . .

She caught Emory's eye, planted the heel of her spear, and flexed her grip. He grinned, tilting his sword outward as if inviting her in, and she knew he'd read her as easily as he did in the thick of battle.

Mira wanted a spectacle. They'd give her one.

At the sound of the whistle, Kat let go. Her spear toppled out of her grasp as she charged forward, and Emory threw down his sword, lunging to meet her. They collided, padded armor barely stopping them from knocking the wind out of each other. Kat grappled at him, fists latching in whatever cloth or skin she could find, desperately, *desperately* trying to ignore the memories conjured at the feeling of his body under her hands. It was crude, undignified, hardly befitting of a proud Telrusian soldier.

And the proud Telrusian soldiers watching them fucking loved it. The noise tripled in volume, and with no weapons to duck, they surged to the edges of the circle, hooting and hollering, yelling taunts, kicking dirt, joyous and completely ungovernable. If Mira had any objections—and surely she had several—she'd have to get them heard over two hundred rowdy voices.

Kat and Emory swayed, stumbled, and toppled over as one, hitting the dirt hard enough that they took a mutual pause just to recover the breath it punched out of them. Emory tried to snake an arm around her torso and get her into a submission hold, but Kat wrenched it back, turning in his grip so she could sling one leg over his hips and lock him in place. He had the audacity to *laugh* at the attempt, and she couldn't help mirroring it. They'd gone from soldiers squaring off with honor to kids scrapping in the dirt, and in the moment, Kat was so blisteringly happy that she barely cared.

She couldn't win Emory his dignity, but she could lose hers alongside him.

They'd become a single panting, heaving creature, entangled by strength so evenly matched it would take the rest of their decade to pry them apart. But Kat had learned a trick or two in the wreckage of Mira's cot two nights prior, and she deployed them without mercy, landing a downright *dirty* pinch that elicited a noise they were lucky only she was close enough to hear. In the space it created, she made her move, wrenching Emory's arms up over his head as she spun him onto his back and slammed her full weight down on his stomach.

For a frozen, delirious moment, there was no difference—they might as well have been back in that tent, doing everything they could to put thoughts of death at bay, nothing between them but heavy breathing, heat, and the feeling that they probably shouldn't be grinning this much.

But the noise *had* fallen away, strangely. The shouts and heckling that crested when Kat pinned Emory had trickled off into a confused wave of mumbling, and the whistle—which surely should have cut through even the peak of the noise—hadn't been blown. Kat tore her gaze away from Emory's flushed face, turning her head to sight Mira on the platform.

"On his back, right?" she called.

But Mira wasn't looking at them. Her eyes were pinned somewhere above Kat. In all their years on the campaign, no matter how daunting the demons she squared off against were, Kat had never seen her centurion look so *rattled.*

Kat turned.

There was a hole where a pack of rowdy soldiers should be, as if the ranks had melted back from the edge of the circle, and in the center of it stood a lone figure, backlit by the late-afternoon sun and nigh indistinguishable from it. He *hurt* to look at, as if the light bled right through him, and it took a few seconds of squinting to see past the brilliance. Beneath it was a young man—*young,* truly, with the same gangly coltishness Kat was used to seeing on the teenage draftees—floppy-haired, pale-skinned, and sharp-featured, his eyes wide as he stared right back at her. He was kitted in ceremonial armor that put all Mira's shine to shame, though it looked slightly ridiculous against his less-than-bulky physique. And around his neck—

There were a few notorious centurions scattered throughout the legions. Every officer had at least one Aurean token to their name, one piece of gold that would help them frontline against the worst demons that tried to hit the troops under their protection, but some, through the blessings of their lineage and the devoted cultivation that had honed their gifts to a peak, carried dozens. When unleashed, they could churn through a battlefield like a rolling boulder, decimating everything in their path, turning tides as if through their power alone, they could reshape the world.

Compared to them, this man blazed like a young star. The tokens layered over his ostentatious chestplate were set in ranks, and though Kat had never been quick at addition, three years of marching in a century had locked in the ability to recognize when something numbered ten across and ten down.

A hundred-token Aurean in the flesh. No wonder he hurt to look at.

But there was one more bit of shine that caught Kat's eye—not on his chest, but on his head, and just as golden. A circlet that could only mean one thing.

This youth staring down at the two of them—at Emory, pinned in the dirt with his hands over his head and looking far too pleased with himself, at Kat straddling him, her hair askew and her token spilling out over her armor—was royalty.

CHAPTER 5

THREE SHORT BLASTS ON MIRA'S WHISTLE HAD NEVER BEEN SUCH a mercy.

The century scrambled to assemble, and in the thick of the commotion, Kat heaved herself up to her feet as Emory rolled out from underneath her. She tried not to feel any sort of way about it, even as the realization escaped, like a knife slid from her gut, that her embarrassment wasn't enough to overpower her reluctance to let him go. There was a fumbling attempt to beat some of the dirt off, but it was beyond hopeless, and their weapons had disappeared somewhere beneath the crowd. They shouldered through the soldiers who weren't a part of their century fleeing the scene now that the entertainment was over—Kat fielding more than a few nods, grins, and knuckles knocked against her training armor—and slotted into their place alongside the rest of their decade.

Some days, being in the first decade was a point of pride. The ten of them were at the fore of the fighting formation, leading off every battle looking the Demon Lord's forces square in the eye, setting the tone for the rest of the engagement with their valor.

Today was not one of those days. As Kat fell in with her fellow soldiers, she registered that their position put her squarely in Mira's sights. She was taller than every shieldbearer who stood in a line before her, and without the length of their spears to even things out, she stuck out between Sawyer and Ziva too.

Ziva leaned in close. "Dirt on your cheek. Actually both cheeks," she corrected when Kat took a swipe. "Actually—"

Kat ducked her head down into the collar of her tunic, scrubbing. It wasn't doing anything to help the furious redness. Hosts, Ziva had been right to warn her not to get too carried away. Now the whole *legion* would be talking about how out of hand that got.

"It's been nice knowing you," she told Ziva from the safety of her collar. She considered going full turtle and staying in her shirt for the rest of the briefing, but the sweat she'd worked up in the fight had a point to argue against it. Kat was forced to retreat, popping her head back up just in time to catch the moment the newcomer—the *prince*—floated up to join Mira on the platform in a display of Aurean power so casual it was difficult to believe it was a Flight of Angels token doing it and not the angels themselves.

In all her years on the campaign, Kat had never seen royalty in the flesh. They'd remained comfortably abstract—an amorphous force she could resent for signing the orders that pulled her name in the draft and forfeited the next five years of her life, provided she survived them. Judging by the age of this young man, he'd had very little say in the matter, but the sight of the crown on his head stuck like a thorn in her side, and she had the feeling she wasn't alone in this crowd.

Mira snapped into a salute, still looking like someone had kicked her in the head, and Kat was briefly, incandescently thankful that this stranger had shown up and absorbed the entirety of the century's attention all at once. He looked . . . *confused* more than anything, then startled suddenly and made a flapping gesture that Mira seemed hesitant to take as a genuine dismissal. After another floundering moment where neither of them made another move, the prince raised an open palm as if to say, *After you.*

Mira turned out to her soldiers. "Third Century," she called.

The assembled thumped their chests as one.

The sight of it locked their centurion's balance back in. "I've called this briefing to address the circumstances surrounding the ending of the war and give an overview of what the next few days will look like. That being said . . ." She glanced sidelong at her strange new guest. "I'm sorry, would you like to say something first?"

The prince's face lit up, like it never would have occurred to him to address the troops. Kat suppressed the urge to snort, succeeding where several of her compatriots failed. "I'D LOVE NOTHING MORE," he replied—and the entirety of the assembled century ducked for cover.

Hosts, Kat had never heard a Voice of Angels token quite that cultivated before. Her ears rang, and she shook her head like a horse, blinking first at Sawyer and then at Ziva to confirm they'd nearly been deafened just the same. A confused murmur rose from the crowd as a hundred soldiers tested their ears against their voices, punctuated by the sounds of snapping fingers and no shortage of vehement swears.

"Sorry," the prince whispered, slightly less overwhelming this time. "So sorry. That token doesn't get a lot of play compared to the rest of my array, and I'm not used to attuning one at a time. Still fine-tuning the particulars. Is this okay?" He turned to Mira, who gave him a vexed, bug-eyed look, followed by a shrug as if to say, *It's really your call.*

Kat was starting to worry the concussion was setting in, because now that she thought about it, this wasn't the first time they'd been blasted with his overly amplified voice.

This, then, was the shooting star who'd shouted "You're welcome!" over the battlefield yesterday.

Which meant that this was the man who'd felled the Demon Lord.

"Okay, great. Hi. Hello. Uh, greetings." The prince straightened, folding his arms behind his back and lifting his chin high. The effect was somewhat lost in the way it jutted out the collar of his ostentatious breastplate, nearly swallowing the bottom half of his face. "My name is Adrien Augustine." He flinched as the metal of his armor threw his too-loud words right back at him, and he immediately abandoned his attempt at posturing.

Ziva leaned in close to Kat. "Is it treason if I say I can't watch this?" she deadpanned.

"I think it's only treason if you laugh," Kat hissed back. It was going to be a battle. In front of her, Emory's shoulders were beginning to tremble.

"Now I know what you're thinking," the prince said, his arms now rigid at his sides. "*I thought the Augustine line had no heirs!* Well, you thought that for a very good reason."

He glanced around as if he genuinely expected someone to ask, *What reason?*

"And the reason w-was . . ." he stammered after another agonizing beat of silence. ". . . that it was a secret!"

At Kat's side, Sawyer feigned smothering a cough. Tears glinted in the corner of his eye.

"Yes," the prince blundered onward, clenching a fist in front of him. "To defeat the Demon Lord, sacrifices had to be made— for only an heir of the Augustine line could successfully unite enough angelic power to smite the High King of Hell. I was born in seclusion and secreted out of the capital to be raised by the finest Aurean tutors the front lines could spare."

Kat could *feel* the crowd's pivot, the suppressed laughter suddenly throttled by the implication of the prince's words. They needed every Aurean they could get on the lines. Every century fought like hell to protect their centurion, and every officer bore the tremendous weight of the responsibility for their soldiers' safety in turn. None of them—and *especially* none of the draftees— had thought that any Aureans *could* be spared.

The prince didn't seem to register the crowd's suspicion at all. "Under their guidance, I took up my first token at the age of five. By the age of ten, I had twenty under my command. There was a bit of a hiccup in my development, and I stalled out at thirty for a few years, but *finally*, at nineteen, I stand before you with a hundred fully cultivated tokens."

Again, he paused, looking expectant.

"You can clap—don't be shy."

A smattering of applause rose from the ranks, strengthening once enough people had decided it might be a direct order they were disobeying. Kat gave him three generously spaced claps. Sure, this surprise royal had temporarily saved her ass from what would likely be the *mother* of all dressing-downs from Mira, but his clueless yammering seemed like a portent of far worse problems.

"So what, he's raised from birth, plied with every token he could carry from the royal arsenal, and turned loose once he'd cultivated them all?" Ziva asked under her breath. "And it couldn't have come any sooner?"

"Least it worked," Elise threw back over her shoulder, drawing a scowl from her battle partner. "Least we get to finish our contracts in peacetime."

"That's an awfully large parade for peacetime," Sawyer said, glancing sidelong at the edge of the ranks.

The prince had arrived with an army of his own. While the century had been distracted by Kat and Emory's scrap, an entire royal entourage had crept up on the camp. Only a fraction of it was visible from the assembly field—carriages on carriages on carriages, some of them already broken open to unleash their cargo. Footmen scurried back and forth, clearing space where the stakes of a tent to rival the scale of the legion's command headquarters were sketched out. The prince hadn't just stopped by to introduce himself. He was putting down roots.

"Thank you, thank you," the invasive species demurred, waving his hands in mock flattery. "Yes, it's true—I united a historic degree of Aurean power, all in the name of ending this war. As you all must have seen yesterday, it worked. The Demon Lord is no more. I stopped his hand as he tipped the crucible, and so the threat of antigold has been wiped from existence. The Mouth of Hell is sealed. Telrus is free to thrive and prosper for the first time in twenty years."

He paused as if fishing for more applause, but all their years at war had made the ranks canny. They knew when an ask was coming.

"Now obviously this is a lot to take in," Adrien Augustine continued. "I'm sure some of you had made your peace with having no heir at all, with the Augustine line crumbling, with demons overrunning this realm. I wouldn't blame you. It looked *bleak* out there before I showed up."

"How would he know?" Carrick muttered. "Unless he was waiting to make his entrance for maximum effect."

"But the bleak years are behind us. And now we find ourselves tasked with something far more important—though slightly less dangerous, I'm thrilled to say. Because you fine soldiers aren't the only ones who need to meet their future ruler. This entire realm must hear the good news and know that Adrien Augustine has arrived to lead them into a golden, host-blessed future. And to that end—"

The prince broke off suddenly, his gaze locking on the edge of the stage, where someone from his entourage was waving his arms desperately and making a shushing gesture.

"To th-that end," he stuttered, holding up one finger, "I invite you all to join me at the *real* assembly where I will announce to the *full legions' forces*"—an approving nod from the relieved-looking adviser—"the next stage in our campaign."

"*Next stage?*" an irate voice thundered from the middle of the crowd. "There'd better not be a next fucking stage. I've marched on the battle lines for nineteen fucking years, and you're telling me you want more out of me?"

A murmur of approving noise chased the old-timer's words, though there were plenty of hisses and tittering to counter it. "You'll shut your fucking mouth and listen to your prince," Mira snapped, though with no token power to boost her voice, her command lost some of its bluster.

"Easy, centurion, they're right," the prince said with a placating palm held up. "Everyone who stands here today marched to the edge of Hell itself, and that feat will not go unrewarded. I know many of you did not get a choice about the weapon in your hands, but I promise you a choice about whether you'll continue to bear it. At the end of the r—" He broke off, glancing at his adviser, who had his head buried in both palms. "That is to say, when the next stage of the campaign is completed, I intend to offer every soldier in the ranks a full release from service."

Kat had seen demon generals plow through an entire century in one devastating maneuver. If there was a hopeful inverse to that horror, this was it. All one hundred soldiers burst into joyous shouts, cheers, applause, and even a few uninhibited yells that echoed over the campground.

Kat felt like she'd just been headbutted. She was eighteen years old again, sinking to her knees in the courtyard of the family forge with her shaking hands rumpling the conscription notice as her father rubbed her back and told her it would all be okay, that it was only five years, that her mother's Aurean token would protect her, that maybe there was a chance to make something good out of this, that it was *only five years*.

She was twenty-one, and just days ago, she'd given up on the idea of seeing him again. On the hope that she'd ever work side by side with him with hammer and tongs, her body not a tool for violence but an instrument that wrung potential and purpose from every molten piece of metal she could get her hands on.

Not even in her wildest dreams had Kat dared imagine she wouldn't be obligated to continue serving those two years she had left on her contract. Only now was she realizing what a *comfort* it had been to leave her fate in others' hands. It hadn't felt like a comfort at the time, only the yoke of an obligation on her back, but in the absence of its weight, she reeled.

Her gaze dropped to Ziva, who had a hand over her mouth. Ziva, who'd been aching, whom she'd caught crying more than once because these lands they marched through were so close to her family's home in southern Kaston and yet duty bound her to walk right by the fork in the road as if it meant nothing. She'd met Ziva in basic training, both of them freshly torn away from the promise of a normal future—and now, just like that, the door had been opened to a new one. If she went back to her village, and Kat to her own home on the outskirts of the capital, would they ever see each other again?

Around them, the rest of the century was ricocheting off similar trajectories, soldiers who'd marched side by side for years looking sidelong at their fellows, mouthing incredulous words and grappling with the notion that they could trade their sweaty, smelly compatriots for their families as soon as the prince put the order through. On her right, Sawyer and Carrick bent close together, wearing matching disbelieving grins.

Kat's gaze slid to Emory. He had his chin slightly tucked, his back squared to her, and he stuck out like a tree among reeds, so rigid was his posture compared to the rest of the shield line flanking him. She reached out, meaning to knock her knuckles against the back of his padded armor, but a thought stayed her hand.

Emory, unlike most of them, had enlisted. He had fifteen years left in his contract, and he'd never once acted like he didn't intend to serve them. Maybe this meant nothing to him. Maybe it didn't change a single one of his plans.

And maybe none of his plans involved her. Their one spectacular night had only been possible because they'd been certain it no longer mattered whether they followed the Telrusian army's exacting rules. In the aftermath of their unexpected victory, Kat had thought she'd have two years to wrangle the consequences and the flutter the thought of them put in her gut. But the prince had opened an unexpected door—one that promised she could go home far sooner than she'd hoped.

When she walked through it, Emory wouldn't follow.

If she could prepare for it, if she could practice ahead of time, maybe it wouldn't hurt as much when the moment came.

Kat let her hand fall.

A long, piercing whistle blast shrieked over the noise, and the century shuffled back into order, though some of the giddy chuckles persisted. "All of you, *quiet*," Mira snapped. "As the prince has said, this will happen when the next stage of the campaign is completed. Until then, you all still answer to me. Unless—" She broke off, frowning, as Adrien Augustine beckoned to her and mouthed something. "Now?" Mira sighed—a *bold* maneuver in the face of royalty, but the centurion was understandably flustered and her high name would probably cover the damage.

"If you don't mind," the prince replied, then turned out to face the crowd. "Now I'm sure I've given you plenty of excitement to take in, so this is where I take my leave. I'm very much looking forward to our future exploits, and to getting to know all of you better."

He tipped a wave and turned to dismount the platform. And his gaze dropped directly to Kat.

She knew, logically, that she was the most notorious person in the legion right now. She'd made an outright spectacle of herself, scrapping with Emory in the dirt, and beyond that, she was remarkably tall and hopelessly scuffed. It was only natural that he'd look at her.

But there was something more in the prince's gaze—in the wide, sincere grin that spread over his face when they locked eyes—that told her whatever nightmarish drills Mira assigned, whatever disgusting chore rotations Kat would be trapped on for the rest of her days in the legion, whatever indignities she'd suffer to pay for her insolence, it would all pale in comparison to the grand plans Adrien Augustine had in store for her.

CHAPTER 6

By THE TIME MIRA WRAPPED UP THE ASSEMBLY, KAT HAD ALMOST started to believe she'd gotten away clean.

After the prince's surprise arrival completely derailed her briefing, their centurion had righted the ship with staggering aplomb, delving into a rundown of the next week's outlook as if a token-laden boulder hadn't just rolled through her plans. Even if the Demon Lord had been defeated, there was still laundry duty, armory duty, kitchen duty, and everyone's favorite, the latrines. Decades were given their assignments and report times, read out by Mira's wisp of an aide, Mobbert—another Morgenstern, one who'd been placed under Mira's protection in a role that many saw as some sort of punishment for an indiscretion that was the subject of *constant* speculation between Carrick and Sawyer.

It was so normal that when Mira hollered, "Dismissed," Kat turned to Ziva and said, "Wonder what's for dinner?"

Ziva looked her up and down. "You might wanna wash up before you worry about that."

Kat frowned down at her arms. They were filthy. They were filthy because—

"Katrien, with me."

She startled, lifting her gaze back to the platform, where Mira glared down at her like she was trying to cultivate a brand-new token that would let her shoot fire from her eyes. "Just me?" Kat blurted.

Emory ducked from under the arm Carrick had slung over his shoulders, moving in to square at her side. Kat wanted to hiss at him to run while he still could, but he stared resolutely up at their centurion with the air of a man who could only be budged by a direct command.

"Just you," Mira said. "Emory, count yourself lucky I've got too much on my docket to deal with you at the moment. Get out of my sight."

Order received, Emory made like a man of duty—but not before he'd leaned in close enough to knock his shoulder into Kat's. "Save you a plate?" he muttered.

"I'll be fine," Kat told him and wished she meant it.

"Been nice knowing you!" Carrick called over his shoulder. Sawyer cuffed him, which Kat appreciated, then pantomimed wiping a tear away, which she didn't.

Mira dropped off the edge of the platform, her Lightness of Angels token making her landing cat-soft. "The prince has asked to meet with you," she said, and under the words Kat heard the obvious corollary: *and until that happens, there's nothing I can do to you.*

Kat would take whatever escape she could get. "Can I clean—"

"No. Now."

She tried to tell herself it wouldn't have mattered much. The prince had already seen what he'd seen, and she doubted he'd forget it. Kat smoothed her battle braids as she followed Mira across the assembly field, fussing with the worn leather tie that gathered them. At least she could tame some of the flyaways before they reached the prince's doorstep.

Over the course of the briefing, an actual doorstep had materialized, a massive red tent looming over its fellows with a single gold pennant flying the Augustine crest—an angel skirted by a radiant crown—on the top. Mira paused at the entrance, glaring sidelong up at Kat. "No gawking. You don't speak unless spoken to. You address him as 'Your Highness' and answer anything he asks truthfully and to the best of your ability. All his ideas are the best ideas you've ever heard. Got it?"

"Yes, centurion," Kat replied, chasing it with a nervous gulp. She'd only ever seen Mira this tense when she had all ten of her tokens attuned ahead of a battle.

"One step behind me."

"Yes, centurion." Kat fell in at Mira's heel as she pushed through the flap.

She immediately failed Mira's first command. Within the tent was a level of opulence that Kat had never seen before, a level that seemed *nonsensical* for the middle of a war camp. The ground was hidden completely beneath a tapestry of intricate plush carpets that made Kat want to lift up onto her tiptoes just to avoid getting more of her hopelessly dusty boots on them. Fabric panels strung from the tentpoles divided the enormous space, carving out a foyer in which two gold-trimmed couches were arranged as a sort of receiving area. The rest was clearly still a work in progress, valets laden with trunks, coats, and casks rushing back and forth, but anchored calmly in the midst of the chaos were four young people sprawled across the seating—and of course Adrien Augustine, placed upon the pedestal of a large wingback chair at the foyer's center.

"Welcome," he said. "Pardon the mess."

"Your Highness," Mira replied, bowing at the waist with a hand pressed flat against her tokens. Kat mimicked her, feeling the shape of her own Aurean gold stamp lightly into the skin of her chest.

The prince flapped his hands. "That's going to get very old very fast. Come, join us." He beckoned to the couches, which were thoroughly occupied by his companions in various states of repose. None of the four looked particularly motivated to make room—in fact, they all seemed alarmed that two soldiers had intruded on their space.

Mira straightened, Kat half a beat behind. "Thank you, Your Highness, but it wouldn't be proper."

"Don't the philosophers say all people are equal under the eyes of the hosts?" he mused.

"The philosophers may say that, but the nobility says otherwise," Mira replied with a deferential nod to the prince's entourage. "I'd do House Morgenstern a disservice not to comport myself accordingly."

"And what about you?" he asked, his eyes settling on Kat. Once again, she felt the weight of it—the way her future was at the mercy of his whims. "Philosopher or nobility?"

Mira glanced back over her shoulder, and the weight doubled.

"Neither," Kat blurted.

A muscle in Mira's jaw tightened.

"That is to say, I'm definitely not a philosopher, and I have no claim to nobility either."

"Oh? But I thought we were all Aureans here? Did I not spot a bit of shine beneath that armor?"

Kat pulled the token out of her collar, letting it catch the candles that lit the space with a warm, low glow. "It's a pauper's token, Your Highness. I have no high name."

Adrien Augustine leaned forward intently, and Kat resisted the instinct to tuck her token back in its safe resting spot. When she'd first been drafted, she'd considered leaving it at home. She'd heard the stories of single-token Aureans robbed for the power they couldn't cultivate enough to defend. Many would argue that a piece like hers, one with very little in the way of combat applications, would do more good in someone else's array, where it could attune with the rest of their gold to enhance their other host-granted skills, and Kat had taken great pains to keep her token hidden for her first two years on the front.

Except from Emory. Emory, she'd told barely three months into their assignment—not because she trusted him, but because it was the only way she could think of to get him to take her seriously.

Theirs had not been a happy pairing at first. Emory had been on the front lines for two years, having enlisted the day he turned sixteen, and he had a deep-set resentment for anyone who had to be forced into soldiering by a random lottery pull. He was fresh off the loss of his first battle partner and in no way ready to accept his replacement, but the war wouldn't wait for that, and of all the people he could have been assigned, fate had given him Kat.

And Kat at eighteen had been, well, *different*. Brighter, always quick with a smile, and so full of hope that it was practically intolerable to someone who'd been grinding through thralls and ground down in turn. Even if physically they were well-matched, her height and bulk the perfect complement to his defensive power, he'd politely closed himself off from any of her attempts to be friendly.

She'd taken it personally. Taken it as a challenge. She'd break down those walls if it was the last thing she did. All it would take was persistence and kindness—with enough of that, her mother had always said, any garden could bloom.

What had happened instead was the same thing war did to everyone. The Telrusian machine marched forward, and Kat discovered that the only way to survive it was to accept your place as a cog. She learned, as every soldier did, that you had to put your head down, had to tune out the screams of the forsaken on the end of your spear, had to pray to the hosts that some combination of your century's discipline and your centurion's gold could keep you alive when the demons came to call. She'd stopped crying for them. Stopped crying at all. It hadn't taken long. Three months in, and she understood why Emory had been cold to her.

But after those three months, she decided she couldn't be both miserable *and* misunderstood. And so one quiet day on the training grounds, when it was just the two of them, she pulled her token out from under her shirt.

"A pauper's token," the prince repeated now. "Fascinating. I've never seen one in the wild before."

If the way he described his upbringing was anything to go by, this young man had known nothing but multitoken Aureans his entire life. If there was anyone in his sphere who carried only a single piece, they probably kept it to themselves.

The Augustine heir's eyes were locked onto her shine now, and Kat felt the prickling needle of Mira's reminders at her jugular. If he wanted it for himself, there was no way for her to refuse him. Especially not in front of his four companions. Now that she'd had a moment to adjust to the prince's weighty glow, Kat could see they were each sporting gold of their own, arranged in gleaming decade ranks that ached just as much to look at. Any one of them could claim her token—and would probably smite her where she stood if she resisted.

"Your name?" the prince asked.

"Katrien," she replied, and thank the hosts her voice didn't shake. It was a mercy she only had a low name to choke out.

"Lovely to meet you, Katrien. You're a spectacular fighter—a real credit to the legions. The moment I saw you, I just *knew* I had to make your acquaintance. Tell me about your token."

She let the order steady her. Orders, she knew how to handle. "It's a Light of Angels. It's not the most useful in battle, and it's uncultivated—"

He cut her off with a gesture, and for a moment Kat feared he was wise to her attempt to talk down its value. But Adrien Augustine only shook his head. "No, not that. I mean yes, it's lovely, but I want to know how a commoner comes into a token like this."

In different hands, the words could easily come off as accusing, but the prince's eyes shone with a genuine curiosity. He didn't seem the manipulative type—more clueless than anything—and Kat was inclined to suspect his request was an attempt to patch that lack of knowledge. He'd grown up sheltered, training relentlessly for a singular purpose. Now that he'd achieved it, perhaps he'd realized how oblivious it had left him about the way the rest of the world functioned.

"It's been in my family for generations," Kat replied. "Probably same as the shine you wear." Mira threw her a consternated look, but she didn't see the harm in drawing a line between Adrien Augustine's hundred-token array and her own small inheritance. Better to remind him that most common people came into their tokens the same way he had, in case he suspected otherwise. "It was my mother's," she added softly.

The prince nodded. "Naturally, naturally. About fifteen of mine are from my mother's vault as well. But you mentioned it's uncultivated? If it was handed down, surely it retains some of the power developed by its lineage?"

Kat shook her head, trying to keep her expression diplomatic. Her play for sympathy had failed miserably. It meant something vastly different to inherit your parents' tokens when your parents had vaults full of them. "No, Your Highness. If it had any power in it to start, my mother had let it go by the time she passed it to me."

Admitting that in front of the most decorated Aureans Kat had ever seen in her life was tantamount to sacrilege. Tokens were *meant* to be cultivated. Squandering the hosts' blessing was as good as spitting in their faces. With the Seal of Heaven firmly in place, Aurean power was the last vestige of the angels' touch upon the material plane, meant to give humanity the gifts they needed to resist the forces of Hell. To be starting from scratch a thousand years after the Forging was an outright *waste*.

But Kat's mother had thought differently. To Kat, the magic of her mom's token had been barely more than a parlor trick, an additional bit of brightness refracted through the already luminous beacon that was her mother. Bronwyn would call on it from time to time—when she needed to bring the winter bedding down from the attic, when a noise in the street in the middle of the night had startled Kat awake. Some nights, she'd use it to cast shadows upon the wall and tell her stories. The classic, grand romantic adventures from the Age of Hosts, folklore that trickled into Rusta's fringes from every corner of the continent, all of it twice as vibrant when whispered like a secret long after the candles had burned down. It was an everyday kind of magic, just as big as it needed to be, and it had seemed perfectly natural to Kat.

Before she'd met other Aureans. Before she'd seen what a truly cultivated token could do.

"So you only hold it for . . . sentiment?" one of the prince's companions asked, wrinkling her nose. She was elegant, but the kind of elegance that seemed to have been assembled out of obligation rather than any genuine interest, her long black hair bound back in simple, straight layers that Kat recognized as a northern style and her deeply dark eyes made deeper and darker by deliberate shadowing.

"Celia," another of the young women warned her from the opposite couch, twisting one of her brunette curls anxiously. "I'm sure the soldier has her reasons."

"And *I'm* sure the token does her about as much good as your metal-softening one," the third woman interjected wryly, nudging Celia with an elbow.

"Let's not make a bad impression," the only man in the group said, holding out his hands in a placating gesture.

Kat's head spun.

"Might be a little late for that," Adrien Augustine said with a sigh. His previous cheer had evaporated like blood spattered on the Mouth of Hell itself the second his companions had opened their mouths. "Katrien, Lady Morgenstern, please excuse my friends. All of you, since you seem so intent on hopping into this conversation, why don't you go around and say your names and a fun fact about yourselves."

"This isn't the first day of High Training," Celia muttered, but she fixed her slouch marginally and made eye contact with Kat. "Lady Celia Vai, Countess of Sprill. Eighty-two tokens."

A beat passed, but Lady Vai seemed to think that was sufficient.

"Tough act to follow," the woman seated next to her said. "I'm Daya Imonde. Pleasure to make your acquaintance, Katrien. Since Celia's already gone and done it, I suppose it's not too gauche to say I have ninety-five, but that's so *boring*. My *fun* fact is that the first token I ever cultivated was one I stole from my family's vault when I was eight years old. Simple Hand of Angels telekinesis— I was an absolute terror pickpocketing the guests of our keep until they figured it out." She tapped the token in her array, grinning proudly.

Kat's grip on her own token tightened, just in case.

"*Daya*," the woman on the opposite couch scolded, then caught Kat's eye. Unlike Celia's detached cool, this woman's presentation—from her prim posture to the careful styling of her curls—was overladen with intention. "I'm Faye Laurent, Duchess of Halston. And since Daya didn't mention it, she's a provincial duchess too."

"Because it's hardly a fun fact," Daya replied, looking sour. "If I were heir to Halston, that would be one thing. Egren's so far from the capital and so sparse I've heard the advisers claim it's hardly worth taxing."

"Well, I'm from Halston, but my battle partner's from Egren," Kat offered, earning a warning glare from Mira that she hardly found fair. Her orders were not to speak unless spoken to, but she'd taken that to mean the prince. Surely she was allowed to make conversation with these nobles, if only to remind them she was more than the token around her neck.

"You'll have to introduce me," Daya said, her smile returning. She was round-cheeked and lovely, and with her hair cropped close to her skull, it made her wide grin all the more dazzling. "I hear we've turned out many a valiant soldier."

"Some might say too valiant," Mira interjected. "Her battle partner was the one being disciplined for breaking rank to defend Katrien in the engagement yesterday."

"Well, then you'll *definitely* have to introduce me," Daya replied, her grin turning wicked.

"*Daya*," Faye huffed again. "Apologies. Some of us have had too much Aurean training and too little etiquette."

"Give us a fun fact about your etiquette training," Celia said, earning her an approving look from Daya and a glare from Faye.

"Fine. Did you know that Hand of Angels tokens have standardized etiquette rules, laid out in the first edition of the *Codex of Manners*?"

"I did not, Your . . . Grace?" Kat hazarded. Her knowledge of courtly address began and ended at the one example Mira had thought to cover before they entered the tent.

Faye gave her an encouraging nod.

"Neither did I," Daya added.

"That much is obvious," Faye replied.

"*Bodhi*," Adrien Augustine interjected, turning to the man at his right. "Would you like to introduce yourself too?"

The final member of the prince's entourage was watching the conversation with the air of a man at a sporting match who'd placed his bets but was mostly just happy to be there. He was handsome past the point of reason, strong-featured and well-built, and though Kat knew very little of Vaya, the allied state that bordered Telrus on the continent's southeastern reach, she knew enough to suspect that the intricately embroidered sash he wore over one shoulder marked him as some form of royalty. "Ah!" the young man exclaimed. "Absolutely, Your Highness."

Adrien pulled a face.

"My name is Bodhi Ranjan, and my fun fact is that it's lovely, just *lovely,* to meet the two of you," he said, nodding to both Kat and Mira over a chorus of groans from his companions. "Fine, fine. My *real* fun fact is that in addition to mastering ninety-nine Aurean tokens"—he gestured over his array, puffing out his chest to be sure they'd noticed—"I have *also* mastered all sixteen forms of Telrusian courtly dance outlined in the *Codex of Manners* that Faye prizes so dearly, and I am very much looking forward to putting that mastery to good use at Adrien's victory ball."

All three of the women stiffened, and Kat got the sense that a deeply treacherous topic had just been broached.

Adrien, too, looked suddenly wary. The prince clapped his hands twice. "There. Done. Miraculous. I've just decided that the four of you exhaust me. Out. Now. Please." He punctuated each word with a flick of his fingers, and the entourage wasted no time in pushing themselves to their feet and rushing out of the tent.

Kat blinked, feeling as if she'd just been spun around. The prince's abrupt change of mood had brought with it a sudden, bitter charge, and she wasn't sure what it meant that any potential witnesses were clearing out. Her only solace was the fact that Mira looked just as disoriented.

"Sit, please, Katrien. Close." The prince pointed to one of the couches that had just been abandoned. Kat lowered herself on the corner of the couch, trying to invite as little contact as possible between the fine plush cushion and her hopelessly dirty ass.

"Everyone else, take a break," the prince hollered, his voice token-powered enough to blast through the tent's arching canopy. Every valet in the vicinity set down what they were doing and rushed to make themselves scarce. "And you as well," he said, flapping a hand at Mira. "Outside for a moment. I'll have Katrien call you back in when I need you."

It might have been the first time Kat had ever seen her centurion look at her with genuine concern, but as always, Mira took her orders without question.

And then the two of them were alone—Katrien, single-tokened, common, Aurean in name only, and the prince of the realm with his hundred-strong array. Mira's order stilled the myriad questions boiling in her throat, but Mira wasn't here to know if she'd spoken out of turn, and Kat was right on the verge of her second drastic act of insubordination of the day when Adrien leaned out over his knees and beckoned her close.

"Katrien," he said, gravely serious. "My life is in danger, and you're the only one who can help me."

CHAPTER 7

Caught hopelessly off guard, she couldn't smother the instinct to laugh in time. Kat clapped a hand over her mouth. It was a small mercy they were in a tent—that the fabric couldn't throw the sound of her catastrophic mistake back at her, though she still swore she heard its echo ringing in her ears.

But Adrien Augustine took having a commoner laugh in his face in stride. "I understand. It's a lot to process. Let me catch you up."

Kat stifled another inadvisable outburst.

"You know, of course, what I've just told the troops. That I was trained all my life for a singular purpose. To free this land from the blight of the Demon Lord. For this, I shouldered the weight of a hundred Aurean tokens—aided, of course, by an Aurean token that makes carrying all that weight a breeze. Now, I'm sure you're all very happy that the war is over, thanks to me, but . . .

that might not . . . exactly . . . be true," he eked out from behind steepled fingers.

Kat blinked, icy dread threading through her veins. She'd *seen* the citadel fall and the Mouth collapse, seen waves of thralls slump into a merciful rest. "Then the Demon Lord—" she blurted.

"Oh, no, not him. There wasn't much left of him, after, well . . ." The prince trailed off, looking pensive. "No, the problem is the generals. The Three Lesser Lords—you've heard of them? Or perhaps faced one in your time on the front?"

Dignity demanded that she speak without trembling, but animal instinct won out. "The First Legion was part of the force that liberated Fallon," Kat said. "I was fortunate to never meet the general in the field. Other centuries were not as fortunate. But I saw it on the city walls once." She cleared her throat, scooting back on the couch to stabilize herself. "The Lesser Lords are still on this plane?"

"All three of them," Adrien said with a nod. "They fled the citadel's collapse while most of their compatriots were attempting to outrace the Mouth's closing. They will be weakened without the Demon Lord himself or any thralls to support their efforts, but even in their weakened state, well—we have a very clear picture of the paths they took through the battlefield, between the casualties and the eyewitness reports. Unfortunately, they've been quite thorough in covering their tracks since then. When the only information we have to go on is the sudden, sporadic disappearance of scouting parties, it's beginning to seem more prudent *not* to hunt for them."

Horror overtook any qualms Kat had about challenging the prince. "Then the strategy is to let the Lesser Lords run rampant through the countryside?"

The look Adrien fixed her with was so dangerously serious that it rewrote him into a different man entirely. This Adrien Augustine must have been the last thing the Demon Lord saw before he was reduced to ashes. "The strategy," he said firmly, "is to draw them out. But to do that, we need to present them with an obvious target. Their purpose, now that they've been abandoned in this realm, is to avenge their foul master. To do that, they'll need to kill me. If I present myself as bait, we can lure each of the three out of the shadows and strike them down."

Kat kept perfectly still. She wasn't about to risk offending the prince worse than she already had, even as every part of her screamed, *If they're coming after you, what are you doing sitting so close to me?*

"You have questions," Adrien said.

"Concerns," she hazarded.

"Name them."

Well, now that she'd been ordered—"Not to put any doubt upon your prowess as an Aurean, but I understand the mechanics of attunement, especially where multiple tokens are concerned."

"Which is to say you understand my array is practically useless unless I've been locked in quiet contemplation for five hours, which all falls apart if I'm interrupted at any point before I've finished attuning every token in my array." The prince nodded. "That's a good one. And it's precisely the reason our defense won't rely upon Aurean strength."

Kat nearly asked what other kind of strength there was, but then the realization hit. "You can't mean—"

"In fact, the generals likely wouldn't strike at all if they knew I was ready to meet them with the same force I used against the Demon Lord, not without antigold. No, we need to present them with a target they think they can win against and beat them with strength they'll never expect."

Kat could feel herself going pallid. "You mean beat them with infantry."

Adrien held up a single approving finger.

"I have a few more concerns," Kat said weakly. "Why not use

the strength of lesser Aureans? Mira only takes half an hour to attune completely. You could build a guard of centurions and a rotation of attunement."

Adrien's eager smile went strained. "Well, first of all, there are some political considerations to take into account. I rely upon the faith of House Morgenstern, and it wouldn't do for me to put one of their most capable daughters in the path of a Lesser Lord."

Kat nearly bit through her tongue. *So you'll protect the Aureans in your forces and risk hundreds of foot soldiers instead?*

"The other consideration is one of optics. There's a narrative we need to establish that gets more difficult when a blazing star of an Aurean is seen grappling with a demon and word begins to spread that evil is not quite as defeated as previously thought."

"Optics," Kat breathed.

"Public opinion," Adrien added, and it took her a moment to understand that he thought he was clarifying the term for her. "While I'm sure you must have been very impressed by my defeat of the Demon Lord, I've got a lot more to live up to as the Augustine heir. Mine must be an era of decisive peace, and the campaign we wage across this kingdom must be one that spreads the good news, not one that's dogged by rumors of demon attacks. Battling with infantry will be much less noticeable, which serves our mission well."

"Our mission," Kat replied, and this time she *was* asking for clarification.

"You and your century are the first of many to hear the good news—that news being that House Augustine has an heir who will take up his father's crown and steward this glorious country into prosperity. Bit of a mouthful, but we'll figure out the short and sweet way to get the message across. I don't want to be one of those useless royals who sits around and does nothing but accumulate bad reputation after bad reputation. I want to use my power for good!"

Kat genuinely could not tell if this young man was self-aware or not.

"The people need to know *me*. They need to see what kind of a leader I'll be. And I know the perfect gift to give to them—apart from my divine presence, of course."

"Of course," Kat repeated.

The prince's eyes lit up so brightly she swore he was using a token for effect. "Public infrastructure," he exclaimed, clapping his hands.

"You mean—"

"A *road*." He said it with the reverence Kat had come to expect from priests speaking of the afterlife that awaited beyond the Seal of Heaven. "Think about it. Our countryside has been ravaged for the past twenty years, turned into salted battlefield after salted battlefield. You've marched through your fair share of them— you've seen it firsthand. If my rule is to be prosperous, it must start with a solid foundation. And what foundation is more solid than a road that connects our countryside from here in Kaston clear to the capital?"

It hadn't been high on Kat's list of guesses for what the prince's so-called next stage would be—namely, because she hadn't thought to guess anything that was genuinely useful. The prince had been locked away training relentlessly to punch clean through the Demon Lord for most of his life. Who would expect him to know the first thing about the essentials of good governance?

And he was right about the road thing. Kat had trooped all over this country, sometimes doing more sliding in the mud than forward motion, and over the course of her service, she'd gained an appreciation for the rare moments when there was solid, hard-packed road beneath her boots. She'd shoved enough equipment carts over uneven terrain to last her a lifetime, and there had been a few tight moments on the campaign where they'd stretched their rations to the breaking point waiting for a supply line that had been promised. A road was food and stability and safety. It was exactly what the people needed.

It was, to put it frankly, *suspicious* that this newly minted royal had landed on the right answer. "That's . . . generous of you," Kat hedged.

"Isn't it? I hope everyone agrees." His grin suddenly dropped. "Seriously. You think it's a good idea, right?"

"Brilliant, Your Highness," Kat replied, maybe a shade too fast.

He pursed his lips. "I think I want you to stop doing that. The title thing—it's so clunky."

"Respectfully, Highness, I'm not looking forward to what my centurion might do to me if I drop it."

"I can tell her you're under my protection."

"I can promise you that'll only make it worse," Kat muttered. "Your Highness," she added after a beat long enough to bring Adrien Augustine's smile back.

"Well then, it can't be helped. I had the misfortune to be born hopelessly royal—I suppose I must bear it." He sighed, slumping back in his chair. "Anyway, on the subject of my first royal decree—the plan is to repurpose our now *grossly* overstaffed military into the labor force we need to build this magnificent road. We have far too many soldiers contracted for peacetime, eating significantly into my treasury at a time when those funds will be critical to the reconstruction effort, and my advisers warn that Vaya and our other neighbors may find our militarism concerning now that it's less justified by a demonic invasion. So you and your comrades will dig and pave your way to Rusta, where, as I mentioned before, you'll be offered a full release from service in exchange for your labor. What are your thoughts?"

Kat sputtered. "*My* thoughts?"

"Will you take the release?"

"It's . . . I *just* found out about it. Your Highness. It's a very generous offer. I'm thankful for the opportunity."

"You're making a simple answer quite complicated, Katrien."

"Are you ordering me to answer?" she shot back. Her hands were clasped in her lap, holding on to each other like something was about to be torn from her grasp.

"Come now, you must have had a gut instinct when I announced it. Hand to the hosts, tell me what it was." He paused. "Tell me or I'll tell your centurion you defied a direct—"

"I'll take it!" Kat blurted. "I'll . . . I don't know how much you already know about me."

"Next to nothing," Adrien replied, waving a flippant hand.

"I was drafted," she said. "Called up in the census the year I turned eighteen. Before that, I worked my father's forge. He'd been a blacksmith, but as the war escalated, our purpose bent to armory. Everyone was doing their part, but a number pull decided I had to put my body on the line too. It wasn't ever something I would have chosen for myself."

She risked a glance prince-ward and found Adrien Augustine staring at his own hands contemplatively. "I don't think I can look at the draft with objectivity," he mused. "I was born into this fight quite literally—one year after the Mouth broke through. I never got a choice either. In one sense, that's just the way it's always been for me. Now that we're faced with an overabundance of soldiers, the practice seems barbaric, but I recognize that when my parents put the policy in place, we were losing. Badly. Against an enemy who could compel the dead to fight for him."

"You don't need to justify the draft to me," Kat said. It was nauseating listening to him try. "I've made my peace with it, and it's certainly easier to stomach on the other side of the Battle of the Mouth."

"But," Adrien Augustine interjected cannily.

Kat took a deep breath, rebalancing her focus from the mire of the past to the uncertain footing of the future.

"It's just, I don't know what my life is supposed to look like now that I get to live it. All this time I dreamed of going back to my father's forge, being able to *make* things again, but never this soon. It's a lot to take in all at once, and I thought I'd have more time with the people I marched beside for these three years. More time with . . ." She stopped herself from saying *Emory*, but it was a near thing. "So it's a yes. I want the release, I'm *eternally* grateful, Your Highness, but—"

"You're welcome," the prince said, and the interruption was halfway to a kindness. "If it's any consolation, I too find the future very sudden and strange at the moment. I was born for something. Two days ago, I accomplished that purpose. Now I must make something of the rest of my life. A road seems like a good enough place to start."

Kat glanced at him sidelong, gathering her courage like she was at the fore of the century. One moment to steady, to root herself, and then she was ready to ask him plainly—"Why are you telling me all this?"

Adrien grinned. "Wanna know my favorite token in my array?" He tapped it twice with a fingertip, sending it jangling against its fellows. In the low light of the tent, it was difficult to make out the glyph. "This one is lucky. I don't mean that in a superstitious sense—I can feel it pulling me toward the easiest solution to my objectives. Its guidance got me to the Demon Lord's doorstep at the moment he tipped the crucible, the moment he was about to alchemize antigold."

Adrien had used that phrasing before in his speech to the century. Kat thought he must have misspoken, but perhaps the prince just didn't know what he was looking at in the moment and decided it sounded impressive. After all, if the Demon Lord had been tipping the crucible, that implied he'd already smelted the antigold within it and was instead in the process of casting it into a mold before it stabilized.

It wasn't worth interrupting to press the issue. The Demon Lord was defeated, the Mouth of Hell had crumbled, and the prince was on a tear. "Now I find myself in need of someone who can defend me when I can't defend myself," he continued, "and lo and behold, it guided me to you precisely at the moment you put a man of that size on his back like you were playing with him. It's fate."

Kat had never been one to doubt the will of the hosts, but this was the will of the hosts as interpreted by a prince who'd popped up out of nowhere. And, in point of fact, she *had* been playing with Emory. "An exhibition duel's not necessarily an indicator of combat prowess."

"Oh believe me, if exhibition duels were accurate descriptions of combat, it would be Bodhi Ranjan's praises you soldiers would be singing, not mine. The point remains. The angels' guiding hand brought me to you." The prince looked her up and down with an appraising eye. "I wonder what lessons they have to impart."

Kat was hardly a vessel for angelic *power*—it seemed bordering on madness to expect her to be a vessel for angelic wisdom on top of that. "Surely . . ." she said, floundering, "surely there are people more blessed by the angels than me. Your friends, for instance."

"Oh no, not them. Anyone but them." Adrien's smile had disappeared.

"Why not?"

"Because all of them want to marry me."

Kat snorted, which only worsened the dangerously distressed look that strained Adrien's face. "Why . . . What . . ." Kat couldn't quite find the words to express the absurdity of it. "Wouldn't that mean they *want* to protect you?"

Adrien shook his head. "You've met me. Like, really met me. You saw me make a fool of myself in front of the troops out there. I'm barely worthy of the crown on my head, and the only good thing I've ever done in my life is behind me now. I am not what you would call a hot prospect—beyond, of course, the fact that my bloodline has held the throne of Telrus for centuries. So anyone who's expressed intentions to marry"—he gestured up and down—"*this* is only in it for the power. And if they'd marry me for power, they might kill me for it too. So again, none of them can be trusted. Not them, and not any of their centurion friends—any of whom could be vassal families to theirs."

The bitterness startled her. He was mercurial, certainly, but her first impression of the prince hadn't allowed for this kind of sharp edge. "So your solution is to trust someone you just met instead?" Kat asked.

"Well, my lucky token hasn't warned me away from it yet. So. What do you say?"

"That it's absurd," Kat blurted. So much for Mira's *all his ideas are the best ideas you've ever heard,* but she couldn't stand it any longer. "I'm just one person, and infantry isn't *built* for taking on a Lesser Lord. On the battlefield, even with a hundred of us, we still rely on our centurion to frontline when the demons strike."

"Which is why it will work!" Adrien exclaimed. "Like I said, they won't strike in the first place if they think they'll be going up against an Aurean."

Kat shook her head. "For non-Aurean troops to face one unassisted, it'd take a whole decade. A whole *century.*"

Adrien nodded, his expression switching over to a thoughtfulness she didn't like. "You're right. You're absolutely right. This is why the token brought me to you. One second." He stuck his fingers in his mouth and blew a short, sharp whistle that brought a valet bursting through one of the tent's back flaps. "There's a centurion outside," he told the man. "Bring her in."

ONE FLURRY OF ACTIVITY AND ANOTHER INTERMINABLY LONG-winded, self-aggrandizing explanation later, Mira sat across from Kat, glaring daggers through her soldier as Kat did her damnedest not to meet that razor-edged stare.

She'd misspoke. Or hadn't realized what she was implying. She'd fucked up—and now not only would she pay the cost, but her entire century would pay it alongside her.

"So you see, Lady Morgenstern," Adrien concluded at last. "I'll need you at the fore of the formation as we lead this project. Your unit will do their part in the road construction, of course— I wouldn't want to deprive you of that honor—but you'll have the *additional* honor of ensuring that I make it safely to the capital in time for my victory ball as we root out the Demon Lord's last remnants in this plane. Any questions?"

Doubtless Mira had several. Kat could almost hear the fluttering of the deck as her centurion shuffled through it, weighing which card to play. But in the end, her commanding officer was a professional—and more than that, Adrien was the heir to the kingdom. There was only one answer he'd hear.

"When do we start?" Mira asked through clenched teeth.

CHAPTER 8

"I THINK THE HOSTS ARE TRYING TO TELL ME SOMETHING," MIRA groaned the moment they strode out of the prince's tent and into the startling discovery that night had fallen over the course of their visit.

Kat didn't know how *not* to provoke her, so she kept her silence and thought forlornly of the hot meal she'd missed at the mess tent. Mira held the kind of sway that could get her fed after-hours, but Kat genuinely feared what her centurion might do if she asked for help making up her lost dinner.

"I made it out alive yesterday. This must be them rebalancing the scales," Mira said, staring pensively into the middle distance.

Kat decided to roll the bones. "So, can I go, or . . ."

And truly, strange things were afoot in the war camp, because Mira flapped a hand and muttered, "Best not to risk it. Get out of here before I change my mind."

Kat bolted. First to the mess tent, where the dishwashers confirmed her worst fears had come true. She trudged back through the camp, finding a rock to kick every time her stomach growled. If she couldn't have her dinner, she might as well have the next thing she craved—and so she made her way to the training field on the far outskirts.

Emory leaned against one of the posts of the makeshift fence that walled off the training ground from the rest of the camp, and even from behind, Kat could tell his usual after-meal drowsiness was hitting him. She softened her footsteps, sidled up to him, and nudged his hip with her own. "Someone should tell her we won," she said, nodding out to the field beyond.

Giselle stood in the middle of the training ground, her pale hair luminous in the torchlight, jabbing her way through spear drills as if the legions of Hell were upon her and it was her personal responsibility to skewer as many of them as possible.

"Tried that," Emory said once he'd recovered his footing and choked down his startled yelp. "Got some line about how we all have to be prepared and evil never sleeps."

"Pretty sure I heard that one a time or two when I was first assigned to this century."

"I was *not* this bad," Emory scoffed, gesturing to where Giselle had just executed a *truly* unnecessary spin of her spear around her neck. "Look at her. She's ready for the Mouth to burp the demons right back out."

"Teenagers," Kat lamented as if she hadn't been one herself barely two years back. "So, here's the interesting thing: She might be a little bit right."

Emory's eyes went wider and wider as she muddled through a disjointed explanation of everything that had transpired in the prince's tent. "So now *we're* supposed to fend off the Lesser Lords themselves because the prince is making himself deliberately vulnerable?"

"Seems that way, yeah. Wanna run a few drills now?"

"No, I want to save my strength for all this road construction,"

Emory deadpanned. "Say what you will about the man, but he certainly knows how to get the infantry on his side."

"Hey, I'll take digging a road over a day on the lines any time," Kat countered. "Provided, of course, my battle partner doesn't go and do something stupid like *break rank* while a shock knight's bearing down on us."

"Are you trying to get me to regret saving your life?"

"Oh, was it saving my life? Because I seem to recall both of us being seconds away from shaking hands with the hosts before the prince swooped in."

"You *are* trying to get me to regret saving your life."

"I'm trying to—" Kat broke off, scrubbing her hands over her face. She was still hopelessly dirty from their wrestling match, though maybe it worked out in her favor, covering up the furious red. "Thank you for saving my life. I'm sorry Mira tried to make you pay for it."

"If she really wanted to punish me, she couldn't have chosen a worse way to go about it," he said, glancing at her sidelong with a knowing smirk that nearly swept her legs out from under her.

"Are you even paying attention?" Giselle hollered from across the training field with impeccable timing.

"No," Emory hollered back. "Run it from the top again, and I'll watch this time."

Giselle let out a long-suffering *ugh* that Kat felt on a personal level for several reasons and trooped back over to the fence. "I feel like I'm not getting the form right."

"Maybe you need a spearbearer's eye?" Emory offered, nudging Kat.

"Have you tried growing a foot or two?" Kat asked. "I find that really worked out for me."

"As did resting properly," Emory added before Giselle could bite her head off. "I know you've got this whole *raging mission of revenge* thing going on, but training late into the night is only going to make recovering your strength harder."

"What else should I be doing with my time?" Giselle asked with a haughty sniff. "Normal teenage girl things? Swooning over pathetic young men?"

"Pathetic's what does it for you, huh?" Kat replied, grinning.

Giselle fixed her with a look so withering she could have only learned it from Mira. Unlike Emory, Giselle hadn't been in the ranks long enough to grow out of her disdain for the draftees, and Kat had turned making it worse into a hobby. She didn't have Emory's patience when it came to helping the youngest member of the decade in her quest to out-drill all of them, but she admired it because she knew where it came from.

Over the course of her three years, Kat had seen fifteen members of their decade killed in action, and none of them took it harder than Emory. She suspected that she'd missed out on the worst death he'd seen, the one that made every subsequent loss knock him off his axis—that of his first battle partner, Nolan, whom she'd never heard him say more than five words about. Every death rattled Emory so badly that Kat had to fight twice as hard to keep the thralls off him, and it was never worse than when it was a young soldier—many of them enlisted, many of them bright-eyed with the notion that they'd be part of the forces that saved the world.

And then came Giselle—small, nearly no muscle to speak of, soft-handed, but with a vicious spark that Emory saw right from the get-go was going to get her killed if he didn't do something about it. He'd decided, practically from the moment she'd been assigned to their unit, that he wasn't going to let her feral teen rage be the death of her.

Miracles on miracles, he hadn't. Here they all were, on the other side of battle—if only for a moment. In battle, Kat knew exactly what to do with a break in the onslaught. How to rock back, regroup, release what tension she could.

If she didn't think too hard about it, this could be the same thing.

"I feel like we should talk," Kat muttered as Giselle started from the top of the drill set, each thrust of her spear punctuated by a grunt. "*Higher,* kid," she added. "Hitting them in the gut is only going to slow them down."

Giselle let out a snarl but took the note.

"I agree," Emory said, once his protégée had slipped back into her flow.

"It seems we'll be fighting one last campaign," Kat said. "And then . . ."

"And then you'll take your release," Emory finished, so matter-of-factly that it hit her like a kick in the chest.

"I should, shouldn't I?" she replied, and immediately hated herself—both for how easily she'd told the prince that she would earlier and how much the hesitation in her voice now made Emory's face light up. "Soldiering was never supposed to be my future, but there's an opportunity in it that I never seized."

"Oh?" Emory asked. She knew she wasn't imagining the hopeful lilt of it.

Kat's hand crept up to where she'd tucked her token beneath her armor's protection.

Emory's brow wrinkled. "But you always said—"

"There was never time. It's a Light of Angels—the most it could do on the battlefield was aggravate a demon and blind the rest of the century in the process. The other Aureans in the ranks were too focused on their own cultivation anyway. It wouldn't have made sense, tactically, to demand their time. And once we hit Fallon . . ." She trailed off, knowing Emory would understand.

Past a certain point in the campaign, it wouldn't have mattered if she'd had a willing tutor. The days collapsed into an interminable grind, and Kat barely had the energy to kick her boots off each night. The idea of mustering the willpower to train her token on top of that was outright laughable.

She'd hoped, once, to walk back through her father's forge door at the end of her contract not just safe and intact but fully in command of her mother's token. By the Battle of the Mouth, she'd have been happy just to walk through it at all.

"Now there's time," she continued. "However long it takes to build the prince's road. But there's not much to be gained from whatever skill I can muster if I'm not going to stay signed on."

Emory nodded. "But if you *were* to stay signed on, one cultivated token alone would be enough to qualify you for centurion."

Of course it was the first place his mind went. So few of the people commanding them had come up through the infantry. Most Aureans entered the ranks as centurions—though not without reason. "I'd get my century killed if it fell to me to defend them from a demon trooper with nothing but a Light of Angels," she reminded him. "Who'd serve under an officer like that?"

"I would," he replied without hesitation.

Kat blinked. "You're just saying that because I put you on your back today."

"I'm just saying that because I've seen what happens when you rally the line. Even this morning in the med tent, you brought the whole decade into focus. You think a light's not much, but sometimes all people need is a reminder that the hosts are on our side."

"And what about the demons strong enough to cut a soldier clean in half? Think the reminder's going to do them much good?"

"Well, no, that's what those magnificent muscles are for," he replied, rapping his knuckles against her bicep.

They did this all the time. Casual touches. Teasing compliments. Hosts above, she'd had him on his back in front of the whole century just a few hours prior, so why was it that this—just a brief touch and a kind word—had her feeling like she'd toppled over the edge of a cliff?

The fraught talk of the future wasn't helping. Kat had dreamed of returning to the forge with something to show for her time away—to walk back into her father's arms and prove to him that these stolen years hadn't been for nothing. But she wouldn't be coming back an officer or even a proper Aurean. All the prince had done was move the timetable up on the moment she'd have to leave Emory behind.

There was no question of what he'd do next. Emory had enlisted the day he'd turned sixteen, practically the second he was legally able to take up arms in service of Telrus, and signed on for twenty years of service. He'd grown out of the teenaged snobbery that had Giselle in its grip, but he remained a loyal soldier through and through. There was no other life he'd ever choose for himself.

And maybe that made it selfish of her to dream that anything could happen between them in the time they had left. They'd had one glorious night. She could—*should*—let that be the ending of something wonderful, not the beginning of something that could ruin them both.

Or at least, that was Kat's line of thinking before Emory reached down to the bag she hadn't noticed on the ground next to him. "Dinner was wet and sloppy, so I couldn't sneak a plate out of the mess for you, but I think I found the next best thing," he said.

The object he pulled from the bag was so impossible that for a moment, Kat couldn't quite *see* it. The pieces she put together—a spiky tail of stiff, waxy leaves, a spiny, almost reptilian skin, a shade of yellow molting into green—didn't add up, even when she finally understood what she was looking at. They were hundreds of miles from the southern coasts.

And yet Emory was holding a pineapple.

"Wh . . . *How?*" Kat demanded, reaching out to prod one of its spines. The confirmation that it was tangible didn't do anything to correct the feeling that she was dreaming.

"The prince brought his own supplies when he rolled into camp, and the kitchens haven't figured out where to put them yet," he said with a shrug. "Before I was a soldier, I was a food-snatching thorn in Miss Ophelia's side. The cooks in this camp have nothing on her. Go on."

Kat gingerly lifted the fruit from his hands, turning it over to inspect its scaly surface. She'd never seen one up close like this. It had always been a dream of hers to eat one, but she figured she'd either need to voyage south or somehow get herself invited to a fancy dinner party to make it a reality. But here she was in a war camp, where they'd all been going for months on strict rations, holding a genuine treasure.

"You remembered," she said wonderingly.

"It was the first thing you ever told me you wanted to eat when this was all over."

"Because it was such a long shot, I figured I had to dream big." Kat laughed, pinching one of the rigid leaves between her fingers. That day was crystal clear in her memory. It had been horrible— not in the bloody sense, but in the tedious one. Their gains were minuscule, every ten feet earned over several rotations through the lines, and it was the first time Kat had ever felt just how dangerous fatigue could be.

In previous engagements, she could always trust that the next rank would be ready to take over and that she'd get the time she needed to recover her breath and rally for her next turn at the front. But on this day, the rest wasn't enough. She'd gotten sloppy, taken a hard knock on the head from the butt of her own spear, and she saw the panic it put in Emory's eyes. Their fates were tied. They both needed to focus.

She'd been disoriented, but she knew on a bone-deep level that they weren't going to make it out of this if she couldn't get *him* to cover for her, and that meant wrenching him out of the spiral his thoughts had locked him into. So in the press of the midcentury, with the chaos of battle clamoring ahead, she had yoked one arm over the back of his neck and said, "Pineapple."

"Pineapple?" he'd repeated.

"I've never had a pineapple. So we're going to get through this, and then I'm going to go on a nice trip to some southern beach and I'm going to find a pineapple and eat it."

"What, just lying around?"

"Don't they grow on trees down there?"

"I don't . . . I have no idea . . ."

For a moment, she'd feared she'd only made his distraction worse. "That's my thing," Kat said hastily. "Now you go. Something to look forward to when all this is over."

She had *felt* the moment the focus took him, his posture steadying under her arm. "Remember when we passed through Valon? The officers wouldn't shut up about that tavern they stopped in that had a strawberry mead."

"Perfect. We're going to get through this, and I'm going to have my pineapple, and you're going to have your strawberry mead."

It had become their ritual. Something to keep them going when the churn got hard. As the campaign wore on, the list got absurdly long and occasionally fanciful beyond reason. They dreamed of shaved ice from the far northern reaches, of spun sugar street food Emory had once heard about from a Vayan comrade, of dining at the king's own table, which Kat promised to tolerate long enough to see what kind of wonderful dishes it must entail. It would take a lifetime to check off every promised reward.

But now Kat found herself faced with an unexpected lifetime of potential ahead—and, as promised, a pineapple.

"How do you even eat this?" she asked with an incredulous laugh.

"May I?" Emory held out a hand, and she hefted the pineapple into it. "I asked around, and one of the guys in the Fourth Century knew the trick to this." He palmed it around until it was, at least to her mind, upside down, and jammed his thumb against the base.

"You asked around . . . just now?"

Emory grunted. "Course not—I just stole this from a prince. It was years back."

"Years back as in right after I said I wanted to eat a pineapple?"

"Had to be sure we'd be ready when the moment came." He wedged his thumb into a seam in the fruit and began working it around the hardened circle that she assumed had once been a stem. Heat rose in her cheeks, and she wasn't sure whether to blame it on the fact that he'd been preparing for this moment for years or the fact that the . . . *thumbing* looked vaguely suggestive. "Hah," he rasped unfairly, jammed the rest of his hand into the base, and tugged, pulling out a juicy, conical plug.

"Guy in the Fourth taught you how to do that, huh?" Kat said with a waggle of her eyebrows.

"Do you want the fruit or not?" he replied, cradling his bounty closer to his chest.

She laughed, holding out a hand. But instead of handing the pineapple back over to her, Emory dropped the plug and dug back into the hole he'd made, levering his thumb against the spiny rind to split off a chunk of gleaming yellow flesh. He handed her the bite, and she took it with the same reverence she might have granted an Aurean token.

"You too," Kat said, hefting her chunk like she was waiting for a toast. "At the same time."

"I don't want to step on your moment."

"I want you in my moment."

The words had rushed out before Kat could think about what she was saying, but before she could teeter into an excuse, Emory blinked, nodded, and dug his thumb back into the pineapple's flesh, splitting off his own chunk. "Together, then?"

Kat brought the pineapple to the cusp of her lips. The sweet smell was overwhelming, bright and fresh like nothing she'd tasted in ages, and her mouth immediately began to water. But she waited until Emory had done the same before slipping it into her teeth and biting down.

She hadn't expected it to be so *fibrous,* but the shock of the texture was immediately washed away by the flavor—sugary, to be sure, but with an acid tartness that offset it, sending a tingling sensation buzzing through her mouth. Her eyes watered. For the longest time, food had been nothing but fuel to her. The only job the cooks took seriously was doling out large enough portions to keep the legions going, and taste was an afterthought—nice to have, but never essential.

"You okay there?" Emory hazarded, and Kat nudged away a tear with the back of her hand.

"I've got to get you back for this," she said, sniffling, then took another nibble from the remaining pulp on the rind.

Wordlessly, Emory handed her another piece.

"Strawberry mead?" she asked once she'd finished chewing it.

"Whatever we find next. As much of it as we can manage before the prince's road is finished."

"We should have been writing them down," Kat lamented.

"Well, that's the other thing," Emory said. "I may have traded a favor with Javi for pen and paper. Might have a list in my pocket."

Kat's eyes widened. "Show me."

He raised his juice-smothered hands helplessly.

For a brief, less-than-rational moment, Kat considered pawing for it herself. "Well, if it's been canonized in writing, we have to do it. No backing out now." She held out her own juice-stained hand to shake.

Emory took it with just a shade too much tenderness, his grasp firm and sticky. "Till the end of the road," he said, and Kat knew she wasn't imagining the hint of sadness in those words.

It was at that precise moment Giselle realized that neither of them was paying attention to her. "*Hey,*" she shouted, and the two of them lurched apart. "You didn't see anything I just did, did you?"

Kat, who was slightly more concerned with what *she'd* seen, sputtered. Emory stowed the pineapple behind his back a hair too slowly.

"What is that?" Giselle demanded.

"Nothing," Emory said, half an octave higher than his usual timbre.

"I saw it. How the hell did you get a *pineapple*?"

He shrugged. "Found it lying around."

Giselle stomped back across the training field, and Kat lurched in front of Emory like she was the shieldbearer and not the other way around. Giselle's eyes narrowed suspiciously. "You guys are acting weird."

"No, we're not," the two of them replied in unison.

"Sure." A canny look came over her features. "So you wouldn't mind if I mentioned this to Mira?"

"First of all, I'm very disappointed in you," Emory said, leaning out from behind Kat's shoulder. "All these lessons mean nothing if there's no loyalty in the decade. Second, loyalty can be bought." He proffered the pineapple. Giselle reached for it, and he tugged it back. "Uh-uh. Let's hear it."

"I will not mention this to Mira," Giselle recited in a monotone.

"Good kid." He snapped off a large chunk and held it out to her, and Giselle snatched it from his grasp.

She bit into it, glancing warily between the two of them, and Kat knew that though her silence had been purchased for the moment, there was no walking back the suspicion that lit Giselle's eyes.

CHAPTER 9

IT TOOK ADRIEN AUGUSTINE A FULL WEEK TO ASSEMBLE HIS PLAN for the road, a full hour to present it to the mustered legions, and only seconds for Kat to decide the Third Century was in deep, deep trouble.

The plan he'd laid out would take the entire span of the summer to complete—which seemed terrifyingly fast for a piece of infrastructure meant to leave a permanent mark on the fabric of the kingdom. All seven legions would participate, thousands upon thousands of soldiers distributed over the seven hundred miles that spanned from the Mouth of Hell's puckered remains clear back to Rusta, the capital. The project would culminate in a victory ball thrown in the prince's honor, and the very next morning, he'd grant a full release from service to every soldier who requested it.

It did little to soften the prospect of months of hard labor in

the full glory of summer, and the chatter rumbling beneath
Adrien's token-assisted oration bent clearly toward dissatisfaction.

And that was before the second assembly, where Mira announced that the Third Century would be singled out as a special
security detail, traveling alongside the prince's entourage. For a
moment, this had seemed to cheer them—and then their centurion had clarified that they would still be digging as they went,
alongside providing nonstop coverage of the prince's camp.

Kat felt guiltier and guiltier as the mood among the century
only got more sour. If she hadn't made such a spectacle of herself, none of them would be in this mess. Worse, it seemed Mira
wouldn't be announcing *why* the prince needed such extensive
coverage. Kat knew that Adrien wanted an uncomplicated, joyous, definitive end to the war, but if a Lesser Lord struck them
now, the century wouldn't know what hit them.

Without that context, the logistical nightmare looked horribly
unjustified—making it harder and harder for Kat and Emory to
play along with their comrades' confusion.

"You're *sure* the prince has evidence there are . . ." Emory muttered over his shoulder.

"Swear on the Seal," Kat replied just as low, but she needn't
have worried about being overheard. Mira had just clarified that
they would be performing this additional surveillance at no extra
pay, and the protesting cries that ensued provided ample cover.

Interestingly, Faye Laurent had joined her for this address,
looking increasingly distressed by the way things were getting out
of hand. It seemed that Adrien's friends were all assigned to man-
agerial roles across the legions, which Kat was sure the centurions
were just *thrilled* about. But, she supposed, out of the four young
nobles, Faye was likely to be the least intrusive. Thus far, she'd
only smiled pleasantly and nodded along to everything Mira said.
Adrien probably could have replaced her with a houseplant and
gotten the same effect.

"This is horseshit," Carrick groaned, drawing a sympathetic look from Sawyer. "You don't *need* thousands of people to build a road. We're not even trained in . . . what's it called? Masonry?"

"If it's going to be stone," Javi offered helpfully.

"Where the fuck is he going to get the stone for it?" Carrick seethed. "Does one of his tokens let him shit it out?"

"I have one final announcement," Mira thundered over the crowd. "Katrien, would you please join me up here?"

For the second time this week, Kat felt the entire century's eyes on her. It was barely a mercy that she was just as confused as they were, and it took a searing couple of seconds for her brain to catch up to Mira's order and comply with it. She eased past Emory, who shot her a worried glance, stepped out of the ranks, and crossed to the base of Mira's assembly platform. Most of the officers mounted it with the assistance of a token, but Kat had to haul herself up gracelessly on the struts, drawing an ominous creak from the structure as she rolled out over the top and got to her feet.

"There she is. Let's have a hand for the hinge spear of the first decade and the spectacle she put on this week," Mira said, holding out her palms with a rare showman's flourish.

Kat took in the century's applause with a wave, struggling to tamp down the flush building in her cheeks. Her own decade added a few appreciative whoops and hollers, and she found an anchor in the encouraging smile Emory flashed her way.

"As you might have noticed, that spectacle caught the prince's eye. And so I thought if Katrien truly wants to represent our century in the eyes of our future ruler, why not make it official? As of today, Katrien will be serving as a special liaison between you and your leadership."

Isn't that Mobbert's job? Kat wondered, her distressed gaze flicking to where Mira's strange little cousin was joining the fresh wave of applause. Mira had always been profoundly unfussy about administration, content to let Mobbert handle all her particulars. Kat didn't know how to handle any of her particulars. She knew how to march in formation and stick evil with her spear.

"If any of you have a grievance with this new state of affairs, I encourage you to raise it with Katrien, and she'll make sure your voice is heard," Mira said.

Ah. There it was. Mira was all about what she termed "practical discipline." An ass-kicking for Emory that would reinforce the combat principles she wanted drilled into him. A latrine rotation for Elise so that while she was contemplating the mistake of spying on the high command, she was also making herself useful. And now this. A "promotion" for Kat that put her squarely in the sights of the rest of her century, since she'd made such a spectacle of herself yesterday, that pulled double duty by keeping that ire off her centurion's back.

Kat had to admire the efficiency, if nothing else.

"The prince will be mobilizing his camp in three days' time. Until then, we'll stay on the same job rotation. Which means all of you already know what you should be doing. Dismissed."

Kat, in fact, had no idea what she was supposed to be doing. She opened her mouth to say as much, but Mira caught her eye and beckoned sharply before dropping from the edge of the platform and taking off toward the officer tents.

Kat clambered down after her, once again wondering why her light token couldn't be a lightening token. She had to jog to catch up to Mira, but once there, she could keep pace with the centurion's shorter strides easily. "Centurion?" she hazarded. "Not to say that I'm not grateful, but—"

"Then don't say it. Be grateful. Yes, this is happening because this little misadventure is all your fault, but you should see this as an opportunity."

"I'm afraid I don't follow, centurion."

"Well, I'm of two minds about it. On the one hand, the prince just happened to see a woman at the right time and decided to totally upend my command as a result. Nothing we can do about that. But on the other, he was right to notice you. After all, you're the only other Aurean in this century. You have serious prospects. It's time we did something about it."

"Oh," Kat said, blinking. "Well. Thank you, centurion."

"I wasn't kidding about what I said in front of the assembly," Mira continued. "You're in a unique position as an infantry soldier with officer potential, and that makes you uniquely suited to be the bridge between the soldiers and their command."

Yes, but that sounds like a lot of work, Kat stopped herself from arguing. Her brain had latched onto the words *officer potential,* turning them over and over in her head like a neat rock she'd found in a river. Like Emory had reminded her on the edge of the training field, a single Aurean token *was* enough to qualify her for command. But her pauper's token was also enough to separate her from some of her comrades who had no chance at all to attain such a rank.

It was exactly the kind of opportunity her father had encouraged her to seek out. Something she could bring back to the forge, some proof the years she'd been drafted hadn't been a waste. A chance to wring something not from metal but from her own inherent talents. It had been a fanciful dream—one that immediately plummeted to the bottom of her priorities when the true grind of the war started.

Maybe in peacetime, it was the moment to try for some proper ambition. To invest, the way her superiors did, in the prospects her token had granted her.

"I'll give it my best," Kat said as they approached Mira's tent. In daylight, she could almost pretend that it was unfamiliar, that she hadn't experienced a moment of brief, unfettered, *true* ambition under its shelter.

Mira beckoned her and Mobbert inside, Kat trying to act like she'd never seen the interior before and Mobbert going straight to the desk in the entryway that Kat knew from personal experience had a slight wobble in one of its legs. "See that you do," her centurion replied with a rare, razor-edged grin. "Now let's talk about the particulars of your new role."

SO MUCH FOR AMBITION. SO MUCH FOR TRYING HER BEST. BARELY an hour into her so-called opportunity, Kat was already seeing it for the curse it was.

She'd tried to grab dinner. Tried to make it through a hearty serving of some of the finest slop the kitchens had cobbled together in ages, tried to savor the miracle that was not having your supply lines raided by demons every day and the additional miracle of the prince's presence guaranteeing an abundance of spice not usually featured in the infantry's staple rations. She'd gotten one single bite into her meal before the first aggrieved soldier threw himself down on her decade's bench and began voicing an onslaught of concerns about their marching orders.

Now five of them crowded around her, with several more lined up to take the spots they vacated. Javi and Emory stood to the side, their bowls cooling in their hands as they waited for their usual seats to clear up. Carrick and Sawyer had given up entirely and wedged themselves in with the second decade at the next table over to watch the show unfold.

"Look," Kat tried to say firmly to her latest adversary, but the word had lost its luster after a couple hundred repetitions. None of them were looking. They weren't even trying to look. "I don't want you to miss your daughter's birthday either. But let me just put it out there that your contract seems to have a full three years left on it, which means that the prince's offer is incredibly generous. Think of all the birthdays that—okay, yeah, I get that ten is a big one. Ten's pretty important. Double digits is huge, I'm not going to dispute that. What's her name? Ayla. Lovely. I'm going to mention that to leadership. I think it's important that they hear this. But I'm also not making any promises."

It had been a full hour of this. Her meal—her *above average meal*—sat cold in front of her. Under other circumstances, she'd consider it an unforgivable sin. She'd challenge these soldiers to a duel on the training field. Some of them had legitimate concerns that tugged at her heartstrings. A tenth birthday wasn't something you could do over a few months later.

Others were . . . less sympathetic. One man considered himself the height of martial prowess after a full six months with the century and thought his talents would be *wasted*, absolutely *wasted* on road construction and guard duty. Some inquired about transfers to other divisions of the forces that wouldn't be working on the road—there were garrisons scattered throughout the land, after all, and wouldn't they be light on soldiers after nearly every trained legionnaire had been summoned to the front for the march on the Mouth?

You're not special, she wanted to shout. *None of us are special.* But she'd been made special, elevated by the prince's attention and her centurion's punishment and the token hanging around her neck that made her inherently valuable. Her job was to make everyone else feel special, even if they didn't have tokens or attention or a punishment.

"My turn," Emory announced suddenly, plunging into the gap left by one soldier with all the skill of a shieldbearer locking into the fore before another man could squeeze in ahead of him. "I have a complaint."

"Do you, now?" Kat asked, suppressing a smirk.

"I have a whole litany, actually. And you're going to hear *all* of them," he declared, loudly and obviously. "My first complaint is that you've barely touched your dinner, so tuck in—I won't mind if you chew while I talk."

Kat didn't need to be told twice. She nearly choked on her first spoonful, her throat raw from speaking about six times as much as she generally did in any given day.

"My second complaint is that there are an *awful* lot of people on the first decade's benches who aren't in the first decade themselves." He shot glares up and down the knot of gathered soldiers.

"Centurion said—" the self-professed great warrior tried.

"Don't give a fuck. You've been on the campaign for less than a year, yeah? Dinnertime is sacred."

"The war is o—"

"The war may be over, but the mess tent still runs on a schedule. Javi?"

Kat startled as Javi dove into the gap between her and the soldier seated on her left, squaring himself to force room. He plunked his bowl down on the table, drew his book out from where he'd tucked it in the neck of his tunic, and held it up, blocking the rest of the petitioners on the bench from Kat's view. The soldier next to him snatched for it, but Javi only flipped it closed, rapped them across the knuckles, and went right back to reading.

Sensing an opportunity, the soldier on her right said, "I have a religious objection to—"

She got no further before an arm looped around her waist and hauled her bodily up off the bench. Carrick, it seemed, had forgone his shieldbearer training and leaped straight to wrestling, and as he hauled the kicking, protesting soldier clear, it was Sawyer who dove into the new gap with the precision of a spear.

"Hey," he said, turning toward Kat so that his broad shoulders formed yet another barrier between her and the persistent masses. "So I've heard you're taking feedback? Personally, I think you should show Emory a thing or two again. The man seems to think he can just butt into your important personal conversations."

Kat snorted around a half-chewed mouthful.

"I think you should start biting people," Ziva offered from the far end of the table, where she, too, had snuck in.

Emory tugged his collar noticeably.

"You guys couldn't have done this sooner?" Kat whined, but she couldn't keep her smile down. Her decade. The people who'd carried her through battle after battle, who'd survived until the end and still fought for her—and none more so than Emory, who had marshaled them all to come to her aid.

It was going to hurt like hell to leave them behind, and in that moment Kat wondered—not for the first time, but with a level of seriousness that startled her—whether she might choose not to.

Whether this was where she belonged after all.

THEY SNUCK HER OUT THROUGH THE COOKFIRES, DODGING shouts and complaints from the kitchen staff cleaning up after a ravenous legion, which were softened marginally by the teetering stack of collected bowls and cutlery Emory deposited directly into the washbins. Kat tried to thank them all for their delicious meal even as she was shunted past the cleaning rags they snapped at her and out into the chill of the night air.

"Not sure that was necessary," she said, glancing around at her compatriots. Most of the century had lost interest once the first decade had begun to wall them off from her, and even the persistent ones had run out of things to say eventually.

"Nonsense," Sawyer said, slinging a friendly arm around her shoulder. "Our new century representative needs strict security. It's nothing but back exits from here on out."

Carrick snickered, and Ziva swatted him before glancing forlornly back at the tent. "I should probably apologize to my kitchen girl."

"And we heard a rumor there's a man in the camp trail running the best dice game we've seen in ages," Carrick added, tugging on his battle partner's hem.

Javi wordlessly held up his book.

And then the rest of the decade scattered, leaving nothing but her, Emory, and the stars above.

"Your guard might be a little light, my liege, but I promise I'll give it my all," he said, knocking his shoulder into hers. "Where to?"

"Well," Kat hedged, teetering on the edge of a dangerous suggestion, "Mira's instructions were to report any grievances I heard to one of the camp scribes as soon as possible. So I should probably do that, before I forget that Ayla's tenth birthday is coming up and it's going to be an absolute shame her father's missing it."

"To the scribes' tent, then."

"Could be a bit of a walk," Kat said. "They've set it up on the far end of the encampment. And it's probably better to walk the outskirts—maybe take the route by the edge of the forest?"

"To keep the rest of the century from spotting you, of course?"

"Of course," Kat replied, matching his knowing smirk.

Their previous misadventure in Mira's tent was a testament to the lack of privacy in the war camp, but for those who were less discerning—or those who only needed minutes, not hours—the fringes were the next best thing. The legions had dug in to what had once been their marching camp, not anticipating a long stay. This had been an all-or-nothing push, and their fortifications amounted to a trench around the camp's perimeter and a clear-cut of the forest edge limning them to put some open ground between cover and the guard posts. Outside of the camp proper, the Silk Row had set up their tents, along with the host of traveling merchants who trailed the army's movements. Most of their escort had fallen off toward the end of the campaign, not willing to risk their lives for their livelihoods in such close proximity to the Mouth of Hell, but a few hangers-on gave any common soldier grounds to leave the camp's boundaries without questioning.

Which wasn't to say that Kat didn't have her guard up. Carrick and Sawyer had mentioned they were headed out here for that dice game, and she wasn't sure how much Emory had told them. If they found out about their little indiscretion, the consequences might be dire—and if they caught them out on their way to another, there'd be no hearing the end of it.

And that's what this was, wasn't it? As they broke from the main path and onto a little foot trail that cut into the edge of the woods, Kat's stomach swooped uncertainly. Making a pact to check off food on the list they'd built was one thing. This was a deliberate attempt at privacy—the first true chance they'd had since the night before the battle. Emory seemed like he'd caught her implication, but she could never be too sure with him. "So," she started, her voice strained a shade higher than usual. "Nice night."

"Mm," he replied, and she resisted the urge to pinch him. They'd been in this together too long for him to be so opaque, but with the forest canopy blocking out the stars and the moonlight, she had little else to go on.

"Mira said the same thing you did."

That put a stutter in his stride.

"She thinks I have potential. This aide role is a punishment, but it's also an opportunity. A chance to get a feel for leadership."

"How's it feel so far?"

Kat scoffed through a weary grin. "Feels like a lot of people are upset with me all the time and there's no way to please all of them. Which, I imagine, is probably how Mira feels every day."

"So you're saying it's good training. But how do *you* feel about it?" he asked.

The sudden intensity of the question made Kat thankful the night had rendered her just as impossible to read. "I feel like it's wasted on me if I'm just going to take my release at the end of this. But when I was first drafted, my father told me I should try

to turn it into an opportunity. If I was going to lose this time anyway, I might as well wring what I can from it. Now I'm starting to
wonder if . . . Maybe if this works out . . ."

Emory's breath caught.

"I don't know. Maybe it's not such a certain thing after all.
Maybe you're right, and Mira's right, and there's more I can make
of myself here."

"I wasn't kidding," he said. "I know I joke about a lot of things,
but never that. You'd be an incredible officer. And if this is what
you want, consider me your aide." There was a pinch on the edge
of his words, and for a moment Kat felt profoundly callous. Here
she was, hemming about a golden opportunity that had fallen into
her lap to a man who'd never had a scrap of gold in his entire life.

"It should be you," she blurted.

"Kat—"

"You were the one who marshaled the rest of the decade to
get the century off my back tonight. And you were the one who
was supposed to be getting disciplined anyway. The only reason
anyone's paying any attention to me at all is *this*." She clasped her
token through her shirt, pulling the fabric taut.

But before she could get another word in, Emory's hand was
covering hers. "Kat," he said, a sudden, unbearable rasp in his
voice. "I can't be jealous over gifts I was never born with or doors
that will never open to a man like me. I'm just happy someone as
incredible as you gets a chance to shine."

In the dark, he was barely more than a shadow, his features indistinct but his gaze unmistakably locked on her. It was impossible
to look his generosity in the eye and feel worthy of it. "Y-You . . ."
she stammered, reaching up with her other hand. Her fingertips
grazed hesitantly along the scruff at his jawline—as if she didn't
already know the shape of it, hadn't already felt it against more
than just her hands. Her voice dropped to a whisper. "You can't
just say things like that."

There was a tension in Emory, the same tension she saw break beside the bonfire on the night that started this. He was holding himself back, even as his grip on her hand tightened. "Kat, I . . . I don't know if we should . . ." he breathed in the narrow space between them.

Her heart sank. This was never supposed to happen. They weren't supposed to survive the Battle of the Mouth. Everything they'd done together the night before it had hinged upon that fact. And yet, a sudden spark of anger lit inside her. "What was the *point* of living through that hell if we don't get to go after the things we want?" she whispered, letting her hand fall deliberately on his stubbled cheek.

"This is what you want?" Emory asked.

Kat fought the urge to grab him by the shoulders and shake him. "Am I not making it clear enough?"

Emory's gaze fell to where their hands were entwined, his shielding hers. "I don't want to be a burden to your ambitions. It was different when we had nothing to lose."

"Is this . . . what you want?" Kat hazarded, stilling.

"Of course," he blurted, and she swore she felt his cheek heat beneath her hand. "But . . ."

"You can't risk your reputation," Kat said, so he wouldn't have to.

"I think we've proven that I *can*," he replied, and Kat counted herself lucky she couldn't quite make out the insufferable sly look that had no doubt come over him. "*Should* is harder to say. And I wouldn't be risking as much as you. You think I'm worth ruining your future over?"

"Hosts, you might be the most dramatic man I've ever met— and we share a tent with *Brandt*. We didn't *have* a future until two days ago. And I'm not sure about a lot of things, but this . . ." She slid her hand carefully into a firmer hold on his jaw, pulling his eyes back up to meet hers. "The future's not promised, and we might not be able to get away with this tomorrow, but we can try, can't we?"

Emory's pulse jumped beneath her grip. On the battlefield, she'd always felt her own fear in step with his, and she understood all at once that this was not the case now. Kat's vision of an uncertain future was a hopeful one, and Emory couldn't match it. He'd only been able to act when there was nothing but death ahead of them.

And she couldn't force him.

Kat let her palm slip down his cheek. She knew the retreat had been called. They weren't far from the scribes' encampment now, and maybe it was better to focus on the future that had dragged her unwillingly forward, not the one that stalled in its tracks.

But as she leaned back, a hand at her waist stopped her. Her sharp breath in was twinned as Emory seemed to steel himself. She could barely see him, but two trembling points of contact were all she needed to understand. Her eyes dropped hungrily to where his lips must be. Dropped shut as he leaned in carefully.

Then snapped open as somewhere out in the brush, a twig cracked.

In a heartbeat, he'd spun to shield her as Kat's fists closed around empty air, longing for her spear. Something was moving out there and getting closer. Something that sounded *big*—too big to be another pair of soldiers stumbling out of the camp trail for an illicit rendezvous.

"You don't think . . ." Emory breathed.

Kat did. She'd been thinking, ever since Adrien told her about the Lesser Lords. Wondering when the first strike would come and how unprepared the Third Century would be. It had left her primed to jump at shadows, and for a moment she was ready to dismiss her paranoia as exactly that.

Then she saw movement.

It was enormous—far bigger than the last shock knight that had rattled their line, bigger than any demon she'd faced on the battlefield before—which made its quiet creep all the more eerie. It moved through the woods like liquid shadow, indistinct through the dark columns of the tree trunks, and for a moment Kat was so fixated on trying to track it that she failed to notice it had company. Not thralls—they would have heard thralls coming, for one thing, and only the Demon Lord's magic could raise them—but no fewer than five underlings skirting its wake.

Kat nudged Emory's shoulder, and together the two of them crept for the nearest tree trunk, pressing themselves into the cool, damp wood of the old growth. Her breath came in shuddering fits as she struggled to keep it quiet, and she held her arms slightly away from her body, terrified that any brush of cloth on cloth might give away their location.

The demon paused, its lungs working like a great pair of bellows as it scented the air, and Kat ducked lower to the ground, pulling Emory with her. She'd never had to worry about a demon being able to smell her—had never thought to wonder if their senses were sharp.

A hand at her chest startled her so badly that she nearly yelped, slipping her palm over her mouth to catch the noise before it could escape her. Emory pressed insistently on her token, and Kat understood. If they were caught, they didn't have a chance—but they could give one to everyone else. If she could call on her token. If she could flood the woods with angelic light.

It was Kat's turn to cover his hand with hers. She thought of her mother, of every night her token had made itself a beacon, of how she'd never had to fear the dark as long as her mom was at her side. She'd never been able to match that light in her own feeble attempts to cultivate her Aurean power, but maybe now was the moment—now, when it mattered more than anything else.

Kat called to the hosts, imagined her voice reaching past the Seal of Heaven, fought back the bile flooding her tongue. *Help me. Let me bring your light forth.*

Nothing answered. She was hollow with fear, inadequate as a vessel for anything else, and the metal beneath her palm was nothing she could shape into a tool. She was on her back beneath the shock knight again, infantry meat in the mortar, waiting for the pestle to drop.

Another *crack*. This time, the noise was farther away. The demon and its underlings were moving again, continuing along the forest path. Maybe the hosts were on her side after all.

"They're after the prince, right?" Emory breathed close to her ear.

Kat nodded—she wouldn't risk more.

"Then why are they headed toward the scribes?"

Dread flooded her the moment she landed on the answer. The scribes' encampment rested on the outside edge of the legions', positioned for efficiency when it came to sending and receiving couriers. It was the beating heart of the army's logistics, managing the supplies necessary to keep the legions fed and equipped. With their sudden pivot to infrastructure, it had become the central hub of the road project. Which meant—

Kat stiffened. "Because they're after the prince."

CHAPTER 10

THEY CREPT UNTIL THEY WERE CERTAIN THEY COULD RUN, PLUNG-
ing through the woods to the clear-cut and sprinting to the trench
that circled the outer edge of the camp. It was dug a full six feet
deep, the excavated dirt piled high on its inward side to form an
additional protective barrier, which handily shielded Kat and
Emory as they slid down to its base and then took off, staggering
through the loose dirt as fast as their feet could carry them.

Kat spent the entire sprint cursing Adrien Augustine and his
entire rotten bloodline. Surely with all his Aurean might, he could
have concocted a strategy that didn't hinge on throwing powerless
infantry against the Lesser Lords. But the prince wanted his
throne and his people's praise, and now innocent soldiers were
going to face a nightmare for which, by his own design, they were
horrifically unprepared.

Worse, there'd been no time to break the Third Century from
the rest of the legions. The temptation to raise the alarm was blis-

tering. If they threw the whole camp into chaos, there was a chance they could secure the prince, even if it would shatter the peace.

But there was also a chance—a slim chance, but a chance nonetheless—that they could react just as Adrien intended. Could take this Lesser Lord out quietly, with no Aurean flash at all. If Adrien was at the scribes' camp, he'd be escorted by at least two decades of the Third Century. Two of them were assigned to him at all times.

Two didn't sound like nearly enough to stop a Lesser Lord in its tracks, but Kat knew they were past the point of picking their battles. Two would have to do.

The scribes' camp was an ember of light, three large administrative tents flanked by a set of smaller sleepers that laid like darkened logs around a campfire. In desperate times, they would be working at all hours of the night, ensuring communications flowed smoothly among the legions, the capital, their suppliers, and anything else necessary to keep thousands of soldiers in fighting shape. They should have been enjoying a much-needed reprieve from all that, but as Kat and Emory approached, she saw they were just as busy as ever.

Part of that impression was formed by the decades standing guard around the central tent. When Adrien had demanded earlier today that at least twenty of the Third Century's soldiers would need to escort him at all times, it had sounded like overkill—especially to the poor bastards abruptly thrown onto the first night shifts.

Now Kat couldn't be anything but cheered at the sight of her comrades. She and Emory clambered out of the trench, their sprint dulled to a jog as they approached. She snuck a glance at the tree line, but in the light that spilled from the camp, it was impossible to tell what might lurk in the shadows.

No one was screaming yet. They had to take the wins where they could get them.

"Kat?" one of the soldiers called as she approached. It was

Paola, the seventh's hinge spear, a sturdy older soldier who held their line together with raw grit every time they hit the front of the formation. "Actually this is great timing. I've been meaning to ask if you could put a word in with—"

"Nope," Kat snapped firmly, glancing up and down the decade lined up outside the central tent. All of them were armed for century combat, the spearbearers with their usual weapons and the shieldbearers with a shortsword sheathed at their hips. It was an arrangement that worked well against thralls, but in unorganized combat, it would be a different story—especially given none of them were kitted out in their usual armor, only a light leather chestpiece and cap.

She caught Emory's eye and knew he'd reached the same sobering conclusion. It would take more than numbers to win this. It would take a leader's hand.

"What are you thinking?" she asked him.

"What are *you* thinking?" he countered.

"You rallied the troops at dinner—"

"Which means now it's *your* turn—"

"What's going on?" Paola interjected, looking wary.

"It's the seventh and eighth here, right?" Kat asked, picking out more familiar faces among the soldiers arranged across the camp. "We need everyone to form up. Get in close, before—"

A sudden shout of alarm echoed across the clear-cut, severed just as quickly by a gargled choke that was all too familiar. On the edge of the tent's light, a soldier swayed, then crumpled into the arms of the demon that had just cut his throat with nothing but a razor-edged nail.

The remaining four underlings were rushing from the trees, the rest of the soldiers lining the outer edge of the camp caught off guard as they struggled to bring their weapons around in time to meet them. Kat had nothing. There were no spares for her or Emory, and they'd be hard-pressed to find suitable weapons among the scholars' bedrolls.

Unless—

"The tents!" she shouted, sprinting to the closest of the sleepers as the rest of the posted soldiers rushed past. She kicked up the stakes and grabbed the canvas in a fistful, wading into the crumpled mess she'd made of it until she found the central pole holding the whole thing up—and an incredibly dismayed scholar rudely awakened by her boot, who could only watch in horror and confusion as she tore their shelter away and stripped the sturdy wooden beam of its rigging.

She glanced back over her shoulder to find Emory doing the same. It was a shorter weapon than the one she was used to wielding, and a longer one than he normally had to manage, but they'd have to do.

Ahead of them, the soldiers were meeting the demon underlings head-on, spears and swords struggling to keep their snapping jaws at bay. Each of the legionnaires had paired off against an enemy, trying to distribute their strength against the five demons they faced, but their true strength—and their only hope—couldn't surface in this disorganized brawl.

"Fall back to me!" Kat shouted, hoisting her makeshift staff.

If she'd had a smidge of Mira's authority or a token like Adrien's to make her voice too loud to ignore, maybe she could have pulled it off. But the seventh had just lost a man, and Kat's command wasn't nearly enough to override the instinct that had taken over.

It was one of the first things drilled into you on your first day on the lines—never let a demon have a corpse. Not unless you wanted to see that person again, puppeted by demon flesh and screaming in mindless pain as they clawed their way through your line. Do whatever necessary—beheading, burning, smashing their spine to bits—but never, *never* let a demon have a corpse.

"There's no Demon Lord left to raise him," Kat hollered, grabbing one of the seventh by the collar of his shirt as he tried to rush to his comrades' aid.

"Davis deserves better than to be left in the dirt," the man protested, wild-eyed. Three of his decade had forced the underling back from the man's corpse, walling up as another slammed the base of her shield into poor Davis's neck with a meaty crunch.

One of the underlings darted for an opening in their cluster, slavering jaw hung wide. Kat's shout of warning was swallowed by the scream the demon let out as Paola's spear found its target, plunging deep into the underling's shoulder and leaving a fountain of black blood in its wake as it tore free and staggered into a retreat.

Kat gritted her teeth and repeated, "Back to me! If we stay spread out, it's going to have us."

"What is?" Paola called over her shoulder.

A low, guttural noise rumbled from shadows of the tree line.

Kat didn't need to say it a third time. The decades scrambled back like there were a thousand thralls on their heels. "Seventh to my right, eighth to my left," Kat called, grasping for a bit of Mira's unshakable certainty. "Mark your target. No advance beyond five feet. Clear?"

"Clear!" the decades replied in staggered shouts, lurching into formation. She couldn't blame them—she wasn't their hinge or their centurion, and they'd all gone soft in the past week. Everyone had dreamed that this might be over and they might never have to face a demon on the field again. Worse, there was no century at their backs, no ranks to rotate through if they flagged, and no chance of calling for reinforcements. They'd have to use every last drop of strength wisely. There'd be no recovering.

And the demons knew it. Their eyes glimmered with predatory hunger as they probed the new formation, all but daring the soldiers to lunge after them and waste precious energy. They'd wear them down first, then move in for the kill.

So their ranks had to move instead. "On my count, march," Kat declared, pounding the butt of her staff into the ground to mark out the rhythm. Four beats, and on the fourth, they stepped as one. Kat could feel the reluctance of it, the way the line dragged with fear—and one notable exception, as Emory matched her without an ounce of hesitation.

Her thoughts flickered to the Battle of the Mouth. To the way he'd broken rank and thrown himself in front of her. To the way she was *certain* he hadn't learned his lesson from it.

Her own steps started to flag.

"Leftmost, striking!" one of the spearbearers on her left called out, and his decade contracted around him as he and his shield lunged forward. The demon tried to skirt back a heartbeat too late, and the spear caught the meat of its thigh. It let out a shrieking rasp, then another ear-shattering squeal as a second spear plunged into its abdomen, giving the first a chance to withdraw. The air flushed with the acidic, smoke-edged tang of demonic blood.

A third spear struck. A fourth. The demon's companions watched impassively. These creatures of Hell had no solidarity in their ranks, only loyalty to those higher up the food chain.

But they could also sense openings. With the eighth decade focused on the underling they'd caught, another decided to try its luck, rushing in so fast that the shieldbearers barely had time to react. It hit the line with scrabbling claws searching for purchase in metal, flesh, leather, *anything,* and one of the soldiers howled in obvious pain, flinching back into the line as their comrades tried to force space for them to shake out their wounded arm.

Emory lunged, and Kat's heart leaped with him as he brought his staff down hard on the demon's skull, scoring a *crack* clean between its curving horns. She fought down the urge to chastise him for the reckless move, for the way it had clearly startled the shields in front of him. It'd worked, hadn't it?

She needed to let her soldiers fight. She couldn't spare them all.

She was out of her depth.

It hit her like a blow to the chest—how she'd thrown herself headfirst into the fray untrained, fueled only by the raw necessity of it. Kat had never seen battle from the core of a century, calling orders and praying she'd made the right choices as they twisted the fate of every soldier around her. Mira always seemed so certain. It had always struck her as unquestionably correct to follow her directive.

Now Kat wondered how any of these decades could have confidence in what she was saying—and she felt how it was slowing her. They'd felled a single underling and scored hits on three of the others, but the Lesser Lord was still out there. It could wait for the smaller demons to tire them out, and it wouldn't care about its losses in the slightest.

Kat couldn't stop caring. Couldn't stop herself from taking it like a wound to her *own* body every time another claw struck flesh. The spearbearers were trying their best, but the demons were starting to circle wider, teasing apart their formation, loosening it up enough to create gaps that might seem obvious to Kat but couldn't possibly be noticed by the shieldbearers, who only had eyes for their enemies.

"Two steps back, my count!" she shouted, thumping her staff's butt again. On the fourth beat, the decades moved—more steadily than her first command, but in a simple backward motion that didn't fix the weakness in their formation. "*Tighten that line!*" Kat corrected, flinching at the obvious stress in her voice. Mira made her orders sound inevitable. Kat's were almost questions.

Her soldiers were getting sluggish, the kind of sluggish where they'd start expecting the changeover whistle at any moment. But no changeover was coming, only another, bigger demon—one Kat had just spotted in the shadows of the tree line.

Her brief glimpse of it in the forest hadn't given her an accurate read on its size—not while it was moving, bent low to the ground, and she was more concerned with staying out of its sights than getting a good look. Now it stood stock-still, drawn up to its full height, only its head distinct in the darkness. Its eyes burned with infernal fire, and its horns curled around its head like scythes. It was easily twice the size of any demon warrior that had hit her line in the past, a full twenty feet tall. Looking at it, she wondered why it bothered waiting. It looked like it could crush her two measly decades with a single blow.

They were tiring. The opening was going to come soon. The only question was when.

"Seventh break right, eighth break left, on my count!" Kat hollered and pulled her token out from beneath her shirt.

Emory's gaze snapped to her from where he'd inserted himself haphazardly in the seventh's formation. He knew her too well to let her get away with what she was about to try.

At least, not on her own.

Kat stamped out the count. On *four*, the decades moved, splitting clean down the middle.

And Kat didn't. She held her ground, eyes locked on the shadow in the tree line. Daring it. Begging it.

It *flowed* more than it moved, spilling from the trees like liquid night, dragging the shadows with it as it lowered that massive head and charged. The Lesser Lords knew what they were made for. They'd only take the field to down an enemy commander.

Which was exactly what Kat had made herself. With her fragment of a century split on either side of her, with Aurean gold plain on her chest, she'd offered herself up on a platter to the demon.

It came to feast.

"*Spears center, shields take the line,*" Kat screamed. Every muscle in her body begged for permission to run, and she very nearly granted it—up until the moment Emory threw himself ahead of her, squared like he had to the shock knight.

He hadn't learned a fucking thing. This fool of a man with his makeshift staff, a hinge shield with no decade but *her* to defend, rearranging her priorities in a heartbeat. Kat reached out, grabbed him by the shoulder, and forced him down.

The Lesser Lord's swipe missed him by a hair. In the same instant, all nine of the decades' remaining spears found their target as one.

Five glanced off, hitting a plated joint, a tough bit of sinew, a bone. Two found purchase in muscle—one through the monster's thigh and the other in the forearm that had been aiming for a second swipe. One lodged in the demon general's gut, flushing the night air with a vile scent as it punctured a bowel.

And one took it through the throat.

Black blood spewed like rain, spattering hot over Kat as the beast let out a gargled yowl. She tried to stagger back, pulling Emory with her, but nine *sticks* barely put a dent in the general's momentum. It toppled, its weight coming down like a meteor, and Kat ducked, braced for impact.

But it never came. She cracked an eye open to find Emory crouched at her side, his tentpole held vertical where it plowed into the ground.

The other end was buried in the Lesser Lord's soft palate, stalling its collapse with only inches to spare.

The bloody rain kept falling, drenching them both in its foul muck. Kat blinked through it, collapsing back on her ass with her heart hammering. She was vaguely aware of the decades rallying, free of her haphazard command. The hinge shields took over, their lines charging after the leaderless, fleeing underlings, but everything was secondary to Emory's eyes on her. To the way he'd refused to accept the risk she'd taken, the way he'd defended her once again like it was the most natural thing in the world.

The way this foul general of Hell had robbed them of their moment back in the forest, and now that it was dead, if she only reached out for him—

A sudden smattering of applause jerked her back into context, and she saw herself with fresh eyes: drenched in blood, awash in the stench of bile, and ready to lay all that aside. She let her head loll back to find the source of the noise.

Adrien Augustine had stepped from the scribes' tent, looking like he'd just been woken up from a very fine nap. His golden curls were haphazardly mussed, and his eyes were bleary, though they'd widened an acceptable amount at the sight of the Lesser Lord's steaming corpse barely ten yards from the flimsy canvas barrier he'd stepped through.

He let his applause fade as his gaze dropped to Kat. Hers couldn't help but lock on the one hundred golden tokens arrayed across his chest, all of them equally useless in the face of this beast. He'd been right, loath as she was to admit it. Infantry alone could take on a Lesser Lord and win. As if sensing her line of thinking, he lifted a finger and tapped it twice on one of his tokens—the lucky one, or so he'd told her.

"One down," the prince said with a toothy grin. "Two to go."

CHAPTER 11

THREE YEARS AT WAR HAD TRAINED KAT WELL IN THE ART OF campaigning. She'd learned to welcome the kind of days where nothing was expected of her beyond taking her turn leading the decade's pack mule in the winding snake of the First Legion's progress through the landscape and arriving on her feet at the camp the scouts had chosen. With a walking song bouncing between the soldiers to buoy their spirits, she could make the miles disappear easily, even if she could never quite bring herself to join in the singing.

Two weeks in, it was becoming clear that the road project was a different kind of campaign. The legions' organization had dissolved under Adrien Augustine's management as centuries were broken out into working units and spread over miles of countryside at a time. Gone were the massive war camps with nightly fortifications dug in around a single legion and all its centuries. The Third Century had been absorbed into the slow, strange pa-

rade Adrien was making along the road as it chewed its way down
through the highlands of Kaston and out into the plains of the
continent's heart. After years of slogging west, fighting and clawing for every scrap of ground gained, it was a relief to walk east
unhindered.

Or at least *less* hindered.

Kat's life had been thrown into utter chaos thanks to Mira's
so-called promotion. She could no longer afford to sleep until the
wake-up call, as she'd learned on day two, when a disgruntled
shieldbearer from the fifth decade latched onto her the second
she rolled out of the decade tent. Sleeping in with the rest of her
rank meant they knew exactly where to find her and could make
sure their particular gripe was at the top of her list for the day.

Instead, she'd begun forcing herself to get up as soon as dawn
began to pearl the sky, stepping over the lumps of her comrades
in their bedrolls, then stealing past the rows of the century's tents
and into the relative safety of the camp's administrative heart that
they flanked. Here lay the intricacies and essentials of the prince's
entourage, from the command tents in which the legions' leadership plotted the Augustine Road's grand advance to the tents that
quartered the second army—the hundreds of workers who kept
the whole operation fed and broke the camp down each day for
the next fifteen-mile march they'd progress along the road's construction.

Here also lay the most important tent in the whole operation—
the one in which breakfast was served.

Being Adrien's purported good luck charm was more of a
curse than a blessing, but it did entitle Kat to eat with him and the
rest of his companions, and her forced early start meant she had
plenty of time to savor the decadence of it. Every morning there
was sizzling bacon fresh off the griddle and pancakes with crisp
edges neatly fried in the leftover fat. Today, they'd pitched camp
close to Palomar, a riverside town nestled in the foothills that
drew the edge of Kaston's border with its neighboring duchy,

Bredol, and that meant that a runner would be arriving soon with the finest selections the local patisserie could provide.

As usual, Bodhi Ranjan was the first to join Kat. He rose and fell with the sun itself, and though he never seemed to need it, his appearance was always accompanied by a steaming mug of milky black tea that she suspected he brewed in the privacy of his accommodations. "Morning, Katrien," Bodhi said as he slotted in at her side on the long bench laid against the dining table. "Hope it wasn't too late of a night?"

"No more than usual," Kat replied, which was a roundabout way of saying it had been. After the first Lesser Lord's attack, Adrien had declared it in everyone's best interests that his lucky charm accompany him through his late-night work. Kat had made the mistake of going along with the order *before* she'd become acquainted with the prince's horrendous sleep schedule. One of the tokens in his array must have given him a boundless wakefulness— that, or the drastic amount of horrible black coffee he'd started drinking after picking up the habit from the officers in the command tent. It left her staggering back to the decade tent long after everyone else had bedded down for the night, feeling less like a soldier and more like a security blanket that had been dragged through the dirt after a clingy child.

Bodhi let out a sympathetic hum. She used to think he asked this kind of question out of concern for her, but then she'd started to notice the undercurrents of the curiosity he directed her way. It wasn't that he didn't care about Kat's well-being—he just also had a keen interest in whatever it was that kept the prince up so late at night.

The answer wasn't all that interesting. Usually, the prince was sorting through his correspondence and muttering over the logistics of the absurd project he'd spearheaded. She hadn't once caught him at anything even mildly salacious, nor anything that might threaten Bodhi's chances of coming out on top in the scramble to secure Adrien's hand. But though the prince hadn't earned her loyalty in the slightest, he did have her pity, and for that reason, Kat protected his privacy to the best of her ability.

Another benefit of Bodhi's disposition was that he was far too nice to ever call her out on it.

Next came Faye, rushing into the tent with a stack of papers clutched tight to her chest. She let them splay over the breakfast table, then pinned them with her plate.

Bodhi craned forward, squinting. "Still running the numbers with the quarries, huh? You know, the scribes could probably handle—"

"Yes, they *could*," Faye interrupted, "but then I wouldn't understand it at all. Aren't you curious where the stone for this road comes from?"

Bodhi and Kat exchanged a dubious glance. He'd chosen good looks and charm. Faye, on the other hand, had decided the way to Adrien's confidence was to make herself as useful as possible or die trying. More than once, Kat had borne witness to an absolute firecracker of a conversation where Faye had tried to engage the prince in a spirited discussion of his logistics and Adrien had nodded along, muttered the occasional word, and glanced about desperately for some excuse to bolt.

Given Adrien's penchant for late nights in the scribes' tent, if anything *should* have captured his attention, it would be the logistics of his road project. Faye was right to try it as an opening and right to be driven slightly mad by the fact it wasn't working.

Kat was beginning to find the prince's companions as tedious as he did—and that was *before* Celia Vai and Daya Imonde swept into the tent, arguing viciously about couriers. Though all four of the companions insisted on traveling with Adrien at the fore of the road project, he'd tried to keep them occupied by giving them a legion apiece to "manage," a task some took to with more aplomb than others. Faye was studious and curious, Celia forceful, Daya frivolous, and Bodhi, Kat thought privately, was the best of all of them because he ignored the assignment and left the management of the Fifth to the commanders who'd been properly trained for it.

"This is the second time you've stolen a rider out from under me this week," Celia seethed as she flung her plate down on the table. Faye shielded her papers without looking up, while Bodhi sat back with his usual spectator's grin on.

"It was very important," Daya replied, all the while wearing the kind of smirk that made it clear it wasn't important at all.

"You're free to mismanage your own resources, but leave mine out of it," Celia groused. "Back me up, Faye—isn't that what you're studying?"

Faye's gaze snapped up with the air of a prey animal who'd just caught sight of a hawk circling overhead. Before she could get a word of defense out, the tent flaps flung outward and Adrien strode in, carrying a teetering plate loaded with a truly inadvisable amount of bacon.

If it weren't for the circlet on his head or the array of tokens rattling around his neck as he plunked himself down at the breakfast table, Kat never would have taken him for the prince of the realm. Maybe an overworked scribe or some lesser cousin like Mobbert, thrown into administrative work mainly to get the youth out of the house. The impression wasn't helped by the way he immediately began inhaling the bacon, a spectacle mercifully smothered by Celia and Daya's arguing, though it didn't stop Faye from staring at him like she was watching her beloved childhood home burn down.

Once the last piece of gristle had disappeared, Adrien laid both hands firmly on the table and shoved to his feet. "*You*," he said, pointing at Daya, "can't possibly have that much to relay to your legion. If there's only one rider available, I want you to think long and hard about whether you really need to send that message. And *you*," he continued, fixing his sights on Celia. "If you have so much of dire import to communicate to your forces, have you considered joining them in the column? Just a thought."

"But then I'd miss all this excitement at the fore," Celia replied flatly.

"Keep that in mind when the next Lesser Lord comes to call," Adrien shot back, and a sudden stillness fell over the table.

"Has there been an update from the scouts?" Kat dared to ask when the silence stretched long.

"Nope," the prince replied with a grating false cheeriness. "Nothing you need to worry about."

Kat narrowed her eyes. "So there *has* been an update from the scouts."

"There's been an update—the update being that they haven't caught on to the trails of the two remaining generals yet."

"Seems suspect," Daya interjected. "They're *huge,* aren't they?"

"One certainly is, going off what they said about the tracks on the edge of the battlefield," Bodhi replied.

"How do we lose something that enormous?" Celia groused.

"The Third Century is getting restless," Kat declared before the highborns could turn this whole line of thought into an abstract classroom exercise. "They're asking me for answers I can't give them, and they trust me less and less every time I come back empty-handed."

"So tell them to knock it off," Daya suggested.

Kat bit back a scathing reply. She'd grown comfortable enough with Adrien's companions, but it was another thing entirely to contradict them, especially with her token's metal warm against her chest beneath her shirt. Thus far, they'd tolerated her presence, but she knew that tolerance was wholly dependent on her good behavior. They wouldn't understand the difference between a centurion and a hinge—between someone who could command a unit like it was her own arm and someone whose authority was only ever a shadow play of her centurion's orders. Kat's promotion to representing the century's interests hadn't come with any authority to *manage* those interests in turn.

"Frame it as a good thing," Faye offered before Kat could work out a more diplomatic reply. "As long as the scouts report no signs of the Lesser Lords, they don't have anything to worry about."

"I hope that's true," Kat said, thanking the angels that there was at least *one* highborn at this table capable of giving her reasonable advice.

"As do I," Adrien added, pulling back from the carafe he'd been fussing with. "Well, this has been lovely. See you all at dinner."

Before anyone else could get a word in edgewise, the prince turned tail and bolted.

Kat snatched up her napkin, folded it around one of the pastries, and stuffed it in her pocket. She had few advantages around Adrien's companions, but none of the highborns could spare the indignity of rushing out on his heels the way she could, and Kat pressed her edge with aplomb, leaving the rest of them to resume their fussing.

"Your Highness," she called, knowing he'd hate it. Though the prince had taken off at a good clip, her longer legs made up the difference easily. "I have something I'd like to discuss with you."

It hadn't been a sure thing until just then. Until her powerlessness ran headlong into the highborns' clear-cut assumptions of agency. She was sick of the past two weeks of dodging her fellow soldiers, of not being able to help them with what ailed them, of knowing that every unanswered woe or worry would bite her when the next Lesser Lord struck and she'd need them to trust her command. She didn't have blood or Aurean power to back up her authority.

She'd need to cultivate it some other way.

"I always find your perspective fascinating, but I've got a bit of a busy day ahead," Adrien said, taking a swig from the mug of horrid black coffee he'd stolen away with. His taste for the commanders' swill ran completely counter to everything Kat understood about the prince. He seemed to not only accept but *crave* the discomfort of a strong, bitter drink in the morning.

Kat couldn't relate. She'd drink the vile stimulant mixture passed around in waterskins on the battlefront, but only because the alternative was the possibility of a thrall getting past her spear. In peacetime, she'd wait for sugar and cream or pass entirely. "This is quick," Kat said. "And important."

Adrien only shrugged as if to say, *What isn't?*

"For when the next Lesser Lord strikes."

That, at least, got his attention like few things could. "You've got my walk to the command tent," he said.

It was early enough that the majority of the camp was still getting their wits about them, but the ninth and tenth decades were on guard duty, dogging their steps as they strode into the heart of the administrative core. Kat eyed them warily over her shoulder. The instant she lost the prince's focus, they'd be on her like wolves—especially now that their camp had landed on the outskirts of Palomar. With a town in sight, there would be ceaseless requests for evenings off, too many to grant at once. Kat could practically see one brewing in one of the hinge shield's eyes as he caught her gaze.

"It may be better to have this talk in confidence," Kat suggested.

She couldn't outright demand Adrien's time, but she'd discovered over the past two weeks that sometimes it was enough just to pique his curiosity, and from the sudden sharp look he gave her, she'd managed it. "I suppose I did leave the breakfast tent a little ahead of schedule, but who can blame me when Daya and Celia were being such nuisances? Very well," Adrien said with a beckoning flap of his hand.

When they reached the command tent, the ninth and tenth took up their posts on either side of the entrance and Kat ducked through on Adrien's heels, biting back the urge to let out a sigh of relief as she found herself once more out of sight of any infantry. This tent had formerly played host to the administrative operations of the First Legion, but Adrien had wrenched it into his orbit and turned it into the hub of his road operation. On the campaign, Kat had always been fascinated by the mysteries that must have been held within it. Here was where the commanders plotted their stratagems. Here was where the war would someday be won—or so she thought.

It had very quickly lost its charm. Maybe some of its grandeur was forfeit in peacetime, where the urgency of troop movements had given way to the mundanity of land use negotiations, deals with local quarries, and preparing for the administrative ordeal of releasing thousands of soldiers from their contracts at once. Behind these canvas walls, the high command was less a group of shadowy architects plotting ten steps ahead, more a chorus of petty, squabbling highborns more interested in their own personal glory than the defense of Telrus, pecking ceaselessly at one another while their staff picked up after them.

At the heart of the command tent was a map—the biggest map Kat had ever seen in her life—painted over a sturdy canvas that stretched in a wooden frame nearly four times as wide as Kat was tall. She wasn't used to conceiving of the world as something this big, especially when her own place in it was nothing but a little wooden marker that stood for a hundred soldiers, nestled against an equally sized marker that stood for the entire town of Palomar. The whole of the continent was staggering to think about—and more staggering, still, when she saw the progress of the road that had been made since they'd departed Kaston. A faint painted line marked the proposed route, winding through the towns and cities, stringing the war-torn duchies together until it found its way to Rusta, whose wooden marker included a gilded crown to signify the kingdom's capital.

In some ways, the length of that line was a profound relief. Yes, it sketched out an absolute mountain of work to be done, but every day it took to do it was a day Kat didn't have to face what taking her release might mean.

Adrien cleared his throat, startling her. "I'm guessing you've noticed the part that doesn't add up?"

"The—huh?"

"I've been thinking about it too. When the first Lesser Lord struck, it was bound straight for the scribes' tent, and we were lucky enough that you spotted it on its way." He tapped his Luck of Angels token twice to underscore the point. "But how did it know where to find me?"

"Can demons sniff out Aurean gold?" she asked, nodding to his array.

"If that were the case, wouldn't it have still needed to scout to be sure it was targeting me and not Bodhi?"

"Maybe demons can sniff out princes."

"Again, the previous point stands."

She hesitated, reeling for another theory.

"Don't you see? They have an *informant*."

Kat couldn't help the laugh that burst out of her. "You think someone would be stupid enough to ally with demons?"

The past two weeks had forged a strange rapport between the two of them—one that was going to get her in deep, deep trouble one day. She'd never dare to speak to Adrien like this out in the open, but in private he'd pestered his way into getting her to treat him like an equal instead of a walking weapon and the realm's future ruler.

From the consternated look that flickered over his face now, she wondered if scorning him like this had finally crossed the line. "You haven't met some of the political minds involved in my parents' administration. Practically demons themselves, and if they could use a rogue Lesser Lord as a tool to further their own ends, they'd do it in a heartbeat."

Kat shook her head. "Not possible. Even if you could reason with one of these generals, even if you knew you could get it to do what you wanted, no one would betray the material plane just for *power*."

"Then how are they evading our scouts so well?" Adrien countered.

She didn't have a good answer for that, but she also needed to get this conversation back on target before something else grabbed the prince's attention. "I actually had a different concern I wanted to discuss with you," Kat hazarded, and she thanked the angels when it got nothing more than a *go on* wrist flick out of him. "I'm honored, obviously, to have been given the privilege of representing my fellow soldiers' interests. I don't deny that it's important work, especially with such an abrupt shift in operations. And in fact, *because* it's such important work, I want to be doing it as effectively as possible—only, what I'm doing right now isn't working."

"Is there mutiny on the horizon? Desertion?"

"Well, no, but—"

"Then you're doing a great job. You're doing exactly the job I need you to be doing."

"But I'm not going to be able to do the job you need me to do when the next Lesser Lord strikes," Kat blurted.

"And why's that?"

"This role has thrown a wall between me and the rest of the infantry. When I was fulfilling my role as the hinge spear of my decade, I knew they'd follow me because I was right there alongside them day in and day out. They could trust me to know what was best for them—to *do* what was best for them. But when I'm working on the administrative side all day long, I lose that trust. And if the first Lesser Lord made anything clear, it's that I need that trust to lead all the decades when the time comes."

Adrien stared down at the map, looking worrisomely contemplative. "So your proposal . . ."

"I need to be out there with them, working side by side, whether it's on a guard rotation or in the trenches digging the road. Not buried in admin, and *definitely* not waiting up every night for you to finish your work."

The prince chewed it over for a long moment. "You can just say you don't like hanging out with me," he groused at last.

"I *don't* like hanging out with you," Kat huffed. "Just because you hate your friends doesn't mean I don't miss mine."

"There it is," Adrien said with an outright smarmy grin.

"Doesn't mean what I said before isn't true." Kat was tired— not just of keeping up with the prince's deranged schedule, but of collapsing on her bedroll each night in the midst of her passed-out comrades. She had no idea how Ziva's flirtation with the kitchen girl was going, what book Javi was reading, and she hadn't had a proper conversation—nor the improper one she was hankering for—with Emory since the road campaign got under way.

"I don't hate my friends, though," Adrien blurted. "I just wish they could be my friends with no strings attached, like you."

Kat sputtered. "Like *me*?"

He showed no signs of not being serious about what he'd just said. "You don't have all this baggage I have to deal with. You're always there for me—"

"—because you've demanded it, and I can't say no—"

"—whereas they're only following me around because they all want to marry me, even though I gave them *jobs*."

"Jobs, the horror," Kat replied flatly. "Look, Your Highness, it's not just about missing them. It's about being able to work with them when the time comes. Because when it was me and the seventh and eighth against that Lesser Lord, I wasn't prepared, and I don't want to let that happen again."

Adrien looked pensive. She didn't like it. "You really felt that you were out of your depth?" he asked.

Kat nodded. "Surely you understand what that's like?"

For a moment, she thought she'd cracked him. That there *was* a kernel of self-awareness underneath all those tokens. But the pause broke only with Adrien shaking his head. "Nope. Can't relate. Clearly we need to figure out how to remedy this, but for the time being, I'll allow it."

She should have felt nothing but raw relief, but Kat didn't like that the prince still looked like he was *thinking*. Thinking was never a good thing with Adrien. "You'll allow . . ." she hazarded, scarcely daring to believe she'd gotten through to him.

"You can return to your decade's rotation—after today, of course. There's no point in sending you back when they've already gotten started for the day."

Kat could have argued that there *was*, but she wasn't about to risk how far she'd come already. "Very wise of you, Your Highness," she said instead. Another thing she'd learned about Adrien over the past weeks was just how susceptible he was to positive reinforcement.

"It is, isn't it?" the prince said, beaming.

Sometimes she worried profoundly about the future of Telrus and the inescapable fact that it rested in this hapless young man's hands.

WHEN SHE FINALLY GOT THE NOD FROM ADRIEN, IT TOOK EVERY-thing in her not to run.

She burst through the flaps of the decade tent, nearly toppling over the structure in the process and cueing a chorus of shouts from her comrades that fell away just as quickly when they saw how brightly she was beaming. "Did the prince trip on his own tails?" Carrick asked, and Sawyer kicked him from the adjacent bedroll.

"He's letting me come back," Kat announced.

It was their turn to nearly take down the tent as Ziva pounced, Javi whooped, Brandt yelled in outrage as he was trampled by Gage's scramble to get in on the action, and the whole decade fell into a chaotic rumple. It terrified Kat a little, how much everything she'd been through felt worth it under the sudden crushing force of her comrades' affection.

It scared her worse that she could be tangled up in them and know for certain whose hand was at her back, firm against her spine, steady, supportive, and never demanding more. She caught Emory's eye, snorting at the smile he was trying to hold back. "What is it?" she needled, reaching through the scrum to jab him in the ribs with two fingertips.

"You're just in time. We start a digging rotation tomorrow."

KAT BIDED HER TIME. SHE FOUGHT HER EXHAUSTION, WAITING until the rhythms of her decade's breathing had dropped to the steady marches she knew so well. When she was certain all of them were asleep, she wriggled her hand into the pocket of her discarded pants, drew out her treasure, and nudged Emory awake.

"You shouldn't have," he whispered as he accepted the irrevocably squished strawberry-stuffed pastry she'd smuggled away from the highborns' breakfast table.

The smile she could hear in his voice told her otherwise.

CHAPTER 12

As the morning shift wore on, Kat began to understand what a grave mistake she'd made.

Though really, it was *two* mistakes compounding. On the one hand, if she'd stuck to Adrien's side, she could have spared herself from the long, exhausting slog that was digging a trench down to bedrock—or at least to the firmest ground they could find. On the other, if she'd done this sooner, she could have built up the strength and calluses necessary to keep up with the rest of her decade.

She was getting left in the dust. But that wasn't to say she wasn't loving it. Even with the sun beating down hard on their backs, even with her palms going raw and red around her spade, she was so profoundly happy to be with her decade, waging a war not against evil but against dirt.

It would have been even better if they'd stopped making fun of her for it, but Kat knew she could only be so lucky. "Keep up, princess," Carrick jeered as she paused to readjust the strips of cloth she'd wound around her hands to protect them.

"Takes one to know one," she replied. It was a bottom of the barrel retort, but she was too tired to think of a real one, and it got a snort out of Sawyer anyway. If she'd had any of their respect as their hinge spear on the front lines, it had vanished within the first hour of digging. "It's not my fault I was missing out on all the fun you guys were having rolling around in the dirt."

"Oodles of fun. *Miles* of fun," Sawyer groaned, driving his next strike deep for emphasis. "You'd better thank the hosts that you lost out on the first days two weeks back. When we started working our way out of Kaston, the soil was so rocky we barely got ten yards per decade laid in a day. I feel like a proper farmer. Never thought I'd appreciate *loam* this much."

Neither had Kat. She'd seen a large portion of the continent in the course of her three years campaigning, but she didn't know how to grasp its beauty until peace fell upon it. Almost instantly, the craggy hills turned from insurmountably difficult terrain to breathtaking vistas worthy of admiration. Their path had wound south out of Kaston's foothills where the Mouth had once made its home, into Bredol and its vast tracts of farmland that had been razed by demons and were only now starting to percolate with greenery again.

From their worksite, she could see clear down to the town of Palomar, nestled along the edge of a river where the skeletal outline of a bridge marked this stretch of the road's end point. She was incandescently glad that she didn't have to sit through another meeting about that bridge and all the debates that went into its construction. Instead, she could merely appreciate it as a bit of architecture that would soon make this countryside both picturesque *and* easily navigable.

"Ten yards is bad?" Kat asked as she heaved another shovelful of dirt over her shoulder.

"The prince expects each decade to get twenty a day," Emory

answered from across the trench. Though nothing seemed to demand it, the decade had sorted itself into the battle formation, shields on one side of the ditch and spears on the other, battle partners paired like always.

"How hard is that to hit?"

"Easier for the other centuries with . . . *less* in their rotations," Ziva said from her left, shooting a wary look down the line to where the next decade's work was staked out. On one side, they were flanked by the Third Century's own second decade, but on the other were unfamiliar soldiers who knew that the Third had been wrangled into additional work as the prince's guards but had no inkling as to why. With the prince's camp now separated from the main body of the legion and the first attack successfully covered up, they had no reason to suspect anything as drastic as two Lesser Lords still at large.

And if the first decade didn't want Mira sending them home in pieces, they'd better keep it that way.

"We'll make it today for sure," Emory said with a steadying grin. "Now that we're back at full strength."

"You know what would have us *really* at full strength?" Brandt called from the far end of the spear line.

Giselle let out an earth-shatteringly teenaged groan.

"I'm just saying what we're all thinking. If the Aureans pulled their weight instead of letting *us* do all the digging, this would go a lot faster."

"Hey, *one* Aurean's pulling her weight," Ziva countered, flicking a salute to Kat.

"Kat hardly counts," Brandt scoffed.

Emory's next shovelful of dirt sailed across the trench and landed at Brandt's feet.

"She doesn't!" Brandt protested, which only earned him another load from Ziva. "That token's not gonna—"

Carrick plucked a thick clod from the dirt and hurled it at him, striking him squarely in the forehead. Brandt seethed in outrage, but before he could put his fury to words, another clod exploded on Carrick's sweat-soaked shoulder.

Carrick blinked—not at Brandt, who'd been shocked into silence, but at Javi, who'd already bent to pick up his next weapon.

Sawyer threw down his shovel and rolled up his sleeves.

It was senseless. It was irresponsible. It was senseless and irresponsible in a way they hadn't been allowed in years, in a way war had completely robbed them of, and even though Giselle fumed and stamped her foot, even though Emory flashed Kat a helpless smile from the middle of the cross fire that she couldn't help but mirror, even though as hinges it was probably their job to put an end to this, nothing could stop any of them from giving in to it.

What was more important, after all? No one would die if they didn't get their twenty yards in. Well, maybe some of them might, after Mira was through with them, and it was only that thought that did the work of sobering them up enough that they went back to their shovels, dirt-spattered, grimy, and fighting smiles—even Brandt.

By the end of the afternoon, their scuffle felt like a distant memory—made more so by the fact that over the course of a full day of digging, the soil they'd thrown at one another had easily been eclipsed by the amount of filth they'd accumulated just by doing their work. Kat was no stranger to getting this dirty, and she counted it as a rare mercy that dirt was the only thing coating her—not blood, not guts, not bile.

And another bright spot to savor: At the end of a long day on the battle lines, there was rarely a river so close by.

The exhaustion that had set in as the day wore long faded the moment her shovel left her aching hands. Carrick and Sawyer led the charge away from the equipment tent, and Kat broke into a run to catch up, the rest of the decade hot on her heels. They raced down a path that had become well-worn in the scant few days the camp had been pitched and spilled onto the sandy river-bank. Half of them had their shirts over their heads, the other half prioritizing kicking out of their boots, and Carrick and Sawyer were already stripped naked and howling as they plunged into the water.

Kat's hands hesitated on her hem.

It was one of the first things she'd had to get used to as a soldier—the way living on top of one another eradicated any shred of privacy she'd once valued. The decade slept ten to a tent and bathed side by side when the rare occasion arose where they had the *opportunity* to get clean. She'd seen every inch of most of them and had learned to think nothing of it.

But now she was thinking. She was thinking very intensely about how her eyes had been skating off Emory for weeks, about how easy it had been to hide that fact in the dark of the decade tent or the focused mission that every chance to bathe became. About how she'd caught him doing the same once or twice and had only wished she could make his blush even worse. About the way the sight of just the slope of his back in the half-light put a dryness in her mouth worse than any thirst she'd ever known.

Ziva saved her, jabbing an elbow into her side before her pause could get any more obvious. "Down, girl," she whispered theatrically, tugging her own sweat-stained shirt over her head. "Though honestly we're all so mudded up I don't know what you *would*—"

She cut off on a squeal as Kat hip-checked her toward the water, then stripped off her shirt, followed quickly by her bandeau. She shimmied out of her pants and underthings—*not thinking, not thinking*—and scuttled over the pebble-studded bank as fast as her bare feet would take her, trying to play it like she was looking *only* at her feet for reasons that didn't go beyond sure footing.

The shock of the water's chill was enough to put most of her untoward thoughts away. On the surface, it was sun-warmed, but the deeper she waded, the more the cold sank in. Any other day, she would have taken her sweet time easing into it until at last she let herself sink fully into its embrace.

Instead, Kat flopped face-first.

She resurfaced to cheers from the rest of the decade and glanced back at the shoreline to find Ziva plunging after her, two fists held triumphantly over her head.

And behind her, standing on the riverbank, looking less like a seasoned soldier and more like a village girl tucked shyly at the edge of some spring festival, waiting to be asked for a dance, was Emory.

Fully clothed.

So he was going to blow this for both of them—that's how it was? Over her shoulder came a bewildered shout as Carrick set his sights on his comrade and nudged his battle partner. "Fuck are you standing around for?" Sawyer hollered.

"Might just enjoy the sun," Emory called back in a voice strained a half octave too high. He gestured to where Giselle and Gage were wading at the water's edge. Neither of them was much for the river—Giselle because she was still acclimating to the ranks' foregone privacy and Gage because they'd acclimated and found that their preferences remained the same.

With Emory, on the other hand, the main problem usually was getting him *out* of the water. The man was born to wallow and would do so until pruned if unfettered by the cruelties of their demanding schedules. Which meant it was glaringly obvious, and only getting more so, that he was doing anything other than tearing off his clothes with the rest of them.

Kat felt a chill that had nothing to do with the water temperature as she saw Carrick and Sawyer exchange a glance. Many of the looks that passed between them were incomprehensible, a near telepathy they'd developed after seven years as battle partners.

This look was as transparent as the crystal-clear water they swam in. They weren't going to let this slide. Emory was about to be dragged into the river—and if his current discomfort was anything to go by, the two of them were bound to notice that his posture wasn't the only thing that had noticeably stiffened.

On the one hand, Kat was far from precious. She knew men got hard all the time for reasons far less drastic than *I fucked my battle partner one time and now she's naked in front of me.* But this wasn't just a boner—it was an alignment of the stars. It was practically pointing right at her. And there might not be a brain cell rattling between Carrick and Sawyer on most days, but they were *primed* to connect this dot.

She knew what she had to do. It might be the worst thing she had ever done to Emory—worse, even, than putting him on his back in plain sight of the legions.

Kat stood. She turned for the shore. And as if Mira had just blasted one long, shrill note on her whistle, she charged.

If Emory hadn't been making such a concentrated effort to look anywhere but her, she probably couldn't have pulled it off. Wading through water took her speed down to barely more than a crawl, and she had to fight like hell to get her feet stable on the silty riverbank. But by the time she'd found her footing, she'd closed just enough distance that Emory could only stammer, backpedal, and—in a win sent straight from the angels—trip over his own feet.

"Kat," he choked as he tried to flail away from her. "The hell do you think you're doing?"

"*Fixing this,*" she growled, low enough that her voice was lost under the whoops and cheers from the rest of the soldiers frolicking in the river. She was the only one who could. Unlike their comrades, it didn't matter if *she* noticed Emory's condition.

So she grabbed her struggling battle partner and hauled him up over her shoulder, staggering step by step through the silt and pebbles, cutting off every half-hearted attempt he made to wrench himself free and deliberately arranging herself between the rest of the troops and the one thing they absolutely could not notice—a problem she herself noticed had been . . . somewhat exacerbated by the manhandling.

"You owe me," she said as they reached the water's edge.

Then, with a mighty heave, she threw him in.

Emory sank like a stone, and for a moment he was terribly still. Kat was a second from flinging herself in after him when he finally pushed himself upright, coughing and hacking. She waded to his side, reaching out hesitantly to steady him. Maybe she'd overdone it.

Then an arm snaked around her neck, and Kat barely had time to shriek before she was unceremoniously dunked.

She twisted free and resurfaced, howling with laughter as she heaved an enormous splash after Emory. Ziva was at her side in a flash, leaping on Emory's back to avenge her—only Emory flopped backward, slamming both of them back under the water. Kat lunged to rejoin the fray, but two weights dragged valiantly at her biceps as Carrick and Sawyer each grabbed an arm apiece and did their damnedest to fight her bulk.

"Okay, okay, easy!" she shouted, and by some miracle it worked. The two of them stopped, Emory and Ziva resurfaced, laughing amicably as she slid off his back, and the churn of the water settled—though not enough that Emory had anything to worry about.

He was a vision though, like this. Kat found it blisteringly unfair how he somehow looked better drenched and clothed than he might have stripped bare. There was something about the way the water clung to him, sluicing down his neck to melt into the fabric of his shirt, which stuck to his thick, muscled torso in ways that made her profoundly grateful for the chill. He mussed at his hair, which was plastered down over his eyes, and Kat found herself resisting the urge to reach out and help him push it back.

She flicked her fingertips at him instead, sending a spray of droplets that earned her a warm sideways glance. Part of her screamed at how *obvious* it felt—hosts above, Carrick and Sawyer were *right there*, and never mind that Ziva was in on the bit and barely bothering to hide it. But maybe it was no different than it had always been. The teasing, the jostling, the give-and-take. They'd been like this for a while, before sex got thrown in the mix. As long as Emory kept the bottom half of his body beneath the river's surface, they had nothing to worry about.

Kat had almost convinced herself of that when from behind her, Mira Morgenstern's unmistakable razor-edged voice called her name.

CHAPTER 13

SHE'D GIVE MIRA ONE THING—THE SECOND THE CENTURION spoke, every lustful thought in Kat's head fled with its tail between its legs.

Which wasn't to say that the fear that replaced them was all too different. If Kat was being honest with herself, there had been stretches of the campaign where she'd entertained a completely delusional crush or two aimed in her centurion's direction for that very reason.

It wasn't the thing to be thinking about with Mira wading into the river, naked but for the ten tokens arrayed over her chest, flinty-eyed, and heading straight for her. Kat stiffened, feeling the eddies of Carrick, Sawyer, Ziva, and—reluctantly—Emory's retreat swirling over her hips. "Centurion," she said weakly. "The prince gave me permission to—"

"I've spoken with the prince," Mira said levelly.

Kat fought not to flinch. Adrien's order superseded Mira's—it was just a little difficult to remember that while standing bare before a woman she'd once seen punch clean *through* a demon underling's spine.

"With me," Mira said, striding past her and sinking into the river's chill with barely a shiver. In a few powerful strokes, she eased into the current, drifting away from where the rest of the soldiers were carrying on as if they weren't trying to listen in on whatever their centurion was about to say. Kat followed at a dignified paddle, glancing over to where Emory could do nothing but pass her an anxious nod.

They'd swum a hundred yards before Mira slowed, checking over her shoulder to gauge the distance they'd put between themselves and the rest of the infantry. "Centurion," Kat hazarded. "Are you sure we need to talk about this *now*?"

"Do you have somewhere else you need to be?"

"Well, no, but—"

"Me neither. Which is a fucking miracle with the way we've been scheduled recently, so believe me, if we're going to talk about this, now is the time. Would you care to explain why, after I elevated you to represent the whole of your century, I find you cavorting with the infantry?"

Kat sputtered. "I'm not . . . *cavorting*. I wasn't doing anything useful trailing Ad—His Highness around, and we both know it."

"You weren't doing anything useful for *him,* certainly, beyond providing peace of mind. But that's not what I'm talking about. You've served under my command for three years. You've been a good, reliable soldier—but you could be a great one. I promoted you. I put you squarely in the sights of the most talented Aureans this continent has ever seen. And you went scuttling back to dig holes and play in the river at the first opportunity."

"If the time comes when we have to fight, I'll do the prince no good living separate from the soldiers I'm meant to rally," Kat countered, battling back the burn of shame that rose instinctively within her at the criticism. "I felt it when the first Lesser Lord struck. You want me to lead, but if I can't earn their trust, I can't command them. Separating myself, elevating myself above them—it doesn't work if you're not a highborn."

Mira righted herself, her chin dipping just below the water's surface as she let her hands tread lazily back and forth. "Have I ever told you about the Battle of False Creek?"

"I know of it," Kat replied. She'd been fourteen at the time, but news of the horrific routing had made it all the way to the skirts of Rusta just days after it had happened, and a pallor had dropped over the capital like few others Kat had seen over the course of the war.

Mira shook her head. "Everyone knows of it, but I've never *told* you of it. It was my first battle. I'd just enlisted. Because I was a Morgenstern and because I wore ten tokens around my neck, they'd placed me in command of a century I had no business leading. I was eighteen. Had only ever seen battle in smoke on the horizon from my family's keep. But I thought I was ready. I thought my gold made me untouchable, and that would be enough."

Her eyes had gone as glassy as the river's surface. With her loose hair sopping wet and not a scrap of clothing on her, she looked so vulnerable that Kat barely recognized her centurion. "And then?" she prompted when Mira's silence stretched long.

"And then it was the Battle of False Creek. You've heard the stories."

Kat had, and she thanked the hosts once again that in all her years on the campaign, she'd never been present for a defeat *that* bad. There had been days where they'd been thrown back on their heels, days the battle discipline collapsed and it became a long, ugly grind back to safety, days she'd had to throw down her spear and *run* when the horns sounded a retreat, but they never compared to the stories she'd heard of False Creek.

"The thing was, I *was* as untouchable as I thought I'd be. Morgensterns start training their gold at the age of ten, and by eighteen I was lethal with it. But just because *I* was untouchable didn't mean I knew the first thing about protecting my ranks."

Another blessing she was never grateful enough for—Kat had never had the misfortune of serving under an incompetent centurion. She'd arrived at the front after her basic training and immediately been assigned to the First Legion's Third Century under a Mira Morgenstern who'd been at war for four years. She found it difficult to imagine any other version of her commanding officer. To Kat, Mira must have sprung from the womb barking orders and waving that glorious sword.

But she'd heard the stories from soldiers who weren't so lucky. Soldiers whose commanders cared more about driving their line forward than making sure everyone came home. Commanders whose orders fell apart the second pressure hit them on the field. Some of these centurions had no qualifications beyond the gold they carried and the recommendation of a powerful ally.

It was too close to the path she was being shuttled down now, rushed along by Mira's pressure and Adrien's senseless enthusiasm. "That's how I felt when the general struck," Kat said. "Well, not untouchable—not at all. But like I couldn't keep everyone safe. Or like I could if they would *listen* to me, and I didn't know how to get them to hear my command."

Mira scoffed. "That's not what the reports told me. Unless every one of those soldiers—and you yourself—lied, you marshaled them into formation within moments of the situation turning hot. And not only that, you figured out exactly how to draw the Lesser Lord out of the shadows and focus its attention solely on yourself."

"I was just trying to do what you would have done."

"Do you want to know what I did at False Creek?" Mira asked, glancing sidelong at her. "I tired my lines. I was holding back, trying to draw out the changeovers, because I could feel things going to shit around me and the only way I thought I could fix it was giving the rear more time to recover. And then the turning point hit, and suddenly my soldiers were dropping left and right, so instead I tried to frontline myself. I'd never stayed in attunement for that long before. I burned hot and hard, too much, too quick, because I had no sense of how to pace myself when it mattered."

She broke off, swallowing thickly.

"I lost fifty people that day, and I had to be carried in the retreat."

Kat shivered. Every soldier had a worst day burned into their memory. For Kat, it was Murdo's Gulch—a brutal slog of a battle that had been fought in rain so heavy it was difficult to tell thrall from comrade in all that mud. Only battle discipline held them together, and in the end, the Third Century lost ten.

Fifty was unthinkable to her. Half a century gone, with the blame falling directly on Mira's shoulders. It shouldn't have happened in the first place, not with a full legion working in tandem, not unless the Demon Lord's foul magic was involved.

There was a part of her that flared righteously angry at the thought—not on behalf of Mira, but on behalf of the infantry who'd been saddled with a fresh-faced eighteen-year-old giving them orders. It shouldn't be possible for an officer that unqualified to take the field, but Telrus's hierarchy was tailored to create these situations. When the prerequisite to become a centurion wasn't length of service but a piece of angelic gold hanging around your neck, there were bound to be some people who got in over their heads—and others who died because of their incompetence.

Mira fixed Kat with a miserable look, one that said she knew exactly what path her soldier's mind had wandered down. "It's fucked. If the hosts refuse me when it's my time to shake their hands, I'll know why."

Kat understood abruptly, in a way she never could have prior, why Mira was so exacting when it came to battle discipline. Kat had always thought she was just a hard-ass—a typical highborn, raised in a military family, with no empathy for common soldiers who hadn't been drilling since the day they lost their first milk tooth. "I'm sor—" she started.

"I'm not telling you this to get your sympathy," Mira interrupted, shaking her head. "I'm telling you this so you appreciate that your first experience of command was after three years of campaigning. You didn't lose a single soldier."

"One man died in the initial—"

"A man died at his guard post before you had given a single order, yes," Mira said sharply. "If you choose to carry that, I can't stop you. But I need you to understand that what you achieved that night was not a failure in any sense. If anything, it was an illustration of what a folly it's been to allow some of our centuries to be commanded by inexperienced Aureans when we've got experienced ones at hand."

"But it felt like—"

"It's always going to feel like that. The important thing is that you didn't let your panic stop you from acting."

But I don't want to feel like that, Kat didn't dare blurt. When she signed her contract of service, she'd understood the implication that for the next five years, her feelings were irrelevant. Failure to follow orders was a failure of discipline, and a failure of discipline was dangerous. "I think," she said instead, after a reeling pause, "that I can be better."

"Obviously," Mira replied so offhandedly that were it not a punishable offense, Kat would have splashed her. "Which is part of the conversation I had with His Highness this morning. He accepted the premise you presented to him yesterday, that there are better ways that you could be using your time, and I've also managed to convince him that I know exactly how to instill in you the discipline necessary to lead. If you truly want to feel more in control, there's one thing you need to do."

"Lead drills with the rest of the century?"

"Cultivate your fucking token."

Kat's hand went to it on instinct, closing around the gold to press the familiar sun sigil into her palm. *Easy for you to say,* she wanted to hiss, but she knew how that would go over with her centurion. "I'm not sure that has anything to do with it," she demurred.

Mira fixed her with a level look. "Why haven't you cultivated it?"

"My mother never—"

"I don't want to hear about your mother. I want to hear about *you,* Katrien."

Fury smoldered in Kat, barely cooled by the river's chill. "I suppose it's different for highborn families," she said, fighting the urge to spit the words from between gritted teeth. "You've never started a token from scratch, have you?"

Fortunately for Kat's anger, Mira looked appropriately cowed. "It's true, I inherited all my gold with at least some power in it."

"And when you took up your first token, there was someone to tell you what to do with it, right? You weren't trying to figure it all out on your own as a ten-year-old. You had your parents. Your family."

"Tutors, too," Mira said with a flippancy that made Kat want to kick something.

"I had my mother's memory and . . . fairy tales. All those old stories of folk heroes who had a dying stranger press a token into their hands and worked out on their own what it meant to channel angelic power from the other side of the Seal. And it turns out that channeling is a lot easier when it's not something you associate with your dead mom."

A brutal, necessary silence stretched long between them, filled with nothing but the lap of the river against its banks and the distant shouts of frolicking soldiers. Kat found that she was breathing quickly, tensed like she was braced for a blow, and she couldn't bring herself to meet Mira's eyes without her own burning. Her entire career depended on the next words out of Mira's mouth and whether Kat could abide them.

"I don't think I fully appreciated your circumstances," Mira said at last, and though the statement had more syllables than Kat would have liked, it passed muster. "I'm sorry about your mother. How old were you?"

"Thirteen," Kat said hoarsely.

Mira sat with that for another long moment, Kat feeling like a raw nerve all the while. Centurions weren't supposed to have this much personal leverage over their subordinates. It was part of why they slept separate from their ranks, and though it resulted in a lot of circumstances going unappreciated, Kat found that she agreed with the layout. It was the natural order of things, wasn't it? She hated the feeling of a highborn sifting through her life, trying to twist her worst moments into the words that would convince Kat to do exactly what she wanted. It pushed her toward caving just to spare Mira the trouble.

"It's not fair that you never had a chance to pursue your own potential," Mira said at last. "But I don't think you do anyone any favors—least of all yourself—by leaning into that unfairness when you have the opportunity to correct it."

"Fuck you," Kat snapped.

Mira nodded. Her lips had thinned to a disappointed line, and Kat braced for the inevitable. Laps. Latrines. Or maybe they'd skip straight ahead to execution—all for the crime of not daring to want for herself what her centurion had been handed at birth. Kat felt *incomprehensible*, like her own desires were something that needed to be picked apart, parsed, translated—like a creature that had broken through not from the hellish plane or the heavenly one, but another place entirely.

There was nothing to be corrected here, but maybe there was something to be forged. Something she could make of herself— if only she could admit that the woman sitting next to her was right.

"It's up to you," Mira said at long last. "Tomorrow morning, I'll be waiting on the field's edge when the dawn horns sound.

Think about it. And one more thing." She fixed Kat with a dangerous look. "Bodhi Ranjan has ninety-nine tokens. One shy of a nice, even one hundred, and I'm sure the Vayans would love to see him in equal standing with Telrus's heroic prince. It would benefit you immensely, I think, to have a good counter to the argument that your token would be better off with Ranjan—or any of the prince's companions. The longer you spend time around them, the more likely it is that one of them is going to get ideas. Something to consider when you decide whether to train with me or not." Mira gave a sharp jerk of her chin. "Dismissed."

CHAPTER 14

THERE WAS NO QUESTION HOW KAT WOULD SPEND HER FIRST night of freedom.

For as long as they'd been approaching Palomar, the Third Century had been talking her ear off about securing permission to spend their leave in town. They were close to a hub of a legion, whose bursar tent was swarmed nonstop with joyous infantry withdrawing their wages to spend on the local wares. Roughly half the complaints levied at Kat over the past week had concerned who was able to live the fantasy of an evening off and when.

What she'd failed to anticipate was just how many of them were living that fantasy simultaneously. Kat had thought she'd get to the tavern early, beating the rush, and had thought completely wrong. The dimly lit barroom was packed to bursting, and there was no camaraderie to be found in these ranks. Every soldier was out for themselves, battling through the lines to the bar, where a harried man and his three gorgeous daughters were running their own operation with military efficiency to rival the troops.

It had taken all her charm for Kat to convince them to give her two pours at once and all her training to keep both of them from spilling as she wedged her way back to a chance for some breathing room. Seating was even more of a fantasy, and she had to content herself with a position on the back wall that gave her ample view of the throng and a clear line of sight to the door.

So she didn't miss the moment Emory slipped through it, his eyes going wide at the crowd, then soft as he picked her out among them.

Part of Kat had been convinced he wouldn't come. After all, hauling him into the river might have made him rethink a few things. She'd invited him as they trod back up the path from the water's edge, trying her damnedest to make it sound casual because there was no telling how far Carrick's hearing extended and Giselle had been giving her suspicious looks ever since she came back from her chat with Mira. This was just two friends spending time together, a decade's hinge pair strategizing, nothing untoward.

And at the moment, with half the legion packed into this tavern, she didn't dare make it anything else.

It took Emory a few minutes to battle his way over to her side, clapping shoulders as he passed and nodding greetings to the comrades he recognized. "Cute place," he said as he wedged himself in next to her, drawing a disgruntled look from the woman behind him.

"Cozy, right?" Kat replied, shifting so he couldn't see the cups she'd tucked behind her back.

"You sure you want to spend your evening here?" he asked with a nervous glance over his shoulder. "This is tighter than the midcentury on a bad day."

"But the midcentury on a bad day doesn't have *this*," Kat said, drawing the cups out with a flourish that only cost her a couple drops.

Most people, when confronted with a cup of unknown liquid in a dubious, packed establishment, would react less with curiosity, more with an appropriate sense of caution, but Emory was not most people. His eyes immediately lit as he took the cup she offered, and she commended herself for barely reacting when his fingertips brushed hers. "And what is this?" he asked, lifting it to his nose.

Kat took a whiff of the bouquet herself, her mouth watering at the lightest touch of sweetness woven through the scent. "A step above what most of these louts have in their tankards, I'll say that much. Go on, try it."

With the pineapple, Emory had insisted they go together, but Kat couldn't resist letting her cup pause on the cusp of her lips so she could fully appreciate the sight of Emory's first sip. His brows shot up, and a dribble of red-tinted liquid escaped the corner of his mouth as it twisted into an irrepressible smile. "That's—"

"Not exclusive to Valon, turns out," Kat said, then tipped her cup back to let it wash over her tongue. The drink was bright, honey-sweet, and flavored with a delicate hint of strawberry that gave it a subtle floral tartness. On any other day, she would have been content to drink the most bottom of the barrel beer her wages could buy, but earlier this week, she'd overheard the high command—possibly the same officers who'd inspired Emory's first battlefield wish—talking about this particular tavern and how it carried a delectable strawberry mead.

One sip and she understood why they couldn't stop talking about it. It had been worth the dent it put in her coin purse. If she came from a family with a vault full of Aurean tokens, she'd drink it every night.

Emory, too, seemed to be having a lightly religious experience about it. He could barely stop smiling enough to get another sip down, then another, then pulled the cup down and held up his other hand as if he had to physically force it away from his lips.

"Worth the fuss?" Kat asked wryly.

"Worth surviving Hell, that's for sure," Emory replied, meeting her eyes with a boyish grin. The droplet of mead that had escaped nestled into the scruff on his jawline, and Kat felt briefly insane with the urge to put her lips to it. They were far too close together for those kinds of thoughts, and her attention must have been transparent, because he ran the back of his wrist sheepishly over his chin, which at least saved her from the temptation.

Some of the temptation. She'd cooled off since the river incident. The sight of Emory shuffling around in his soaked-through clothes had gone from enticing to a little pathetic past a certain point, which helped. But they were still packed in tight by the crowd, his shoulder joined with hers in the gap they'd managed to create for themselves along the wall.

It felt obvious—a dare to the world for someone to catch them, someone to yell that this wasn't allowed.

Kat took another hurried sip of her drink, then blurted, "So Mira wants to train me."

Their centurion's name was a shield thrown up desperately between them, putting a furrow in Emory's brow. Kat launched into a summary of her conversation with Mira, lightly tongue-tied by her own flusteredness and hampered by the fact that by the end of her explanation, the barroom had gotten so loud that she was on the edge of shouting to be heard.

"So what are you going to do?" he asked.

"Hosts if I know," Kat huffed. "I . . . I understand every point that she's making, but I can't . . . I feel like . . ." She took another pull from her cup as if *that* was going to be the thing to clear her head. "I have to. I know I have to. Even if it's only for the summer, even if my token's never going to be properly useful, I'll never have access to Aureans of this caliber again. I can't go back to the forge without something to show for the last three years.

But I don't feel called to it—not the way I should be if I really mean to take up my mother's legacy. It should feel like the hosts are reaching out, asking me to channel their power. So why am I not feeling called?"

"You know I can't answer that for you," Emory said gently.

"I know, but you're called to soldiering, right? You've known what you wanted to do with your life since you were sixteen."

"Earlier, actually," he said, then shrugged when he caught her puzzled look. "Sixteen's just when they were legally allowed to take me on."

"How'd you get it figured out so early?" she groaned.

It was difficult to tell in the low light, but she swore his expression had just gone *wistful*. "Guess I've never told you about Von, have I?"

"Someone I need to be worried about?" Kat asked with a daring, flirtatious smirk.

"Hah. Well." Emory blinked. "Hosts, that might have been part of it, now that I think about it. But no—first of all, you've got nothing to worry about," he said with a nudge that made her stomach swoop, "and second of all, I was a kid and he was a grown man. When I was growing up in the orphanage, I used to skip lessons and go watch the garrison practice. Most of the soldiers would chase me off if they caught me at it, which was probably the right thing to do, but then there was Von."

"A bad influence?"

"From a certain point of view. But I think he knew what I was after, and he didn't see the harm in giving it to me. He called me little brother. Or Scraps, if he wanted to knock me down a peg. Told me I could stick around and watch the drills if I hauled equipment for him."

Kat snorted. "Guessing you didn't see that as a raw deal?"

"Wasn't smart enough," Emory said. "Probably should have stuck around for those lessons, huh?"

"What was it about the garrison that caught your eye?"

"Apart from all the handsome soldiers?" He stared out at the barroom, the seething mass of joyous people celebrating the end of yet another long day where their only weapons were spades and their only enemy was the soil. "I was too young to remember my parents when I lost them. Too young to ever feel like I was part of a family—of anything, really. There were plenty of us in that orphanage, more and more every year as the Demon Lord's raiders began to push into Egren. But it felt like we were bonded because of what we survived, not what we'd chosen to do about it. The garrison was full of people who chose to stand together against the hold evil was trying to take on our lands."

"You wanted to choose," Kat said, and he nodded.

"The way I saw it, I had a chance to choose—what mattered to me, who mattered to me, who I wanted to protect. I had to find something worth choosing. And Von showed me how to make that choice because he chose *me*. He saw that I was lonely and searching, and he invited me in. Made a home for me. Showed me my home could be here in the ranks."

"Sounds like a hell of a guy." A looming question tugged at her, and it took Kat a long moment to muster the courage to voice it. "What happened to him?"

Emory shook his head. "No idea. Egren was a safer duchy, relative to the Mouth, but as the war escalated, they called up every trained soldier in Telrus. I looked into the rolls after I enlisted, but with no high name to track him by, I couldn't find where he'd been posted after his garrison was absorbed into the legions."

"He could be marching with us."

Emory offered her a weak smile. "Suppose so. It's certainly what I'm hoping for." He took a long, considered look at his cup. "He would have loved this. Any sweetness with his drink, he couldn't resist."

Kat offered hers. "To tracking him down and letting him know what you chose in the end."

"To getting to thank him, the way I never could have when I

was a stupid little kid," Emory replied, clinking the rim of his cup with hers.

They both drank, Kat taking a far deeper pull than any of the ones that had preceded it. She'd hoped talking to Emory would give her clarity, but she found herself more conflicted than ever. He made his path sound inevitable, a perfect summation of all the things that had created him, but when she tried to follow the same throughline in her own history, she hit a wall—the one that had dropped into her life three years ago when her name got pulled in the draft.

She could barely imagine the person she'd be if that moment had never happened. It had rewritten her story down to its very bones. Kat was no longer the forge girl, working diligently at her father's side, untouched by the war but shaped by it all the same with every new sword that passed beneath her hammer. She was a spear—a *hinge* spear at that, holding her line together as she pushed them through horde after horde of thralls. But the real guilt wasn't in coming back different. It was in coming back not different enough to make up for the three years she'd left her father alone.

If she accepted Mira's training, she could forge yet another new version of herself out of the twist of fate she'd never wanted.

But she needed to be able to see the shape of that future—the person she could be at the end of the road.

Emory had Von. A man who'd shown him the kind of life he could make for himself, shown him what a man could *be,* and gave him hope for the kind of man he could become.

Kat thought of who that person was for her, and only one face came to mind.

It had been eight years since her mother's passing, but the version of her mother that Kat had done her best to enshrine was one from years before that—before she got sick, before that sickness began to chip away at her no matter what they tried. Bronwyn had been full-cheeked and bright-eyed, and the combined force of the two made every smile a knockout. She'd whistled off-key as she swept the forge, and Kat had always thought it flustered her father because, well, that was his wife—he was *supposed* to go crimson at the tips of his ears when she was charming. It wasn't until Kat was much older that she realized every song she'd only ever heard in haphazard notes had lyrics that would make even a Silk Row worker blush. Nowadays, Kat could only mouth the words every time one of them started up in a rowdy bonfire circle and never explained to anyone why her eyes were leaking at the corners.

Her mother had taught herself to use the token, the family heirloom passed down from a grandfather Kat had never met without a single drop of cultivated power in it. She'd taken hold of its angelic magic and made it useful in little ways—reading to Kat by its light, giving herself a safe pool of brilliance anytime a delivery had her walking the roads at night—and the assumption had always been that one day, when Kat was old enough and Bronwyn had no more use for the gold, she'd hand it down to her daughter with that power enshrined.

But instead, she'd gotten sick. And the sicker she became, the further the notion of preserving the token's power got from their minds. The token was a thing to pray over—to ask the hosts to infuse it with magic it didn't hold—but asking Bronwyn to pass it on was as good as accepting that she wouldn't get better, and none of them wanted that.

It had happened anyway.

Kat knew—and had been trying to deny for a long time now—that her mother probably would have wanted her to start over with the token. Probably would have laughed and swept her into a hug and told her it was *fine,* it was honoring her memory, not tarnishing it, to do what she hadn't been able to. To forge a power worth handing down to the next generation, instead of leaving the hosts' gift squandered. Her mother would have been so excited to see what Kat could do with it.

And for years, the idea that she never would had put the taste of bile on Kat's tongue anytime she tried to call upon her token's power.

But if she thought about it from a different angle—from Emory's angle—she could see a way forward. The world had been robbed of Bronwyn too soon, but not so soon that she hadn't enshrined herself in Kat's memory as the sum total of everything her daughter wanted to be. A brightness in people's lives. A barroom song so bawdy it left the whole room flustered. A light to those who needed it.

It had taken only a few months on the front for Kat to believe that dream was dead. War had ground her down with its horror and its monotony equally. But in the new world, she could take up her hammer and tongs once more.

She could forge herself into everything that had been taken from her.

"It's good, but it's not worth crying over," Emory said softly, and Kat jolted back to the crowded room and the cup starting to tremble in her hand.

She dabbed at the corners of her eyes, shaking her head. "Sorry, it's just . . . I realized I've got an early start tomorrow."

His brow wrinkled, then smoothed in sudden understanding. "Well then. Guess we've got to make the most of tonight."

She glanced at him sidelong, a familiar, dangerous heat building in her. They were in plain sight, but there was a kind of anonymity in crowds like this, details swallowed by the torrent of face after face after face, body after body after body. It almost made her believe they could get away with something, could fulfill the unspoken promises they seemed to be accumulating. "Make the most of it, huh?" she muttered, and this time she let her shoulder fully settle against his, even though nothing was pushing her from behind.

Emory leaned in closer, close enough that she could smell the river in his hair, close enough that she couldn't tell whether the hint of strawberry sweetness was coming from her lips or his. "As much as I enjoy what is clearly the premier establishment for infantry making bad decisions, I can't help but wonder if this town has more to offer."

"I dunno if we can beat this mead."

His eyes dropped unambiguously to her lips. "I can think of a few things that might."

She reached for him, letting his bulk shield the hand she slid around his waist. She'd fought tooth and nail to gain this ground, and there was no retreat now. For weeks she'd been starved for this—for how easy it was to touch him, how natural it felt to let him steady her or let herself be steadied.

This wasn't a steadying touch. It was a push at the top of a precipice. A promise of a fall.

"Gimme a second," Emory breathed, then lifted his cup to his lips. She snickered into his shoulder as he gulped down the rest of his drink, watching his throat work with an idle fascination. "Sorry," he gasped between swallows, "it's just *really* good."

"Don't choke," Kat warned, though the hand she had on him was wandering in a way that made it a difficult command to follow. Her head was going a bit fuzzy, and she could feel her decision-making starting to slip. The sweetness of the drink had masked a dangerous factor now coming into play. That mead was *strong,* and it made her bold.

"Knew we'd find you here," a voice called, and any notions of boldness evaporated in an instant. Kat jolted away from Emory, her hand clipping the wall as it beat a hasty retreat behind her own back. Before she could fully disentangle herself, Emory was shoved forward, forcing her to catch him again as her own drink sloshed precariously. Carrick had draped himself over Emory's back, his head nestled on top of her battle partner's shoulder, and before Kat had time to scope out her surroundings, Sawyer had jammed himself in at her side, one arm slung comfortably around her.

"The hell are you drinking?" Sawyer asked, his nose already halfway buried in her cup. "The prince put you on to the fancy stuff? Too good to drink swill with the rest of us?"

"Hosts forbid we try to expand our horizons a little," Kat replied, jostling him in the hopes he wouldn't notice the terrified kick his appearance had put in her pulse.

"You're back with the infantry now, Kat," Carrick said, reaching over Emory's shoulder to muss her hair. "You wanted to be one of us, you prove it."

Kat caught Emory's eye, and he gave her a rueful shake of his head. "Fine then. One round of swill, on me, coming right up."

Carrick cheered, Sawyer clapped her on the back, and Kat knew with bone-deep certainty that any notions of getting back to camp at a decent hour had just been thoroughly quashed.

CHAPTER 15

"I JUST WANT TO SAY," KAT MANAGED OVER AN UNCERTAIN BUR-ble in her throat, "that I think the fact that I'm *here* is what we should focus on."

"Is it?" Mira retorted, eying her up and down.

Kat hadn't made time for a run-in with a reflective surface this morning, but surely she couldn't look as bad as the face her centurion was giving her implied. She'd wiped the drool from her cheek. She'd even gone through the trouble of putting her hair in proper battle braids, though that was mostly because the tug of them did *something* for the headache drilling into her skull. There had been an attempt, was the point.

The fault was with Mira, if anything, for getting her hopes up. Kat had staggered back into the decade tent only a few hours ago. Making it to the field that bordered the marching camp at sunrise was a complete triumph. "If I wasn't serious about this, I'd be sleeping in. Or throwing up in the road trench. I'm ready to give this my all. Or, well." Another hitch, this time accompanied by a flush of bile she had to swallow back. "As much of my all as I can give at the moment."

Mira's lip curled. "If you're so eager, then I suppose we should get started. With laps."

Kat wilted.

BY THE TIME THE SUN HAD RISEN COMPLETELY, KAT WAS STARTING to suspect Mira had no intention of training her as an Aurean, only punishing her for having a bit of fun last night. Twice she'd had to pull over to the edge of the field, where no one could fault her for leaving a mess, and the token hanging around her neck went unmentioned as Mira ran exercise after exercise side by side with her. The centurion wasn't verbally extolling the benefits of temperance and getting to bed early, but Kat could hear the lecture all the same and was starting to think she had some good points.

She was on the verge of begging the hosts for an intercession when Mira finally drew up short at the fence. "Now that the body is ready, the mind can follow," she said.

Kat would have argued that both were in pretty rough shape, but she'd resolved to grit through Mira's nonsense.

"Tell me about your token," her centurion continued.

"It does light," Kat said.

Mira pinched her brow. "I'd picked that up in the past three years of campaigning with you, believe it or not."

"I don't know what more I'm supposed to say. You know the rest. It's a Light of Angels token, and it's uncultivated."

"Have you drawn on it before?"

Kat hesitated. She wasn't certain what *counted* in this scenario.

She'd managed flickering glimmers from time to time, but she was never sure if they were more on account of her own effort or the angels' power. "Maybe?" she decided after a long minute.

"Helpful," Mira deadpanned.

"I thought we'd been over this," Kat snapped. "Some of us didn't have tutors to guide our every move."

"Your token *lights up*. It should be obvious."

"Fine. Yes. I've had a few times where it listened when I tried to call on it. But it never felt like something *I* did."

"It never does," Mira replied.

"Something I might have known if, again, I had some help along the way. What does that mean?"

Mira ran an idle hand up the chain that held one of the tokens in her array. "The power a token has is not yours. It starts to feel like yours the more you use it, but the base truth is that these tokens are pinpricks in the fabric of our plane that channel power from the heavenly realm." She paused, taking in Kat's dumbfounded expression. "Surely someone's explained this to you?"

Kat snorted. "Makes no sense. The token has the power, doesn't it?"

"The token is a *conduit* for the power."

"But cultivated tokens are more powerful."

"Cultivated tokens are more easily able to access power. Hosts, what are they teaching in schools these days?"

"Reading. Writing. Addition. Useful skills for a tradesman's daughter."

"So then it was your *mother* who neglected your education," Mira said with a lancing degree of flippancy.

"Do you want me here?" Kat spat.

"I'm trying to see how badly you want to be here. I'm not going to teach you if you're not committed to the work. Hosts know I'm busy enough as it is."

Kat's dignity frayed, and for a harrowing moment, she thought it might snap. She was on this field of her own volition, and she owed Mira nothing. When she took her release at the end of the road, she'd probably never see this woman again.

But the real problem was what Kat owed to herself. This was her last chance to wring something more out of the three years of her life that the draft had stolen, to make herself into the kind of woman who could face her father and tell him it hadn't been for nothing. She didn't have years now—she had one summer to turn it all around before she walked back through his door.

And if there was one thing Mira had taught her already, it was how to straighten her back and take a hit. "Tokens are conduits of power from the angelic realm?" she asked through gritted teeth.

Mira's approving look scraped like gravel on skin. "That's correct. Power is not inherent to a token but is instead drawn through it from a different plane by creating an alignment of intention. Understanding that is key to being able to wield that power yourself and is the first obstacle most people need to overcome to become functional Aureans."

Kat would have argued that the first obstacle most people encountered was not being born with a token in their lineage, but she was trying to be a team player. "And cultivating isn't about increasing a token's power, it's about . . . easing that access?"

"The visualization my tutors used was one of a hole. When a token is in its natural state, it's a pinprick of access to the heavenly plane. Cultivating is the process of widening that hole, allowing more power to channel through."

Kat held up her index finger curled into her thumb's first knuckle, then slid it until she had her fingertips pinched together. In principle it all made sense, but . . . "How do you make the hole bigger?" she asked.

Mira looked thrown. "Well, you just . . . I mean . . . Let's focus on the basics of channeling before we worry about cultivation."

"Got it," Kat said, not at all reassured. "So how do I channel?

Because I can tell you from experience, holding on tight and begging the angels for help has not been working out for me."

Again, Mira looked as if she'd just been asked to join the engineers building the bridge over the river.

"Oh, I *knew it*," Kat snapped. "All this talk about how you're going to teach me and you don't even know how to explain the things you do."

"I can explain them fine," Mira snapped back. "I'm just trying to figure out how to get that explanation through *your* meathead skull."

"If it's that complicated to wield a token, how do eight-year-olds do it? Or was Daya Imonde making shit up?"

Mira snorted. "I wouldn't put it past her, but you're right. If an eight-year-old can do it, you should be able to pull it off too." She folded a hand over one of her tokens, her eyes going distant. "It sounds like your concept of Aurean magic was always based around the idea that the power was stored *in* the token. If that's how you conceptualized what you were attempting to do, it's no wonder your attempts didn't succeed. When you *did* succeed, you likely chanced into alignment and didn't even realize you'd been thinking about it differently. When you put out the call, you're opening a pinprick of a hole between our realm and theirs, a hole the angels themselves forged a thousand years ago. Power can only pass through that hole in . . . it's sort of like a straight line, so the hole has to be lined up with the power's direction . . ."

As Mira droned on, Kat began to lose the thread. She let her fingers play over her own token, trying to get her thoughts into that precious *alignment* Mira was talking about. It still felt too abstract for her to grasp, even if she tried to visualize a wall, a hole in it, and a spear jammed through the opening.

It felt delicate, and Kat had never thought of herself as meant for delicacy. Delicacy was for smaller people. More refined people. Not girls born in a forge or women who took up a spear on the front lines. Kat didn't think about her next move—she was ordered into it by a blast from Mira's whistle.

But her mother had done this, and if the stories were to be believed, she worked it out on her own. If Bronwyn, crass and bright and maybe not quite as big as her daughter, could work this out, Kat had no excuse.

Hole. Spear. One correct angle of attack. Kat squeezed hard on her token.

And light momentarily speared from between her fingers.

It was gone just as quickly as it came, but the impression it left streaked over her vision was unmistakable. Mira's monologue had broken off, her centurion rendered momentarily speechless. "That . . . *Yes, that.* Do that again."

Put on the spot, Kat could only flounder. She reached for alignment, but it was as if the hole had moved, as if she had to recalculate that angle of approach all over again. She swore out loud, her fingers aching around the gold as if she was trying to flatten it, but nothing answered.

This was the moment she'd dreaded. The churn in her gut was already awful on account of last night's choices, but it swelled to a dangerous peak as Kat felt the echo of the moment her mother had slipped away from her. For one glorious instant, she'd harnessed the magic that had told her stories in shadows on the walls, that had made her feel safe in the depths of a cold winter night— and then she'd lost it all over again.

"What was it? What did it?"

Kat shook her head, her eyes burning. "Not sure."

"But you felt it. You can feel it again—it should come easier."

"Yeah, funny how it's not," Kat ground out.

"Unclench, hosts above. It hurts to watch you."

A bullheaded part of Kat wanted to resist just to stick it to Mira, but if she strained herself any more, she worried something in her body was going to *pop*. She forced herself to take a long, slow breath instead, letting her token fall and nestle, warm, against the fabric of her shirt.

"It's not something you can force," Mira said. "Alignment is only the first step, and it needs to be natural—otherwise, you can't hope to keep multiple tokens attuned at the same time. Becoming a seasoned Aurean is about being able to operate precisely at a moment's notice. You need to be honed like a fine sword so that—"

"Good morning, ladies!" a much too chipper voice called from the training field's far side.

Kat and Mira muttered the exact same oath under their breaths.

Adrien Augustine had materialized at the edge of the field, a mug of violently black coffee held haphazardly in one hand as he waved with the other—as if there were any chance they'd miss that it was in fact the heir to the realm who had called out for them. He was dressed far more casually than Kat had ever seen him, wearing nothing but a loose shirt and sturdy pants, though if this was an attempt to blend in among the common soldiers, the effect was somewhat diminished by the Aurean token array still worn proudly around his neck.

"Your Highness," Mira said with the kind of brightness that could only be trained into you by high etiquette lessons starting from the age of six. "How generous of you to join us."

"It is very nice of me, isn't it?" he said, sauntering over. "Got a jam-packed schedule today, but I couldn't miss out on Kat's first day of Aurean training. Especially since the whole thing was my idea in the first place."

"*Was it?*" Kat asked with a sharp look at Mira.

"She didn't tell you?" Adrien looked put out. "Yes, we had a wonderful little chat yesterday about your prospects, given that you'd be missing out on all the fun in my retinue, and I suggested that if you were feeling less than capable of doing your duty, the solution was clearly to get you competent with your token. Mira agreed."

"I felt it was the kind of suggestion Kat would take to better if it came from a comrade, not from her prince," Mira said mildly.

"Well, I'm glad you convinced her," Adrien said, oblivious to the glare Kat had shot sidelong at her centurion. It was true. If Mira had told her the idea that she should begin cultivating came from *Adrien,* she'd be happily curled in her bedroll and dead to the world at the moment. She was strongly considering making a run for it as it was, and the headache needling into her skull was only underscoring the impulse. But then Adrien's bright grin landed on Kat. "Show me what you've got so far."

"She's struggling with the basics, so I don't know that there's all that much to show," Mira said.

Kat *knew* she was being goaded, but it wasn't like a cart horse could argue with the touch of a crop. She took her token back in hand, closed her eyes, and let out a long breath. It was simple. It had to be simple, because kids did this. Kids casually threaded a perfect hole between planes of existence, guided only by instinct and the desire to make something *new* in this world.

To say nothing of the hundred tokens arrayed across Adrien's chest. Over the past weeks, she'd gotten to know him better and had come to respect his honest effort, even if he'd been handed almost every advantage he'd ever accrued. But the fact remained— he was a bit of a fool. And if this numbskull could master a hundred Aurean tokens, surely Kat could master one.

She called. Somewhere out there, across the boundaries of reality and all the angels and demons sealed beyond them, there was a hole. And if that hole was a point, there was a single linear path between it and her token, and that was the trajectory she had to draw power along. She saw it as a thread. She pulled that thread tight.

And she didn't have to open her eyes to know that beneath her fingertips, her token was glowing with soft, angelic light.

Someone was clapping, and it certainly wasn't Mira. Kat cracked an eye open to find Adrien beaming. She almost caught herself smiling back, but then the prince turned to Mira and said, "*Truly* incredible work. To take a soldier who could barely use her token and in the span of a single morning set her on her cultivation journey? I see great things in your future, centurion."

"I do hope so," Mira replied graciously. Kat wished she could kick her without getting court-martialed for it.

"How does it feel?" Adrien asked eagerly, his attention swinging back to Kat.

"Like I can't breathe," she managed through her teeth. "Your Highness," she added, though it cost her dearly. The tension had crept back into her body while her focus had been honed elsewhere, and she'd returned to a balancing act that felt one wrong move away from shattering every plate stacked on her head.

"In High Training, our instructors used to tell us half the battle is figuring out how to balance the divine with the mundane, and that the real victory is in understanding them as one and the same," he said.

Kat's lips pursed.

"Breathe, Kat. Breathing's part of it. The angels quite literally cannot work through you if you're not breathing."

It felt like ceding ground on a slope, like one wrong step would leave her sliding and vulnerable, but Kat let herself draw that breath, let it flood her lungs just as the light was flooding from her token. The alignment held, the light unwavering, and as a bonus, Kat no longer felt like she was about to keel over. Her next breath came steadier, if not a little too quickly.

And her light was still there when she exhaled.

"Never gets old, does it?" Adrien asked, prodding Mira with a comradely elbow in a gesture that would have had any member of her century mucking stalls for a week. "How blessed are we to have the angels on our side, huh? Well, I've got a meeting about quarries on the books, but this was worth the detour. Excellent work, can't wait to see more!"

And just like that, the prince trotted off, swigging from his mug as he went.

Kat blinked, her token finally winking out. "Why did *that* work ten times better than anything you said?" she asked.

Mira glared after Adrien. "Who am I to question the will of the angels?" she muttered.

CHAPTER 16

WITH SUMMER EASING TOWARD ITS PEAK, THE EVENINGS stretched long, the hours after dinner filled with just enough daylight that there was time to grow properly bored.

Boredom was a rare delight for the ranks. There hadn't been much of it to go around in the last year of the campaign, once the fight to liberate Fallon had started in earnest. They'd had downtime, of course, but not the sort where the mind could be idle, not when the forces of evil loomed on the horizon and every breath felt perilously close to being your last.

It left Kat uncertain how best to enjoy it. She lay flat on her back in her bedroll, staring at the decade tent's slope and wondering how her body could be so tired with her mind so far from sleep. Most of the decade was out and about—Emory and Giselle training, Carrick and Sawyer up to their usual mischief, Gage and Brandt unaccounted for, but no doubt occupied. Ziva and Elise lounged idly on opposite ends of the tent. Across from Kat, Javi, the unit's leading expert when it came to staving off boredom, was paging through a book he'd acquired in Palomar, some heretical pamphlet that he'd been arguing about with Gage at dinner for the past week straight.

Kat was right on the verge of asking him whether he really believed all of it—that the hosts came from the stars, not the heavenly plane, and that their true purpose in Telrus had been to mine some mysterious ore from the very place where the Mouth of Hell had broken through—when Ziva sat up abruptly from her bedroll, reached into her marching pack, pulled out a leather ball the size of a melon, and dropped it in Kat's lap. She pointed at the open tent flap and said, "Goal."

"This again?" Javi sighed.

Kat stared down at the ball. The cracks and stitches across its surface were exactly as she remembered them, but she'd last seen this ball disappearing over the horizon more than a year ago. "You—I thought Mira—"

"Punted it a mile when she got sick of us turning into absolute children every time we played this game?" Ziva finished, flashing a bright grin. "Turns out Haileen over in the fourth found it on a scouting patrol."

"And gave it to you?" Elise asked from the tent's far corner, rolling over.

"Guess she must have liked me better," Ziva replied, her smile gaining a diabolical edge.

Kat knew from experience that she had roughly five seconds to head off the spat before it became a full-blown incident. She snatched up the ball, tossed it out the front of the tent, then pointed at the matching flap in the rear. "Goal," she said.

Ziva and Elise scrambled for it.

The rules of Goal were, in theory, simple. It had started as an easy way to pass the time and burn off the nervous edge that tended to chase any hard day on the campaign. Any opening large enough to pass the ball through could be declared a goal. Whoever got the ball through it first got a point, declared a new goal, and sat out the next round while the rest of the players tried to score on it. The game could go to a point threshold, but more often than not, it ended just shy of the moment the officers got wind of how out of hand things had gotten.

It had been over a year since the last time they'd played it, and not just because Mira had attempted to kick their ball into the sun. They'd been on the approach to Fallon at the time, and they couldn't have known that from then on, the campaign would only ramp up in intensity—that there wouldn't be much time for frivolous games, and even if there was, no one would feel like playing.

Ziva and Elise crashed back into the tent, the ball squashed between the two of them as they each tried to pry it away, nearly trampling Javi as he dove to protect his books. On the battlefield, the two of them were well-matched, Elise as stalwart and immovable as Ziva was agile. Off it, turned against each other, they ground to a standstill—at least, until Javi tugged hard on his bedroll, pulling Elise's footing out from underneath her. Ziva twisted, wrenching the ball free, and pitched it out the rear flap before Elise could get in a word of protest.

"I thought outside interference was against the rules," Elise panted.

"I'm playing," Javi replied mildly. "I'm just very bad at it."

Elise cut her gaze to Kat.

"Don't look at me," Kat protested. "I'm the reason Brandt won't play until we start requiring helmets."

"Which would take all the fun out of it," Ziva said.

"Exactly."

"Fine," Elise conceded. "Call it."

Ziva turned back to the fore of the tent, pointing at the legs of the rack that held their training gear just outside the open flaps. "Goal."

Kat sprang from her bedroll, thanking the hosts that she hadn't bothered to kick off her boots when she'd flopped down in it an hour ago. Elise lunged for her but couldn't make the intercept before Kat had thrown herself through the tent's rear flap. The ball had settled against the side of the adjacent decade tent, and Kat checked her momentum just in time to stop herself from taking out its stakes as she skidded on top of her prize and tucked it safely into the cradle of her elbow, pinning it against her hip a second before Elise caught up.

She could have sworn she was tired—if not in mind, certainly in body. But some reservoir within her had been unleashed, an extra bit of spark she hadn't felt in . . . well, it had been at least a year, hadn't it? Part of her despaired, thinking of all the times on the battlefield she'd *needed* just a little bit of push and hadn't been able to call it up, but it was easily overwritten by the relief that flooded her, the knowledge that her appetite for play hadn't been destroyed completely.

And she needed that push now, because Elise wasn't holding back. The shieldbearer fell on top of her, one arm threading beneath her armpit in an attempt to pry the ball out. Kat rolled, trapping that arm in place as she bore her weight back and used the momentum to wrench herself back on her feet. She staggered sideways, trying to round out behind the wall their decade tent presented and get a line of sight on the training gear rack, but before she could find her target, Elise tackled her sideways, and this time the ball popped free.

Elise tried to scramble away, but Kat latched onto her ankle before she could get clear and held on tight.

"Oh *no*," she heard from over her shoulder and glanced back to find Ziva sidling out of the tent, grinning wickedly. "Two beautiful women wrestling for my entertainment. Whatever will I do?"

"Depends on whom you'd rather fight for the next point," Kat ground out with a smirk of her own, then pulled hard, hamstringing Elise's attempt to get back on her feet. With deliberate ease, she pinned the shieldbearer, getting herself up and clear of Elise's shorter reach in the same move. From there, it was a quick scramble to where the ball had rolled, and this time she had her line of sight.

The shot was long—twenty paces, at least—but Kat's aim hadn't failed her yet.

She loosed, and the ball sailed clean through the gap in the rack.

"Hah!" Kat crowed, though she reached down to help Elise back on her feet before the shieldbearer could start another argument over the rules. Now that they were out in the open, the options for her next target had expanded significantly. She had to make a good choice.

Another decade tent was too risky. She wasn't about to piss off the rest of the Third. Outside the infantry encampment was similarly perilous—she'd never live it down if she lost their ball to Mira again. But parked at the end of the infantry row was the equipment wagon that carried their tents on the march.

Kat pointed to the gap between its wheels, and announced, "Goal."

The word had barely left her lips when Ziva threw herself in front of the cart, blocking the ball as it whizzed past Kat's ear. Elise bolted after the rebound as Kat turned, just in time for a tiny blond blur to dart past her and kick the leather ball even farther away from Elise's outstretched fingertips.

Though the action spilled down the road, Kat kept turning, and found Emory straightening from where he'd bent to pick up Giselle's discarded training spear, his practice shield slung over his back.

"I don't think you're working her hard enough," Kat called over a series of shrieks and the sound of boots scrabbling against the dirt. "Clearly she's still got some fight left in her."

"She'd run me off my feet before she lost the last of her energy," Emory replied. His smile was warm, but there was a wary cast in his eyes as he tracked the game's action.

"Don't," Kat warned.

"Don't what?"

"Don't be the hinge shield," she replied, jerking her chin at the equipment rack. "C'mon, only Ziva and I have points so far."

He set down the training gear. "I'm not being the hinge shield, I'm being appropriately cautious. It's harder to get away with Goal under Mira's nose in a small camp."

"There's a lot worse Mira could string you up for," Kat said with a waggle of her eyebrows. Emory was already flushed from drilling, but even in the late evening sun, she could tell he'd just gone pinker. She backed away from him, spreading her arms invitingly.

"Not too close!" Ziva yelled, and Kat startled before she could register Ziva meant *to the wagon*. It was another hotly contested Goal rule, born of far too many bouts where someone picked an easy target and then camped in front of it until the ball came their way again.

"She's fine! It's ten paces," Emory hollered back.

"Oh, so you'll *referee,* but —"

"Actually it's looking like nine," he corrected.

Kat mimed a scandalized gasp. "My own battle partner, ruling against me?"

"Maybe you should break the rules in more interesting ways," Emory replied, leaning against the equipment rack as his attention slipped to Ziva, Elise, and Giselle's dust-up. With Giselle in the fray, it had turned to a kicking game, each of them trying to get distance and run with the ball long enough to scoop it up. None of them could manage it without getting cornered by the other two, and all three of them were so focused on the intricate dance of it that they failed to notice the new threat lurking on the sidelines.

"Heads up!" Kat shouted, and all three of them turned toward her.

Carrick and Sawyer saw their cue.

Carrick went for the ball and Sawyer went for Giselle, who had just broken away with it. Giselle shrieked as her fellow spearbearer scooped her up and threw her over his shoulder, and she shrieked louder when Carrick snatched up the ball and broke into a sprint. "Where's the goal?" he wheezed as he tore past Kat and Emory with Ziva and Elise in hot pursuit.

"Don't tell him!" Ziva wailed.

"No team-ups!" Elise shouted.

"Your battle partner's right there," Sawyer observed.

Giselle kicked her feet limply, floundering without a hope of escaping Sawyer's grip. "C'mon, you guys. Gage always talks about this game—I thought I was finally going to get a chance to play."

"If you really want to play Goal, play dirty," Emory said.

"Noted," Giselle chirped, flashing her mentor a grin. Sawyer's smile dropped, and he let out a shout of dismay as her elbow went for the kill.

"You're a terrible referee," Kat said, pointing at the gap between the supply wagon's wheels.

"But a great player," Emory replied and lunged just as Carrick cocked his arm back and loosed. Kat, unable to participate on this point, could only stand back and watch, beaming despite herself, as Emory snagged the ball out of the air, spun with its momentum, and pitched it through the wagon wheels.

"You weren't playing!" Carrick protested.

"You think I'm going to let you two knuckleheads terrorize the rest of the decade?" Emory shot back, then pointed to one of the crates that had been left out after the tents were set up, now empty of the stakes it had carried. "Goal."

The six of them were off like a pack of hunting hounds— Sawyer still trying to dislodge Giselle, who'd turned herself into dead weight in an effort to stall him, Carrick abandoning his battle partner to scrap with Elise and Ziva, and Kat fast on their heels, fresh after sitting out the previous round.

It had taken her the whole of her time on the front lines and then some to arrive at this moment where she finally understood this game—both why it was so fun for all of them and why Mira had put so much energy into keeping them from playing it. Every element of the Telrusian army, from the legion down to the battle partner pairings that made up each decade, was optimized for cohesion. It was only natural to prioritize unity and order when squaring against wave after wave of thralls and all the chaos that entailed. Day in and day out, they were commanded to work in perfect harmony, and any threat to that harmony that didn't impart a lesson, like Mira's exhibition match, was a threat to the legions themselves—whether it be fighting, fucking, or stupid ball games that turned them against one another.

As a soldier, Kat understood that sometimes command was wrong. They couldn't be in synchronicity all the time. The infantry *needed* to get rowdy on occasion, to bounce off each other a bit, if only to prevent the pressure on their shoulders from breaking them when it mattered most. But now she'd seen the other side— seen what happened when cohesion fell apart under her command as they'd squared off against the first Lesser Lord. Even as she wrestled back Elise's attempt to keep her from prying the ball out of Ziva's grasp, she could feel a part of herself, in her own words, *being the hinge spear.*

There may not have been any more thralls to fight, but there were still two Lesser Lords out there.

She and Emory threw themselves into the fray anyway. In some ways, it was the role of the hinge made manifest, to regulate the decade from the middle of its ranks. In this case, it meant wedging themselves between Elise and Ziva anytime it looked like they were close to tearing each other's hair out and between Carrick and Sawyer anytime it looked like they were close to teaming up unfairly against the rest of them. And if they stole a little fun for themselves in the midst of their duties, where was the harm?

The harm, Kat reminded herself as she stiff-armed Giselle, *is when Mira gets wind we've gotten the ball back.* She was ready to bear the consequences if necessary. She suspected Emory would be ready as well. The hinge's job was also to keep the line together, whether it was against demon troopers or their own centurion. It was something she'd been doing far too little of recently, with so much of her time and energy consumed by Aurean training, something that was at the front of her mind as the game picked up pace.

Carrick scored, then Sawyer. The moment the ball flew through the target his shieldbearer had declared, Kat caught Emory's eye. *Guard Carrick,* she willed him to understand. *Don't let the two of them walk away with this.*

But instead, Emory raced after the ball, neck and neck with Ziva, leaving Carrick to hang back near the open flap of the decade tent, which Sawyer had just declared as the next goal. Kat frowned. Maybe Emory was getting swept up in the game, but usually he understood her better than that—usually *he* was the one thinking in troop movements while Kat thought in single targets.

She pushed in close to Carrick, jostling him with her shoulder as they both waited for the scramble to resolve itself. "Swear on the Seal, if this game just becomes you and Sawyer trading points . . ." she warned.

Carrick smirked, shoving right back. "Sounds like someone's mad her battle partner didn't give her an easy opening."

Down the row, Emory broke away with the ball, staggering into a sprint as Elise, Giselle, and Ziva rounded on his heels. "Speaking of easy openings," Kat replied and shouldered hard into Carrick's flank. He pushed back, rooting with all the unerring skill of a shieldbearer. It would take more than her bulk to ram him clear of the goal.

Later, Kat would wonder what possessed her to do it. It was

less a lapse in judgment, more rote muscle memory after a week under Mira's unrelenting tutelage. In the moment, the only thing she clearly registered was a bone-deep certainty that if she grabbed her token and sought alignment, she would find it.

She sidestepped Carrick's next shove, grasped her gold, and called.

Light blazed from between her fingers, sending Carrick reeling back as he threw an arm up over his eyes. Kat dropped to one knee, leaving Emory with an unmissable shot.

Only, he didn't take it. In the corner of her vision, she caught his boots skidding into a stop. Kat snapped her head up to find every member of her decade frozen in place, staring at her with expressions that ranged from incredulity to wary suspicion.

She pushed back to her feet, then reached out to Carrick, who was still blinking and scrubbing at his eyes. "Sorry," she said through a grimace.

"I'm okay," he reassured her, patting the hand she anchored on his shoulder. "Just looked into the sun for a moment—it'll wash out. Wish Brandt had been here to see that. No way he'd say you don't count as an Aurean after that display."

Kat caught Emory's wide-eyed stare and felt a part of herself crumble. "Too dirty, huh?"

He shrugged helplessly, still clutching the ball to his side. The thing was, she hadn't put him in an impossible position. There was one correct call here, and no one would fault him for being the hinge shield about it. The only thing staying his hand—obviously, in front of half the decade—was the fact that it was *her*. "So the training's working out," he offered.

"You don't have to—" she started, but faltered. "Look," she tried again. "New rule. No Aurean magic allowed. I can take my token off, if it helps."

But she knew it wouldn't. The damage was done, and it had only taken a week to get here. She'd set herself apart from the rest of the infantry by choosing to accept Mira's offer, sided with the centurion instead of her own ranks, and this was the natural consequence. Every bit of distance she felt from them now, she deserved.

And tomorrow morning, bright and early, she'd roll out of her bedroll ahead of the dawn horns and trudge to the training field to make it worse.

CHAPTER 17

IN WARTIME, A MONTH FELT ETERNAL. A MONTH COULD BE CAMP-
ing in the same rotting field where the only thing that seemed
more permanent than the scars the tents had carved into the earth
were the constant screams of thralls over the hills as century after
century held them back from their ceaseless advance. There was a
point where you simply stopped counting the days, where it was
no longer worth it to know the difference between twenty-three
and twenty-four. Kat expected the road project to be the same
kind of monotony, just differently flavored. Days that bled together, but at least none of those days were life-threatening.

Instead, the first month of road work had felt like a blink.
Blink and the Augustine Road had crossed the four-hundred-mile
mark. Blink and every decade was laying *thirty* meters on average.
Blink and one morning, Adrien sauntered past Kat's exercises
with Mira while sucking down his black coffee, paused mid-sip,
and said, "Tomorrow, you should train with me and my friends."

Then he continued on his merry way.

"Was that an order?" Kat asked under her breath once he'd gotten out of earshot.

"Do you want it to be?" Mira replied.

Kat wasn't sure, but she knew her status quo badly needed the shake. Though her skill with her token had progressed significantly over the course of her training, she couldn't say the same for any other aspect of her life. It had been two weeks since the Goal game that had driven an undeniable wedge between her and the rest of the decade—and nowhere was that wedge more painful than in the distance that had grown between her and Emory. They'd already gone back to sleeping in the same tent as if nothing ever happened that night at the tavern, as if they *hadn't* been on the verge of sneaking out into the back alley and fraternizing to their hearts' content, but now that Kat was focusing on cultivating her token, Emory seemed bent on keeping himself out of the picture. If she asked, she was sure she'd get some line about how he didn't want to distract her, how it was probably better for everyone this way.

She didn't ask.

He'd thrown himself into Giselle's training instead, spending every spare minute he wasn't digging roads putting his pupil through her paces. The two of them were enlisted through and through, clearly not taking Adrien's offer of release, and it occurred to Kat one morning watching them drill together that Emory wasn't just training Giselle up to keep her alive. If Kat was taking her release, he would need a new battle partner—a new hinge spear to hold his line together.

Kat tried not to let it sting, tried to appreciate that even if they couldn't spend time together, he was on the training field alongside her and Mira every step of the way.

Then again, he couldn't have chosen two worse babysitters to keep them honest: their centurion and one of the most judgmental teenagers Kat had ever met in her life.

She snuck a glance over her shoulder to where Emory and Giselle were in the midst of a warm-up lap around the field. They were too far away to have heard Adrien, but they had to have seen him and seen that he said *something*. They'd know who to blame when Kat disappeared tomorrow morning—if they weren't already set on blaming Kat for choosing the Aureans over the infantry.

Giselle, she wouldn't put it past. Emory, though—

Maybe this distance was for the best. To practice, to prepare, like she'd thought before, for the moment they'd have to separate for good.

"I suppose it couldn't hurt to get some perspective," Kat said.

Mira gave her a wary look. "Just be careful about what perspectives *you're* offering. Remember what I told you. Any one of them has space in their array for your shine, and so far all you can do is blaze it in their eyes a bit if they try to take it."

The only good outcome of the Goal game had been proof that blazing her token's power in someone's eyes was, in fact, an effective deterrent. "Yes, centurion," Kat said with a flippant salute and was already running before Mira fired back with a flat, exhausted, "*Laps.*"

ADRIEN HAD GIVEN NO INSTRUCTIONS ON WHERE TO MEET HIM and his companions, but instructions weren't necessary—all Kat had to do was follow her ears.

Even from a distance, the sound of the five most decorated Aureans in history putting themselves through their paces was unmistakable. Kat set off into the woods at the edge of the camp, following the shattering *booms* for what she estimated to be about two miles of uphill scramble. She was used to marching with her gear on her back and felt strangely naked fording undeveloped land unencumbered save for the token hanging around her neck.

As she got closer and closer, she spotted the distant shiver of the treetops that accompanied each noise, feeling it more and more in her throat with every step.

Finally, she broke into a massive clearing—and didn't dare take another step forward.

In the center of the open field stood Daya Imonde, and suspended over her was a boulder the size of the command tent. It rotated slowly above her head, and she held one palm outstretched and tilted skyward, unwaveringly still.

Daya flipped her hand, and Kat shrank back as the boulder rocketed skyward. Her breath stalled in her lungs, but Daya only tipped her head back, watching its progress, then neatly stepped to the side a second before it slammed into the ground with a crash that rivaled a shock knight smashing through a century's fore and put a shudder in Kat's knees.

Daya lifted her hand again, pulling the boulder up with one clean gesture and setting it back into position over her head.

"She thinks she's so impressive," Adrien said, and Kat nearly elbowed him in the head where he'd snuck up to her side. "That's an ordinary Hand of Angels token at work—her very first token, in fact. Stolen from her family's vault completely uncultivated, so all that ability is nothing but Daya's raw talent. Which would be *incredibly useful if she attuned the rest of her array,*" he hollered across the clearing.

Daya gave him a cheeky grin and a wave. The boulder didn't move an inch.

"Well, I think it's impressive," Kat offered, mainly to worsen the vinegar in her prince's expression. *Impressive* wasn't the right word for it. *Terrifying,* maybe. *Infuriating,* if she thought too hard about how Daya probably could have put that boulder clean through a pack of thralls and crushed the demon shepherding them in the process. No wonder the Demon Lord had been so keen on alchemizing antigold.

"She has ninety-five tokens. Do you have any idea what kind of power she's leaving on the table by using just one to get very good at throwing rocks around? Actively reinforcing alignment in a single token makes it more difficult to chain its power to the rest of her array."

Kat supposed Adrien couldn't help seeing it that way. His entire existence was centered around the goal of achieving the most powerful token set the world had ever seen. He looked at Daya and all he saw was wasted potential.

Kat looked at Daya and wondered what the war would have been like if more people on the front lines had the opportunity to cultivate a token. Not an array, like so many of their officers—just one, pushed to the outside edge of its power. How many tokens sat in the Augustine family vaults, waiting for a far-off moment in the sun that would only come when the time was right to compound their power?

"How's it coming with the rest of you?" Adrien asked, and Kat realized that the other three companions were settled on a blanket that had been laid out at the edge of the clearing.

"Halfway," Faye replied with forced cheer. She knelt with her eyes closed and her head bowed, and she flinched visibly as the boulder dropped like a thunderclap once more. Next to her, Bodhi sat cross-legged, a beatific smile on his face.

At his side, Celia appeared to be asleep flat on her back.

"Lady Vai," Adrien said with the assistance of his Voice of Angels token, drawing another flinch out of Faye.

"Had a late night," the young countess grumbled, cracking one eye open. "And it's not like I'm going to get anywhere trying to attune while *that's* going on," she added, flicking her fingers at Daya.

"I think it's wonderful practice," Faye said. "We can't always be expected to attune in perfect conditions. True readiness hopes for the best but prepares for the worst."

"Thought we left all those philosopher platitudes back in High Training," Celia groaned, letting her head fall back onto the blanket.

"Was it always like this?" Kat muttered as Adrien turned back to her. "Training together during the war?"

"This is mild," he said, shaking his head. "Imagine six years of this, day in, day out, locked in a freezing monastery up in Sprill, all of us trying to grow our arrays faster than each other with no one but a bunch of crusty monks for company."

Kat could see the downsides, but watching Daya, she couldn't help but feel a prickle of envy. Kat had scant few hours to practice in the morning before her digging rotation, during which she'd been able to cultivate to the point that the light came consistently when she called it. To get to Daya's level at Daya's age—to be a teenager capable of heaving that much mass around with nothing but angelic power—took years, years in which Daya did nothing but train her gold, with all her other needs taken care of to allow for it.

In some ways, it stung even more than the notion that some of the tokens these Aureans carried had power within them that had been cultivated for centuries. Anyone could take up a token pressed into their hands by a generous relative, but it was another thing to have the time to cultivate that power yourself, a luxury Kat could scarcely conceive.

But she knew what Adrien meant by it, and so all Kat said was, "I've never met a proper host-devoted monk, but I can't imagine them being more exacting than a centurion."

"And how has it been coming with Mira?" Adrien asked.

"It's been . . . a process." On the one hand, Mira had her loyalty, even if it hung by a thread during many of their mornings together. They'd been through too much over the past three years for Kat to ever throw her to the wolves just because she took Kat's training seriously.

On the other, Mira was not the most effective of teachers, and the patterns from Kat's first day had only become more entrenched as their sessions wore on. Mira had started her Aurean training over a decade ago, and there were many aspects to wielding a token that she now found so instinctive she couldn't properly explain them. Worse, when she tried, she ended up parroting things she remembered from her tutors, who had been working on the presupposition that their pupil had a proper classical education. Sometimes Mira tried to explain with scientific theory, others she took a crack at literary allusion, and all of it went clean over Kat's head.

She'd realized after that first day that Adrien, for all his eccentricities, had a different kind of instinctive approach. And though she wouldn't admit it even if the High King of Hell tried to burn it out of her, Kat had come to accept that in all likelihood, *he* was the better teacher.

It was probably confession enough that she was here on this hilltop.

"Well, there's only so much a ten-token Aurean can teach you," Adrien said nonchalantly, and Kat reconsidered.

"I would imagine ten tokens is closer to what I'm working with than—" She jerked her chin at his array.

"In principle, every token was created at the Forging from an equal weight of gold. I can tell you from my experience wrangling a hundred of them that, although *attuning* all of them at once is one matter, the process of bringing each of them into alignment is identical no matter what kind of token it is. The *ease* of that process is the only difference, and that's a matter of cultivation. And it's gotten much easier for you, hasn't it?"

In answer, Kat brought her hand up to clutch her token, and light flooded through her fingertips as her call was answered. She'd fought hard to gain this ground over the past month, but when she glanced over to Adrien, she found a furrowed brow, not the easy wonder she'd come to expect from every drop-in he made on her sessions with Mira.

"What's wrong?" she asked, letting go of her alignment.

Adrien shook his head. "It's nothing. It's . . . I don't want to say it's too advanced, but it's just—"

"Out with it, Your Highness," Kat said with a daring edge.

"*Fine*," he groused. "In my training, I was told our fundamentals are essential to everything we do, and part of good fundamentals is recognizing bad habits before they can take root."

"I've got a bad habit?"

Adrien reached up to his own array and smushed his hand against the tokens. "My instructors called it 'grounding.' Creating a physical action that accompanies the act of coming into alignment. I'm guessing Mira didn't call it out because she was more focused on getting results out of you. I don't begrudge her for that, but I bet you can do better."

He dropped his hand and nodded for her to do the same.

Kat found that she did so with great reluctance. It felt like she'd hiked a massive hill and Adrien was asking her to roll down it and start all over because she'd led with her left foot instead of her right. And yet, she wasn't certain she could make it to the same heights if she switched up her gait. The principle should have been the same, the alignment made spiritually, but when she reached for it, she hesitated.

Adrien nodded. "So you see what I mean."

It annoyed her, in all honesty. She'd have to be hit over the head to lose the same amount of progress when it came to her skill with a spear. Her hands curled taut at her sides and she reached again. Light flared, unprotected by the cage of her fingers.

"Breathe, Kat."

The light flickered out, and Kat huffed. "Why?"

"Because you've taught yourself to do it one way and one way only."

"But the alignment has nothing to do with my body."

"*Exactly.*"

"No, but then why is it harder?"

"Why indeed?"

Kat took back everything she'd secretly thought about Adrien being a better teacher. She understood the principle of letting the student work through a problem on their own. Hosts, she'd certainly let her fair share of green recruits go uninstructed so that they learned *properly* when they ended up hitting themselves in the face with their own spear.

The sudden thud of Daya's boulder slamming back into the ground jarred her from thoughts of putting Adrien through a few spear drills and seeing how he fared. Kat glanced at the young duchess, frowning as Daya pulled the boulder back up with another sweeping gesture. "Daya's doing physical gestures," she said with a truly restrained amount of petulance.

"Conducting is a little different," Adrien replied. Noting her blank look, he continued, "When a gesture is bound to the action of drawing a connection between our plane and the realm of the angels, it becomes a crutch. But gestures can guide our intentions when it comes to what we do with the power we've accessed, and *that* is what you see Daya demonstrating every time she tosses that boulder *so incredibly loudly*," he concluded, shouting his last words over his shoulder and earning him a cheeky blown kiss from the other Aurean.

"And that's called conducting?" Kat asked.

"Mira didn't teach you that?"

Kat threw him a consternated look. "Maybe she didn't think it was relevant. Or that I could grasp it."

"I think I'm starting to understand why this has been so hard for you."

"Because I can't understand simple things like the difference between conducting and . . . and . . ."

"Grounding," he supplied. "No, not at all. You didn't even know what they *were* until I told you just now. You've been trying to figure out *Aurean magic* without any framework for what you were doing. It's one thing to get instinctive alignment locked in—

it's essential, obviously, but anyone can pull it off if they grit their teeth and strain the way you do. It's another thing entirely to have no theoretical foundations to organize the process of drawing power from the heavenly plane and applying it."

Kat felt she was owed damages for hearing the words *theoretical foundations* before getting a solid breakfast in her. It reminded her of Javi's heretical theories that framed tokens as less of a magical gift, more of a technology beyond humanity's understanding— the idea that there was a core logic, a mechanism beneath it all. But she kept circling back to one sticking point. "No one taught those words to my mother, but I never once saw her struggle to call on this token."

Adrien's eyes lit up. "That's incredible. She must have been a prodigy. My studies turned up a few cases of pauper's tokens whose wielders could perform like a trained Aurean, almost as if they heard their instruction from the angels themselves. Obviously that's a lot of folk superstition, but maybe your mother just had the aptitude."

Kat wasn't sure what she expected—all she knew was that some quiet hope inside her had started to curl up like an untended plant. Maybe she'd thought that her mother's skill with the token was a sign there was another path she could take, one with less stodgy terminology, one a simple forge girl could learn, just as her mother had. But if Adrien was right, Bronwyn was simply born with a natural skill—and as evidenced by Kat's struggle to reproduce her talent, it wasn't something she'd passed on to her daughter.

"Guess I'll just have to learn the basics like everybody else," Kat tried to joke, but her throat was tight. "So! Grounding is bad. Conducting is good?"

"Let's not think that way. Grounding is limiting. Conducting is directed."

"Why can't grounding be directed? Why's conducting not limiting?"

Adrien opened his mouth, then closed it. Kat could practically hear ungreased wheels spinning in his head. "Great questions," he said at last. "Light up that token without grabbing it and we'll see if you can figure out the answers."

She'd almost had him.

By the time Kat made it back to camp, the sun was sinking into the horizon.

She tore through the tents on a beeline to the mess and the hot meal she was owed after a full day of having her brain scrambled by *frameworks*. She'd missed out on a day of digging—a fact she had no doubt Brandt would run with—and she was already lost in the argument she'd need to counter his jabs about the high and mighty Aurean skipping out on a day of honest work.

As a consequence, she ran headfirst into Emory.

The hit was hard enough that he nearly went down, and only the hand Kat snaked out to grab him by the hip saved him from collapsing on his ass. "Oh," he managed, looking just as disoriented and frazzled as she was—perhaps even more so, given the amount of dirt he was covered in. "Just the spear I was looking for."

"For . . . me?" Kat replied. A heartbeat later, she remembered that it might not have been the best idea to be caught with him like a pair of dancers frozen mid-step, and she released his waist with no small amount of reluctance.

"You vanished. Thought Mira might have taken things a step too far and left you dead in a ditch somewhere."

Kat scoffed. "Dead in a ditch? *Mira?* You know she'd parade my corpse around as a lesson to the rest of you louts. Could probably pull it off without looking like an overburdened donkey, too, with her Strength of Angels token."

He fought for a straight face, and relief nearly took her feet out from under her. She couldn't remember the last time she'd seen him battle to keep from showing that she made him laugh. "So you're training as an Aurean full time now?" Emory blurted.

"Hosts, I hope not. I wouldn't want to miss out on the joys of digging," Kat countered, but the lightness in her tone was forced, and she was certain he knew it. "No, today was a . . . strange exception. Adrien invited me to train with him and his companions."

Emory's eyebrows shot up. "*Adrien,* huh?"

"He makes me call him by his first name," she clarified.

If anything, that made Emory look even more concerned. "Makes—"

"He fusses about it. As long as Mira doesn't catch me doing it, I figure what's the worst that could happen?"

She was getting her answer. *This* was the worst that could happen. The gulf between her and Emory had widened since the Goal game, but it was another thing entirely to feel it get wider with every ill-considered word that tumbled out of her mouth.

He'd wanted this for her. He'd said so himself, all those weeks ago. But that had been before she knew what it would feel like, losing him more and more with every step forward she took.

She reeled for a way to fix it. To prove to him she was still the same woman who'd fought by his side for years. "It was illuminating," she offered, "but I'll be back in the dirt with you tomorrow. C'mon, let's get washed up for dinner."

Emory nodded, flashing her a taut smile as he fell in at her side and they set off toward the mess.

"We'll be in Fallon three days hence," Kat added. She'd come to a decision all at once. "You and me, we're going into the city."

"Oh, are we?" Emory replied.

Fallon had once been overtaken by demonkind and used as a base to advance their Lord's foul agenda, a factory from which his armies of thralls were issued. Liberating it had been warfare unlike any Kat had experienced before or since, fighting not on sprawling battlefields but within the narrow confines of city streets, her century broken down from their usual split formation to advance one decade at a time over the cobblestones their enemy had shattered to slow their approach.

She'd never forget the *crunch* those cobblestones made as the people of Fallon hurled them from their rooftops onto the skulls of the demonic forces. The Battle of Fallon had shown Kat the folly of thinking that only trained soldiers could muster the kind of valor necessary to fight back against the unceasing evil of the Demon Lord. There was valor, too, in the way the people of Fallon cared for them and kept them going in the months it took to root out the demon occupation. They helped establish supply lines, built barricades, sang songs that kept the darkest part of the night away.

And one of them—one old man Kat was *desperately* hoping survived the rest of the war—had given Emory a gift that he kept thinking of through the desperate fighting in those streets. He'd kept *describing* it over and over until, during the press of a turnover, Kat had leaned in close and told him if they got through this, she *had* to know what the fuss was about.

"We're going to the city because you would not shut up about those fucking hand pies for a week straight after the Battle of Fallon, and they're on our list, and I'm finally going to see what was worth all that noise."

Emory stopped dead in his tracks. "*The hand pies*," he whispered with a longing that made Kat want to hiss, "*Not here*," even if it was only directed at a pastry.

"Yeah, the hand pies. With that savory filling you wouldn't stop going on about—"

"Onions, peppers, ground beef, dunno about the spices, I think there were olives?"

"Stop describing them. I'm hungry enough as it is," Kat pleaded, elbowing his side. But no amount of feigned distress could over-write the relief that surged through her at the spark in his eye and the knowledge that she'd caused it—that she'd given him something to look forward to.

Something that almost made up for the fact that she was slip-ping away.

CHAPTER 18

THEY'D STARTED EARLY. STARTED HUNGRY. BUT TRACKING DOWN a single food vendor in a city of thousands was a tall order, one that had Kat wishing she'd planned this excursion on less of a whim by the time the sun was high in the sky. They'd spent all morning traipsing up and down Fallon's streets with nothing to show for it, leaving several perfectly good food stalls tragically unpatronized in their quest to find the *one*.

"You're sure?" Kat groaned after the latest near miss, shooting a longing look at the display cabinet full of savory pastries.

"They had a very particular folding style," Emory said despondently. "And besides, it was an old man selling them."

"Maybe he passed along the family business to a daughter?" she countered, but Emory wouldn't hear it. Kat's wish had been specific, and he was determined to hunt down that exact pastry or, apparently, starve to death trying.

But even with hunger gnawing at her, Kat couldn't find it in herself to be let down by disappointment after disappointment. It was a beautiful day in a healing city, and she found she didn't resent the opportunity to see more of what Fallon had become in the year since the war had loosened its grip on it. The cobblestones beneath her feet were a little uneven, the concrete that threaded between them a patchwork river of repairs. Many of the roofs were tiled with mismatched shingles, and the buildings' walls bore obvious bulges where damage had been plastered and then painted over. The citizens she passed all had a familiar cast to their faces—hollowed out but optimistic, like they hadn't dared imagine a future where their city had been freed and the war was over.

Fallon had opened the door to that victory. During its occupation, it had served as a pen for people the Demon Lord rounded up to convert into thralls for his armies. When the army had liberated it, the High King of Hell had lost the ability to produce a significant portion of his infantry—enough to turn marching on the Mouth of Hell itself from a far-off fantasy to the sole focus of their campaign.

Crimson banners hung from the balconies, proclaiming the victory of Adrien Augustine and welcoming him to the fair city of Fallon, which made Kat snicker a little. The prince was far too absorbed in the particulars of negotiating the path his road would take outside the city to ever see the favor of his people.

And Emory was at her side for all of it. She'd missed this—the feeling of moving in sync with him, their strides matched as they meandered up and down the city streets, trying to figure out what vendors parked at which plazas. It steadied her, knowing that even after a month that had done nothing but put distance between them, they could always come back to the foundations of their partnership. There was a certain joy in seeing the world twice over—once through your own eyes, and once through the eyes of a man whose mind worked in harmony with yours.

A certain annoyance, too, because that harmony never worked

out to perfect unison when it came to canvassing the city's food carts. Kat wanted to go about it methodically, checking off square after square, but Emory seemed convinced he could find this *roving food cart* on pure instinct. *It's not a stag,* Kat wanted to shout after his third "*This* street, definitely, this has to be it—I've got a feeling." She'd heard tell of Thread of Angels tokens that could lead hunters to their prey. Now that she had a solid handle on her Light of Angels, Kat wondered if she couldn't somehow track one down, add it to her arsenal, and use it exclusively to hunt the foods she wanted to eat.

Of course, there was another solution to the problem of Emory's ranging, one that was getting more and more tempting with every abrupt swerve Emory took to hound down an alley Kat hadn't even noticed. Kat's focus had started to slip from the bustle of the city surrounding them and narrow instead on her battle partner's hand.

It was frankly embarrassing how much her cheeks were heating at the mere thought of sliding her palm into his. Hosts above, she'd fucked this man, and she very plainly wanted to do it again. Something as innocent as hand-holding couldn't be sending her spiraling. But it wasn't just the notion of that physical contact that had seized her imagination. With their hands joined, the push and pull of their haphazard adventuring would go from something she sensed to something she *felt*. The tug of every side street that caught his attention. The glance back over his shoulder to confirm she'd followed, and the way she knew he didn't *need* to check but wanted to.

He'd still look back at her with their hands joined, she thought. Just to look.

But Kat resisted and tried to tell herself her caution was correct. Though a city gave the soldiers more room to spread out, they'd still crossed paths with a fair number of legionnaires out to spend their discretionary funds and cause trouble. She didn't want a repeat of the tavern incident, and knowing that somewhere out

there Carrick and Sawyer might be roaming these streets was reason enough not to risk it.

It wasn't because she was afraid she and Emory had grown too
distant over the past month. Certainly not.

In her hesitation, she'd lost sight of Emory. He'd rounded a
corner ahead of her, and she jogged to catch up, breaking from
the alley out into a bright, open plaza. Though in construction it
was nearly identical to many of the ones they'd traipsed through
this afternoon, two things set it apart.

The first was that it was absolutely swarming with children, all
of them running, shouting, shrieking, and generally carrying on
like a herd of farm animals turned out into sunlight after a long
winter in the barns.

The second was that on the edge of the square sat a small
wooden cart, on a stool next to that small wooden cart sat a com-
panionably small elderly man, and Emory was already halfway
to it.

"This is the one!" he shouted, the unfettered smile he threw
back over his shoulder blending right in among the joyous kids.

By the time she caught up, Emory was already deep in conversation with the vendor, who'd clasped him by the hands like a
penitent as Emory tried to get one free to fumble for his coin
purse. "Kat," he said over the tussle. "Want you to meet Roberto.
Finest purveyor of hand pies in the city of Fallon."

"Pleasure to meet you, Roberto," Kat said, grinning as the
old man returned her nod. "Since my friend seems otherwise
entangled—"

"Don't you dare," Emory yelped. "You got the mead last time.
It's my turn. *You* put this on the list."

"Neither of you pays a penny," the old man said, shaking his
head vehemently. "It's the least I can do for the heroes of the
realm."

"Think his eyesight's bad," Emory whispered theatrically over
his shoulder. "Makes up for it with a hell of a grip, but the man

seems to think we're the Aureans who took down the Demon Lord."

Roberto scoffed. "Didn't see any of those Aureans when Fallon was in the foul one's grasp, but I remember your face clear as day," he said, jerking his chin at Emory.

"I don't know what he's talking about."

"You had a religious experience eating one of my pies. Said the hosts had blessed you personally to have given you this meal at that moment. A man doesn't forget a compliment like that, nor the person who gave it."

"He wouldn't stop talking about it for weeks," Kat confirmed, and Roberto beamed.

"So not only did you rid my city of demons, you also gave my stall free advertising. Again, I insist."

"How are you so strong?" Emory whimpered as yet another attempt to pull his hands away was foiled. "Fine, you win. You've ruined my dream of treating Kat to your magnificent pies. I hope you're happy with your stolen valor."

"Exceedingly," Roberto replied. "Now, miss, I must ask you the most important question you've been asked all day." He released Emory's hands and swept behind his stall with a flourish. "Beef or chicken?"

"One of each," Kat replied without hesitation.

Roberto nodded approvingly. He grabbed a pair of tongs, reached into the belly of his cart, and pulled out a plump pastry, its edges crumbling slightly in the grip of his implement. Kat cupped her hands, but Roberto wagged a finger at her. "Needs one more finishing touch."

He brought his free hand under the pie and flipped its palm heavenward. Even if Kat hadn't spent the last three days figuring out the difference between grounding and conducting, she could have spotted the movements of an Aurean from a mile away. One breath passed, and then the pastry began to steam.

"You didn't mention that part!" she exclaimed.

"And ruin the man's theatrics?" Emory replied.

"Go on," Roberto said, holding out the tongs. "Don't worry—the wrapper stays cool enough to hold."

"Then you must have fine control of the angels' gifts," Kat said, taking the pie as gently as she might hold a newly hatched chick. True to his word, the shell of it was pleasantly warm, a promise of the heat the vendor had infused inside it.

"You're versed in the golden arts yourself?" Roberto asked cannily.

Kat pulled her token out from under her shirt with her free hand. "I'm just getting started, and it's only a pauper's token—"

Roberto's nose wrinkled. "Do I look like a pauper to you?"

"No, no!" Kat backtracked. "I mean there's only so much I can do with a single token—"

He looked like he might change his mind about giving them the pies for free. "With one single token, I make the best meat pies in the city of Fallon. 'Pauper's token' is highborn thinking. Dragons, sitting on their hoards, who never have to be properly creative because they rely on numbers to solve their problems. And then they dare to act like they know everything about Aurean gold."

"They do, don't they?" Kat muttered, weighing the pie in her hand. She'd been training first under Mira, then with Adrien and his companions, who were even more deeply entrenched in the philosophy that Aurean power was better off in the hands of people who could attune handfuls of tokens at a time. She'd seen firsthand the way that Mira's tokens chained together to enhance her power—speed, lightness, that thing she did with the glowing sword. Compared to that, what could Kat hope to achieve?

Maybe this was her answer. She lifted the pie to her lips and took a bite.

She'd developed a sneaking suspicion over the years that Emory's dedication to this long-lost perfect meal was a bit—and if not a bit, then a fixation colored by the Fallon campaign's unique horribleness. It made perfect sense that he'd found a miracle—something decent to eat in a city that had spent fifteen years as a cesspool of demonic suffering—that had given him a reason to keep going when reasons to keep going were few and far between. It followed that she'd built up this hallowed meat pie in her mind, based on nothing but Emory's over-the-top description of it, and that reality could never compare to the fantasy that she'd latched onto mid-battle.

But with one bite she knew. If she had no other reason to visit Fallon, if she was on the far end of the continent and there was no prince dragging her around, no festival worth coming for, no once-in-a-lifetime event that called her to the city, she'd make the journey just for this pie.

The crust was somehow both sturdy and elastic enough to keep the filling from escaping its bounds, but crisped and flaky on the outside, melting in her mouth. The beef inside had been cooked to perfection, finely ground without even a hint of gaminess, the fat rendered down just enough to bind it to the rest of the diced vegetables, which were seasoned with a spice medley she couldn't hope to replicate even if she were given full run of the royal kitchens. Roberto had heated it flawlessly with his little flourish, so flawlessly that she had to hold herself back from wolfing the rest of the pastry down before it could cool.

She caught Emory's eye.

"So you see now," he said.

"I see now."

Roberto had every right to look as smug as he did. "*Pauper's token,* eh?" The old man scoffed.

Kat's hand dropped to her coin purse, doing a strenuous mental calculation as she eyed the pastries remaining in the cart. "How long do you usually park here?"

"Until I sell out or sundown, whichever comes first."

"And if I bought every last pie in your cart, would you teach me everything you can in the time until sundown?"

Roberto looked her up and down. "You're quite a vision, miss, but I worry if you plan to eat the rest of my inventory all by yourself."

She glanced back over her shoulder at the kids playing in the plaza. It wasn't hard to guess where they'd come from or why there were so many of them—not in a city like Fallon, not when there were only a few older caretakers watching over them from the sidelines. "Think there's enough for everyone?" she asked Emory.

Her battle partner beamed.

THERE WAS AN ATTEMPT AT AN ORDERLY LINE, BUT THESE WERE no legionnaires. Kat did her best to make sure no one got shunted to the back of the pack, grabbing a few little scamps by their collars when they tried to shove back in for second helpings. As she marshaled her tiny troops, she watched Roberto work with more intensity than she'd ever spared for Mira or Adrien. There was something hypnotic about it, a sleight of hand she was *sure* she'd catch if she could just keep her eyes focused on the right part of the trick.

Having Adrien's words to describe everything she saw happening made a world of difference. The breath Roberto took preceded coming into alignment, he made a conducting gesture when he flipped his hand beneath his target, and the total effort allowed him to flow seamlessly in and out of the focused state that maintained his connection to heavenly power.

It reminded her of her father, of the forge—a thought that came all too readily at the sight of heat being steadily applied, over and over. Her training thus far had been focused on the practical application of Aurean magic, on honing it as a weapon or a tool, but nowhere in the past month had there been a mention of artistry, and that was all she could think of at the sight of Roberto's skill.

"How did you start?" Kat asked once the last pie had been delivered into an eager pair of tiny hands. "Family business?"

"Manner of speaking. Married into it, you might say. And then divorced from it, when it turned out the Aurean tokens we exchanged with our vows were the only thing the two of us had in common." Roberto barked a laugh at Kat's incredulous look. "Decades ago—before the city fell. No idea where she's ended up or what she's done with the token that used to be mine."

"So you already had foundations as an Aurean before you started working with this token in particular?"

"Suppose you could say that, but my first token was a Water of Angels. It felt like learning to walk again after breaking a leg, trying to figure out how to wield this one." He tugged on the chain as if it were a collar, but the smile on his lips was fond. "I suppose the principles are the same, but the practice—manipulating a quality instead of a quantity—had so little overlap that I would have pawned the sucker if I didn't have my ex-wife to guide me. And if she hadn't been relying on me to guide her through the same process. Nothing strengthens you like a complementary."

Across the square, Emory was tussling with some of the older kids as they kicked a ball around, one tiny scrap of a girl draped over his shoulders and shrieking in his ear with every jolt and spin. It made it extremely difficult for Kat to keep her attention on Roberto's words.

"What kind of token do you have?" he asked, and from the sly look in his eyes, she knew it hadn't been the first time he'd said it.

"Light of Angels," she blurted.

Roberto let out a low whistle.

"What's that supposed to mean?"

"Maybe it's my thinking as an old man set in his ways, but that sounds like a hell of a thing to wield. I started with water, which was both physical and perceivable. Then I swapped to heat, which you can't quite cup in your hands but you can *feel*. But anchoring yourself in the concept of light? That's no small feat."

Kat's brow furrowed. "You're telling me this is *supposed* to be hard?"

"No one's told you it's supposed to be hard?"

"Everyone I've ever trained with has at least ten tokens. They've always made it sound like *that* was the feat. Like managing one is the bare minimum."

"And of course they only think of you as a soldier. To a high-born, you're a tool, and they're teaching you as if they're going to use you like a tool. But the angels didn't just give us these tokens so that we might be *productive*. I think I'm starting to understand what's wrong with you," Roberto said.

"Do you think it can be fixed?" Kat replied.

"Probably not before sundown, but it's worth a shot."

BY THE TIME KAT AND EMORY WERE MAKING THEIR WAY BACK down the worn dirt path that led to the Third Century's encampment, night had fallen completely and the moon was a bare sliver overhead. Part of this was Kat's fault, for she'd wanted to soak in every last second of Roberto's rough but incisive tutelage, but in the end it was Emory who'd had to be pried away—though not before emptying his coin purse to match Kat's, some of it into the hands of the orphanage matrons and some distributed individually to the kids he'd been playing with to soothe the broken hearts he'd left in his wake.

She would have thought him dead tired after all the walking they'd done to find the pie cart and all the roughhousing he'd added on top of it, but Emory moved with a lightness she'd never before seen in him. Kat had spent half of the walk in silence, trying to puzzle out the difference.

There had been plenty of kids on the campaign trail, and Emory had never held himself back from doing whatever he could to take care of them. He'd dried tears, carried them on his back as the troops helped guard civilians fleeing a demon raid, grabbed stuffed animals and jogged like a persistence hunter after the cart they'd fallen from. But all of it had been infused with a somber sense of duty. A fear he could never shake. It was wartime. He could let himself help, but he could never let himself get close.

In peace, that restraint was gone, and now Kat saw a whole new side of her battle partner. Without the looming threat of thralls and demons, he could let the man win over the soldier, let himself be loose and lighthearted, let something shine through that had been part of him all along. Kat had been contemplating her own future for months, but now she wondered about Emory's—about whether the only path he could see for himself was that of a solider. When he'd told her about Von, about the way he'd come into the vision for his life, she'd been awed at his certainty.

But that vision had sprung fully formed from the mind of an Emory who'd grown up under the shadow of the Demon Lord's invasion. An Emory who might never have considered the possibilities beyond the doors that soldiering opened for an orphan from the far east of the continent.

Kat's eyes had dropped to his hand, swinging loose at his side, barely visible in the low light. The road was empty, the noise of the camp still distant on the horizon, smothered completely by the sound of their footfalls, which had fallen in step with each other naturally the moment they set off on this path.

She considered her own possibilities.

Ever since she'd become aware of her grounding gesture, calling on her token without it had been a fight. Part of her had accepted this—tokens, after all, were gifts the angels had once given to humanity to allow them to fight back against demonkind. It was only natural that utility came with a burden. If it were easy, everyone should have a token, not just the elites.

Roberto hadn't been burdened. He saw his gift as artistry, as letting something *loose* from within him, and though Kat knew it would take decades to get to the natural ease with which he wielded his magic, just that notion had unlocked a bit of the tension that came upon her as she reached for her alignment and struggled to keep her hand at her side.

The light came gently, a glow that crept up her throat, but for once she didn't pull like an anxious cart horse, didn't fear that her alignment would falter, didn't try to drink every last drop of the connection to the angels' power before it slipped from her grasp. It wasn't about building a perfect channel, Roberto had told her. It was about figuring out exactly what you wanted to express in this world and inviting the heavenly plane to help with that process.

Kat brought her palm up, cupping beneath her token. She'd never tried conducting like this, but after watching Roberto do it, she'd begun to wonder what it might feel like to project her power the way he did—not localized to his token, but somewhere different where he'd set his intention.

She spread her fingertips.

Her goal had been five, but the angels had their own surprises in mind. The light from her token split into hundreds of tiny beads, like the pinpricks of stars, and spread outward from her in a slow, circling swarm. Kat spun as they whirled around her, her lightheadedness nearly toppling her before she remembered she needed to breathe.

When she finished her turn, she found Emory stopped in his tracks, staring at her.

He'd seen her magic before. Every morning on the training field. During that disastrous game of Goal. He'd seen the fits and starts, the slow scrape for progress, and he'd seen that every step she took carried her further and further away from where he stood with the rest of the infantry. But he'd only ever seen her magic under the highborns' guidance.

This was different. This was *her* magic. Her token's gift, not as her commanding officers or her future rulers wanted it to be, but powered purely by Kat's own desire.

To bring something beautiful into the world. To light up the night. To share her gift.

With him.

"Kat," he said hoarsely, the awe of it almost unbearable.

It was alignment—the same as the feeling of drawing that connecting thread between herself and another plane. Of knowing she could have what she wanted. Of everything falling into place.

She'd been preparing to lose him. He'd been doing the same. But on the battlefield, you didn't prepare to lose. If you did, it was already over. They'd both learned the trick of this long ago—to fix in your mind's eye the thing that you wanted, even if it was as small as a perfectly warm meat pie.

Then you dug in. You fought to your last breath for a chance at that scrap of goodness. You made it worth the risk.

Kat reached out and took his hand.

CHAPTER 19

EVEN WITH THE GUIDANCE OF KAT'S LIGHTS, THEIR PATH THROUGH the woods was ungainly. They fought through the brush, which only got thicker the farther they got from the road, until at last they burst into a moss-spackled hollow, which had them tripping on nothing but the sudden lack of obstructions in their path. Only by clinging to each other did they manage to stay upright, shushing their breathy laughter like a pair of drunken teenagers trying to sneak beneath their parents' notice.

"If another Lesser Lord comes stomping through here, I swear on the Seal—" Emory started, and he got no further before Kat had snuck her hand around the back of his neck and pulled him up into a kiss.

The last time they'd done this, they'd been desperate. Feverish. Fumbling in the dark. Barely taking time for the niceties once they'd ducked into Mira's tent. There was urgency driving them now, certainly—more than a few things Kat wanted to do to

Emory immediately or she was sure she'd die—but it could wait while they savored this moment. The drag of his lips as they parted for her. The firm hand he snuck around her waist, the other coming up to tangle in her hair.

Death no longer loomed on their horizon. There was no certain end urging them to take what they could while they could. Every moment of slowness was one that promised a thousand after it, a constant, reassuring refrain that they had time. Kat found herself grinning too much to kiss him properly, which only got worse when he pressed a frustrated peck into the corner of her mouth.

"We're gonna get in trouble," she singsonged.

Before, those words might have yoked him back, reminded them of what they had to lose, but instead Emory stepped in closer, his hips shunting against hers as her back met a tree trunk she'd barely noticed looming behind them. "I intend to," he rumbled into the join of her neck.

They might have been the sweetest three words she'd ever heard him say. Emory, who calmed the troops in the chaos of the fore, who kept them in line, who held himself back whenever it was proper, *that* Emory committing himself to both her and the consequence of having her in no uncertain terms.

She couldn't possibly ruin it by checking if he was sure, so instead Kat let one hand drag slowly down his chest, over the lacings of his pants, her breath catching as he pressed into her touch. He dropped his forehead to her shoulder as she ran a knuckle up and down the seam he strained against.

"Taking your time, hmm?" Emory whispered—which would be one thing if he weren't also letting his hand work a slow, pacing path up and down the curve of her waist.

"As much of it as I can," Kat replied. This wasn't hesitancy. This was indulgence—as much as they could spare, for as long as she could stand it.

Past a certain point, it became a dare, an impossible challenge for both to hold themselves back. Emory's hand wandered down, toying with her lacings as he leaned back up to recapture her lips. She sighed into him as he worked one hand into her waistband, pushing through her curling hair to find the heat and warmth and wet of her.

Not to be outpaced, Kat fumbled with his ties—losing, some distant part of her brain was aware, the war it was taking to keep this slow—and wrapped her hand around him. "Hosts," he gasped at her touch, the rough pads of his fingers falling into step with the leisurely pace she set as she began to work him up and down. There hadn't been time, last time, to figure out what he liked, how he liked it. She'd had to ask for the answers.

If the past month had proven anything, it was this: Kat was nothing if not a tenacious learner.

It cost her dearly to pull back from his touch, but it was worth it for the soft noise Emory made as she sank to her knees. "Not . . . fair," he keened, and she had to wonder how the lights still dancing around them made her look. The reverence in his eyes said it was somewhere in the vicinity of *blasphemous,* and that was before she took him in her mouth.

Kat knew there was only so much he'd let her get away with, so she took to her task with gusto, determined to keep his brain from catching up with the rest of him for as long as she could manage. The hand he had in her hair went taut, and she felt him lean forward to brace the other against the tree behind her as his breathing got more and more ragged, barely smothered by the obscene, wet noises her mouth made as she worked him over. With one hand on his hip, she could feel the tension in him starting to build, and for a moment she dared to think she could coax him right over the edge far earlier than he'd ever consider dignified.

Just as that thought had begun to transform from a whim into a goal, Emory pulled her back abruptly, a groan spilling from his lips as he dropped to his knees and crushed his mouth over hers.

Kat let herself be pushed back into the cradle of the tree's roots, forgoing her grip on him to shuffle until she'd found a position where nothing dug uncomfortably into her flesh. As she settled, Emory's lips began to wander down her body, his nose tracing over her collarbone as he left feverish kisses against whatever skin he could find.

She nearly murmured a warning as his hands began to tug down her waistband, but he seemed to sense her objection a second before she voiced it. He leaned back, pulling off his shirt and coaxing her hips up just enough to slip it underneath her. Mollified, Kat took a moment to settle and enjoy the sight of his muscles on display as he worked her pants and underthings down to her knees.

She didn't know what she'd been thinking back at the river. This was far better than the sight of him soaked but still covered up.

Emory sat back on his heels, his shoulders gilded by the light of her magic. "Tell me," he rasped.

"Need instruction?" she fired back, though something in her was distantly glad for the chance he'd given her to breathe, to cool.

His lips quirked. "Orders," he corrected.

Sprawled beneath him, indecent and flushed, Kat could barely hide how intensely that had *worked* on her. She drew up one knee, laying herself open for him to find out exactly what he'd done, and breathed, "Fingers."

He put them in his mouth first, and by the time Kat's brain had re-formed itself from the absolute disarray the sight threw her in, he was sliding one inside, letting his thumb circle gently over her as she twitched around him. "Hosts, Kat." Emory sighed.

That alone was almost enough to undo her right then and there. It had been a long two months since the night they thought would be their last alive, months of living on top of each other in the decade tent without a scrap of privacy, months of aching for the feeling of him inside her again, for the way he *moved,* the way that battle partner tandem paid dividends when he found the place that made her arch and push her hips urgently into his grasp.

"Mouth," she managed between her teeth, then whimpered as he withdrew his hand. But Emory only grappled her hips up until her knees could hook over his shoulders, her back scraping against the blanket he'd made of his shirt as he drew her hard against him and bent his head between her legs.

Demon that he was, he stopped just before contact, his breath sending a shudder through her. She kicked one still-booted heel impatiently against his back, and he took it for the command she was far too winded to verbalize.

He went slowly, teasing along her folds, savoring her like she was another meal on that list he'd waited the whole war to try. Kat knew beyond a doubt she wasn't the best thing he'd tasted today, but he almost made her believe otherwise. With her body clutched against his, she could feel every motion he made echoed in the shifts of his weight, and she loosed one hand from where she'd braced herself just to stroke along the firm, thick line of his thigh.

Emory groaned against her, the vibration of it making her weak in the knees. With blood pooling in her head, she was starting to go dizzy, starting to worry she might faint, but she'd be damned before she let that happen.

She also wasn't sure she had enough air left in her lungs to do anything but pant along with Emory's attentions. The lights around them wavered, a subtle reminder she'd kept her alignment despite everything. She wondered if the angels were enjoying the show.

He had one arm wrapped around her abdomen, his other hand helping her thigh brace on his shoulder, and in the end, that was what did it—one shift of his weight where he gripped her tighter, and suddenly Kat was arching off the forest floor, heels dug hard into his back as she bucked against his mouth and cried out. Her lights, impossibly, flared the brightest she'd ever seen them, then fell away to nothing as she crashed through wave after wave of pleasure.

Emory fought through her writhing until she forced herself up and jammed a palm against his forehead, tearing him away from her with a wet, ragged gasp. She anchored her grip on the back of his neck and pulled herself up to crush a kiss over his glistening lips. "Easy," he grunted against her, and she took a moment to breathe as he soothed a hand up and down her side.

"Your . . ." she groaned.

"My?" he murmured into her neck.

"Your turn."

With a lightning-quick move, she'd toppled him onto his back, pinning him as handily as she had that day they'd wrestled in full sight of the century—though it was admittedly leagues easier to pull off when Emory was doing absolutely nothing to fight back. He flinched, shifting uncomfortably against the leaves and sticks that made up their improvised bier, and Kat sat up on her heels.

"We can stand if that's—"

"It's fine—"

"At least let me get the shirt—"

"*Kat,*" he said sharply, fixing her with a look that stilled every argument in her throat and sent another shiver of heat up her still-trembling thighs. "I would lay my back on the Mouth of Hell itself if it meant I could have you over me."

"Still, let me try a little chivalry on for size," Kat countered, then grabbed the hem of her own tunic, tearing it up over her head and tossing it in his face. As she sank into the pause of watching him shuffle it beneath him, a thought occurred to her. "We . . . weren't exactly forward-looking the last time we did this, but you should know I'm gentled."

It had been an easy call when she'd reported for the physical evaluation that cleared her for duty after she'd been drafted. An Aurean healer's hand on her abdomen, a quick flash of pain on each side of her pelvis, and no more worrying about conceiving until she decided to have it reversed.

"I am too," Emory said. "Which I should have let you know, but—"

"Wasn't a problem," Kat blurted. Consequences had been the furthest thing from their minds on the night before the war ended. There was no future to face, only certain death and whatever they could do to stave off its inevitability.

It should have daunted her—the reminder that this time there *would* be a tomorrow they'd face together at the end of this night. A dawn that promised many more after it. Possibilities that went beyond the two of them dead in the mud by the end of the day.

But having felt that alternative, that narrow path, that promised end, the edge of its blade pressed against her throat, Kat could only see the wonder of having a choice at all. Everything could go sideways tomorrow. They could be found out, could have their careers torn out from under them, could die in some surprise demon attack—or by tripping on a shovel and falling into the foundations of Adrien's ridiculous road. They could check off another item on Emory's list of foods they needed to eat or discover something that should have been on it all along. They could find a quiet moment, a secret place to escape to, and do this again—possibly even with a proper bed beneath them.

What comes next? used to be a question that had only one answer. Now they were limitless.

Kat called her lights and let the warmth of their glow trace up and down Emory's body. Alignment came naturally when there was a purpose to guide her, an artistry she meant to enact, and in that moment she wanted nothing more than to outline the sturdy shape of his waist, his chest, his powerful shoulders. He watched her with a wretched degree of patience, his breath settling to a slower, almost soothing rhythm.

"Orders?" she whispered, when she couldn't take it any longer.

"Ruin me," he replied.

CHAPTER 20

IN THE END, THERE WAS ONLY SO MUCH THEY COULD DO TO MAKE themselves decent—which wasn't to say they didn't give it their best shot. Dirt was hastily beaten out of clothing, sticks and leaves were plucked from hair, but all the desperate finger-combing in the world couldn't hide what was, at least to the two of them, flagrantly obvious.

"We'll stagger it," Emory said as Kat roved a light over his skin, rubbing despondently at what was either a persistent patch of dirt or a developing bruise she could do nothing about. "You go first. I'll take a beat, then follow. Night air will do me some good anyway."

"And when the decade asks what wild beast you got in a fight with?"

"I'll tell them we took care of one of the Lesser Lords on the way back as a favor. They'll be singing our praises."

Kat snorted, knocking her shoulder into his. The giddy fizz in her bloodstream had her half convinced she could take out a demon general single-handedly, powered by nothing but raw joy and several good orgasms.

That fizz had sputtered out entirely by the time she'd reached the Third Century's encampment. At this hour of the night, there should have been more than enough rowdy noise to cover her return, with soldiers chatting around the fires and Adrien's administration bustling at its usual clip. The fires still burned, but the noise that skirted them was nervous and muted, and Kat found herself stepping soft to match it.

So when someone shouted "KAT!" she nearly jumped out of her skin. Ziva was on her in an instant, grabbing her by the elbow and dragging her down the rows of tents. "We've been looking everywhere—where the fuck were you?"

"What's going on?" Kat warbled, still at the mercy of a heartbeat that had been spurred into a breakneck gallop.

"What do you mean, *what's going on?* We were attacked."

"*Attacked?*" Kat yelped.

Ziva shushed her. "Mira's told us to keep things orderly in case we get any unexpected arrivals. This time it's going to be harder to cover up."

What, exactly, they were meant to be covering up became apparent as they approached the far end of the officer tents, where Adrien's ridiculous circus contraption of a living space had been set up.

The key word being *had.* The whole confection was ripped clean in half, leaving a raw, gaping wound flanked by fluttering, singed silken edges. Great ruts had been torn in the ground surrounding it, the scars of a battle Kat could scarcely imagine. The first Lesser Lord's attack was a stealthy, precise strike—one that only required the cooperative silence of the scribes who'd witnessed it and the healers who'd dealt with the aftermath.

This was a detonation.

"Did . . . Is everyone . . ." Kat faltered.

Ziva gave her a grim look. "This way," she said and pulled on Kat's elbow.

Kat had never felt more relieved in her life to see a demon corpse. It was unquestionably one of the Lesser Lords—no other spawn of hell could grow to such a size. The body was riddled with spears, the ground beneath it muddy with black blood, as if the fiend had been stuck over and over again until finally it had been drained.

Next to it, Adrien looked impossibly tiny. He lay on his back in the dirt, his hands folded over his chest, and for an awful moment, Kat thought he was dead. Then she realized how utterly nonsensical it would be for anyone to leave the prince's body laid out on the ground. The soldiers of the Third Century who'd gathered to form a perimeter kept glancing back over their shoulders at the young man like he was a bit of roadkill they were trying not to think about.

"Is he . . ." Kat began.

"Being dramatic," Ziva confirmed.

"Kat, is that you?" Adrien called.

She had the sneaking suspicion he was fully capable of raising his head and looking himself, but it seemed like the kind of moment in which he needed humoring. "It's me, Your Highness," she said. "I see you've had a bit of a night."

"Oh, it's been lovely. Got the coffee on, got dragged into a drawn-out tiff with a local stonemason, was just getting ready to tuck into the latest reports from the capital, and then wouldn't you know it? The strangest thing happened."

"Did it now?" Kat asked, staring unblinkingly at the body of the demon general. It looked molten in places. It was still steaming.

"This . . . *piece of shit,*" Adrien spat, flopping an arm at the corpse, "came plowing through my tent. Already had a few spears in it by that point, so I think it just had a heading and *ran*. Wasn't particularly smart of it, but I don't think this one was the brightest of the bunch. Luckily—*hah*—I keep my Luck of Angels attuned out of habit, and so its aim was just off enough. Thank the hosts we didn't end up needing you. Where were you, by the way?"

"Out," Kat croaked. "Sorry, did you say it came *through* the camp?"

Adrien lifted an arm and pointed. Kat followed the line his finger drew and saw that the damage to Adrien's tent was only the tip of the spear. The prince hadn't been exaggerating when he said the Lesser Lord had a heading. The trail of destruction left in its wake was nothing if not linear.

That was troublesome. It was one thing for the generals to target Adrien, another thing entirely for them to target him precisely.

"My token kept me slippery enough that it couldn't get a blow on me," Adrien snuffled, as if that was even in question. "The Third closed in right after. They did . . . *okay*, all things considered."

"What's *okay* mean?" Kat asked under her breath, glancing sidelong at Ziva.

"Three," she replied just as quietly. "All from the ninth decade, all in one bad hit, all at once. Beyond that, a few broken bones, some bruising and scraping. And I think Brandt's concussed again."

Kat's stomach turned. She'd gotten used to peacetime. To swimming in rivers and playing stupid ball games and hunting food carts through cities. To the biggest source of stress and doubt in her life being the token hung around her neck. The Lesser Lords were in the back of her mind all the while, but every time they camped near a city, she allowed herself to relax a bit. There was no way they would strike so brazenly here, especially not with Adrien tucked safely in the heart of the camp.

And yet, one had charged right in, and now three good soldiers who should have had long lives ahead of them were dead. Part of Kat tried to reason with herself that even if she *had* been here, there was probably very little she could have done. She would have been just as caught off guard as the rest of them.

But she would have recovered. Would have done exactly what she'd been training for—would have taken charge. And maybe it would have made a difference this time.

She'd never know now.

"Katrien, would you mind coming over here a moment?" Adrien asked with so much feigned politeness that she nearly didn't, just to spite him. But too many soldiers were crowded around them, too many witnesses to a potential act of insubordination, and so she left Ziva behind with a reassuring pat on the shoulder and went to crouch next to Adrien.

Up close, the prince looked so tired that she might have given him a pass for lying in the dirt like a fed-up toddler who'd had a big day. She'd always seen Adrien as one of those people who came pre-stocked with a boundless supply of energy. Even if there wasn't a magical explanation for his bottomless well, the amount of sludgy black coffee he was constantly sucking down could have done the trick just as easily.

In this moment, she didn't have to ask to know Adrien had hit a wall. That all at once, the mechanisms keeping him upright had crumbled. Worse, she knew that by being *allowed* to see him like this in the first place, Adrien was only cementing the place he'd carved for her at his side. For everyone else, he was impenetrable and assured. But as Kat peered down at him, he stared back with watery eyes she could barely bring herself to meet.

"Someone did this, Kat," he said, low and urgent.

"I can see who did it," she replied dryly, jerking her chin at the smoldering pincushion of a demon corpse.

"Do I have to spell it out for you?" he hissed. "The first Lesser Lord attacked when I was in the scribes' tent—vulnerable, on the outside of the camp. The second took its shot straight at my personal quarters. Which would be one thing if I was ever *in* my tent. I'll fully admit it's not the subtlest of accommodations, but it has its uses. Namely being a reliable signal fire for where *not* to find me on most nights. The fact that they attacked now *could* be lucky, but . . ."

Adrien palmed over a token in his array—the same one he used to insist that Kat was his lucky charm. Luck may have saved him tonight, but it didn't *feel* lucky. Especially not when the demons had gotten lucky twice in a row.

"Someone's giving them intel?" she murmured.

"It's worse than that," Adrien said, staring at the sky. "Only four people in this camp knew I planned to read those reports in my tent tonight. I'm sure you can guess which four."

It was at precisely that moment Faye Laurent strode through the soldiers and dropped to her knees at Adrien's side. "I've sent a rider down the road to the main body of the legion's camp. They'll intercept and redirect anyone approaching."

Adrien flashed Kat a wary look. She wasn't sure what to give him in return. It was a serious accusation he'd just levied—and one currently at odds with Faye's immediate, effusive effort to help cover up the impact of the Lesser Lord's attack. Could that itself be a cover-up for some part she'd played in this?

Faye laid her hand on Kat's forearm, startling her from her thoughts. "Thank you for protecting him. It must not have been an easy fight," she said, looking her up and down.

"Oh, I-I—" Kat stammered, then shut her mouth before anything else incriminating could come out of it. For all her earlier worries about sticking out like a sore thumb coming back from her tumble in the woods, Kat now blended right in among the battle-haggard soldiers.

"We'll double your security," Faye said decisively, her attention already back on the prince. "Four decades at all times. We can shift schedules. Pull them off digging."

Adrien frowned even deeper. "I will take that into consideration," he grumbled, then gestured to the path the demon had torn through the camp. "We'll also need a good explanation for the damage we leave in our wake."

"We could say it was a training accident," Kat offered. When the suggestion earned her nothing but puzzled looks, she clarified, "An *Aurean* training accident. One of you practicing, and things got out of hand."

"Daya," both Faye and Adrien said in unison. Something told Kat that Daya would find it flattering she'd been the first one they'd thought of.

Provided Daya hadn't orchestrated this in the first place.

Kat caught movement on the edge of the crowd—a new arrival among the soldiers. Emory had finally made it back to camp to find that their carefully planned staggering was completely unnecessary. Kat watched, her guts in a twist, as he tapped Ziva on the shoulder and bent to let her talk in his ear.

She had thought—with an optimism she believed she'd finally earned—that things would be different after tonight. That she and Emory had finally figured out what they wanted from each other. That they'd *taken* it, and all that remained was to hold fast to that dream until the end of the road and take all the pains they could not to be caught in the process.

But things were exactly the same. They stood on either side of a vast divide—Emory with the common infantry, and Kat with the prince of the realm. And she knew, with a growing sense of dread, that until the last Lesser Lord was defeated, this was where they'd have to stay.

Emory caught her eye. It felt brazen to hold his gaze, daring the whole century to notice the two people who hadn't been involved in the battle but were smudged and rumpled anyway. But in it, there was a promise.

Even if nothing had changed, it still *could*. Someday.

Perhaps even someday soon.

"Help me up," Adrien said, flapping his hands at Kat. As she took the muddy, blood-splattered hand he offered, the prince leaned in close to her ear. "Stick with me. Keep an eye out. Figure out who it is," he whispered.

She pulled him to his feet and gave him a stiff nod. Orders received.

"Well, then," he said brightly, turning and spreading his arms to the rest of the onlookers. "Two down, one to go!"

CHAPTER 21

TWO WEEKS INTO HER NEW ASSIGNMENT, KAT DECIDED SHE WAS even less suited to the role Adrien had foisted upon her than any of the other responsibilities she'd been saddled with since he upended her life. She had no leads on who their traitor might be and no idea how she was meant to scrounge them up.

She did, however, have an excuse to rejoin the highborns' fancy breakfast. Under the guise of acting as Adrien's full-time security, she mopped up the sunny, golden yolk of a perfectly poached egg with a slice of bread still steaming from the cookfires and watched as the prince forced himself to sit through a civil meal with four people he thought might be passing information to his enemies.

If Kat hadn't known, she never would have suspected Adrien didn't want to be there. She kept catching him ducking his head into the crook of his elbow when Bodhi said something charming, Daya said something brash, or Celia did nothing but try to maintain her air of casual nonchalance. When Faye scolded Daya for her table manners, he made a show of mirroring her mannerisms, holding his fork and knife *just so* until she caught on and scolded him as well.

The more time Kat spent with the highborns, the more she understood how deeply the roots of their friendship ran. The five of them had been through six years of monastic training side by side, had no peers but one another, and were all confronting a sudden introduction to the wider realm as best they could.

And with every mile that collapsed between their advance and the capital, they were getting closer and closer to the end of it all. Taken like that, it was no wonder the highborns had refused to take up their posts with the legions Adrien had assigned them to. This was their last chance to squabble over meaningless quibbles at the breakfast table before those quibbles became full-blown political issues that would take fraught meetings and careful negotiations to solve.

She couldn't fault Adrien, even as he rolled his eyes and pulled sour faces every time he was dragged into an argument, for savoring something he knew wouldn't last.

There was just the small matter of the investigation. The little thing where the prince suspected one of these people—these people who, though Kat would never dare say it out loud, seemed to make him happy—was actively trying to get him killed.

Then it happened. Bodhi cracked a joke. On its own, it never could have made it through Adrien's defenses—he had six years of practice while locked up in that monastery, training himself not to laugh at Bodhi's jokes. But when he'd said it, Faye had hitched in surprise, and the egg-laden toast she held dropped unceremoniously into her lap.

Faye paused, flushing, and it felt like the whole table held its breath.

A bright, sudden laugh burst out of her, so winsome the hosts themselves would have a hard time not mirroring it, and though

Adrien wore enough of their gold to scour the Demon Lord from this plane, it wasn't enough to save him from the grin he cracked. It was a lightning strike, gone just as soon as it came, but from the way everyone around the table blinked, its impact was just as searing.

"He's having fun," Bodhi whispered.

"I'd be having more fun if the two of you sorted out whatever it is that's *still* going on with your couriers," Adrien replied, eying Celia and Daya, but the blush that painted his pale cheeks was stark, obvious, and damning.

AFTER BREAKFAST, KAT TRAILED THE PRINCE TO HIS MEETING IN the command tent, taking up a post outside the entrance with the rest of the forty soldiers now arrayed in guard positions. She could have followed him in—and probably should have, given that the heat was starting to swell into the full bloom of a late-summer afternoon that had her longing for the more arid climate they'd left behind in the midlands. But time away from Adrien was sparing, and she had to take as much of it as she could, especially when it meant more time with her fellow soldiers. Today's assortment was from the fifth, sixth, seventh, and eighth decades—all of them separated from her by the usual order of the ranks.

But if she'd been hoping to bond with them, and in the process convince them she was a humble member of their number and not the prince's pet spearbearer, the effort was thoroughly spoiled by Faye Laurent sweeping up to her side and asking, "May I have a word, Katrien?"

Kat fought not to let her alarm show. None of the prince's companions had ever tried to speak to her alone before, and her thoughts immediately stumbled into Mira's warning about token thievery. Surely Faye Laurent found that sort of thing beneath her—or at least, that was what Kat hoped, as she was in no position not to oblige her. "Your Grace," she said with a nod and allowed herself to be beckoned to the edge of one of the nearby supply wagons, which was parked close enough that she could keep eyes on the command tent's entrance for the moment Adrien emerged.

"I've been thinking about you since you rejoined our number," Faye declared. "Forgive me for saying this, but I don't think the prince has been very considerate with your time."

Kat made a valiant effort to keep a straight face and a tactful tongue as she replied, "Well, there have been higher concerns lately."

"True as that is, I thought you were making great strides with your token before, and I've noticed that you haven't gotten any time to practice recently. I wanted to check to see if there was anything I could do to help make that time for you."

In answer, Kat slid into alignment, her token shining radiant through the fabric of her tunic. Faye was right enough—in the time since they'd departed Fallon, Kat hadn't been drilling with Mira, but there were plenty of long hours standing behind Adrien in logistics meetings where she'd had nothing to do but hone her understanding of Roberto's artistry. Putting it into practice was becoming as natural as breathing.

Faye straightened, clasping her hands as a cheery smile spread over her lips. "Oh, that's *wonderful*," she said, and though Kat wasn't feeling charitable, it was impossible to read the noblewoman as anything but sincere. "You've come so far in such a short time. It's a pity you don't have another token to begin working on. Your grasp on your first is good enough that it's certainly prime time to start cultivating a second."

"Maybe I'll ask the prince to loan me one," Kat joked.

Faye's smile dropped, replaced with first a horrified look, then a flustered one. "I'm so sorry," she said, cupping one hand over her mouth. "I must admit, though it's been months on the road,

I'm still not used to the rough ways of . . . the common," she finished, pulling a face at her own lack of tact.

"Did I say something wrong?"

"Not wrong, per se, just a little uncouth," Faye replied. "It's not proper to speak of adopting another's gold, given the means one must go through to acquire it."

"Because I'd have to beat him up to take it?" The quip was risky, given their circumstances, but Kat needed the temperature check on the duchess's intentions.

Faye hid a decidedly unladylike snort behind one hand. "That's one way, yes. But the other would be to somehow join the ranks of his family and entitle yourself—quite literally—to a portion of the Augustine vault."

Kat blanched. "I didn't mean to imply—"

"No one would have thought you did," Faye assured her hurriedly.

What's that *supposed to mean?* Kat wanted to blurt, but she needed to take the outs where she could get them. "I can assure you, I have no designs on the prince's hand." After a beat, she added, "You've got nothing to worry about."

It was a bold bit of bait to dangle before the duchess, but Faye surprised her with a self-deprecating scoff. "It's very kind of you to think the prince would consider me," she said. "I know it's the game we're all meant to be playing, but there's little I can do to make myself a realistic prospect."

"What makes you think that?" Kat asked, hoping it wasn't rude to do so.

Faye laid a hand over her array. "The others will tell you about their family vaults—about all the cultivated tokens their lines hold in reserve—but for the Laurents, I'm afraid these seventy-five are all there is. Though we have domain over Halston and Rusta within it, though these lands we walk are technically my inheritance, my house has very little to show for it in the way of Aurean power. I've done my best with each and every one of my tokens, but it can't make up for the fact that I've reached the limits of my potential as an Aurean and can only hope to better myself through marriage or brutality—which is to say that I can only hope to better myself through marriage."

"Are you sure about that, Your Grace?" Kat asked. "I don't know many who'd fare well against an Aurean more decorated than Magnus Lythos. Present company included," she added with a nervous chuckle.

"My objection to brutality isn't because I'm afraid I won't be capable of it," Faye replied. "Quite the opposite. I find myself in a position where there is no possible honorable way for me to usurp another's token. I can only hope for generosity, which I find to be the worst sort of pity."

"Well, I suppose that's very nice of you," Kat said, resisting the urge to fold her hand over her own token in equal parts relief and reassurance. For all Faye seemed to value propriety, Kat wondered if she was aware how much it was strangling her. All these rules, all of them, at least to Kat's mind, made up, and none of them could help Faye's prospects. "You make it sound . . . calculating," she hazarded.

"I realize this must be very strange to you," Faye acknowledged. "These are the games we were raised in, and none more so than the four of us. It helps to stay pragmatic about the math. After all, the Imonde family has a vault to rival even the Augustines. Bodhi's a prince in his own right, and there's a lot to be gained by legitimizing the alliance with Vaya. Celia, well—Celia's not really in the running, either, being merely a countess, and a countess of Sprill at that, even if the Vai are laden in tokens. No royal in their right mind would stoop to marrying either of us."

"That's implying Adrien's got his head on straight in the first place," Kat blurted, then immediately stiffened. She could get away with those kind of cavalier remarks around the prince, and the fact that he allowed such talk in the first place had made her sloppy. If there was *anyone* in his cohort less likely to tolerate jokes at the royals' expense, it was Faye Laurent and her *Codex of Manners*. "Forgive me, Your Grace. My infantry tongue got the better of me there."

But Faye, to her surprise, was smiling. Between this and her self-deprecating laugh at breakfast, Kat was beginning to wonder if the duchess was coming down with something. "Believe it or not, I understand that there are different standards for politeness among the infantry. It would be absurd of me to expect you to behave as one of us highborns. That expectation is something I put upon myself, even if it seems nonsensical sometimes. The only hand I have to play is to excel in all these silly rules. I don't have the luxury of pretending they won't impact me."

She paused, and in that pause, Kat felt a sudden, sharp awareness of an incoming blow.

"I might go as far as to say I envy your audacity where your battle partner is concerned."

Faye hadn't said it very loudly, but Kat glanced around anyway. They were far enough away from the decades posted outside the command tent, but the wagons provided ample cover for eavesdroppers.

"That's . . . I don't know what you . . ." Kat faltered, buttoning down a hysterical laugh.

"You don't have to lie," Faye said, giving Kat's arm what she clearly meant to be a reassuring pat. "I couldn't help but notice after the Lesser Lord's attack. The two of you are always joined at the hip."

"Because we're battle partners. We're the hinge of our decade," Kat assured her hastily. Hosts, of all people—Faye and her *rules* were a recipe for disaster.

"Battle partners who weren't at all involved in the fight to take down the second Lesser Lord and ended up just as disheveled as the soldiers who were?" When Kat opened her mouth to try to protest, Faye cut her off with a gesture. "I know you think I'm naive to the ways of infantry, but *please* do me the courtesy of not denying what I could plainly see with my own two eyes."

"It was dark that night," Kat said flatly. "Who knows what you saw?"

"Could you please stop panicking and listen to what I'm trying to tell you? Your little secret is safe with me. I *understand.*"

"Why?" Kat asked. "Even if you had evidence—which again, you don't—doesn't it go against your . . . codex, or whatever it's called?"

Faye scoffed. "The *Codex* is for high society. They're rules that govern the proper behavior of highborns, because people with that much wealth and power need to be properly managed. It always struck me as unnecessarily restrictive, the binds your leadership puts on common infantry—and none more so than fraternization laws."

"You've never seen what happens when battle discipline falls apart," Kat countered.

"Aren't you supposed to be agreeing with me?"

Kat blinked incredulously down at the noblewoman. "I'm *supposed* to be a good soldier. And what you're accusing me of—"

"—has no bearing on that, in my eyes."

"Who are you and what have you done with Faye Laurent?"

At that, Faye laughed—once, bright and belly-deep, a laugh like she'd been holding it in for years, the same laugh that had pulled a smile from the prince at the breakfast table. "Hosts, you're just like the rest of them. Six years and all they see is the girl who stumbled into High Training clutching a stack of books and praying that one of them would have the answers she needed."

"I see a seventy-five-token Aurean," Kat countered. "I see the fifth-most-decorated Aurean in *history.* And someone who could ruin my career with one word to my centurion or my prince."

Faye shook her head, still fighting a smile. "I'm not going to do that. Of course I'm not going to do that—not when we can be useful to each other. I see it as my obligation as your duchess. We both have rules we have to abide by, and rules we have to work around. And, if we play our cards right, rules that can be rewritten."

Kat bit back a frustrated huff. Of course highborns could rewrite things. They were currently in the process of rewriting the *map*, etching a new line clear across Telrus's countryside. All she could do was rally her rank to meet the changes and hope they all survived. "I'd like to believe that's possible," Kat said. "But until then, I suppose I don't have the luxury of pretending the rules won't impact me either."

"Would that more of my friends shared our convictions," Faye replied with a dry smile. "I can't believe Daya and Celia are *still* making a spectacle of the courier issue this far into the project."

Kat let some of her tension loosen. Both noblewomen had been a plague on the camp logistics for the entire length of the march, constantly stealing riders out from under each other to send messages to the legions they were supposed to be managing—to what end, Kat still didn't understand. "I'm not even sure which one of them started it."

"Oh, it had to have been Daya. She's been a pigtail puller for as long as I've known her. I'm fairly certain she keeps her hair cut so short just to stop anyone from doing it back, and I'd bet you two gold crowns she isn't even sending the riders anywhere useful. She's probably just giving them orders to take their horses out for a turn in the countryside long enough to get under Celia's skin."

Kat frowned. "It's strange, though, that Celia needs the riders just as frequently. She's never struck me as actively involved with the leadership." It went against everything she'd come to understand about the two of them, even after weeks of close observation. In fact—

"They're both being frivolous," Faye said despairingly. "It's a wonder the prince still takes them seri— Oh, what's wrong?"

"Sorry, Your Grace," Kat called over her shoulder, already hustling toward the command tent. "I just realized I have urgent business with His Highness."

CHAPTER 22

"I THINK I HAVE A LEAD," KAT DECLARED AS SHE STRODE INTO THE inner sanctuary of the command tent—then froze in her tracks.

For a gut-wrenching moment, she thought she was too late. The prince was slumped flat on his face in the middle of his correspondence and hadn't moved an inch despite the bluster of her entry. A second before she swept in to check for a pulse, he peeled his head up from his desk, a golden seal coming along for the ride plastered to his cheek. He picked it off with a scowl, then flicked it back down on the pile of letters. "Ah, Katrien. Sorry about the mess. What was it you just said?"

"I think I have—"

"I've just gotten some mail, as you can tell," he interrupted.

"Actually, this concerns the ma—"

"A letter from my parents has arrived."

Kat stilled, all thoughts of couriers and conspiracies shunted abruptly backward. Adrien, for all his grand ideas and outlandish, expensive maneuvers, rarely communicated directly with the crown. She'd gotten the sense that his sequestered upbringing had created a distance between the prince and his parents, one both parties were struggling to navigate in the new world where he no longer needed to be kept a secret. With the physical distance between the royals shrinking on their approach to Rusta, Kat should have been bracing for this moment.

And probably should have gotten her thoughts in order beforehand. Royalty was one thing when it was Adrien. Prior to the Battle of the Mouth, Adrien had no say in policy, as it would interrupt his two highest priorities: cultivating one hundred tokens and making sure no one knew he existed. With the king and the queen, it was different. If it hadn't been for them, Kat never would have gone to war in the first place.

Three years in, it was difficult to latch onto the seething resentment she'd felt toward the crown when she was first drafted. There was no going back to the person she was before she'd been called up to fight—and *that* left her stewing in a far more complicated emotion that couldn't be boiled down to a simple approval or disapproval of the current royals.

So she fought to school her features and asked, with as much neutrality as she could muster, "What did they write?"

"You know, of course, that our arrival in the capital will culminate with a ball to celebrate my victory and introduce me properly as their heir."

"And you're saying this like it's a death sentence because . . ."

"Because they're insisting that it would be best for everyone—*for the greater good of the realm,* as my father's written here—that I declare my intentions to wed that very same night."

"Ah," Kat replied tactfully. "That seems . . . sudden. At least, in my simple commoner's perspective." Granted, half the shadow plays her mother had raised her on that involved princes ended with the gallant young man falling helplessly head over heels in love at first sight and packed off to swear vows at the hosts' altar not long after, but Kat had outgrown that romantic notion of royalty years ago.

"Believe me, I find it sudden too. But they think it would be good for morale. Optics. Whatever you call it. Apparently what I'm doing with the road project—which, may I remind you, *concretely benefits all people of Telrus*—isn't high-profile enough. They want something with more staying power in the minds of the rabble, and the only thing that will satisfy them is a royal wedding."

Her thoughts snagged on *rabble,* but Kat did her best to nod along sympathetically. "Something tells me this isn't how you envisioned your marriage."

"Envisioned *what* marriage?" the prince countered with a frustrated flap of his hands. "I thought I was doing something good, something *productive*. I don't know what the rest of my life is supposed to look like, but it can't be just . . . this. I should get some say in it."

Must be terrible, she thought, *to have your plans for your life thrown totally off course by a royal decree.* Kat wrestled the sentiment down before she could get herself in trouble. "It sounds like they're giving you options, at least," she said instead. "And I may have a lead on which one of your options might be trying to kill you."

She'd thought it would cheer him, but Adrien took the news like a soldier taking a fatal wound, careening forward into the scattered correspondence with a despondent huff. "Could you tell whoever it is to hurry up and get it over with?" he groaned.

"Your Highness," Kat chided.

He rolled his head to prop himself up by the chin. It struck her all at once how dangerous this was—both that the future ruler of Telrus was showing his belly and that *she* of all people was the only one to bear witness. "Sorry," he said, another damning piece of weakness Kat was stuck with. "I'll endeavor *not* to throw away all your hard work, though I am tempted severely. You must understand, simplifying the choice to people who don't want to kill me will not simplify it to any options I'd prefer."

"You favor none of them?"

He sniffed. "Maybe I've soured on the concept because I'm sick of the people who should be my closest friends courting me for political power, but I don't see a lot of appeal in the notion of favoring anyone. It's times like this I envy you."

"Envy *me*?"

"I imagine for the peasantry it's relatively uncomplicated. You don't *have* to do anything, whereas there's an entire kingdom riding on me striking the right political alliances."

"Doesn't mean it's not complicated."

"Oh? Enlighten me."

The imperative hit like a slap, waking Kat up to the fact that the conversation had somehow spun around to focus on her. "Well, it's . . . it's . . ." she floundered. "It's nowhere near the scale you deal with, but the problems remain the same. How do you find someone who can be your partner through thick and thin? How do you forge a life that supports that partnership without sacrificing the things that are most important to you? How do you commit to a person and every possible future they carry inside them? How . . ." She caught herself rambling and trailed off as she realized Adrien was staring with a suspiciously canny look in his eye, his chin now cradled on his interlinked fingers.

"No, go on," he said. "This is so much more interesting than *my* problems."

"Your problems impact the whole of the realm."

"Yes, but my problems are math problems at the end of the day." He leaned forward, eyes sparkling. "Tell me, Kat, have you ever been in love?"

"I . . . I don't . . ." she said, reeling. "I don't get to—"

"Come now, *I* don't get to. You, on the other hand, what's holding you back?"

Kat sobered. "Three years at war, for a start," she said, her tone severe enough to catch Adrien's gossipy air by the throat. "Nothing's promised on that battlefield. Many of the soldiers I fought alongside when I was first drafted three years ago are dead now. The bonds we forge—they're fierce, but they're fragile. Anyone could be taken from you at any moment."

"Sure, but people want what they want, even when they know it's delusional," Adrien countered. "Actually, *especially* then. My companions are proof enough of that. At least, the ones you're certain aren't conspiring with demons to kill me."

Kat dove on the out. "If my suspicions are correct, we might be able to narrow it down to two."

"Oh?"

"For as long as we've been on the campaign, Celia and Daya have been fighting about the couriers, but have you ever looked into why they need to send so much mail back to their legions in the first place?"

"Well, half of nobility is creating the impression that you're very busy to cover for your life of leisure," Adrien said, but his expression had gone thoughtful. "You're suggesting they're leaking information to the enemy. Schedules, troop positions—it could all look quite innocuous if we interrogated their mail habit directly."

"And if you were to put a hold on their access to the couriers?" Kat asked.

Adrien nodded. "Then we could pay close attention to them. See which one of them it upsets more. It's not a foundation for an accusation, but it could prompt whichever of them it is to act in more obvious ways."

Kat had a brief, dizzying moment of unreality at how easily he had taken the suggestion. Having Adrien's ear was a dangerous game of chance—one in which sometimes she was ignored and sometimes her words shaped the future of the kingdom. She never knew when to press her luck and when to hold her tongue. All she knew for sure was that her efforts would be thankless.

"And if what you say is true, then I have two safer options to consider in the effort to appease my parents' whims," the prince mused. "Not that either of them is appealing."

"You truly couldn't see yourself wed to Faye or Bodhi?"

Adrien grimaced. "I don't think either of them realize what being wed to me would entail. They're far too ambitious. During wartime, it was useful—it's what pushed all of us through High Training. It's the reason we're all loaded with gold."

The reason you're loaded with gold is because your family had gold to load you with, Kat restrained herself from interjecting.

"I can't see them being content with a lifetime as an Augustine's right hand, beholden to the duties of my line. They'd be setting aside all the work they've done, demoting themselves, *shrinking* themselves. It'd kill them in all the ways that mattered."

"Even Faye?"

"Oh, especially Faye. Faye may try to make herself useful to everyone at every possible opportunity, but you should have seen her apply that same diligence in High Training. She lagged behind all of us for the longest time, but there was this moment where it clicked for her that if she didn't get her act together, the rest of us would be carrying *her*—and she couldn't possibly abide that. There was a period where she was picking up a token a *week* trying to scramble up that distance."

"Doesn't sound half bad to me," Kat offered.

Adrien shook his head. "No, she's still deathly afraid of inconveniencing anyone. There's just a rare alignment of the stars sometimes where that works out in everyone's favor."

"And what about Bodhi?"

Adrien let out a decidedly unprincely grunt. "He's my parents' favorite, that's for certain. A formal link between the royal houses of Telrus and Vaya would put aside many fears on both sides of the border. The Southern Reach was an essential ally during wartime, when much of our farmland was lost to demon raids. In peacetime, we're now a grossly overmilitarized neighbor, and the

Vayan crown is just as eager as I am to see our forces cut back down to a rational size. Marrying Bodhi would reinforce our commitment to alliance—at least, that's what my parents keep telling me," he finished, plucking at the letter on his desk.

"So you won't do it, simply because they want you to?" Adrien scoffed.

"He's the kindest, most decorated, and most handsome of your options."

"I can't be seen with a king consort who's better looking than me. Pass."

"Well then, if we suspect Daya and Celia of collaborating with demons and Bodhi's far too good of an option for you to ever pick him . . ."

The prince frowned. "Faye?" he said with a sudden, serious weight.

"Faye," Kat agreed. If she had the prince's ear, she might as well use it to push him toward the Duchess of Halston, the humble, hardworking young woman who'd cultivated every single token at her disposal to the outside edge of its capacity, who'd spent her formative years in the shadow of far greater Aureans and never let it stop her.

And if Faye had meant what she said about rewriting the rules, it couldn't hurt to do her this favor and put her in a position that made it possible.

It was no fairy tale, no shadow play, no grand romance—only mercenary logic, perfectly suited to the machinations of royalty.

Adrien gave her a long, considered look, and for a moment Kat wondered if she'd finally overstepped. *Royalty* could be mercenary, but she wasn't royal, and maybe it wasn't her place to think like them.

"Perhaps I've been thinking about this all wrong," the prince said at last. "My parents have tried to box me into the confines of their expectations, but that hinges on me accepting their premise in the first place. They've never been out among the common people like this. They've never seen things from your point of view, and so they lack perspective. Maybe I can give it to them."

Kat would never dare say it out loud, but it was remarkable how far Adrien had come from the flippant princeling who barreled into their camp with his grand delusions of a better world. He might even be a good king one day, if such a thing was possible.

"But of course, there are more immediate and pressing concerns," Adrien declared, drawing his finger down the page and tapping a word twice. "Ball in my honor. No matter what unpleasantness precedes it, it will be the party of the century. We must alert the tailors at once."

"Of course, Your Highness," Kat replied.

CHAPTER 23

"I NEED HELP REACTING TO SOMETHING," KAT ANNOUNCED AS she slotted herself in at Emory's shoulder.

Ever since the Third Century had been released from digging in favor of furnishing guard rotations for the prince, Giselle had taken their newfound free time as an opportunity to double down on drilling, and Emory had been dragged along for the ride. Kat had found him leaning on the edge of the fence that demarcated this camp's training grounds, watching as Giselle stomped her way through a familiar set of spear drills.

Kat couldn't help but wonder whom Giselle was picturing at the end of her spear when she practiced century tactics like this. The Demon Lord's defeat had wiped the notion of thrall armies from this plane completely. Staying signed on as a soldier meant that the next enemy you faced in tight ranks on the battlefield might be just as human as you were.

Once they defeated the last Lesser Lord, that was.

"Hello to you too," Emory said, tearing his eyes from his pupil to flash Kat a boyish, almost sheepish smile that had her fighting the urge to check over her shoulder and make sure no one else could see it.

The past two weeks had been a unique sort of torment, with Emory suddenly remarkably underscheduled and Kat pulled relentlessly back into the prince's orbit with orders to uncover a traitor in their midst. There'd been no time to continue the conversation they'd started in the woods outside Fallon, and Kat could barely look at him without feeling the itch to drag him into the first dark corner she could find. Duty had reared its ugly head to remind them of their true priorities.

It was that duty she tried to focus on now as she leaned in and muttered, "I just had an illuminating little chat with Faye Laurent, and now I think we might be able to narrow our investigation down to two. It has to be either Celia or Daya."

Kat filled him in on the details, bent close enough that he could hear her without raising her voice but not so close that any passerby could accuse them of anything untoward. She couldn't help second-guessing every inch of distance between them now. Faye had seen clean through her. How many of their compatriots were just as savvy?

She could feel the same tension in Emory as he listened, attuned as she always was to the way her battle partner moved and reacted. It had been months since the last time they were in battle together, but she recognized this rigidity and hated feeling like she was the cause of it. They were supposed to be in peacetime. Why did it feel like they had more to fear now than when the High King of Hell was blighting their land?

"So the prince's plan is to put a hold on the couriers and . . . wait?" Emory asked after a long beat of silence filled only by Giselle's distant grunts. "Surely there's more that can be done."

"Not without incurring their suspicion," Kat replied. "Unless . . ."

"Unless?"

"Their focus has to be on the prince, and they'll be paying close attention to any action he takes that might indicate he's on to the traitor. But the infantry is nothing but background noise to them. Our own could observe them beneath their notice."

"Say the word and I'll marshal the troops," Emory muttered, low and serious. Then he reached into his pocket and pulled out a small cloth bag. "Candy?"

Kat let out a startled chuff at his sudden about-face. The bag was stamped with a familiar confectioner's seal. "But these . . ."

He pushed it toward her insistently, and she took it. "You spotted them in Fallon on the day we went looking for the hand pies."

Several other things had happened that day that had shunted her memory aside until this moment. Kat unraveled the string wound around the bag and tipped the package over, shaking a handful of small candies into her palm. They were pale white, and the scent of mint and sugar wafted from them. *This* she did remember—the way the sudden whiff had done nothing to help with her borderline insatiable hunger as they hunted the city for Roberto's cart.

"You were a little busy in the day following, but I doubled back before we broke camp to see if they were worth the fuss."

"You didn't have to," Kat protested, even as she resisted the urge to cram them in her mouth immediately. "They aren't on the list."

"We could add to the list," he suggested. "It's not set in stone."

"You haven't even shown it to me," Kat reminded him. Something about the notion of expanding their ambitions rankled at her. It was no insult to the ground they'd already covered, but it felt like the kind of thing that could easily get out of hand. They couldn't be making up goals just to check them off. She didn't even know how long the list was, and she got the sense Emory was afraid to show her—that he worried it might scare her away.

"Hey," he said firmly. "The list is a rule we invented to give ourselves a reason to treat each other. But I don't want it to be the only reason."

"Oh, am I being rewarded for something?" Kat asked slyly.

The tips of Emory's ears had reddened, and he cast a distressed look over to Giselle, who was mercifully still focused enough that she hadn't noticed her mentor's attention slipping away. "Can't I do something nice for you just because I want to?"

Yes, she wanted to say. *Forever,* she would have added. What a wonder it would be to be spoiled for the rest of her life by this man's generosity, but that thought was *far* too big for this moment and the tiny candies nestled in her palm. They were barely a week away from the capital. Barely two weeks away from Adrien's victory ball. The day Kat would decide the shape of her future was almost upon them, and the dread was only getting more and more concrete by the moment.

For years, soldiering had been an obligation, which meant she'd never had to think about what she'd be without it. She missed the forge. Missed her father. Missed the feeling of a hard day's work going toward *making* something, not advancing an arbitrary line on a map on the orders of someone who wasn't risking their life the same way she was.

But she was so much more than a forge girl now. She'd put in the work to hone her token. There was a door open, and the temptation to walk through it was only growing day by day.

Kat held her palm out, offering it to Emory.

"I got them for you," he insisted, holding up his hands.

"And what did you get for yourself?" she asked.

"Honestly, my purse was a little light after our last excursion together," he said sheepishly. "But I had a few pennies, enough for something small."

Their last excursion together. Where he'd nearly fought an old man over being able to buy her a meat pie, then emptied out his coin purse for the orphanage matrons and their charges. Suddenly it was all Kat could see—the way this man gave himself away ceaselessly. The way he enlisted the second he was able to. The way he spent his spare time training up a teenaged girl to make sure she'd survive the front lines. He gave and gave and gave. He left so little for himself.

And what had Kat done? She took. She took his offerings. She took the prince's attention and brought her whole century into the line of fire in the process. If she walked through the door that had swung open for her, she'd take the place that Emory deserved, the officer position only *she* could qualify for with the golden token around her neck.

Again, she pushed her hand toward him, and this time he didn't resist as she tipped one of her candies into his palm.

There were so many things she didn't dare say out loud. That half the joy of this little quest they'd constructed for themselves was sharing a good thing together. That now that there *was* a future to consider, she wanted to spend as much of that future as possible finding every good thing in the realm they could share. That nothing since the end of the war—not even the threat of the Lesser Lords hunting them—had made her feel dread like the moment Faye insinuated that she knew their little secret.

"Together?" she breathed instead, and maybe that was the heart of it. This question that was lurking in the space between them, the one they kept needing to answer over and over again.

Emory popped the candy in his mouth, and as always, she moved in tandem with him.

It was delightful—it couldn't be anything else. A burst of sugary sweetness, balanced perfectly with the crisp cool of the mint flavoring. She knew she could always rely on Emory to find the best of the best, and she wasn't even sure if she'd ever told him just how much she loved mint.

"This had better not be a commentary on my breath," Kat said, just to see him nearly spit his out in a panic as he shook his head.

"What have you guys got there?" Giselle called from across the training field and they both straightened like schoolchildren who'd just been caught by a teacher.

Emory snatched the pouch out of Kat's hands and tucked it behind his back. "No idea what you're talking about."

Giselle trotted over, and if Kat didn't know any better, she'd swear the kid sniffed the air like a dog. "Did you finally give her the mints?"

"No," Emory blurted, just as Kat said, "Oh, *finally*?"

Giselle flashed a smug little grin. "He's been carrying them around for weeks waiting for the right moment. Did he try to pass them off as something he just happened to have on him?"

Emory shouldered in front of his self-appointed charge. "Don't listen to her. No idea what she's talking about. Heat must be getting to her after all that drilling. Hey, Giselle, want a mint? They keep your mouth very occupied."

"Who am I to complain about my silence being bought so deliciously?"

So she knows for sure, Kat thought as Giselle folded her hands out eagerly for Emory to shake a few candies into. Of course she knew. From the pineapple incident alone, she must have been able to tell *something* was going on, and if that didn't seal the deal, morning after morning training with Emory would have. At least she seemed content to be bought off with sweets.

But unlike with Faye, Giselle's awareness steadied something in Kat. Sure, the girl's origins were mysterious and almost certainly noble, but she'd proved herself time and time again in battle, fought side by side with them, and never backed down from an opportunity to be a better soldier—not in the stickler-for-the-rules way that would spell certain trouble, but in a way that made Kat trust this kid with her life.

Giselle caught her eye with a wry smirk. "You know, I'm finding myself exhausted from a long day of drilling, as my teacher has so wisely pointed out. I think I might go nap somewhere out of the way before the dinner call goes out and tell everyone I was drilling with Emory if anyone asks where I was."

She sauntered past them, setting her practice spear back on the rack. Emory stared after her. "I've never seen her call a practice early. Do you think she's feeling well? Maybe I shouldn't have given her candy—"

Kat was already dragging him by the hand in the opposite direction.

PRIVACY IN A WAR CAMP WAS ONE THING. BUT IN THE CONVERGENCE of the Third Century's operations with all the chaos of Adrien's road project, Kat had begun to notice gaps. Consistent gaps, now that she was stuck with the prince long enough to check them day in and day out. It was into one of those gaps that Kat pulled Emory, barely certain they were out of sight before her lips sealed over his.

He tasted of mint and grit and the salt of his sweat, and she realized somewhat sheepishly that he might have appreciated some forewarning and an opportunity to freshen up. But from the way he drew her firm against him, she also understood that any further delay would have been torment—or an opportunity for one of their obligations to rip them apart unsatisfied again.

"You're sure . . ." he groaned against her collarbone as her wandering hands began to pull at the lacings of his clothes. "Sure this is a good spot?"

"Can never be too safe," she panted. "But this is Lady Laurent's storage wagon, and I'll wager she's off trying to make herself too useful to notice."

"Fair, but if someone else notices a wagon rocking . . ." he countered, bucking his hips a little into hers for emphasis. The wood beneath them creaked worrisomely, but the heat of him growing hard against her made a fierce counterargument.

"Then we're going to need to be fast and creative," Kat re-plied, and from the wicked curve of the smile her lips found in the dark, she knew her challenge had been accepted.

It was different from the first two times they'd been able to have each other properly—no less desperate, but so much more urgent. Kat felt a little wild with it, with how much she had to let go all at once. There was no slow lead-in, no long night, no lazy walk back to the camp. They could be caught at any moment. They had to take everything they could all at once.

There wasn't the fear of the first time, and a surprisingly com-fortable folded spare tent made it a huge improvement on their second, but as Kat tried to let herself sink wholeheartedly into the pleasure of everything Emory had to give, she found that a new sort of desire was starting to build to a much less satisfying peak in her. She craved, more than anything, a chance to be *lazy* with this man. A slow morning. A soft bed. No war hurrying them to scramble from the wreckage of Mira's tent, no duty dragging them back to camp after their tumble in the woods. They'd made it to peacetime against all odds. She wanted to enjoy it.

Which wasn't to say she wasn't enjoying herself now. In fact, she wished she could let Emory know *exactly* how much she was enjoying herself without alerting the road camp to the fact that two people were currently defiling a storage wagon. It was an-other maddening way this was *good* but could be better. Maybe to love someone was to workshop, whether it was their dogged pur-suit of their food quest or the relentless need to have this man in pieces over her body.

That was it, she decided in the aftermath of the second shud-dering orgasm he'd coaxed from her in mere minutes. That was the impossible future she craved above all others. A chance to pursue perfection, and to share it with him.

CHAPTER 24

RUSTA LOOMED ON THE HORIZON, STARK AGAINST THE SETTING sun, and even if she hadn't been told, years of experience on the campaign had Kat gauging a simple truth from one look alone.

They were only a day's march away.

She expected Adrien to be mired in dread, but the prince was in shockingly good spirits, surveying the last stretch of roadbed being dug out with a lopsided, almost charming grin on his face. She had to hand it to him—for once, a royal had been more than just talk. Over the course of barely two and a half months, Adrien had carved a line clean through the map of the continent, paid every soldier a fair wage for their contribution, and was offering a release from service with no strings attached that, if nothing went sideways between here and his victory ball, was only a couple days away.

And, as if the promise of the victory ball wasn't enough, Adrien had decided to throw a feast for the Third Century and spared no expense to do so. He'd sent the porters out to the local farms surrounding the capital, and each of them had returned with a veritable bounty that the cooks had been working tirelessly over with just as much vigor as the soldiers digging some of their final trenches. The mess tent was torn down for the night, sending the smoke of their cookfires high into the starry skies above and leaving the rows of tables open to the soft breeze that whispered through the camp, carrying with it the last gasps of summer's warmth and the promise of autumn's chill.

Kat had been salivating for a solid hour, barely able to focus on Adrien's meetings as she caught whiffs of the food being prepared. The farmland around the capital had borne only the slightest of incursions by the Demon Lord's forces, and this late in the season, it spilled over with abundance. Tomatoes, corn, even gourds already falling off the vine. Kat had grown up sustained by these fields, and the smell was enough to rocket her back to childhood memories of lightly seasoned squash roasting over coals her father had brought in from the forge.

Adrien had also seen fit to procure around forty casks of ale for the festivities. He'd hemmed and hawed over whether it would be enough, and Kat had not-so-subtly encouraged that anxiety until he'd decided it would be better to overestimate than fall short. She had a sneaking suspicion that they'd need to add an extra day to their schedule to account for the hangovers that were about to be incurred.

At long last, the sun plunged toward the horizon. The mess bell tolled, the tables were set, and the first casks were cracked into as the century passed flagons around under Adrien's patient eye. He'd floated himself up to stand on the table at the heart of the arrangement, straddling a whole roasted hog as he looked on with merry eyes and his own cup propped on his hip. His circlet was notably absent. Tonight, he was just a man.

A man with a hundred tokens arrayed across his chest, but Kat found she appreciated the gesture all the same.

"Places," he called as soon as it seemed everyone had gotten their cup.

Kat and the rest of the first decade packed in around the table at his feet, as around them the century followed suit. Shields on one side, spears on the other—though at this point, all the organization felt like a play they were putting on. They were so close to the capital and the moment when many of them would no longer have to care about sticking to their formation.

Emory sat directly across from her, catching her eye with a subtle smirk as Adrien knocked his signet ring against his cup and whistled for quiet. Under the table, her battle partner's boot pressed unsubtly on top of her toes.

"My friends," Adrien declared as the noise of the century finding their places settled. His Voice of Angels token was working its magic, but he'd mastered the art of finding a middle ground with its power, taking his projection down from ear-shattering to sufficiently loud. "I've gathered you all here tonight to celebrate your magnificent accomplishment. Not only have you built the finest road this continent has ever seen, but you've also seen me safely delivered from the Mouth of Hell itself all the way to Rusta's gates. Tonight, I celebrate you. I toast to you. I thank you for every drop of sweat you've given to this kingdom. And I reiterate my solemn vow. On the morning after the victory ball, every last one of you will be entitled to a full release from the contracts of service that still bind you. We've all worked hard to bring about a world at peace. All of you are free to enjoy it."

He tipped his cup up, and the century raised a hearty cheer in answer. It was a far cry from his first stumbling attempts to address them, and Kat couldn't help the pride that warmed through her at the sight of the prince, bright and steady and ready for his future. She met his toast and drank deeply, letting out a satisfied grunt at the crisp, cool, malted ale—one she knew Emory must have mirrored.

"I also want to raise a toast to the leadership that has helped make my vision a reality," Adrien continued, pivoting to face the long table that was set up at the far edge of the feast. At it, Mira, Mobbert, and the rest of the prince's advisers flanked Adrien's four companions, each of them resplendent in their gold and dressed in Telrusian red to mark the occasion. "Without you, my ideas would be nothing but vague whims of a better world."

Kat caught Emory's eye across the table, tamping down a snort. The important thing was that Adrien saw where credit was due and acknowledged it, already a huge stride from where he'd started. They toasted along with the prince, drinking deeply and eagerly.

"And finally, to my dear companions," Adrien said. Kat wondered if she was the only person who'd watched him closely enough to see the mountain of tension that had come crashing down over his shoulders as he narrowed his sights on the four highborns. "Though it was I who struck the final blow on the evil that blighted our land for the past twenty years, it was only possible because I had the four of you at my side. You've challenged me in every way. Made me the Aurean I am." He folded a hand over his array for emphasis, as if to make sure no one forgot just how many tokens sat on his chest. "If they call me the hero of the realm, if they feast to my accomplishments, I must reject it wholeheartedly. We have done this together, and I'm forever in your debt."

Celia looked bored. Daya was already draining her cup, heedless of the prince's toast. Neither of them seemed to find it ironic that the prince was singing their praises—but then again, neither of them had cracked when Adrien cut off access to their couriers. If they were playing a game, they were playing it well—well enough that none of the infantry Kat and Emory had organized to survey them under the guise of extra protection had reported anything untoward.

They were only a day from the capital. Surely the traitor would have to reveal themselves before then.

"Oh, and one more thing!" Adrien announced, snapping Kat out of her scrutiny. "A very special toast to the Third's own Katrien, who has been by my side through thick and thin on this project. It has been a delight to watch her flourish, and I cannot wait to see the illustrious future that awaits her."

Kat froze under the sudden, all-too-familiar weight of the century's attention. *No,* she wanted to protest. *This isn't right.* She was supposed to be laughing along with the rest of them at Adrien's overblown speeches—she wasn't supposed to be a *subject.* There was a horrible pause, a moment where none of them knew what to do.

Then Emory surged up from his chair. "*TO KATRIEN,*" he hollered.

The decade followed their hinge shield. The century roared in reply. Tankards hoisted, Ziva and Sawyer crushed in on either side of her, and the first decade alone made so much rowdy noise that it could probably be heard from Rusta's city wall. She may have been an Aurean, may have set herself apart from them, may have been elevated again and again by the prince's attention, but the decade had Kat's back—on the battlefield and off. It was a profound relief to be reminded of it.

Kat could barely get her own tankard to her lips through all the jostling, and half of it ended up sloshed down her front. Sputtering and thoroughly overwhelmed, she barely caught the moment Adrien activated his Lightness of Angels token and stepped off the table, tipping her a cheery salute as he floated back down to the ground.

They fell on the feast like wild dogs, hardly caring that a few yards away, Mira was staring resolutely at her plate and shielding her eyes from the spectacle her soldiers were making of themselves. Half of them didn't need their centurion's respect, anyway—not if their releases were on the horizon.

Kat had to remind herself to slow down. No one was going to pull her away from her plate. There was no mess schedule to stick to, no orders breathing down her neck, just her and the most generous meal she'd had in ages. The pork was so fatty she could barely get it to stay on her fork, so salty she could have spent the whole night suckling one slip of it on her tongue. The roasted vegetables, too, were a revelation, the late summer harvest's bounty seasoned to perfection. On the campaign, meals needed to be efficient—not only in the time it took to hork them down, but in the value they provided. They ate heavily, loading up on meats and grains, and though the occasional vegetable snuck its way into the preparation of the cooks' stews and roasts, it was another thing to see them laid out as dishes in their own right. It felt foolish to see a miracle and a promise in a squash dish, but it was a kind of foolish she was allowed to be, now that peace was upon them.

And it wasn't as if her foolishness lacked company. The soldiers around her were on a heaven-sent mission to drink their way clean through Adrien's anxious overbuying, and it seemed like every three bites another rowdy toast was being raised to something or another.

"To never marching again!" Carrick hollered, lunging across the table to clack his tankard against Sawyer's. At his side, Emory took a measured sip from his own drink, catching Kat's eye warily. Carrick and Sawyer were a foregone conclusion. The two of them had declared their intention to walk from the moment Adrien made the announcement.

"What's the first thing you're going to do when you get your papers in hand?" Elise asked, her question lobbed over Emory's head.

Carrick smirked. "Can't say. But the *second* thing I'm going to do is buy a horse and make use of this lovely new road until the fork in Fallon. Then it's another day's ride south to Brista where my folks are. What about you?"

Elise's troublesome smirk spread across her lips as she jerked her chin at Ziva. "Guess that depends on which one of us gets to that kitchen girl first."

Ziva sucked her teeth. "It's cute that you think you have a shot."

"I don't just have a shot—I have a contingency. I've got my exits marked and my route drawn."

"Gonna make it more embarrassing for you when she shoots you down and lets you know she's waiting on someone else."

"Ladies, ladies," Brandt said from Ziva's other side, spreading his arms in a gesture he probably thought was helping. "Let's keep tonight joyous."

"I don't think you fully understand that this *is* joyous for the two of them," Javi countered from opposite his battle partner, looking up from the book he'd snuck under the table.

"Thrill of the chase," Kat confirmed, nodding sagely at Brandt's confused look. "Honestly not sure how the poor girl is going to live up to the sport you two have made of pursuing her."

"I'm sure I can find some ways," Elise replied with a cheery grin, and Ziva scowled into her next swig.

"Cover your ears," Emory said, catching Giselle's eye.

"I'm not *five,*" Giselle huffed, prompting snorts from every corner of the table. "Hosts, I'll be happy to take my release and leave you losers behind."

Emory stiffened. "You're taking your release?"

Giselle shrugged as if she hadn't just completely upended his world. "I mean, the world is saved, right? I keep thinking about the rest of my life. Like, I always imagined I'd meet a boy on the battlefield. Him cowering pathetically under a demon, me charging in with my spear, him swooning over my perfected technique. But it's never going to happen that way now, so I might as well enjoy peacetime like the rest of you."

"You're saying you've been making me train you for the *entire* course of this road campaign just to give up your position as soon as we reach the capital?"

Giselle straightened, sobering. "I . . . I wasn't in the best place when I joined up. I had a brother. Older. He went to war five years ago, and when . . . The way my family talked about it . . . I felt like I was the only one seeing clearly. Felt like I had to avenge him in some way, carry on what he was trying to do, so I marched myself right into the local garrison and demanded they put a spear in my hand."

Kat shot Emory a *did you know?* look. He shot her a *not a clue* one right back.

"And it's not just that I never got a chance to live up to what he could have been and pay the demons back for taking him from me. I don't think I ever *could.* I mean, look at us. Look at all of us—even Kat has a token, and she's barely a drop in the bucket compared to the prince and his lot."

"Thanks, kid," Kat muttered under her breath, but she wasn't about to stop Giselle from calling it like it was.

"I just . . . I wonder how my family made peace with it. I think I should go back and talk to them—see if there's any peace for me there too."

A weighty silence swept over their table, made all the more potent by the background noise the rest of the century provided. After a second, Kat lifted her tankard and caught Giselle's eye. "What was your brother's name?"

Giselle never had much tolerance for prying questions. She always deflected anything of the sort with her ceaseless commitment to honing herself as a spearbearer. So it was new for all of them, the softness that came over her eternally pinched expression as she said, "Henry."

Kat lifted her tankard. "To Henry. May his bravery not be forgotten and his legacy stay lit in you."

"To Henry," the rest of the decade echoed. Giselle's lip wobbled as she met their hoisted tankards, then ducked behind the shelter of her drink.

When she resurfaced, she'd schooled herself back into her usual neutrality, though her gaze darted suspiciously around at the rest of the decade. "Don't look at me like that. There're far too many other dead people for you to pity me and me alone. Let's toast to them, yeah?" She twitched her mug at Emory, as if desperate for a lifeline.

Though he still looked somewhat shaken, he sat forward gamely and raised his mug. "Some of you remember my first battle partner, Nolan," he said, nodding to Carrick and Sawyer. "Before I was your hinge, I was a fresh recruit about to shit my pants on the verge of my first battle, and he was the one who showed me how to bind my shield on right. That little kindness has probably kept me alive to this day. But Nolan wasn't so lucky. He fell to thralls at the Battle of Belin, and he left a hole in our ranks that I've been trying to fill ever since. I wish he could be here tonight, sharing in this bounty he helped create."

Kat exchanged a glance with Carrick across the table. Three years at Emory's side, and this was the first time she'd heard him say more than five words about the man whose place she'd taken. It had gone from an unspoken resentment that hovered between them to an unspoken ache she'd learned to let lie every time they lost another member of their decade on the front lines. At last, the dam had broken.

"To Nolan," Kat said, pushing forward across the table to knock her mug into his.

"To Nolan," the decade rumbled.

They continued on like that for some time, each of them taking a turn to memorialize one of the fallen soldiers whose memories they carried. Though the thought of how many they'd lost was sobering, by the end of it all of them were grinning, swapping every story they could recall of the people who had once made up their unit. It seemed a peculiar arrangement of fate that this was their final configuration—so arbitrary, that the war's end had happened to fall on this group of ten. And with the capital looming, with the threat of a third Lesser Lord still on the prowl, all Kat could think as she got deeper and deeper into her cups with every fallen soldier's name, was that she desperately hoped—hoped *be-*

yond hope—that all ten of them were done with war and free to choose whatever future best suited them.

The decade had moved past both the sobering business of honoring the dead and sobriety itself as a whole for some time when Emory lurched up from his seat. "Back in a moment," he slurred, then strode unsteadily across the clearing where the banquet had been set and into the cover of the woods.

"He knows the latrines are dug back that way, right?" Ziva asked, hitching a thumb over her shoulder.

"Man that drunk can piss where he pleases," Sawyer replied with a shrug.

Between them, Kat sat in crisis. A tension had been building in Emory as the night went on, but she wasn't sure what to make of it—whether it was just a natural by-product of so much melancholy or something more. She didn't want to add to his woes by calling attention to it, but at the same time—

"I'm going to make sure he doesn't get lost," Kat declared, plunking her tankard down a bit too loudly and shoving herself up. Across from her, Carrick's lips pursed toward a salacious whistle, but a distinct *thud* underneath the table had him wincing instead. Kat patted Sawyer's shoulder gratefully, then shunted her chair back and made off in Emory's wake.

She knew she'd been drinking heavily, but it was another thing to feel the alcohol hit her all at once as she struggled to keep her feet on a straight path. That task became even more difficult the second she hit the brush at the edge of the clearing, and she found herself bracing trunk by trunk for balance as she moved through the trees.

She didn't have to go far. With her utter lack of elegance, it was no secret she was following him, and Emory had paused to give her a chance to catch up. "Kat," he warned, his voice lowered and his eyes fixed somewhere off in the dark.

"Emory," she replied evenly. "What's going on?"

"I'm fine," he said in the strained tones of a man who was plainly not.

Behind them, the raucous noise of the party carried on. They hadn't gone too far into the trees, and the spill of the torches that surrounded the festivities cut deep enough into the woods that she knew the two of them were still visible to most of the revelers. Even so, she reached out, laying a less-than-steady hand on his shoulder as she pulled him around to face her.

"Don't," he said gently. "I just needed a moment to breathe."

"It got heavy back there," she offered. "All those losses, all together. Tonight's supposed to be joyful."

Emory grimaced. "That's . . . not quite it."

"Whatever it is, I have your back. You know that."

"I do," he said, his eyes meeting hers at last. "But I've been thinking a lot recently about what the end of the road means. For you—for a lot of you—it's the opportunity of a lifetime. Most of the people who march with us did so because they had to. Whether by draft or by calling, we needed to defend Telrus from the grasp of evil. So you played your part, but you dreamed of a world where you wouldn't need to. You dreamed about the shape of your life without a weapon in your hand. The forge, right?"

He let out a long, bracing breath, and Kat tightened her grip on his shoulder.

"It's a bit fucked-up that a soldier is the only thing I've ever wanted to be. That even when we were neck deep in blood and mud, I couldn't imagine myself anywhere else. I know we tried. I know we said all these amazing things we'd eat when the war was over, and I could at least imagine that bit and get through the day. But I think a part of me always knew I was right where I wanted to be. And it wasn't until these past two months that I figured out why that was."

Her throat had gone dry, the remnants of the feast ashen on her tongue. "Why was it?"

The look he gave her was quietly devastating, the sorrow and care that welled in his warm brown eyes. "This is my whole life. These people, this army, this mission. And it's ending."

Kat blinked. "Because I'm—"

Emory shook his head vehemently. "No, not because of you. Hosts, I couldn't live with myself if you did anything *but* go after everything your heart desires. But you heard the rest of them. Carrick and Sawyer have a plan. Ziva and Elise have their kitchen girl. Even Giselle . . ."

Kat laid a hand on his shoulder. "You trained her so well. You thought she was sticking with it because she was going to stay signed on past the end of the road."

"She's free to make her own choices, that's the thing," he said, pinching his brow. "It's not that I resent the time I spent, I just thought . . . I'd have *someone*—"

Kat was past caring about the potential onlookers. She stepped in close and snaked her arms around Emory's shoulders, pulling him tight into her chest. He caught her around the waist immediately, returning the hug with so much fierceness they might as well be wrestling. In it, she felt every drop of what he'd just confessed, what she'd failed to notice all this time. How badly he didn't want to let go of the wonderful thing he'd built for himself in the hell of the war.

He was an orphan who'd chased the shadow of a kindly man, wrapped himself in the armor of a soldier, and found a family to fight by his side. They'd never known a world without the war, but now that it had arrived, the life he'd built for himself was on the verge of crumbling around him. He was helpless to it. Probably thought himself selfish for wanting things to stay the same.

In this moment, all Kat wanted was to be the one thing that could never slip through his grasp.

But just as that thought settled, a shrill whistle blasted from the clearing. It took a moment for her thoughts to arrange around it—to soothe the initial jolt that came from expecting Carrick's heckling, register that this was blown on metal, not fingers, then process the confusion of the automatic response that had her snapping rigid and stepping back from Emory anyway. They hadn't heard this whistle in months, but its meaning had been drilled into them for years.

It was Mira's. It was an order. It was a call to arms.

CHAPTER 25

KAT AND EMORY BURST FROM THE TREE LINE TO FIND THE FEAST in chaos—the smallest of mercies, given the circumstances, for it allowed them to rejoin the century discreetly. Drunken soldiers staggered in every direction, and over the throng, Mira stood on a table with her hands cupped around her mouth. "This is our chance!" she hollered. "To arms, you louts—or don't tell me you've forgotten how to muster."

The two of them exchanged a grim look. "I've got the decade," Emory said. "You find out what's going on."

Kat nodded and set her sights on the feast's high table, where Adrien and his companions were gathered in an anxious knot, heads bent together so they could mutter back and forth. Adrien immediately brightened at the sight of her, waving her over to join them. "Katrien, thank the hosts. It's the most auspicious news we could have hoped for."

"Which is?" she asked warily. She couldn't help checking both Celia and Daya, but for once the two of them wore the same inscrutable, focused expression, and Kat had no idea what to make of it.

Before Adrien could answer, Mira blasted on her whistle once more. The centurion rocked back on one heel, then lunged forward, one of her tokens granting her a burst of speed and power that had her sailing clear over the heads of her troops and into the heart of the camp. Distantly, the whistle trilled again—this time in a staccato beat that usually meant *move your sorry asses, so help me hosts.*

"Well, remember that Lesser Lord we still haven't dealt with?" Adrien asked, looking shockingly cheerful for the words coming out of his mouth. Kat privately wondered if the prince had been drinking just as much as his soldiers in yet another foolhardy effort to prove he could keep up.

"Difficult to forget," Kat said, glancing back to the woods she'd just plunged out of. Part of her expected the final general to lunge from their depths right then and there, but the prince was far too calm.

"Our scouts just found its camp only a few miles from here."

"You're saying we can strike first?"

"It's the perfect opportunity," Adrien confirmed, beaming.

None of his companions seemed to object—but Kat wouldn't have taken it that far. It was unquestionably valuable if they could muster, march, and quash this problem once and for all. But most of the soldiers staggering toward the camp to grab their armor and weapons were barely walking in straight lines. A hard, driving, battle-ready march was sure to have half of them emptying their guts on the way there. More than half, if Mira was leading the charge.

"We're a single century," Kat warned him. "We're built to work in a ten-by-ten formation on an open field. And even if half of us weren't drunk off our asses, we're down by several members. The woods will thin us even more, and the night will make tactics nigh impossible. And Mira needs half an hour to attune to full power."

Adrien leveled her with a serious look. "And if your prince said he's sick of feeling hunted and wants this war over once and for all?"

Kat grimaced. "Then who am I to refuse an order?"

THERE WOULD BE NO SUBTLE APPROACH UNDER THESE CIRCUM-stances, but Mira had elected for an attempt all the same. They'd fractured into four groups, and Kat thanked the hosts that she'd been placed in one with three decades instead of one with two. The holes in their numbers left twenty-seven of them bent low as they stole through the forest. Kat's heart jumped into her throat at every snapped twig, her nerves fraying worse and worse as their advance progressed.

Through the trees ahead, something glowed softly. From a distance, it could almost be mistaken for the inviting light of a bonfire, but the closer they got, the more distinct its infernal red tint became. It was hellfire that awaited them, and some primal part of her keened to turn back from its light.

Kat only tightened her grip on her spear and the back of Emory's collar. He had his shield up and ready, his free hand tucked in Carrick's belt just as Elise had latched on to his. This was the only way to coordinate a decade formation under the cover of night—all of them holding on, the shield line belted together, moving with the man at the center as a guide. It turned them into one living unit—not the most graceful beast, but one that could contract into a protective formation at a moment's notice.

The second and third decades were out to their left. Somewhere in the dark, the second unit—composed of the fourth, fifth, and sixth—was rounding out behind the fire that marked the heart of the demon camp. The third and fourth units, paired off from the last four decades of the century, were flanking, ready to pincer in the instant the order came.

Mira was out there somewhere, too, fully attuned by now. Kat kept stealing glances at the treetops overhead, though she'd be hard-pressed to find the glint of Aurean gold among their shadows. Their centurion was their greatest asset. Possibly their only hope, given that she'd barely had anything to drink.

Their orders were simple. Pin down the Lesser Lord. Cut off any means it had to run. And then Mira would drop from the trees and use every last drop of Aurean power she could summon to run the beast through. If they did it right, it would be over in seconds.

But even with the blaze of the infernal fire still over a hundred yards away, Kat had already started to sweat.

It was too obvious for something that had been tracking them the entire course of the campaign. It smelled like bait, and they were walking right into it.

As they got closer and closer to the light, a shape emerged beyond the trees—one that at first Kat mistook for an ancient, gnarled bit of old growth. She had never seen a demon quite like this one. The first Lesser Lord they'd fought had been enormous and muscular, the second built much the same. But this one was wiry, more bones than meat. It sat rigid next to the fire it had lit, a twin ember burning in the center of its chest. The flesh around that bit of fire was blackened at the edges, as if the monster's gauntness was owed to the flame consuming it. It looked as if the flame had been consuming it for a very long time.

It sat still. So still that it felt as if they were intruding upon some old and horrible shrine, disturbing a cultist in the midst of its meditation. Its eyes were closed, but that felt more like a dare than anything. *Test your luck. See how close you can get. Win a prize.*

And yet, they took the dare. They crept closer. Close enough that *breathing* felt like it would awaken the beast, close enough that

the decade had started to compact around one another as if presenting a smaller target would stave off the inevitable moment
they were sighted. The second unit was visible now on the far side
of the Lesser Lord's clearing, making the same approach, and Kat
fought not to resent them for being assigned the rear.

She glanced again to the treetops, praying for the sight of a
shadow crossing over the moon above—some indication that
they, with their piddling little spears and shields, were not alone.

Closer. To the edge of the very last trees, the last sentinels
standing between them and the beast. It seemed impossible they'd
made it this far without the monster so much as flicking an ear.
The only explanation was the worst one.

It had to be a trap.

The moment Kat had convinced herself of its inevitability
was the moment Mira's whistle screamed from the trees.

There was nothing for it—and no way to resist the siren call of
the order without being left behind as the decade surged forward.
The other two groups that accompanied them were tight at their
side, shields up, battle cries loud. Kat let Emory's collar slip from
her fingertips, bringing her hand up to catch the haft of her spear
instead. He squared in front of her, his shield locked end over end
with the other four flanking him.

And in the heart of the grove, the Lesser Lord's eyes snapped
open at last, liquid black and star-flecked. Kat braced for impact,
but the beast's head only wobbled as it took in the puny humans
who'd come charging into its camp. She swore she could *feel* its
gaze in the hairs that rose on the back of her neck, that burning
stare moving right over her like she meant it no threat at all.

She swore, too, that it smiled.

In the span of a breath, Kat saw it all play out beat by beat.

First, the blaze of Mira's sword lighting with angelic fire overhead.

Second, the demon's sights locking on its true target.

Third, one gnarled hand moving—not toward the soldiers

who charged it, but to the blazing campfire that the Lesser Lord sat next to.

Its palm slammed down, a fury of red sparks spattered over the shield line, and the clearing plunged into darkness.

Save for two things. The burning red heart at the demon's center, and the golden glow of Mira's sword.

It should have been an even match. A target and the weapon meant to plow clean through it. But in that honey-slow moment where every soldier in the clearing flinched back from the scattershot embers, Kat saw exactly what the demon had been waiting for.

The fire was the real trap. Without it, they were grasping at the darkness, and even Mira, with her sword to see by, had lost the markers that guided her descent. There was no way for her to see the beast's claws in the dark.

But it was starkly, horribly clear when they hit her. The beacon of her sword snapped sideways, the crunch carrying over the confused shouts of the century. Their centurion was wearing armor. That had to have mattered. The alternative was too terrible to think of.

And just like that, their plan was ashes. It had all hinged on having the might of an Aurean warrior to finish the demon off, but Mira was crumpled somewhere in the dark. Her sword's light had disappeared the second she was hit, and now the clearing was nothing but indistinct shadows, lit only by the last embers of the demon's smothered fire and the red glow of its infernal heart impossibly high above them.

It let out a quivering, guttural noise.

Kat had never heard a demon laugh before.

Her hand fell from her spear. Their strength as a century had conquered two of these Lesser Lords, but the third was a different beast entirely—one cunning enough to bait them in and powerful enough that it had dispatched Mira like it was swatting a fly. They had nothing but strength and steel to stand against it.

Strength, steel, and the token hung from her neck.

Multitoken Aureans always attuned ahead of battle. In the chaos of the lines, there was barely any room to think—only to react and follow orders. Bringing more than one token into alignment was near impossible in the heat of the moment. But the flow Kat slipped into as she centered her focus on the demon's hulking, twisted shadow took very little from her conscious mind. It was survival instinct, plain and simple, and in that moment, Kat knew exactly what to call for.

The gate to the heavenly realm flung open, and angelic light blazed overhead.

It poured down over the Lesser Lord like molten metal, flooding the clearing with its golden warmth. The beast gave a rattling hiss, its star-stained eyes flinching closed against the overwhelming luminance.

There was no whistle to drive them forward. Only Emory straightening ahead of her and bellowing, with all the authority of a hinge shield, "*CHARGE*."

And like the good, trained soldiers they were, every last rank of the Third Century lunged.

Every soldier but two. As the spears locked in behind their shields and the lines closed on their target, Emory held back, his sword at the ready, his shield raised to cover Kat as she maintained her alignment. The sight of it nearly knocked the light from her grasp. He hadn't learned a single thing from the moment she'd put him in the dirt all those months ago.

But maybe that wasn't quite it.

He wouldn't even follow his *own* orders if it meant leaving her unshielded.

She wouldn't squander his devotion—not when this was their last chance. Kat found the edges of the hole her focus had pried between planes and *ripped* with every last bit of strength she'd gathered over the course of her training. She raised one arm. Conducting, not grounding. A movement to guide her intention. Her fingers spread, and overhead, the light matched her motion, splaying into a sheet that whited out the night.

It made it impossible to miss the inevitable consequence that came for her. She'd been careful when she first called the light to pin the source away from herself. No grounding gesture had given her token away. But this clever demon saw the ranks of soldiers charging for it, saw the two that weren't, and knew exactly where its next strike should fall.

It was the same trick in a horrid reversal. As the gnarled claws reared back for the blow, Kat felt the choice she could make like a wound that had already speared her clean through. Drop the light. Dodge. Draw the demon's ire away from Emory even as he squared steadfastly to meet it.

Or hold. Hold with every drop of bravery she had left, hold with the knowledge she might never walk back through her father's forge door, that Emory might never taste Miss Ophelia's strawberry rhubarb pie, that the life in peace that had been promised to them at the end of this road was nothing but a dream. Hold and give the rest of the Third the chance to strike true.

It was the choice she'd been making ever since her first battle—but it had never hurt this much before to make that call. To let the future be ripped from her teeth and grin through it. To keep performing, a proud soldier to the end.

She fixed herself on the view she'd always expected to see when the end came. On the back of Emory's neck, the solid wall he'd made of his shoulders as he squared to the incoming blow. Anything that got to her would have to go through him first.

But impossibly, the demon's hand stalled in its arc. It took Kat a full second to blink her own light from her eyes and register that it hadn't just *happened*—that four spears had rammed clean through the demon's sinewy palm and lodged, sending their wielders digging into the forest floor with every last ounce of their strength.

The Lesser Lord, too, seemed confused about this turn of events—a confusion worsened by the rest of the Third's efforts to stick it like a pincushion. It operated in a world of hierarchical power, power that cascaded down from a lord to its generals to its underlings to its thralls. It only understood the power of its enemies within the same framework. It had gone for the first Aurean that had lunged at it. Its next logical move was to eliminate the second.

It had ignored the simple human soldiers. Kat had drawn the monster's attention so completely that it hadn't bothered dodging the spears that came its way. Hadn't even *seen* the first decade's spear line lunging to step between its mighty swing and their hinge spear.

Ziva, Sawyer, Brandt, and Giselle—Kat could have tackled them all into a hug if she weren't so busy maintaining the overhead light show. They'd held their line, and now they held the demon's outstretched arm aloft on the tips of their spears. For a moment, she feared it would wrench back and disarm them all at once, but then her gaze flicked over to the beast's body.

Where no fewer than eight of the century's spears were buried through its infernal heart.

The Third Century piled onto the beast, taking no chances, but the red light of its fire had gone out, leaving nothing but Kat's brilliant gold. Their battle cries went from vicious to joyous, the tumult from furious to a tangle of arms and limbs as the soldiers began to slap each other on the back and pile into chaotic hugs.

Kat fell to her knees—but she held her light.

And then Emory was on her, joined by the rest of the decade, the ten of them on the ground in one seething heap, a dream she never wanted to wake from. It was over. The third Lesser Lord was cooling at their feet, and it welled up in Kat all at once that she would never, *ever* have to fight again if she so chose. That with this blow, the last stain of evil upon the material plane was wiped out. Telrus would be at peace.

She would be at peace.

Only one thought wrenched her from the complete joy she

found herself buried in. "*Mira,*" she gasped into Ziva's elbow. She tried to fight free from the tangle of her decade, but Emory steadied her with a hand to the shoulder.

"They've got her," he shouted into her ear. "She's . . . I wouldn't look, if I were you, but they've just landed with a healer in tow."

Who had just landed was made abundantly clear as a token-assisted voice blasted over the clearing, "Three down, none to go!"

Adrien Augustine got little more than exasperated groans in answer as he dropped himself squarely on the crown of his downed enemy's skull. Kat's hard work was doing him all sorts of favors, his tokens catching her light greedily and his mop of golden hair grabbing whatever was left over. The prince stood tall, triumphant, and finally unburdened from the weight of the fear that had been dogging him all these months. He'd dug his circlet out from somewhere just for the occasion.

"I feel like some sort of speech is in order," he said, clapping his hands together. "*But,*" he continued after more than a few emphatic stares, "I also feel like the lot of you might have had more than enough of that back at the feast—and not *nearly* enough of the fine ale I sourced to compensate you for the glorious work you've done tonight!"

The fist he flung in the air was met with enthusiastic cheers—though they were nothing compared to the roar that went up when Bodhi Ranjan and an Aurean healer lifted Mira Morgenstern gingerly to her feet. The centurion's face was half bloodied, one arm dangled limply at her side, and the glorious battle armor that had seen her through seven years on the campaign was crumpled so badly it would take a master crafter months to set it to rights and restore the detailing. Her eyes were unfocused, and the healer had one hand on the back of her neck, the other white-knuckled around their token. Kat got the sense that Mira's spine was the very first thing they'd seen to.

"Weren't you louts in the middle of a party?" their centurion spat, along with a tooth. "Start acting like it."

And who were they to refuse a centurion's order?

Only this time, the casks were rolled miles from the camp into the woods. A pyre was built, the demon's massive corpse hauled atop it—an effort that would have taken a quarter of the century if they'd been sober, but as it was, took half. Gone were the tables, the stuffy ranking they'd created, the barriers between the legion-naires, the aides, and the Aureans in their midst. There was only joy and merriment, and one song in particular that Mira wasn't around to stop, another of Bronwyn's old favorites, which Carrick and Sawyer belted with so much enthusiasm that they blew out their throats by the end of it and finished in croaking gasps like prepubescent teens with the rest of the decade howling in laugh-ter piled at their feet on the edge of the fire.

It was in this state—red-faced, tear-streaked, and convinced she'd never breathe properly again—that Kat realized she had a shadow. She glanced back over her shoulder and caught Adrien's eye. The prince had kept his distance. Not just from the common soldiers, but from everyone, even Bodhi's persistent attempts to draw him into the toasts the rest of the highborns were making together. Adrien had barely touched his drink, though he seemed to be clinging to it to keep up appearances.

He jerked his chin—ambiguously enough that Kat could dis-miss it if she chose. It was so generous of him that she figured she might as well oblige. "Gimme a second," she said, patting Emory on the shoulder as she pushed herself reluctantly up from the warmth she'd found sandwiched between him and Ziva.

"Can we speak privately?" Adrien asked, nodding to the cover of the clearing's edge.

"We can try," Kat replied with a dubious look at the rowdy, drunken antics playing out on all sides of the demon pyre. She caught the concerned glance Emory threw her way and dismissed it with a subtle salute as she followed Adrien into the brush.

"So here's the thing," Adrien said once he'd decided they'd

gone far enough, clapping his hands together. "I think tonight might have fixed everything."

"It better have. Even if we don't know which of your companions was sending them, there are no more Lesser Lords for them to throw at you. And if there are, so help me hosts—"

The prince held up his hands, chuckling. "I swear to you, you will never fight another demon as long as you live. But I'm afraid I may need to ask something far worse of you."

Kat couldn't imagine anything much worse than the terror of battle. She was properly drunk, buoyed still by the adrenaline of living through the fight, and part of her took it like a challenge. A dare. *You say you've found something worse? Let me at it.*

She was about to say as much, but by the time her inebriated brain had found the words, Adrien had already barreled forward. "Now that peace has been achieved, it must be sealed. The kingdom must believe in a future again—one that all people can enjoy under the prosperity my rule will bring. The road is an excellent first step, but there's more I can do. I didn't understand that very well at the outset of the campaign. I thought it was up to me to think in big-picture terms. Things like roads, infrastructure, policy. That, after all, is the domain of kings."

Kat fought back a snort at the dramatics. She didn't want to interrupt this fascinating tear Adrien had found himself on.

"But as we've traveled through these lands, I've seen those massive policy decisions through a different lens entirely. All these little negotiations about where we'd lay the foundations for the road. All the logistics that go into making sure every soldier is fed well and kept happy. All the ways that the separation between the high and the low *limits* the possibilities of this kingdom. And I've seen so much of it thanks to you."

He met her eyes. She'd never seen the prince so serious. If he were anyone but the future ruler of the realm, she would have pushed him, told him to knock it off. Instead, she was trapped under his focus—and for the second time tonight, she realized her fate was in the palm of a being whose power far overshadowed her.

"Your perspective has been absolutely vital these past few months. I thought at the start that the pull of my lucky token was because you were meant to defend me from the Lesser Lords, but I've come to understand it's so much more than that. There are things I just don't see—*vital* things, perspectives on the upkeep of the realm that are never my first thought when I confront these kinds of problems. You, though, you see it right away. Sometimes I can tell, even when you don't say it out loud. You'll squint or frown a little and I'll know I need to take a new angle. I think I'm getting better at it. I *am* getting better at it, right?"

"You are," Kat replied, and it wasn't just to soothe his ego. She'd seen it in the recent weeks, the way Adrien had begun to shift his approach to land usage negotiations from using local councils to strong-arm the rights he needed out of their citizens to approaching those citizens directly and presenting *them* with generous offers that made the deals equally prosperous on both ends. The road he'd built was as much his people's road as it was his, and she found herself, annoyingly, proud of the part she'd played in it.

Adrien grinned. "I'm better when I'm with you. The *realm* is better for your part in my governance of it. And I think that makes one thing starkly clear to me."

Kat froze. Being a foundational part of Adrien's evolving consciousness was a heavy enough responsibility as it was, but she didn't think she was cut out for his advisory—especially as a woman without a high name to cement why anyone but the prince should listen to her.

She'd opened her mouth to say as much when Adrien sank to one knee.

CHAPTER 26

"So I don't have a ring—"

"The hell do you think you're doing?" Kat muttered through her teeth, ducking down to join Adrien in a crouch on the forest floor. Her gaze darted back to the light of the pyre flickering in the distance. No salacious jeers had risen from the celebrations, but that didn't mean no one had spotted them.

"I'm doing the right thing for Telrus," he said as if it was obvious, taking in her panic with an infuriatingly bemused smile. "If there's one thing I've learned over the past months, it's that the realm is better off with your input. You've proven you can tackle weighty problems—like the problem of my marriage, in fact—and come up with innovative, concrete solutions that put the people first. So if I elevate you to the role of princess—"

"Do you hear yourself?" Kat interrupted. She hadn't taken a single blow in the fight against the final general, but she felt like she'd just been hit over the head. "I'm *common*. There's elevating and then there's dressing a . . . a *horse* up as royalty."

"You're not a horse, Kat."

"I'm infantry. I don't even have a high name. It's basically the same thing."

"First of all, you're an Aurean. That token you wear around your neck and the way you've trained yourself to wield it make you far more potent of a warrior than you give yourself credit for, and the Telrusian high court runs on gold. They've turned it into this elaborate game, played out over generations, all with the end goal of amassing as much angelic gold as possible in a single lineage." He gestured to their obvious success, splayed over his chest. "Which is why it would be *perfect* to throw all of that back in their faces by marrying a single-token Aurean—one who took down *two* of the Demon Lord's fiercest generals."

"*Took down* is generous," Kat said weakly.

"Every soldier here would vouch that this is your victory. Don't pretend otherwise. Even Mira Morgenstern would swear it."

Kat grabbed desperately at the line he'd strung past her. "If it's just a low-tokened Aurean you need, Mira's right there. She's quite literally ten times the warrior I am."

"And saddle myself with the Morgenstern family and all their ambitions in the process? No thank you. They'd probably want *heirs*," he added with a shudder.

"You don't want heirs?"

"I'd have shockingly little say in the matter if I were to marry anyone *but* a single-token commoner. Another point in your favor," he said, as if it was supposed to be anything other than horrifying. "Look, I know this is a lot to take in, and I want you to know I hear your concerns."

She barked a laugh.

"However, for the good of Telrus, I'd like you to at least consider it. Sleep on it. My victory ball is in ten days. Just let me know before then if I should ask again—this time in front of a proper audience."

"By a proper audience, you mean your parents. The king and queen of the realm. Who drafted me," she added, in case it wasn't clear how she felt.

"I would *really* love to see the look on their faces." The prince seemed nothing but gleeful at the prospect of placing Kat's thorny political opinions squarely in front of their source. "Just think about what Telrus has become in these months with you by my side. Imagine what it could be with a woman like you shaping policy as a queen. It's a realm I'd be proud to rule."

And before Kat could put together an answer to *that,* Adrien Augustine launched from his crouch and shot into the night sky, disappearing past the darkened canopy overhead.

Kat shoved to her feet, feeling feebler and more plainly human than ever before. How else was she meant to respond to a hapless princeling overladen with divine power asking for her *hand in marriage*? She'd been sent away to war with instructions to make the best of it, to find some bright side, something that would improve her prospects instead of stalling her future in its tracks.

A marriage proposal from the heir to the realm certainly qualified. And a pragmatic voice in the back of her head warned her that the real mistake was considering anything *but* taking the hand that had been offered to her. She'd watched Adrien's companions spend the past months falling over themselves trying to court the opportunity that had spontaneously landed in her lap. Short of breaking the Seal of Heaven herself, Kat would be hard-pressed to find a better improvement of her circumstances.

Worse, Adrien was correct about what she might be capable of. A commoner rising to the rank of queen was something out of a hopeful folktale, not something that happened in real life, precisely because of how much it could shake the foundations of the world. In her mother's fanciful shadow plays, these commoner queens never did much beyond enjoying their sudden change in

social status, but Kat would never be one of those queens—
especially not when Adrien had made it clear that he would glee-
fully support the consequences of giving someone who'd worked
and marched and fought for a living that much power over the
realm's fate.

She could block senseless policy decisions. She could *reverse*
them. She could go straight to the high command and demand
that they tear down the requirement that all officers in the Telrusian military must carry a minimum of one Aurean token.

That policy being the first place her mind went shook her fully
awake. The first thing she'd thought about was Emory's future.
Emory, who'd just confessed to her that he felt as if the life he'd
built was slipping through his fingers with every new member of
the decade who announced their intention to take their release.

Emory, who was losing everything he held dear.

Emory, whose fate she could change, whose future she could
guarantee—if only she took the prince's outstretched hand.

"So, are you gonna do it?"

Kat nearly screamed, whipping around to find Carrick and
Sawyer leaning over a toppled tree like it was a bartop, chins in
their hands. "You—how long—" she choked out.

"Essentially the whole time," Carrick said cheerfully, even
though it caught him an elbow from Sawyer. "It's shockingly easy
to sneak around a prince locked in a soliloquy."

"You let him go on for a while," Sawyer added.

"He tends to do that," Kat muttered sourly. The hosts' mercy
wasn't going to be enough to save her from this one. "I don't suppose it'd be too much to ask you two to keep this between us?"

Carrick and Sawyer exchanged a glance.

"As comrades," Kat added. Three years of serving side by side
had to count for *something*.

"As comrades," Sawyer repeated slowly. "I suppose we could.
But Kat . . ."

"Don't look at me like that," she seethed. "He sprang it on me.

How was I supposed to know he'd think something as senseless as marrying me is the answer to all his problems?"

"Kat—" Carrick tried to interrupt.

"It's so ridiculous. So *transactional*—they're all so transactional, these highborns. They think everything can be bought, whether with favors or with the weight of these stupid little gold tokens." She pulled despondently on hers, tamping down the urge to tear it off and pitch it into the woods. "And maybe it's a good trade. That's the worst part. I'd get a say in the shape of the kingdom. I'd get to advocate for all the soldiers this realm is determined to forget in favor of their glorious Aurean saviors. I could do so much. I could *be* so much. And all I'd have to give up is . . ."

"Emory," the two of them breathed.

She grimaced. Of course he'd told them by now. They were his closest friends—the ones who'd looked out for him when he first joined the ranks, who'd survived battle after battle locked side by side with him. It was dangerous to give intel on his indiscretions to these two clowns, but maybe it was more dangerous to let them sniff out the secret themselves.

"Look, Kat," Sawyer started, rounding behind the log and approaching her with the caution of a hunter moving in on a wounded animal. "We didn't dream of being soldiers either. The only good thing it ever did for me was introduce me to this knucklehead over here. I certainly wouldn't have made it to this day if I hadn't met him. So I think I understand a bit of what you feel. The bit that's not a prince asking you to marry him," he added after a beat.

Kat blinked. It seemed she'd failed somewhat spectacularly in her duties as a decade's hinge. She was supposed to know the soldiers in her line well enough not to miss something like this. "The two of you . . ." she hazarded.

"—were on our way to see what kind of delightful dark corners these woods offer," Carrick finished.

Sawyer threw his battle partner a long-suffering look but didn't dispute it. "And I suppose we neglected to mention back at the banquet table that when we have our releases in hand, we'll be going to Brista together," he added.

Kat bit down on the urge to point out that this, too, was transactional. They didn't need to offer up their own intimate details to convince her they'd keep her secrets. "That's wonderful," she said instead. "I wish I could say I had half as much of a plan for what the future holds."

"Care for a suggestion?" Carrick asked, sidling up to his battle partner and propping his elbow on Sawyer's shoulder. "We didn't just wake up one day, face-to-face in that tiny decade tent, and announce with perfect synchronicity, 'Ah, of course. We agree.'"

"What my esteemed battle partner is *trying* to say is that you need to talk to Emory," Sawyer interjected. "And maybe tell him a thing or two before it's too late."

"And by 'too late,' we mean if you don't tell him about this whole prince proposition thing straightaway, we will," Carrick added with a wolfish smile.

"Your shieldbearer is a menace," Kat muttered to Sawyer.

"Wouldn't have it any other way," he replied, but the levity slipped from his expression and he laid a sturdy hand on her shoulder. "It . . . wasn't hard to guess where his head went back at the feast. Giselle's little announcement was a surprise to all of us. If you're going to let him down, maybe it's better to wait."

"*No,*" Carrick said vehemently. "This has gone on long enough."

Kat shook her head, biting back a smile. "I think you're right. I'll talk to him, I promise. *Not* right now," she added as she saw Sawyer about to open his mouth again. "Tonight is for revelry. Tomorrow is going to be a march. But if I haven't started the conversation before sunset two days from now, after we've arrived in Rusta proper, you two have permission to ruin my life exactly as much as I deserve."

Carrick and Sawyer exchanged the kind of glance only battle

partners could share—a look that was a conversation and a decision in the span of a second. Both of them nodded.

Kat let out a long, relieved sigh. "How long have you two known, anyway?"

"Years," Carrick blurted, just as Sawyer said, "Known?"

"That we hooked up—*years*?"

"*Hooked up?*" Carrick sputtered. "When?"

"Before the Battle of the Mouth. And again— No, hang on, what did you think I meant?"

"We didn't—" Sawyer tried to interrupt, just as Carrick replied, "Well, *Emory* has been in lo—"

Whatever words he might have said next were smothered by his battle partner's palm. "*That*," Sawyer said over Carrick's muffled protests, "is something Kat should hear from her battle partner first. Speaking from experience," he added with a wink that only drew an even more irascible flurry of wrestling attempts to get free.

"Hosts help me," Kat muttered, but a part of her felt as if she'd just taken flight in Adrien's wake.

CHAPTER 27

IN BATTLE, IT WAS EMORY'S JOB TO PUSH FORWARD INTO THE thick of the fighting and Kat's to follow him like she was glued to his back, matching him step for step.

This afternoon saw them starkly unprepared for the reversal. Kat charged on a bullheaded path through the market day crowd, and Emory fought to keep up in her wake, dodging pedestrians and calling apologies over his shoulder to the elderly women with wicker baskets of laundry twice their size strapped to their back whose path Kat had unintentionally plowed through.

She couldn't help herself. Not when the day she'd been waiting on for *months* was finally here. And not when Carrick and Sawyer had permission to ruin her life the moment the sun set tonight— if she didn't have a very important conversation with Emory first. Kat was already starting to sweat.

Though part of that wasn't her fault. It was uncommonly warm for the onset of autumn, and the pleasant weather had drawn a larger than usual crowd to the South Bank Market, the weekly assembly where tradespeople hawked their crafts on the edge of the river that defined the outer limits of Rusta proper. Under the auspices of the bright sun overhead, the cobblestones baked and the throngs of people trapped the heat.

Kat used to spend all week looking forward to market day. When she'd left home, she hadn't been any smaller, but after seeing so much of the world, after marching to the Mouth of Hell itself and back, she felt twice as strange as she once had towering over these crowds. She found herself scanning the faces she passed for childhood friends, chastising herself when she turned up nothing. All she recognized was older neighbors. People whose numbers hadn't been pulled when the draft hit their assembly house. The young had been scattered, and the old stayed planted.

She'd done her best to cultivate a healthy mindset, but it was so hard to hold on to here in the capital's outskirts. The war had barely touched these people, even when the Demon Lord's armies pressed close to Rusta. And if Kat had her way, she would have been one of them—would have spent the last three years holed up behind the city's outer wall, grateful for the hard work of people like Emory who'd stepped up without being pressed into service.

Now she strode into the market square wondering if she was just as unrecognizable as the place that raised her had become. There weren't a lot of towering platinum-blond women passing through every day, and though her training as a soldier had packed more muscle onto her frame, she hadn't started from zero as a forge girl. But she noticed as she moved through the crowd that one inescapable thing *had* changed. She wore her Aurean token outside her tunic, and every eye that might have otherwise recognized her lodged on it and stuck.

Until she arrived at one stall in particular, a stall with a spectacular array of expertly crafted knives laid end to end and a banner hung over it that read, in the same inelegant red scrawl she remembered, "Honnold's Honed Edges." The man sitting behind it, sheltering from the sun under both a parasol and a floppy straw hat, took one look at her and lunged clean through his displays, sending the gorgeous knives scattering in utter disarray as Honnold himself nearly tripped over his sandals to wrap his only child in a bear hug.

"Dad," she gasped into his shoulder. This, too, was different. Last time she'd hugged him, he'd felt solid all the way through, but three years had seen a sudden reversal in both of their compositions. She put it to the test, grappling him hard and swinging him up off his feet in a haphazard circle before setting him carefully down on a patch of knife-free dirt.

"Bean," her father sobbed, pulling her back by the shoulders so he could get a good look at her.

"*Bean,*" she heard snorted somewhere near her boots, where Emory was already in the process of helping pick up the scattered cutlery.

Kat let her father drink in the sight of his kid, intact and back from the front lines. His eyes roved up and down as if to verify she still had all her limbs, lingering here and there. First on the scar on her forearm from a demon underling at the Battle of Bolsun, one of the few places she'd been wounded enough that not even Aurean magic could wipe away the mark. Then on her eyes, for a minute that felt both interminable and far too brief for him to possibly understand the weight they now carried. Finally, they dropped to her token. "Well, that's new," he said, pinching the chain where it sat on her neck and tugging it gently.

Kat grinned, slipped into alignment, and watched the light she summoned reflect in her father's wondering eyes, brightening the sudden tears that welled there. Before she could apologize, he was pulling her back in for another hug, and this time she let him give grappling the life out of her his best shot.

By the time her shoulder was thoroughly soaked and they both had reached a mutual agreement to let each other go, Emory had all the knives collected and was carefully laying them back on the booth's resettled tabletop. "Sorry," he called back over his shoulder. "Didn't want to interrupt, but I'm not certain where each one goes, and I'm sure you have a system—"

"Dad, this is Emory," Kat said, biting back a grin. "My shield-bearer and battle partner. Wouldn't be alive today without him."

"It's very nice to meet you, sir—" Emory started, but didn't get a chance to finish as Honnold sideswiped the hand he offered and pulled Emory *hard* into his chest.

"Nice to meet you, too, Emory," her dad replied, sounding vaguely snotty from where he'd tucked his head over her battle partner's shoulder. Emory had frozen up like a dog that hadn't been petted in an age, and it was only after an encouraging nod from Kat that he wrapped his arms around Honnold's barrel of a torso.

Kat felt something inside her settle at the sight. She hadn't been sure about bringing Emory along today, given what she was obligated to tell him by the end of it. But she'd feared she wouldn't find her father at his usual market stall—that somehow in the three years she'd been away, something might have happened to him—and if the worst came to pass, she knew she couldn't confront it alone.

Instead, she was treated to the sight of the two most important men in her life meeting for the first time. Her dad looked ridiculous in his market getup, between the patchy hat he'd never let go of and the sandals she'd fretted over time and time again. The man worked with *knives, hot metal,* and yet he never seemed to be able to tolerate a close-toed shoe for long. Emory, too, looked out of his depth, if his panicked glance, once it became clear Honnold wasn't letting go any time soon, was anything to go by.

Sorry, she mouthed before hiding a smile behind her knuckles.

's fine, he mouthed back, though he was plainly being crushed.

"Dad, okay, that's enough," Kat said, stepping in and laying a hand on her father's shoulder. He released only a single arm, and

Kat huffed as she was drawn back into his embrace, shunted awkwardly against Emory's shoulder as her father held them tight. "We're making a scene," she hissed, passing a strained smile to some of the bystanders.

"You think my daughter gets to march back home a victor after three years on the battlefield and I'm *not* going to make a scene about it?" Honnold said, clapping her on the back. "You hear that?" he called out to the rest of the market. "My kid's back!"

His words were met with a few scattered cheers and claps, though from the way his face lit up one might think the whole crowd had burst into applause.

"Hosts, I can't take you anywhere," Kat grumbled. Across from her, Emory was looking dazed. Throwing the full force of her father's affection at a man who'd had very little in the way of fatherly affection in his life might have been a lot to handle all at once. "We're quartered in the city proper ahead of the prince's ball, but I have a free day to visit," she said.

"Well, then, c'mon, you two," Honnold replied, tugging on their shoulders. "We've got some catching up to do."

"Dad, the booth."

"Lance can watch the booth. *Can't you, Lance?*" he hollered, and the basketweaver at the adjacent stall flashed him a thumbs-up without lifting his eyes from his craft. Kat had her doubts about Lance's attention, but it wasn't enough to stop her from following the gentle squeeze of her father's arm finally, *finally* around her as he guided them onto the familiar path home.

THE FORGE WAS JUST AS SHE REMEMBERED, THE SMOKY FUG OF IT welcoming her in the courtyard. Kat knew she shouldn't linger—the sun was starting to dip from its zenith already, and she didn't want to waste a single second with her father—but she couldn't help taking a moment to breathe it in deep. Her feet had stalled at precisely the spot where she'd read the conscription notice, and it felt as if the next step she took was the first step of a brand-new life.

"Might have tidied the place up a bit if I knew I'd be having such esteemed guests," Honnold joked as he waved the two of them into the cramped little kitchen on the first floor of the home.

Kat couldn't help feeling a pinch at that. There wasn't much that *could* be tidied. The house felt far emptier than when she'd left it, and not for the first time, she pictured her father sitting all by himself at a table that had once been reliably set for three every night. Now Honnold settled the two of them at that same table as he fussed with the cookfire, hunting for an ember in the remains of this morning's ashes. "You don't have to—" she started.

"'Course I have to. Your old dad doesn't get a chance to play host all that often, much less one to heroes. Now, is there a particular sort of tea you prefer, Emory? Still got plenty of water in the pot from this morning, and I may not have much in the cupboards, but you can bet I've always got Katrien's favorite brew on hand."

Something traitorous was happening in the back of her throat.

"Then that's what I'll have," Emory declared, passing her a soft smile she wanted to pinch off his face.

"We're not heroes," Kat said. She'd meant it as a self-deprecating jab, but when her dad's eyes squinted in confusion, she realized there may have been some critical context he was missing. "I mean, surely you've seen all the fuss they're making about the prince and his companions. They were the ones who defeated the Demon Lord in the end."

"Oh, of course," Honnold said, flapping a hand in a way that reminded her disconcertingly of Adrien. "But I'm told the real heroes on the battlefield were the Aureans who led the centuries. You must have done quite a lot of heroics in three years at war."

Kat stared at her hands, folded together in front of her. She could feel a tremble starting up in them, one that was liable to shake the whole table if she didn't get a handle on it. "It wasn't . . . wasn't quite like that."

Emory, too, had gone stiff across from her. No doubt he was remembering the mission she'd been tasked with. The mission she'd failed. "Kat was absolutely essential on the battlefield," he said, landing a comradely pat on her shoulder. "She held our line together too many times to count."

Honnold had paused in his puttering, his brow furrowed. "But your token—"

"I didn't start cultivating it until after the Demon Lord was slain," she confessed, still staring at her hands. "I spent the whole of the war as a spearbearer on the front."

Honnold nodded. "And, Emory, you were her battle partner? Her shieldbearer?"

"Yes, sir."

Her father's eyes darkened, his mouth going tight as the scales rebalanced. "I see," Honnold muttered, then straightened abruptly. "It's no small feat for both of you to survive to see the war's end—especially not as infantry. I . . . thank the hosts you weren't lost. I can't imagine how much death and destruction you must have seen."

"Dad, sit down," Kat said, pushing herself up from the table. Honnold had gone abruptly gray in the face, and he swayed slightly as he took her advice, staggering over to the kitchen table and plunking himself down at the third chair. Kat scooted herself over next to him and wrapped a steadying arm around his shoulders. "I'm here. I'm okay."

"But with your token . . . You were supposed to—"

"I . . . Dad, there isn't a lot I could have done with a Light of Angels token. It wasn't like I could just present it uncultivated and expect it to act as some sort of ticket out of danger. Even if I had known how to use it, I'd barely hold my own compared to some of the other Aureans on the battlefield. Our centurion, Mira, she's got ten, and even she had a few close calls."

"How many close calls did you have?" he croaked.

"More than a few," Kat said, unable to stop herself from glancing down at the obvious scarring on her arm. She caught Emory's eye. "Could you give us a moment?" she asked.

He softened. "I'll be outside," Emory said, rising from his chair—though before he moved for the door, he hesitated, his hands flexing at his sides. She jerked her chin at him before he could do anything so drastic as try to comfort her. Kat may have needed it, but she needed this moment with her father more.

When Emory had shut the door behind him, her father fixed her with a look that sank her heart like a stone. "You said. When you left, you said you'd make this into an opportunity. They drafted you into the infantry, but you had your mother's token. You could have leveraged it—"

"I had an uncultivated bit of Aurean gold," Kat retorted firmly. "They don't just go around handing out opportunities to people with tokens."

Even as the words left her mouth, she knew how false they were. Her time at Adrien's side had shown her just how much of the world could be laid at her feet for no other reason than the fact that she had inherited a bit of gold from her mother. The only thing holding her back was herself—her own fear, her own hang-ups, her own exhaustion.

It was one thing to disappoint her father, another thing entirely to place on his shoulders all at once the weight of three years he should have spent fearing for her life. She wanted to do everything in her power to spare him from it, but all she could do was feel it alongside him in the subtle shake of his shoulders and the shuddering breath he took as he finally turned to look her in the eye. "You're safe now," he said after a long moment. "You've cultivated your token. You found that bright spot in all this ugliness, and the war is over. You'll serve the rest of your term, but—"

Kat brightened. "Actually, the prince has vowed to release us if we choose. He'll be announcing it at the victory ball later this week."

Honnold gave her a weak smile. "That's wonderful. Do I need to get your room ready, or do you have another opportunity lined up?"

Kat's breath caught in her throat. She'd walked right into that one, but she couldn't exactly tell her father the strange new path that had sprouted before her. "I . . . There are a few choices I could make," she said, sitting back in her chair. "Developing my token after the war's end opened some doors for me, but . . ."

Her eyes betrayed her. She couldn't help the glance she threw toward the kitchen door where Emory had disappeared, and she felt the moment her father's gaze sharpened. "Katrien," he said firmly.

"Dad," she replied petulantly. Hosts, she sounded like *Giselle*.

"You—"

"It's not what you're thinking."

"No? Because I haven't seen you this blatantly moon-eyed over someone since you were thirteen years old and desperately in love with that farmer's daughter."

"I'm not *moon-eyed*."

"I just think it's telling that I asked about your future and you—"

"He's my battle partner. We've been to the Mouth of Hell and back together. It would be stranger *not* to consider him."

"But that's not how you were considering him."

"Do we have to talk about my love life?" Kat said testily.

"We might. I'm serious, Kat," her father replied, leaning in and laying one hand over hers. "I understand. I wish it had been otherwise, but I can't change the fact that you experienced the war on the front lines. But that doesn't mean you have to *stay* a soldier, especially if it's only to preserve something you forged in the heat of war. You said you had other opportunities, opened by cultivating your token, and you made it sound like the thing holding you back was *him*. Do I have that right?"

Kat pursed her lips. "I'm an adult. I can make my own choices."

He squeezed her hand. "I know that, Bean. But I just hope you're not making the same mistakes as your mother."

Kat had spent many a sleepless night imagining what it must be like to be a thrall on the end of her spear. This was, perhaps, the closest she'd ever come to the sensation she'd imagined— a sudden punch clean through the gut, so fast that the pain caught up seconds later. "What do you mean by that?" she asked weakly.

Honnold shook his head. "When I met your mother, I found her humility striking. I'd always pictured Aureans as these lofty, brilliant, untouchable people—people blessed by the angels themselves. When this clever, down-to-earth, absolute *sunbeam* of a woman revealed to me that she had a token, my first thought was that she must have stolen it from somewhere. She probably should have been insulted, but instead she laughed herself hoarse."

The kitchen felt unbearably small.

"It was a miracle she fell in love with me after that, honestly. I couldn't understand it. She could have been a centurion. An illusionist. A fixture in the high courts of Rusta, not just because of her gold but because no one could resist her charm, myself included. Instead, she chose a life as a blacksmith, covered in soot and surrounded by more and more blades by the day. I never doubted her happiness—and I never want you to doubt it either. We had a brilliant, beautiful life together. But I could never shake the feeling that . . . that *I* was the thing that had ruined her prospects. That I dragged her down into a common life."

"Dad," Kat croaked. "You don't seriously think that."

The look he fixed her with told her everything. That he meant it. That it had haunted him for years. That it was the voice whispering in his head when he suggested, as he consoled a shuddering, fearful, eighteen-year-old Kat when her name was pulled in the draft, that there could be a bright side to all this. She'd known he had great expectations for her. She'd let them drive her in the rush to cultivate her token over the past months, all so that she could come back and show her father that she'd made it. That the time he'd spent sitting at this table alone had been worthwhile.

Now she saw that making it, in his eyes, could never exist side by side with coming back home. Not when he thought himself the dead weight that had sealed her mother away from a far grander destiny.

Kat pushed out of her chair and knelt at her father's side, wrapping her arms around his torso and pinning his arms down like she used to when she was a little kid. When she was small, he'd fight and gripe and pretend he couldn't break her hold. It always made her feel like the strongest girl in the world.

Now Honnold sat quietly, his chest heaving beneath her ear, and Kat squeezed him as if that alone could get her point across. "I know you want what's best for me. But don't turn yourself into a regret she never had to justify it."

"Bean," he said weakly.

"We're haunted enough as it is," Kat declared, giving him one last firm squeeze before shoving to her feet. "I think . . . I think I need some space. But I'll be back after the victory ball. I have some things I need to sort out before then."

She left just as the kettle he'd hung over the cookfire finally started to wail.

CHAPTER 28

"WE'RE HEADING BACK TO THE BARRACKS," KAT SAID AS SHE breezed past where Emory had propped himself against the courtyard wall.

He startled, then hesitated. "But the tea—"

"It's a very common peppermint blend. You can get it almost anywhere in the continent. We could even grab some in the South Bank Market before we head back."

A hand settled on her shoulder, and she glanced back to find Emory fixing her with his worst mother-hen look, the one she usually saw pointed at Giselle after she'd had one of those training days where no amount of spear drills could settle the seething rage she always kept just below her surface. "What happened?" he asked, low and serious.

"Not here," Kat replied, her throat tight.

He followed her gamely down to the river's edge, past the docks where the trade boats offloaded goods shipped from up and down the river that shared Rusta's name, to a quiet set of steps built into the riverbank where marketgoers gathered to pick through their spoils and locals brought their washing. There, with the water to cover the sound of her confession to anyone but the closest ears, Kat did her best to explain what had gone so wrong.

"But you've cultivated your token now," Emory said, when she finally took a moment to breathe. "You have all the opportunities he'd hoped you might. He should be thrilled."

She hadn't told him everything. The one opportunity that no one but a prince and two very troublesome comrades-in-arms knew about, the reason she couldn't look her father in the eye and tell him she'd done everything she could to make the most of her time away at war. How could she face Honnold, knowing everything he feared about himself and everything he dreamed for her, and tell him that she was considering throwing the opportunity of a lifetime away?

Moon-eyed, he'd called her. This thing she had with Emory may have started as an eager infatuation, unexpectedly spurred by a last chance hookup and the surprise end of the war, but its foundations were far more solid than anything that deserved the word *moon-eyed.*

Of course, if that was the case, she should have told him that a long time ago.

"There's another opportunity, isn't there?" Emory said when her silence stretched on long enough. "A transfer? Did one of the Aureans offer to pull you into a leadership position in another legion?"

She snorted, but she couldn't tear her gaze from where the river lapped teasingly over the edge of the lowest stairstep.

"I figured it has to be something really big. Otherwise you would have told me already."

"Or it's something so small it's not even worth considering."

"If it was that, it wouldn't have been enough to make you storm out on your dad."

"I didn't *storm*. I . . . lightly breezed." She paused. "I should go back, shouldn't I?""

Emory scooched closer to her, pulling her hand from her knee and threading his fingers through hers. "You should tell me," he said firmly.

Kat huffed. She fought back the part of her that balked at the contact. The Third Century was quartered in the innermost district's barracks, a solid two-hour walk from where they sat. If any of those hundred soldiers and the dozen other attachés who might have known them had followed the two of them all the way here, they were dealing with far worse problems. "You're going to laugh at me," she said, tightening her grip on him.

"Wouldn't be the first time."

Kat knocked her shoulder into his. "I'm not even going to take it." The moment she said those words, she felt the truth of them. The burden they lifted from her back. She had given Telrus three years of her life unwillingly. She didn't have to choose to give the kingdom the rest of her life, too, just because the opportunity had fallen at her feet.

"Then you should tell me," Emory said, giving her hand a gentle squeeze.

She drew a deep, steadying breath, staring out over the water. "Adrien asked me to marry him."

With her eyes on the ducks milling hopefully around the distant bridge, where children often threw their scraps in the water, she only had her periphery and the feeling of Emory's hand in hers to go on. The initial hitch of his surprise, followed by a soft "Huh."

"Like I said, I'm not . . . It wouldn't be right for me. He has this lunatic idea that he's going to stick it to his parents by marrying the most qualified commoner he can find, so he can usher in an era of equality with a common queen by his side. Something about how a commoner will govern from a place of understanding to cover the gaps in his fancy noble education. I just happened to be the single-token Aurean he knows best."

"So you've already turned him down?"

Kat grimaced. "Well, no. He told me he'd await my answer at the victory ball. I'll do it then."

Emory let out a long sigh of relief. Before Kat could let herself savor it alongside him, he squeezed her hand again and said, "Then it's not too late to change your mind."

Her ears rang.

He couldn't have said—

He didn't—

But one look at Emory and she knew he'd meant every word. It was his turn to stare off into the middle distance, not meeting her gaze so deliberately that she was tempted to do something drastic about it. "You want me to . . ."

"It's not about what I want," he said roughly. "What I want to say isn't what I *have* to say."

"I want to hear what you want to say."

"Kat," he warned.

"How much longer are we going to dance around this? After the victory ball, we'll be out of excuses, but that doesn't mean we can't get our stories straight before then. Like Carrick and Sawyer—yes, they told me," she said as Emory opened his mouth to interject. "We can have everything we want if we just *say it*."

"It's different for them," Emory said. "They're each other's best option. The best possible future either of them can have is the one where they're together."

She tightened her grip on his hand. "Don't you dare say what you're about to say."

"Kat—"

"I *just* got done having this conversation with my dad. I walked out on him after *years* apart because—"

"Kat, do you think I could live with myself, knowing I held you back from this kind of greatness?" He still wasn't looking at her.

"What *greatness*?" she sputtered. "The thrilling opportunity to be trotted out like a prizewinning horse every time the crown needs to prove it's invested in the common people? The chance to spend the rest of my life shackled to Adrien Augustine, as if the past few months haven't been bad enough? He's insufferable. I don't want to suffer him any more than I already have."

Emory's brow furrowed. She gave him time to gather his thoughts, time which she also desperately needed to quiet the thundering of her fearful heart. "Do you remember how it felt after we found out about Adrien and his companions?" he asked at last.

"Exhausting," she replied immediately.

That got a slight twitch at the corners of his lips, which she'd take as a victory under these conditions. "That too. But I was more thinking about the helplessness. We'd been through so many fronts. So much mud and gore and days we didn't think we'd make it back. And for what? For these people to come out of nowhere and end the war in one blow?"

"That blow wouldn't have been possible if we hadn't liberated Fallon and pushed to the Mouth," Kat countered. Part of her cringed away from repeating command's constant refrain to them on the long march west, as more and more soldiers questioned why Telrus was throwing all its resources at a campaign against the heart of the Demon Lord's foothold on this plane. From a legionnaire's perspective, it made no sense. It had felt like they were nothing but meat stuck in a mortar, waiting for the inevitable grind of the pestle.

Emory's eyes finally found hers. He looked like he was back in those exhausting weeks before the Battle of the Mouth, where they were marching toward a single, awful ending. "We made a difference. I won't deny that. But Adrien made a difference for the whole of Telrus. And that's the kind of difference you could make as queen of this kingdom."

"And when do I get a say in what kind of greatness I get to share with the world?" Kat countered. Furious tears were finally starting to burn behind her eyes, and she folded her free hand over her face, trying to press them down. "I went to war out of obligation. I spent the last two months thinking I would be free from it at the end of the road. Free to make my own choices, free to decide the shape of my life, free to give my heart to the man who's made these past three years worthwhile."

Emory's breath caught.

"And right when I thought I'd finally earned the right to lay down my spear, instead I'm called on to . . . what, to be the people's champion? And if I refuse, I've let down every person I've spent the last three years fighting for, so I'm not *allowed* to choose anything. It's just another fucking draft."

They sat in a lingering silence as the world moved around them. The washers wrung out their work and loaded it up into their baskets. The ducks fussed and squabbled over every scrap flung their way. Farther in the distance, the market's constant rumble set a comforting, familiar blanket over all of it—a quiet promise that life went on.

"If I loved you any less," Emory started, then broke off, squeezing her hand again.

"Don't," she whispered, but for once, her order didn't take.

"If I loved you any less, I could be selfish. I could put myself above you. Beg you to stay by my side—to not go so high above me that I couldn't possibly follow. But, Kat, I love you." He reached over with his free hand, cradling her jaw and drawing her in to press their foreheads together. "Too much to let myself be your worst option."

He leaned back slightly—just enough to pull her head down and press his lips to her forehead. "I love you too," Kat warbled. It was the only true thing she knew how to say.

One last squeeze of the hand. One last press of his shoulder into hers. And then Emory stood, turned away with a hitching breath she wished she didn't hear, and made his way back up the steps to the heart of South Bank.

There on the river's edge, beneath the ducks and the washers and the market's comforting hum, Kat let herself cry, at last, for every future that had been stolen from her.

CHAPTER 29

MIRA MORGENSTERN'S WORST QUALITY WAS ALSO HER BEST ONE, depending on the circumstances. Some days, hell was hammering at your door and you were about to piss yourself in fear. Others, you'd won a bet, had a spectacular night at the tavern, and woke up marvelously well-rested. Either way, Mira did not give one singular shit about your feelings.

This was how Kat found herself settled primly at her centurion's side on a cushioned bench, watching as Bodhi, Daya, Celia, and Faye made themselves comfortable on the couches in the middle of the tailor's suite. From the glimpse she'd caught of herself in a mirror at the entrance, she knew her eyes were red-rimmed. Mira hadn't asked.

"If we're not careful, they'll mistake us for the valets," Kat muttered under her breath.

"The tailors have received the prince's instructions," Mira muttered back. The centurion was looking far better than she had just a few days prior, after the Lesser Lord's attack, but she still moved with a stiffness that betrayed how recently the healers had stitched her back together. "He wants his Aureans presentable for the ball," she continued. "I tried to impress on him that Mobbert would be far better at this sort of thing, but he insisted we join his companions for a proper fitting and instructed us to bill the damages to his own account."

From the look of this place, the damages would be significant. The salon where they'd been settled was grand and elegant, with high arching ceilings and angelic figures sculpted into the moldings that lined the walls. The rest of the Third Century would be issued fine dress uniforms for the parade and ball, but those would be mass-produced in a range of sizes that would encompass the needs of the unit. Whatever fine craftsmanship they produced in these halls would cost months of Kat's wages.

She'd thought herself acclimated to wealth by all the time she'd spent with the highborns on the road campaign, but now she realized she'd only ever been sticking her toes in the water. If she was to go through with the only serious option left to improve her prospects, she'd have to accept this plunge.

"You're going to have to tell me what the order of operations is here," Kat muttered to her centurion under her breath.

"Well, first there will be treats and tea," Mira said, nodding to a young girl who'd emerged from the shop's rear with a set of tiered trays. "As Faye would tell you, it's part of good hosting and better business according to the *Codex*. Next, they'll bring out the racks and let us browse for cuts and colors. Once they've put together an idea of our preferences, the head tailor will guide us through our options and whatever alterations might be necessary to have the garments ready by the end of the week."

"Something tells me I might need quite a few," Kat said.

Mira snorted. "You and me both." She caught Kat's incredulous look and flexed her shoulders subtly, smothering a wince as she strained the fabric of the loose shirtsleeves she wore. "Most tailors don't style for a muscled body, no matter how large or small. House Morgenstern keeps a particular artisan on retainer because they're one of the few in the capital that dedicates a portion of their line to high-ranking soldiers."

"Then why didn't we go to them?"

"Why indeed," Mira said with a dark look at the Aureans, who had fallen onto the tea service like a pack of wild dogs. "Apparently this tailor owes the Ranjan aristocracy a favor or two."

"They need discounts?" Kat asked.

"They do not," Mira replied. "But calling in a favor has its own weight among the upper houses."

Kat's memory reeled for any past favors she might have promised to any of the highborns. She wasn't comforted by the blank she was drawing, but before she could begin to fret in earnest, the young girl approached with her bounty of baked goods.

"Beg your pardon, my ladies," she said in a trembling voice. She couldn't be more than ten. "There isn't a table, but if you'd like . . ." The girl held the tiered trays up in front of them.

Kat leaned forward eagerly, scoping out the offerings. She'd never seen such a variety of pastries outside the windows of the inner-city bakeries, and the delicate aroma that washed over her was nigh impossible to parse—a wave of buttery, sugary, fruit-tinged excellence. She was almost afraid to lay her fingers over some of the finer confections, and instead narrowed her evaluation to the sturdier-looking scones.

One was flecked with strawberry bits. She nearly reached for it, then hesitated and instead laid claim to the adjacent scone dusted in shaved orange peels.

As Kat had been making her choice, the serving girl's eyes hadn't moved from the token that hung around her neck. "Thank you," Kat said gently, and the girl jolted. "Do you like Aurean magic?"

The girl's gaze flicked nervously to Mira, who was wholly occupied with the fruit tart she'd grabbed. She nodded once, decisively.

Kat slid her free hand under her token and held it out to the end of its chain. "Let me take that off your hands, and you hold on to this for me," she said, laying the scone down in her lap so she could relieve the girl of her burden. The kid's eyes went wide, but the hand she held out was eager and her tiny fingers closed over the gold.

It was the most natural alignment Kat had ever fallen into. Pure artistry, loosed from somewhere deep within her, the angels invited along for the ride. Not even the thought of Mira looking on could tense her up, and she released a long, slow breath as warm light speared from the little girl's grasp.

The kid let out a soft *oh,* an eager grin spreading across her lips. She leaned in close enough that Kat tamped down the light just in case she was in danger of burning the poor girl's eyes out. There was a rightness to this—to the ease with which she'd melted away any hint of the girl's prior timidity. If she didn't have places to be and royal balls to attend, she could have done this all day.

Maybe this was how her mother had felt every time she made the shadows dance on the walls.

"Katrien," Mira said firmly, and Kat stiffened, snuffing her light. "Let's not take too much more of the young lady's time. Thank you, miss," her centurion added as the girl let Kat's token slip from her grasp and took back her serving trays.

The prince's companions waited until the girl had scurried out of the room to make their thoughts known. "You shouldn't taunt them like that," Celia said idly.

"Don't be a bitch," Daya snorted.

Celia rolled her eyes. Kat got the sense both that very little on this continent could keep Celia from bitchiness, and that Celia wouldn't have it any other way. "I just mean that it's cruel, dangling what they can't have in front of their faces."

Kat let the undefined "they" go unchallenged, but only barely. "I thought it might brighten her day," she offered.

"I'm sure it did," Faye interjected. "And it was very kind of you. I think the rest of us have been reared with a sense of . . . let's call it responsibility."

"I was going to say *class*," Daya chimed in.

"Now who's being a bitch?" Celia sniffed.

As the two of them fell into the old, comfortable rhythm of a squabbling match, Faye beckoned to Kat, then patted the space on the couch next to her. "This is your first time at an establishment like this, is it not? It's only polite that we show you the ropes."

Kat caught Mira's eye, but her centurion only jerked her chin the way Mira tended to when she couldn't be bothered to verbalize what would otherwise be a direct order. Kat nodded, downed her scone in a single bite that left little room to enjoy the subtleties of the orange flavoring, and crossed the salon to settle herself carefully on the couch next to Faye.

"What cut were you thinking?" Bodhi said from her left, leaning in eagerly to place his elbows on his knees.

"I'm afraid I don't know much about cuts," Kat replied. "I'm not even that handy with a sword," she added, which got enough light chuckles to be worthwhile.

"In the Vayan courts, many Telrusians have taken up a fusion of styles I could see looking quite magnificent on your figure," Bodhi said. "It's a more billowy silhouette, which can be read as an attempt to take up more space than you're owed, but in a case such as yours, I believe it would be justified."

Faye had already summoned the tailor. An assistant whisked into the salon with a rack of colorful vestments, all of them just as billowy as promised. Kat tamped down the heat in her cheeks as she rose to peruse them. She should have been more delicate with the pastries—she barely felt worthy of running her fingers over the fine fabrics.

Pulling out a dress that caught her eye immediately clarified Bodhi's statement. The garment was pleated such that its folds swelled out from the loose band that gathered them at the waist, and the bodice drooped generously from the collar. An outer jacket went over the whole ensemble with wide, flowing sleeves. The cut would certainly *work* on her, though the jacket on the rack would be lucky if it survived an encounter with the broadness of her shoulders and the hem would call it a good day if it could make it to her knees.

"It's nice," she said. "I just think it's a bit small."

"You'll never know until you—" Bodhi started.

Kat held the dress up against her body for emphasis.

"—I see what you mean," he concluded.

"Maybe we start from what fits and then go from there," Faye suggested.

The list was not long, and Kat hated all of them. She knew part of it could be solved with tailoring that would take in what little needed to be taken in and let out almost everything else, but there was something more to it that rankled at her. It wasn't the skirts, she was fairly certain. Before she'd been a soldier, she'd loved a good skirt. She'd worked in one many a day in her father's shadow and had never found them uncomfortable. Going back to skirts after three years in the stiff tunics and pants that all soldiers wore would be one of the highlights of handing in her papers.

No, it all came back to the cuts. The *intention* she could sense behind each and every garment, none of it quite aligning with the parts of her body she wanted to show off. She knew, objectively, that she had a wonderful body. It had served her well and carried her through the war. But none of these dresses seemed to care that she had broad, muscled shoulders, lats that thickened her torso significantly, and legs that made Emory go starry-eyed every time he'd been between them. The only point they could seem to agree on was showing off her generous bodice, but even there she had a disagreement about the priority it seemed to take.

"But you'd look *incredible* in that one," Daya whined as Kat turned her nose up at yet another dress. The highborns all seemed far more invested in this than she was. Most likely it was the novelty. For them, fashion had never been so much of a challenge, and all four of them were practically bred to compete. She was already seeing it manifest—the way Bodhi's usual smile had dropped to a canny, thoughtful look as he hunted through rack after rack that was presented to them, the way Celia and Daya got into increasingly specific snits over the smallest of details, and of course the way Faye kept trying to rein them all in like an anxious sheepdog.

A desperate glance at the bench against the wall found Mira slumped in obvious boredom, her legs spread wide and one hand pressed gingerly against her ribs where the healers had elected to let her bones mend naturally rather than force the issue. The centurion caught Kat's eye and gave her a grin she'd know anywhere—one that said, *You just let me know when you want to tap out.*

Ordinarily, the goad would work in the other direction. Kat would pull herself together, dig for some inner strength she didn't know she had, and finish the fight. But that was a wartime necessity. One where they'd all had to band together and do the best they could with the worst options.

Now they could band together in other ways. "What do you think, centurion?" Kat asked, quieting the latest round of bickering between Celia and Daya and snapping Bodhi from the calculating trance he'd sunken into.

"The blue one," Mira said. "You can make that work, can't you?"

It was exactly the spur she needed. There was only one thing left that could make it perfect. "I suppose," Kat said, drawing out the last syllable in obvious challenge.

"The blue one," Mira repeated. "That's an order."

It was the best and worst thing about serving under Mira Morgenstern. The thing that had carried them all through countless battles, that the decade constantly joked about in a morbid sort of way. The easiest way to make anything possible was to have Mira command you to do it, because Mira didn't care about your feelings.

"The blue one, then," Kat said. It had a structured bodice that, with enough spacers in the lacings, would accommodate her torso and emphasize the strength of her chest and shoulders, covered only by a gauzy layer of tulle. Her lone token could almost pass for simple jewelry with the way it dropped between her breasts. The dress's skirt was layered in a flattering swell that, by some miracle, reached the floor without tailoring. It was functional. It would carry her through the night.

"Oh, someone's going to be *very* pleased," Faye said with a wink that had Kat checking nervously back over her shoulder to confirm Mira was sufficiently distracted by her own browse through the racks. Guilt racked her, but she couldn't set the record straight with the room's current population listening in.

If Faye noticed the sudden tension that came over Kat, she'd probably blamed it on the discomfort of the dress and moved right along. As the Aurean noblewoman fell easily into a conversation with Bodhi about fabric trends, Kat let out a long, slow breath, smoothing her hands over her skirts.

Mira's order made it starkly clear. Kat didn't belong in this world. She was a soldier, through and through, no matter how they trussed her up. She was built to march, to die, to do as told, and the luck that had brought her here wasn't even her own. Why did it have to be *her* burden, to cross the gap from where she'd started into this strange, opulent world?

For the good of the people, she reminded herself.

For that little girl's smile when she saw that magic was something she, too, could hold in her hands.

CHAPTER 30

WHEN MARCHING ON A CAMPAIGN, STAYING IN STEP DIDN'T MAT-
ter. The most important part was keeping your head up. Any time
they were organized into ranks and made to hold them as they
processed along worn country roads, it was done to show that
Telrus's strength hadn't flagged, that the soldiers were still hale
and hearty and up to the challenge.

Marching down a city street in a victory parade was another
matter entirely.

Adrien had the fool idea to move an entire legion through
Rusta, and so the First Legion's sixty centuries were arranged end
to end, dressed in their formal uniforms, and told to make it look
convincing—which here meant *keep your feet on the drumbeat if it's
the last thing you do.*

They could have done with some practice, but the Third Century was giving it their all. Mira led them with her head held high,
and if she could do it battling through the damage the third Lesser

Lord had done to her body, so could the rest of them. As the victory drums pounded, they advanced through the tight streets of the capital's interior, drenched under the stiff dress uniforms they'd all been made to wear. It was a small mercy Kat had been assured there would be time to change and freshen up before the ball itself.

Rusta greeted them with open arms. Red streamers soared through the air overhead, the common folk lined the streets and hung from rooftops just to get a good view, and some Aurean wind magic must have gone toward keeping a constant churn of petals lofting above the ranks as they swept along the well-cobbled avenues. Even as the dread began to build in her, Kat couldn't help smiling at the sight of every cheering kid perched on their parent's shoulders.

She may have been forced into this, alongside many of her compatriots, but it soothed the ache of those lost years to be properly celebrated for once—even if the public would never know that the fight had continued all the way to the capital's doorstep. With all three Lesser Lords conquered at last, nothing stood between the legions and the praise they'd earned for a job well done.

At the royal palace, the rest of the legion marched onward and the Third Century split off into the magnificent, manicured courtyard just beyond the outer wall. Freed from the view of the public, half the century tore out of their uniform jackets without hesitation and began squabbling over the waterskins being passed around.

For Kat, there would be no catching of breath. Mira, even worse for wear and panting like she'd just sprinted a circuit of the city wall, caught her eye and whistled, and the two of them rushed off with the escort sent to take them to their evening attire.

Kat had seen dire wounds on the battlefield dressed with less urgency than that with which the two of them were wiped down and stuffed into their outfits. She hadn't spared a thought for her hair, but fortunately there were attendants for that, too, stylists who swept her long platinum-blond locks back into an elegant twist at the nape of her neck after weaving the smallest, most ineffectual battle braids she'd ever seen in her life through them. Any impulse Kat had to complain about the accuracy of their hairstyles—clearly meant to wed the practicalities of keeping long hair on the battlefield with the sensibilities of the city's fashion—were broadsided by the sense memory that hit her at the feeling of another person's hands moving carefully over her skull.

It had been eight years since the last time she'd felt it.

It must have shown on her face, because Mira gave her a look that promised disciplinary action if she didn't start acting like she was about to go to a party.

Said party was already in full swing by the time the two of them arrived. Their escort led them through the vaulted halls of the palace proper, where Kat couldn't help craning her neck back and ogling the tallest ceilings she'd ever seen. That ogling proved incredibly premature when they stepped through the massive doors to the ballroom.

Aurean craft must have gone into building this room. Nothing but the hands of the angels could possibly raise a structure so grand, much less suspend a ceiling of magnificent glass panes overtop the whole thing. The part of Kat that was a blacksmith's daughter through and through was captivated by the distant ironwork overhead, the lattices that had been built to support the substantial weight of the glass. After months as an accessory to the logistics of laying a road, she couldn't help imagining how long it had taken to coordinate all the materials, craftsmanship, and vision that had gone into this masterwork of stone, glass, and iron.

"Mouth closed," Mira muttered at her side, and Kat's attention snapped down to the rest of the room.

Four hundred, her legionnaire's brain said immediately. A sea of glittering nobility, punctuated here and there by darkened clusters of soldiers in their dress uniforms. Tables were set throughout the hall, laden with the finest finger food the castle kitchens could produce, and servants roved throughout the crowd to keep glasses full, pouring from frost-encrusted bottles that had Kat's freshly marched throat aching. A dais at the center of the room promised to be the focal point of the spectacle to come.

Their entrance to the hall had been quiet and unannounced, but as Kat descended the steps to the ballroom's main floor, she felt eyes on her all the same. One pair of eyes in particular. Her gaze darted to a knot of soldiers huddled together near one of the towering pillars that supported the ballroom's ceiling.

Someone else needed to keep his mouth closed.

They'd already marched in rank together—quietly, business-like, focused on keeping in step. She'd already seen him in the trim dress uniform that emphasized the swell of his shoulders and the sturdy thickness of his torso. But her breath caught all the same at the sight of Emory seeing *her,* dressed in finery, every inch Aurean nobility if not in name. Not yet, anyway. Guilt and pride tangled within her at how often she seemed to be capable of devastating this man.

"KATRI*EN,*" Ziva hollered, jarring her from the moment, and she broke into a sheepish grin as her fellow spear darted to her side, grabbed her by the elbow, and dragged her into the thick of the decade.

"Kat? Where?" Carrick asked, craning his neck until Sawyer jabbed an elbow in his side.

"You look good," his spearbearer said. Any sympathetic, knowing look he might have spared her was immediately over-written by Sawyer continuing, "Emory, tell her how good she looks."

"It'll go right to her head," Emory quipped, tensing even worse. Hiding their flustered little romance had been hard, but it occurred to Kat now that it would be harder still to hide the hole that had been left in its wake.

"If you're jealous, I can ask the highborns if they've got another pretty dress in reserve," she replied, and the chuckle it raised from the rest of the decade was enough to smother her worries—at least for the time being.

"Scraps!" a voice called from behind their cluster. Ten of them blinked in confusion, but only one turned, and Kat had barely a moment to wonder at a man Emory's size responding to "Scraps" before another man was colliding with him in a hug so forceful it nearly took out both Brandt and Elise.

"I'll be damned, it *is* you," the newcomer exclaimed, wrestling out of Emory's grip and shaking him by the shoulders. "Hosts, you filled out." He was dressed in the same uniform as the rest of them, though his shoulders were striped in golden braids that marked him as a garrison captain.

He was also—and Kat was simply being objective here—the most handsome man she'd ever seen in her life, with a magnetic smile, rich brown skin, and tightly coiled hair impeccably styled into short twists. She understood, even before Emory turned out to the rest of them and said, "Everyone, this is Von."

"A pleasure," Von said, ducking his head to each of them in turn. "I knew this one back when he was, oh, about this high," he said, measuring with his hand and chucking Emory's sternum in the same motion. "Can't believe you made it from Egren all the way to the palace proper."

"Can't believe *you* made it," Emory replied, awestruck. He'd looked, hadn't he? He'd mentioned he kept checking the rosters, but he had never been sure of the man's fate.

"Takes more than a few thralls to put me in the ground, little brother," Von replied, but beneath his cavalier tone there was an undeniable softness, an understanding. He laid a gentle hand on Emory's shoulder. "And you made it, too—that's no small thing. You enlisted?"

"As soon as I was able," Emory replied. "Had to catch up to you somehow."

Von barked a laugh. "Classic Scraps, always dogging our heels.

But I assume you've heard the news? The prince is going to offer full releases from service to anyone who wants one."

"We've been traveling with the prince himself," Emory said, nodding to the rest of their circle. "My century was tasked with protecting him on his campaign to build the road."

Von's eyes widened. "Then you must have known for *months*— what am I even saying? You have everything all planned out, then?"

"Planned out?"

"What you're going to do when you take your release?"

Emory's eyes flicked traitorously to Kat, then back. "I . . . I hadn't been planning on taking my release."

"Ah, so soldiering's your true calling. I should have known, the way you were always stomping around in our wake."

"It's not yours?" Emory asked, sounding rattled. "You were enlisted, I thought."

Von sobered. "Well, there's the draft and there's the *draft*. I chose soldiering for steady coin. Made it work for me for many a year, and at least before we were called up to the fronts, I was happy to do it. I imagine it's the same for a lot of you," he said to the rest of the decade.

"Taking mine," Sawyer confirmed, and Carrick echoed with a nod that reverberated through the rest of them. Emory's eyes skimmed uncertainly from face to face. On the battlefield, he was steady, even when outnumbered. Here was another thing entirely.

"Well, *I'm* staying signed on," Brandt announced. "Good coin, *and* I don't have to contend with any more demons on this side of the plane."

"It's going to be a bit different when it's living people on the other end of your spear," Javi muttered.

Von nodded sagely. "That it is. I've still got five years left on my contract, and I'd rather get that time back than a pension, a pat on the head, and the potential to get caught up in a future campaign. Plus, I've got dreams that go beyond marching. In fact, there's a baker based out in Sprill I met toward the end of the campaign who told me they'd been looking for a deliveryman who could spend his downtime tending the ovens. I figure it's as good a foot in the door as any, so that's where I'm headed once the ice firms up for the season."

"*Baking's* your calling?" Emory said, incredulous.

"Baking's what I'd love to be doing right now. Need to give it a try before we can say anything about a calling, but the odds are looking good. Doesn't hurt that the baker's cute. But really, I owe it to myself, same as any of you, to make something of the fact I made it back."

"Cheers to that," Ziva said, raising her glass, and the rest of the decade followed her in the toast. Kat, having only just gotten there, was stuck lifting her knuckles and trying not to overanalyze the dazed expression written across Emory's face.

It didn't have to mean anything. That the man who had been the foundation of his drive to be a soldier was himself leaving soldiering. That the end of the war was a promise of a new beginning for practically all of them, and Emory was exempting himself from what looked increasingly like an inability to imagine a future outside of the path he'd already been walking. But Kat swore, as she cast her gaze about desperately, looking for a servant with one of those trays laden with tempting drinks, that she could hear the squeaky waterwheel of Emory's thoughts suddenly kick into motion.

Maybe there was a passion out there for him. Something he felt called to do instead of obligated. Some mark he could make upon the world. Something that wouldn't break his heart—or would break it in all the wonderful ways a heart could be broken. Maybe he could find it, given time and freedom.

Kat's own broken heart could only mourn that she'd slipped from his grasp before she could be a part of it.

It was at that precise moment a squadron of trumpeters blasted an exuberant fanfare from the hall's entrance. Every head wrenched from its business to find the royal procession, headed by Adrien Augustine, striding forward into the hall. Cheers and applause crowded out the horns as the prince grinned and waved to all his guests. Behind him, the king and queen walked arm in arm, swathed in golden robes held together by ribbons of bright Telrusian red.

To Kat, the crown had always been an abstract concept, a force beyond her reckoning that dictated the shape of her life without any consideration for how she might feel about it. By contrast, even with all the trimmings they'd been wrapped in, these two people were almost painfully human. There was a bit of Adrien in both their faces—the king's nose, the queen's brow. Both wore arrays of Aurean tokens, but she doubted either of them put much practice into the gold. High houses distributed angelic gold from their vaults to their scions, who wore it in rotations to ensure the work that had gone into cultivating their power for generations would not erode.

In the back of her mind, a thought snagged—that if she accepted Adrien's hand, one of those tokens could very well pass to her.

Her focus slipped to her would-be fiancé, who wasn't putting nearly the same effort into appearing stately and dignified. After months on the road with his legions, he'd developed a natural ease with the people underneath him, hard-won after the years of his life spent isolated in monastic training. He smiled at his courtiers. He shook hands as he passed people and shot salutes to those he sighted in the back of the crowd. Kat braced herself to receive his attention as the procession drew near.

She never did. Adrien walked right past their decade with nothing but a glance and a nod, his eyes skipping clean over her as he moved on to the next group of people clustered along the walkway, a knot of youthful nobility who waved eagerly and were eagerly waved at in turn. It took Kat an extra second to register what had just happened, and a second more to understand it.

Part of it was Adrien's showmanship, no doubt. A good magician would never draw your eye to a rabbit before he pulled it from its hiding place, and that didn't even account for the possibility that Kat turned him down before he had a chance to introduce her as his future queen.

They'd discussed it the night prior. She'd told him to ask again.

But the part that stuck in her craw as she watched him chum it up with another patch of token-wearing nobles, none of them dressed in soldiers' uniforms, was that it wasn't just Kat Adrien had skipped over. The first decade had marched side by side with him since they departed the Mouth of Hell. Had fought off Lesser Lords bent on rending the prince limb from limb. Had built his stupid, clever road, and done it well.

And Adrien Augustine had nothing but a nod for the lot of them.

Was it all for show? This integrating himself with the legion, this commitment to the common people? Maybe a grand celebration like this wasn't the right occasion for waging his little war— but if he really meant all the things he'd said when he asked her to marry him the first time, then this *was* the occasion. Instead, Adrien Augustine was playing to the gold in the crowd, the dark wool of the legion's dress uniforms a handy guide to every face he could filter out.

"Unbelievable," she muttered. The king had issued an order that had forced her, by random chance, to put her body on the line for the world's sake. Many of the soldiers in this room had done the same, and even the ones who hadn't been forced had, *by choice,* marched on the Mouth of Hell. They were there as set dressing, nothing more. Charity, by which the nobles could reassure themselves that they'd done their due diligence in showing some measure of gratitude to the people who had wrought their victory.

A vicious, bilious anger rose in Kat, fury that it had taken her this long to notice that Adrien Augustine only ever noticed *her.*

She tracked him across the ballroom, a process made staggeringly easy by the fact that she was a head taller than many of the people in the crowd and easier still when he mounted the dais in the center of the room to another swell of thunderous applause.

"My friends," he said, his Voice of Angels token projecting him so clearly that an echo rang from the glass ceiling high above. "We assemble tonight to celebrate my victory over the Demon Lord, but I look out at this room, and I see the faces who made that victory possible."

A passable start. He'd clearly learned to lead with humility.

"I see Bodhi Ranjan, scion of the Southern Reach, who I know is hoping I rush this speech so he can get to the dance floor quicker. Young nobility of quality, I advise you to stake your claim on him early, as I expect he'll need to be wheeled out of the ballroom in a hand cart by the end of the evening."

The crowd laughed amicably, and she saw Bodhi wave to a smattering of applause from his position at the foot of the dais.

"I see Faye Laurent, Duchess of Halston. Never was there a more polite Aurean warrior capable of freezing a horde of demons in their tracks from a hundred paces. If I use the incorrect address for anyone over the course of the evening, just log it with her and she'll take it out of my hide later."

Faye, too, waved to the crowd, looking decidedly distressed at the implication that she'd ever lay hands on the prince.

"I see Daya Imonde, Duchess of Egren, whom I almost didn't recognize in the finery she's decked out in tonight."

Kat couldn't find Daya from where she was standing, but from the swell of titters and the way Faye looked liable to vomit, she could assume the duchess had just flashed Adrien an uncouth gesture.

"And of course I see Celia Vai, Countess of Sprill, who looks positively thrilled to be here," Adrien concluded, earning him an eye roll visible from clean across the ballroom. "My companions, who were at my side every step of the way. We trained together. Made each other sharper. Made each other strong enough to accomplish what no other Aurean could in the twenty years since the Mouth first opened. Were it not for their might, I wouldn't be standing before you today."

Another vigorous round of applause rolled over the crowd.

Say something about the soldiers, Kat urged him silently. *About how it was their might that got you safely to the capital.*

"However, before the dancing starts in earnest, we have an important bit of business to attend to," Adrien said, and only then did his gaze slip up from the nobles crowded in his immediate vicinity. Only then did he search the crowd of soldiers he'd invited until his eyes landed squarely on Kat's unmissable height.

The prince smiled.

"The fact of the matter is, there were significant obstacles along the long march home—obstacles that went far beyond the Augustine Road's construction. Three of the Demon Lord's generals remained in this plane. These Lesser Lords hunted us on our journey across the continent, and though they were defeated"—through her confusion Kat had just enough presence of mind to note he'd left off the agent of the Lords' defeat—"they had help along the way. Help from one of my four closest companions."

The ballroom's noise shifted abruptly to a miasma of confused muttering that Kat wholeheartedly seconded. Had Adrien uncovered some evidence in the final days of the campaign? Something he hadn't told Kat? Of course the prince had reserved the accusation until the moment he could make theater out of it.

"Guards, if you would, please escort Lady Daya Imonde from these chambers."

"Sorry, *what?*" Daya shouted over the crowd's clamor. Kat finally got eyes on her as the people in her vicinity surged away from the accused young duchess, whose ninety-five tokens suddenly seemed less a display of wealth and status, more an immediate threat. "I'm loyal to Telrus. I flew into battle side by side with you!"

As the guards closed in, their polearms lowered as if confronting an escaped zoo animal, Celia Vai shot from the crowd, skidding between Daya and the royal dais. "You don't know what you're talking about," the countess called, a rare urgency blazing in her eyes.

Adrien looked thrown, but only momentarily. "Remove them both," he said, his Voice of Angels easily overpowering the young nobles' protests and the crowd's shocked murmurs.

Everything was happening too fast for Kat to process. She'd expected a proposal and instead gotten an abrupt, confusing end to the mystery that had been plaguing her for weeks. But none of it felt right. She'd suspected Celia and Daya, but neither of them was behaving like an enemy of the crown. Both followed the royal guards' directives, lifting their token arrays from their necks and holding them out to prove themselves disarmed. Both complied when guided out the ballroom's massive doors, Daya still seething and Celia holding her arm to steady her.

Kat wanted to pull Adrien aside and ask him how he'd been sure, but the prince was still up on the dais, grinning uneasily out at the crowd. "I hate to darken such a joyful occasion with such unfortunate business, but now we're free to celebrate without the specter of the lady's sedition hanging over us. And we have much to celebrate. The Augustine Road is my first gift to the people of Telrus, but it will not be my last. As your prince, as your future king, it is my duty to rebuild this kingdom. To peel back the Demon Lord's scars and heal from the evil that has been wrought upon us. And to that order—"

Before Adrien could get another word out, a shadow flickered overhead, followed by an almighty crash. The height of the ceiling gave the ballroom's denizens just enough time to look up and register the shattered glass fragments plummeting toward them, and not much time more to duck, cover their heads, and lunge for whatever shelter they could find.

A single, soul-shattering roar smothered the screams and confusion as an enormous demon—a *fourth* Lesser Lord—tore through the gorgeous iron struts and plunged into the heart of the ballroom.

CHAPTER 31

THE ORDER OF THE WORLD REWROTE ITSELF IN THE SPAN OF THE Lesser Lord's fall.

There had been three Lesser Lords serving under the High King of Hell for the entirety of the war. Kat had seen the corpses of all three of them laid low. But the beast that crashed to the floor in the center of the ballroom was unquestionably of the same caliber—if not something higher. It drew itself up tall, triumphant, its forked tail thrashing, its many-horned head cocked to one side. It wore a writhing cloak of shadows that occasionally parted to reveal its thick muscle and leathery hide. In its hand, it held a sword that dripped something viscous and oily-looking, and its very presence seemed to gutter the torchlight.

"Back, everyone, *back*!" a high voice called over the crowd's screams. In a flash, Faye Laurent had lunged to square with the beast, resplendent in her red gown, all seventy-five of her tokens radiant across her chest.

All seventy-five of them attuned. As if she'd known this was coming.

"I have a confession," Faye announced to the room. Her fists glowed a molten gold, and the Lesser Lord had locked its eyes on her like a deer frozen in a hunter's sights. "I have shamed my house, hoping to spare us from the greater shame of being ruled by a man so horrifically unsuited for the crown that he's currently trying to crawl under a table rather than defend the people he's assembled here tonight."

Behind her, Adrien offered no counterargument from the shelter of his fortifications, flanked on either side by his parents.

"It wasn't Daya Imonde," Faye continued. "Over the course of the Augustine Road's construction, I conspired with the remnants of the Demon Lord's forces, hoping to place the prince in their sights and ensure that a more appropriate successor could take the throne. That plan plainly failed, outmaneuvered by the efforts of our infantry—but the three Lesser Lords were working under the orders of a Final Lord, the Demon Lord's own heir, who refused to accept that failure despite my efforts to convince it that there could be no path to victory. It insisted on striking this celebration—and so it falls to me to redeem the good name of House Laurent and face the consequence of my arrogance."

She was teeth-rattling to look at, blazing with Aurean power, and once again, Kat was astonished this woman could only see her seventy-five-token arsenal as fundamentally weak.

The demon lowered its head. Its lips spread, baring a rictus smile. And from its cloak of shadows, it drew a silvery medallion that burned with cold fire.

Kat had grown well-acquainted with fear over three years of war. Most fear she could weather with her line at her side and the rest of the Telrusian forces at her back. Fear had kept her sharp and alive when little else could.

But the fear that gripped her now was of a different sort. Because the moment the Final Lord's claws closed around that strange medallion, Faye's magic winked out like a hood had been dropped over its fire.

Kat reached for her own alignment and found nothing. She *reached,* grounding herself with a hand around her token, but not even the amateur gesture could connect her to the heavenly plane.

All her life, she'd been told that Aurean magic was proof the angels watched over them from beyond the Seal of Heaven—that divine power could still protect this plane from the forces of evil.

It had never not been true.

But it seemed that before his defeat, the Demon Lord had succeeded in his quest. The crucible hadn't been tipped, but the matter within it had already been smelted, and this Final Lord had recovered it as the citadel collapsed. The High King of Hell had alchemized antigold—not in time to save himself but in time to wreak his vengeance on them all.

Starting not with the Augustines, but with Faye Laurent, now irrevocably defenseless in the Final Lord's sights. She seemed to have hoped for a glorious redemption, to atone for her mistakes by wiping out the last stain of evil on this land in plain sight of the nobility whose respect she'd spent her whole life clawing for with her *Codex of Manners* and her measly seventy-five tokens.

In the end, she didn't even have a weapon to block the oil-slick sword that took her through the gut.

The ballroom's panic boiled over, the screaming tripling in volume as highborns scrambled in every direction. The royal guards had immediately tasked themselves with ushering the fray of gold-trimmed nobility with their now-useless tokens out of harm's way. Even if they'd made an attempt, they wouldn't reach the prince in time—though the Final Lord was currently preoccupied with drawing its sword almost surgically back from Faye Laurent's limp body.

But the hall was full of others—those used to squaring off against the legions of Hell with nothing holy, only a weapon in hand.

Their centurion was in no shape to lead them. Even if her tokens weren't smothered by antigold, Mira had barely recovered from the blow she took against the third Lesser Lord. Kat found her in the chaos, a fixed point rooted to the spot among the scrambling highborns, her eyes blazing with equal weights of fury and frustration.

Until her gaze locked on Kat's. She'd served under her centurion long enough to know exactly what Mira meant by the firm nod she passed her.

Kat drew a deep breath, pursed her trembling lips, and let out a long, piercing shriek of a whistle. A call to assemble, the same one she'd heard from Mira a thousand times before. She saw it echo through the soldiers still picking themselves up amid the shattered glass, heads snapping back to find the source of the noise, overriding the overpowering instinct to keep their focus on the most deadly thing in the room.

"THIRD CENTURY TO ME," Kat hollered at the top of her lungs.

The Final Lord whirled. Its teeth were long, needlelike, and awful to look at as it leered at her with what could almost be considered a grin. She could see in those ink-black eyes that it wasn't just surprised—it was delighted. This was the sort of beast that craved a fight, that wanted its prey to kick and screech and beg for a mercy it wasn't capable of giving.

Well, she'd give it a fight. With everything she had, because if she didn't, there would be no lifetime of peace. Not while this evil still walked their plane of existence. Not without the prince she'd spent the past few months protecting and all his misguided but generally correct ideals sitting on the throne.

It would have been easier if she had a weapon or two, but as the rest of the soldiers packed in tight around her, she spotted the tables that were scattered throughout the hall—tall enough for the partygoers to lean against them and sip their drinks, supported on three sturdy legs apiece. "Grab those," she ordered after another sharp whistle.

Emory was the first one to follow her command. The wedge driven between them couldn't change the fact that he'd trained relentlessly for moments like this. Within seconds, the rest of the troops had followed his lead, tearing each table down into three passable weapons to hand out among the rest of them and a surface that, in a pinch, would have to do as a shield.

Kat took hers up with a swallow of trepidation, a feeling that only worsened when Emory slotted into place in front of her. The tabletop he held didn't look substantial enough to survive against the Final Lord—who seemed to be waiting patiently for them to get themselves in order, its tail flicking from side to side.

"Shields to the front," Kat commanded. If the hosts were absent in their tokens, at least *something* out there was keeping her voice from shaking. "Everyone with a weapon, line up behind them. Everyone else, brace them with everything you have. Or find something to throw."

She settled behind Emory, side by side with Von, who'd taken up his own table leg with a wary look back at her. She wanted to tell him to run. To go live his bakery dream. The rest of them could do their best to handle this. There was no need to be brave. But she got the sense that the second she opened her mouth, she'd make a fool out of herself. The camaraderie of soldiers with nothing but sticks in their hands was a powerful bond, and one not soon broken.

No matter how terrifying it looked when the Final Lord bent low and braced itself to charge. Its nostrils flared, its cloak of shadows spinning wide enough that it darkened the torchlight. It was a simple creature, like all its fellows. It went for the largest, the most powerful. And with every Aurean token in the room deadened, that role went to Kat and her patchwork century.

"*Brace,*" she shouted as the demon lunged.

Over the course of the campaign, she'd taken many hits from shock knights, but none as unarmored as this. The Final Lord tore clean through the heart of her century, and Kat felt the rattle of its impact in every single one of her bones. It cleaved a gap between her and Von, tossing its horned head like a bull, and she narrowly avoided being gored by one of the points on its rack as she was thrown clear. She hit the ground knowing there would be no second chance—that this was the moment to give everything she had left. Her beautiful dress had torn. Her fancy shoes scrabbled for purchase on the marble floor as she fought her way back to her feet and lunged, her snapped-off table leg raised high.

She saw her opening and hated it. There would be no chance for a fatal blow—only a weakening one, one that would make the Final Lord *furious*. But she was well past the point of being able to choose her battles.

Kat charged and gored her weapon deep into the back of the demon's calf.

She was expecting a backhand. She'd forgotten the beast's tail. It snapped like a whip, catching her in the gut and sending her skidding across the unforgiving stone of the floor. The entirety of her breath was driven from her lungs, and she gaped like a fish, floundering uselessly to replace it.

She'd kept her grip on her weapon. She didn't have much else going for her, but at least she had that. As her vision went spotty at the corners, she leveraged herself up on the butt end of the table leg.

There had been a moment there, brief but glorious, where she'd been everything Mira had ever hoped from her, everything Adrien had expected, everything her father had dreamed, the sum total of every bit of potential that had been placed upon her shoulders. She had called the century to her. She had made a clear plan of action, had communicated it, had the trust of all her soldiers, and never once doubted that the calls she made were the correct ones. For one shining instant, she had been a centurion in everything but rank.

Now Kat felt the moment she blew it. The moment she knew in her heart of hearts she would never be able to live up to those grand expectations. The moment the Final Lord straightened, its tail thrashing as its gaze reeled back to the wreckage of the century scrambling for order. Emory was thrown clear in the hit, and he was still down, slowly—*too slowly*—trying to get his feet underneath him. Kat lunged on instinct—not for the century, not for the prince, not for the demon, but between it and the love of her life.

Months ago, she'd been one of a chorus of voices berating Emory for making the same mistake. She'd told him—and helped Mira prove to him by putting him on his back before the entire century—that she could hold her own. That the priority on the battlefield was always larger, loftier things.

But damn the century, damn the legion, damn the kingdom. If she had a bit of strength left in her, she wouldn't waste it on anything but keeping him safe.

"Kat," Emory groaned as she skidded to her knees next to him. He'd been trying to prop himself up with his makeshift shield, but she tore it from his weakened hands and squared to the Final Lord with her table leg raised high. "Don't . . . You'll . . ."

"Brace me," she said. If she wasn't going to be a perfect soldier tonight, at least one of them was, because Emory took the order without question, a quavering hand coming to rest at her hip as he leaned his shoulder against the column of her spine.

The Final Lord regarded them with a faint, amused chuff. Then it turned its back and broke into a sprint, heading straight for the dais, where Adrien and the Augustine crown still cowered. A shout went up across the ballroom from the onlookers, from the soldiers who'd been scattered by the general's blow, from everyone who could do nothing but yell as the general charged with single-minded focus.

Kat had one singular second to reckon with the depths of her failure. She'd had an opening—another chance to keep the prince safe. Instead, she'd shown her hand.

And then the golden blur struck.

It moved so fast, for a moment Kat thought it couldn't be anything other than Mira. But Mira, for all her toughness, relied on her tokens for that kind of strength and agility. Mira had fallen to the wayside, felled by the quelling of the angels' magic and too injured to fight.

Into her place stepped the only soldier who'd kept training tenaciously long after the war had ended. Who'd stayed sharp, who'd waited for her opening, who now took it with so much vicious gusto it quieted the hall's tumultuous noise in an instant.

She'd found herself a spear—one of the sturdy iron struts that had been torn from the ceiling. Luck, fate, or perhaps the will of the angels had rendered the shaft of metal perfectly sized and sharpened for her purposes. She'd thrown herself between the demon and the royal family with every last ounce of rage in her tiny body.

And Giselle put that makeshift spear clean through one of the Final Lord's inky black eyes.

CHAPTER 32

THE STILLNESS AND THE SILENCE HELD FOR JUST LONG ENOUGH that everyone in the ballroom heard the demon's last breath rattle out of it.

Then chaos descended from all sides. Kat and Emory were nearly trampled by the surge of soldiers rushing in to help confirm that the massive, slumped corpse was well and truly dead. As they staggered clear of the tumult, a knot of golden-haired, well-dressed nobility followed in a second wave that crashed headlong into Giselle, who looked disconcerted but not at all surprised by the people clutching at her dress uniform and weeping at her feet.

Emory hitched forward like there was something his bruised, battered ass could do to defend his protégée, but Kat stopped him with a hand on his chest. "Guess there's our answer," she said, nodding to the older woman with three Aurean tokens in her array who had clasped both hands around Giselle's skull, shrieked in disbelief, and then promptly pulled the girl, demon blood and all, into her bosom.

"Secret nobility," he replied. "Who could have guessed?"

Kat snorted, but the surge of relief she felt nearly took her own shaking legs out from underneath her. If Emory was well enough to deadpan, he was going to be okay.

Her gaze slid inevitably to Adrien, who was helping his mother to her feet and blinking as if a bright light had been flashed in his eyes. The royal family hadn't cleared the splash zone, and their ostentatious finery was spattered with blackened blood that looked like it might be tricky to scour. It was the kind of mess that would have sent anyone spiraling under normal conditions, but the conditions were decidedly not normal.

Underscoring that point, the prince hadn't taken his eyes off Giselle once—not even when his mother produced a handkerchief from somewhere and began scrubbing aggressively at the blood splattered over his face.

Maybe there was something to Bronwyn's shadow plays after all.

"I take it the family's important?" Emory asked. He, too, was staring at his protégée, less in unvarnished admiration and more like he wasn't sure if the people currently swarming her needed to be beaten off with a stick or not.

Kat had the stick in question but was reserving judgment. "From the gold alone, they've gotta be," she said. Most of the people fussing over Giselle were decorated in tokens and only slightly less well dressed than the royal family themselves.

"Oh shit, Giselle's a princess?" Carrick said, startling Kat as he rounded out on her unoccupied side.

"No, that's a ducal signet," Sawyer replied, clapping a hand on Emory's shoulder and nodding to the livery of the servant hovering nervously behind the large man who'd folded both Giselle and the weeping woman who had to be her mother into a crushing hug.

"Called it," Ziva said, squeezing between Carrick and Kat.

"You called secret royalty. No one called secret duchess. Or duchess-to-be. However it is in their family," Kat countered.

"Hear that, Carrick? It's the sweet, sweet sound of someone who owes me money but doesn't want to admit it."

"She's going to be okay," Emory muttered under his breath. Kat squeezed the arm she had around him and felt him lean just a little bit more into her.

They were all going to be okay. The Final Lord—and this had *better* be the final one—lay cooling in the heart of the ballroom. The antigold medallion's smothering power had released with its death, proved well enough by the lights Kat called with barely more than a thought. The road was complete, the prince safely escorted to his capital. The world had needed them one last time, one more time than any of them had expected, and they'd answered the call.

If it dared ask anything more from them, Kat would give it a piece of her mind.

As if the angels had heard her vow and decided to test the premise immediately, Adrien Augustine staggered off the dais, heading straight for her. "Katrien!" he called, waving a hand.

Her decade contracted instinctively around her, but Kat shrugged herself free from their protection. "Your Highness," she said, snapping her heels together so neatly that she desperately wished Mira had noticed, even if the affect of a soldier looked slightly ridiculous in her ostentatious dress with a bloodied, broken table leg in her hand instead of her usual weapon.

"I was wondering if I could have a word with you in confidence," the prince said. "If you're not too busy."

Kat cast her gaze helplessly about the debris of the ballroom, but no prior commitments reared their heads—only the worried furrow between Emory's brows. She leaned, knocking her shoulder into his, their old battle-worn reassurance. *I'll be fine,* she willed him to understand.

He pressed right back into her, his chin jerking in an almost imperceptible nod.

There wasn't much "confidence" to be found in the aftermath of a full-blown national security crisis, but Kat followed Adrien to one of the grand pillars that supported the now-ruined ceiling and nodded along when he proclaimed, "Well, this'll have to do."

"So," Kat said. "Daya."

The prince grimaced. "There was *evidence*! You should have seen how furious she was when I took the couriers away from her. I would have explained it better, only then the ceiling came down and it turns out that . . ."

Both of them cast a somber look to the knot of people who had gathered around where Faye Laurent fell.

"I messed up too," Kat offered. "I did my best, but—"

Adrien flapped a dismissive hand. "You couldn't have done anything. Anything at all, really. Not when the monster had antigold. I appreciate the effort, of course," he added, seemingly sensing that Kat's grace was starting to wear thin. "But look, something's come up."

"Something," she said flatly.

"Now I know we had previously discussed some ideas for your future," Adrien hedged. "And while they were *ambitious,* perhaps they were a little too forward-looking. It's my turn to apologize—sincerely, truly sincerely—for getting your hopes up."

Kat tried to rearrange her features to reflect a disappointment she was nowhere near feeling. "You don't mean . . ."

"I'm afraid that I might have overpromised on some things."

"Some things being specifically the part where you pro—"

"Proposed a *fruitful* future partnership," Adrien interjected with a nervous glance at the bystanders. "Now obviously this isn't to say that I don't want to work with you in the future. I value your insight immensely, and I don't think I'll be half the kind of king I want to be without your input. That being said, the method by which you give your input might not be, shall we say, exactly what we discussed previously."

"So we're calling it off, then?"

"Well—"

"Your Highness," Kat said, drawing a pained look from Adrien. "I understand the effort to spare my feelings, but I'm afraid I need you to be direct about this."

"Well, it's just that my priorities were rearranged. Rather recently, in fact." Adrien rubbed his nose nervously, glancing back at the dais as if to make sure Giselle hadn't vanished into the ether. "So the position we previously discussed might not be as available as originally thought."

"That position being . . ."

"Katrien, I know you know exactly what I mean," the prince snapped.

"Us lowborn infantry types are a little slow on the uptake, you know? I wanted to be sure."

Adrien gave her a sly look. "You would have been a troublesome queen, let's face it. Maybe the good kind of troublesome. But the realm's had enough trouble to last a generation, and you'll be just as adequate a thorn in my side as an adviser, I think."

Kat gave him a gracious curtsy, one Mira had drilled her on with the intensity she normally reserved for spear exercises. "I appreciate the wisdom of my future ruler."

"Yes, it is wise, isn't it?" Adrien said, stroking his chin. "Now, as your future ruler, I have only one command. Would you . . . mind telling me that girl's name?"

Kat barked a sharp, bright laugh and every head in the vicinity turned.

ONCE SHE'D EXTRICATED HERSELF FROM ADRIEN'S OVEREAGER questioning, Kat went in search of Emory.

She didn't have to look far. Despite the stiff way he'd moved that seemed to suggest he'd broken at least a couple of his ribs in the Final Lord's attack, he'd joined in with a small cluster of sol-

diers who'd taken it upon themselves to help clear the jagged
chunks of glass still scattering the ballroom. Every sweep of the
broom in his hand looked painful, but she got the feeling it would
take nothing less than a direct order from a commanding officer
to get him to stop.

"Hey," she said, laying a hand on his shoulder. He startled,
then winced, and she immediately regretted sneaking up on him.
"They've got more than enough people helping out with this.
Mind if we talk?"

The ballroom's far end played host to a balcony that looked
out over the flickering lights of Rusta and the glorious sprawl of
the stars overhead. It wasn't the most private place for a conversation, as roughly half the partygoers had decided they needed some
air after the demon attack, but there was an opening along the
balcony's edge where the two of them could fit, shoulder to shoulder, and lean out into the night.

"You saw Giselle coming, right?" Emory asked.

"Saw . . ."

"When you covered me instead of the prince. I assume that's
what you had to clear up with him?"

Kat snorted.

"What's so funny?"

"I hope you realize the only reason I'm not shaking you by the
shoulders right now is that you're grievously injured."

"I don't understand."

That only made Kat laugh harder.

"Are you saying that wasn't a feint?" Emory asked. "But that
makes no sense. You'd have to be an absolute idiot . . . You . . .
He's the prince. You deliberately covered *me* over the prince? The
prince who's about to—well, you know."

"He's not."

Emory blinked.

"He just told me. It's off. He's not going to."

"But that's ridiculous."

"Oh, it's ridiculous that he wouldn't want to—well, you know?"

"*Yes,*" Emory blurted. That furrow between his brows was back with a vengeance.

Kat resisted the urge to put her thumb in it. "Are you *mad* that he's not going to?"

"Maybe?"

"Why would *you* be mad?"

She wouldn't have been surprised if steam started leaking from his ears. "It's . . . it's . . . *wasteful,*" he concluded. "Extremely wasteful. Like throwing out a whole roast when it's fresh from the oven."

"Oh, I'm the roast in this metaphor?"

"Forget the metaphor. To ask a woman like you to marry him, then not follow through? I worry for the future of his rule if these are his choices." He paused, tamping down a hiccupping, almost hysterical laugh. "Anyway, back to the part where his life was on the line and you covered *me.*"

"What's that all about, huh?" Kat replied, propping herself up on her elbows and hiding her smile behind the knuckles of one hand. "I mean we already knew that I'm prone to bad choices. But fortunately, as is the wont of royalty, the prince has done us the favor of making it not a choice at all."

"Kat," he warned.

"You've been upgraded from worst option to last," Kat said, nudging him with her shoulder.

"Kat, there's no world in which you have *no* other options. Hosts, look at you. You're dressed in a ballgown, and you took on a demon. Half this party would take your hand in marriage the second you asked."

"Oh, so you want me to be sincere about it?" She leaned closer.

It was difficult to tell in the dark, but she swore the tips of his ears had gone even redder.

"I wouldn't be alive if it wasn't for you. I wouldn't have made it through the war if you hadn't had my back at every turn, on every battlefield, even when we were young and stupid and you didn't like me for some reason."

"I did," he muttered quietly.

"What's that?"

"I did like you. I was just terrible at showing it. You confounded me."

"Oh, every young woman aspires to be confounding."

Emory ducked his head, his shoulders coming up as if trying to shield his blazing ears. "Can we go back to the thing you were just saying?"

She could have happily teased him for another round or two, but it would have amounted to psychological torture. "The thing where I wouldn't have been able to picture a future for myself outside of all that blood and death if you hadn't lifted my head from it? The thing where I couldn't have made it to that future if you hadn't kept me going? The thing where you still want to argue that there could be someone better for me out there than the man I'm looking at right now?"

He opened his mouth, then wisely closed it.

"There's no ranking. There's no contest. The Aureans want it to be—to them it's a calculation, adding up all their gold pieces and seeing how high they can get that number. I don't want to play by their rules anymore. All that'll ever get me is cast aside when the math calls for it. I knew it was bullshit from the moment that math told me I was better off without you."

Emory tipped his head back and let out a long breath. When he lowered his gaze back to hers, there was a faint glimmer in the corners of his eyes. "Can I say something?" he asked, the words half caught in his throat.

"I need a moment to breathe," she said, waving him on with a frighteningly Adrien-esque gesture.

"I'm sorry," Emory murmured. "I've gotten so used to following orders, to *accepting* orders that I think sometimes I see commands where nothing is written. I thought you could change the world within the confines of the cage I built for myself, and all you wanted to do was pull me out of it. The last thing I wanted was for you to live in that cage with me—but you've never seen a cage at all."

"Might have been because I'm not bright enough to recognize it."

"Katrien, you have no idea how bright you are. The angels knew exactly what they were doing when they fated that token into your lineage. There were days on the campaign where I might have faltered, might have let the line break if I hadn't known that when the whistle next blew, I'd get to turn and see you. I thought it was enough just to be near you, to let you keep giving me all these little things to look forward to. You wouldn't believe the number of nights I spent staring at the canopy of the decade tent, trying to come up with the next dish I could tempt you with when the going got tough. I was so afraid of forgetting them, I had to start writing them down."

"You still haven't shown me the actual list."

"I have it here," he said, fumbling into the pocket of his dress uniform until he drew out a battered piece of paper folded several times over on itself. His large hands unfolded it so delicately that it might as well have been a book of prayer from the Age of Hosts. Kat called up a light as he laid it flat on the battlements, leaning in close to peer at it.

It didn't do her much good. "You can read this?"

"You can't?"

"Does that say 'milk steak?'"

"No, that's—" Emory broke off, frowning. "I'm not actually sure what that says. But the line above it is the hand pies. See the check? So it must have been something I was thinking about in Fallon."

Kat leaned closer as if that would magically rearrange Emory's handwriting into something legible.

"Stop laughing."

"I'm not laughing," she protested, but it came out garbled and even worse of a lie. "I'm . . . so ridiculously happy that you wrote this down. I never would have been able to remember all of them myself. I'm not sure this does us much good, but—"

"Oh hush."

"*My point,*" she continued over his scolding, "is that there's barely anything checked off here. We had months on the road and very little to show for it. I think we need to get serious."

"Serious as in . . ."

"As in forget that deadline we gave ourselves. Forget only seeing how much we could get away with between the Mouth and here. You and I are going to check off every single item on this list. As long as we can decode them all," she added, just so that he'd knock his shoulder playfully into hers.

"That's going to be a tall order," Emory said, tapping another piece of illegible scrawl. "This is a teahouse I heard an officer talk about once. Said it took a month of *their* wages just to get a seat. And this one's all the way in Sprill."

"So we'll save our money. We'll make a trip to Sprill—we can visit Von and his baker."

"It'll take a lifetime."

"Now you're getting it."

He turned to face her fully, his mouth slightly agape.

Kat felt it—that same opening she sometimes saw in battle, where she knew the moment had come to drive her spear home. Here in the half-dark of the balcony, surrounded by the nervous chatter of the other partygoers, they could easily be taken for a noble heiress and a brave soldier.

And even if they weren't, even if Mira spotted them and finally realized why she'd needed to requisition a new cot all those months ago, they'd both be taking their release tomorrow.

So she moved, her lips coming home to his as she curled one arm around his neck and used her other hand to tilt his jaw up. He opened for her eagerly, letting out the softest of groans as he threaded his arm tight around her waist in kind.

When she pulled back, she saw that his other had stayed on the battlements, white-knuckled as he kept their list pinned to the stone. She grinned, and grinned worse when he mirrored it.

"You know," Kat said. "I think I have an addition. But I don't know what to write for it—I haven't eaten all night and I saw platters of *something* that smelled heavenly going around before all the screaming started. Want to hunt them down?"

Emory was already tucking the folded paper safely back in his pocket.

CHAPTER 33

WHEN THE ROAD CAME TO EGREN, IT ARRIVED WITH SO LITTLE fuss that the residents of the duchy had begun to doubt Adrien Augustine's involvement.

It had been a full year since the prince of Telrus had completed the first part of the Augustine Road at a truly astounding clip. Much of the sparkle had faded from it by the time it made its way to the eastern duchies—partly because it was no longer combined with a victory march for the prince's troops and partly because it had taken so damn long to get there in the first place. *A full year,* the townsfolk grumbled. *Took him two months and change to cover the west, but when it comes to us, I suppose the prince thinks he can take his sweet time.*

Instead, the road marched along at a downright languorous pace, led by surveyors who laid out markers that were sketched in by the crews of laborers shoveling out the tracts. The grunts of the workers and the *skitch* of their shovels into the dirt was the only fanfare that announced its approach.

It was one of those late summer mornings where the sun poured through the bedroom window of their little apartment and made it downright criminal to do anything but enjoy the way it pooled on the sheets and burned off the chill of a night that was edging dangerously close to the first frost of the year. If shovels were *skitch*ing at this hour, they did so quietly and politely.

Kat had once dreamed of mornings like this. She'd never grow tired of waking up whenever she damn well pleased, without the peal of a horn or the shriek of Mira's whistle to command her.

And that wasn't even starting on the wonder that was waking up next to Emory. He'd never struck her as a heavy sleeper when they were on the campaign together, but she'd soon discovered that he was simply *that* good at following orders—and that without anyone breathing down his neck, he'd laze about well past noon if the day allowed.

It gave Kat ample time to take in the view every time she woke first. She'd let her nails skim over the broad slope of his shoulders, the swell of his waist, the places where he'd gone soft over a year without drilling and the places where he hadn't—mainly his arms and back, which he still put to good use almost every day. The sheets pooled around his waist where he'd tossed them off at some point in the night, and she'd let that hand wander lower, teasing over his hipbone, tracing the edge of the heat that radiated from him until she saw a smile start to tense the corner of his lips.

That was usually the point at which she stopped caring if she woke him up.

They could happily pass the whole morning in bed if Miss Ophelia had given them the day, but more often than not, duty called—not with horns and whistles, but with shouts and yells and the thump of small feet on the stairs outside. Today was technically supposed to be one of their indulgent off mornings, but Kat knew simply from the amount of excitement already filtering through their window from the courtyard outside that there would be very little rest to be had.

Not on the day the road was coming to town.

The kids had been worked up about it for a week, and Emory had led a few of the older ones out on an expedition to watch the survey team at work. The younger ones fed off that excitement, even if they didn't understand the economic implications of having a solid piece of infrastructure connecting Egren to the rest of the continent.

None were more excited than Kat. Less than an hour after waking—a record, on a day where she had leeway to take the entire morning off—she was thundering down the steps and sweeping into the kitchen, where Miss Ophelia was running breakfast with a level of skill and efficiency that would have swept Mira Morgenstern off her feet. "There she is," the old woman crowed, shoving a plate in her hands. "Big day today, isn't it?"

"Depends," Kat replied, ducking to the side as the twin boys Amos and Vicks rocketed past her and up the stairs. "Hey, careful!" she called after them, as if she hadn't very deliberately left the door to their rooms unlocked for exactly this reason. Half a second later, Emory's wordless shout of surprise confirmed the hunters had found their prey.

"What do you mean *depends*?" Ophelia asked, doling out another serving into an eagerly proffered bowl.

"Kat doesn't think he's going to show up," Marcy interjected helpfully from the breakfast table.

"Let's pray he doesn't if you're talking with your mouth full like that," Kat replied, wedging in next to her on the bench.

Marcy stuck out a porridge-laden tongue. Kat mirrored it. She was still getting used to the rhythms of the orphanage, even a year in. As an only child, her experience with kids was limited, though her experience as the hinge of a rowdy decade was plenty applicable on some days. On others, she clung to the advice her father sent in his letters—and made sure the expertly honed kitchen knives he'd also mailed stayed far away from tiny fingers. She lacked Emory's natural ease, but with older kids like Marcy, she felt like she was getting close. At twelve, Marcy was starting to come into a sharp wit that made her a terror and a delight in equal measure.

"Of course he's going to show up," Miss Ophelia tutted. "He wrote that he was. And you've seen the progress on the road. Barring the Mouth of Hell opening for a second time"—the old woman flicked her fingers toward the Seal in a superstitious gesture—"he has no other excuse."

"Oh, I'm sure he could come up with something," Kat muttered.

"Coming through!" Emory called, shouldering into the kitchen with one squirming, squealing boy under each arm. "Caught some pests. Gonna put 'em out in the yard for you if you don't mind."

"Noooo," wailed Amos from under his right arm. Vicks echoed the sentiment. Both of them made gagging noises as Emory leaned in to plant a kiss on Miss Ophelia's cheek that worsened when he crossed to the breakfast table and dropped one on top of Kat's head. She gave him a playful smack on the side—no lower, though she was tempted—and he continued past the breakfast table and out through the side door into the yard.

No fewer than three kids excused themselves and shot off in his wake.

Miss Ophelia shook her head ruefully, peering out the kitchen window. "One of these days, that man is going to sit down and enjoy a hot meal I prepared all the way through, and not a single person is going to disturb his peace. I just hope I live to see it."

"If he wanted to sit down and eat a hot meal all the way through, no power in the material plane could stop him," Kat countered. No higher order could interrupt the perfect little life they'd built for themselves—and it wasn't just the two of them, if the letters that trickled into the orphanage's postbox were anything to go by.

· Carrick and Sawyer wrote often from their new home in Brista, bragging about the joys of married life and asking none too subtly when Kat and Emory were going to give their sweet little ceremony a run for its money. Javi had found work in a bookshop he'd scouted out in Palomar, free to hunt down heretical theories to his heart's delight and debate them viciously in a correspondence he'd struck up with Gage, who'd veered in the opposite direction and dedicated themself to the priesthood. Brandt had taken up the duties of the first decade's hinge spear, boasting of the rebuilding effort he was leading under Mira's command in the far reaches of Kaston. Also in Kaston—and writing, curiously, from the same address—were Elise and Ziva. It wasn't clear if the kitchen girl was still in the picture.

All of them were finally free to pursue their own destinies without the weight of duty binding them, without royalty, demons, or the hosts themselves upending the course of their lives.

It was at the precise moment that gratitude settled that the knock on the door came.

"Told you," Miss Ophelia said. "Ask him if he wants breakfast," she called after Kat, who was already halfway down the hall.

"Back, back, you fiends," Kat grunted, wrestling her way through the overexcited pack of kids who had rushed in to fight for a chance to peer through the keyhole. Half of them were too little to open the front door themselves, and the other half lacked the temerity. It was on her to slide back the bolt, pull hard on the handle, and swing it open.

On the other side, Adrien Augustine waited, a coach flanked by a veritable half-century at his back and a sheepish grin plastered across his face that got more and more strained with every new child who peered around the doorjamb. "Katrien!" he cried.

"Your Highness," she replied coolly. "You're on time."

"Why, of course I'm on time. I wouldn't miss out on a single second of our reunion—especially not with the way they've got me scheduled for this provincial visit. Daya's been an absolute nightmare, as you can imagine. Accusing a woman of sedition has the most peculiar consequences. I've never once known the Lady Imonde to keep a schedule *apart* from when it's horribly inconvenient to me."

"So what I'm hearing is there's no time for breakfast," Kat said with a smirk.

"I believe to say otherwise would be heresy in your book," the prince replied. "However, I'm not sure I can stick around to see the fruits of my labor fulfilled."

With a flourish, he produced a woven basket from behind his back, absolutely overflowing with rich, red strawberries. Kat took it by the handle he proffered and did her damnedest to make sure that it looked smooth. No one in his retinue would suspect there was anything but fresh-picked berries in the basket, though it easily weighed thrice what it should have.

It had been unusually easy to guilt Adrien when push came to shove. He felt badly about the whole retracted proposal thing, for starters, and even though he was by all reports absolutely enchanted with Giselle Koros, who had become his fiancée within weeks of their introduction and would officialize her role as future queen of Telrus before the year was out, his rebellious streak was still alive and well. It left him remarkably suggestible when Kat wrote with her proposition. The hardest part had been convincing him of the delivery method, but Kat had made her orders clear. It was late in the summer, and the fields were still abundant. Adrien wouldn't come to her as a cleanhanded benefactor, dropping off his donation like a dress at the tailor's. If he wanted to do this, he had to get his hands dirty.

And he had. Kat would have no grand say in the future of the realm, but she could have a small one. One she cultivated and shaped right here at Ophelia's orphanage, one that went hand in hand with a future spent eating her way through that illegible list Emory kept in his pocket, which had only gotten longer over the past year. It felt like true alignment. Clarity of purpose, paired with unwavering intention. The Augustine coffers had so many Aurean tokens sitting in reserve, wasting away uncultivated, and Egren had so many orphaned children who needed not only an open door but a steady hand to forge their potential when they walked through it.

Already Kat was thinking of Marcy, and which of the angels' blessings she might take to.

The weight of the gold in Kat's hands was the promise of a long road ahead. But first there would be strawberries, and if Miss Ophelia could be convinced, a pie, and one more item checked off on a list long enough to last a lifetime.

ACKNOWLEDGMENTS

Starting out in a brand-new genre is no small task. Rewiring my brain to write not just fantasy, but romantic fantasy, after ten years publishing science fiction action/adventure books was a huge effort, and I couldn't have done it without the help of my own brave century of incredible people.

Enormous thanks to my agent, Thao Le, for riding the tides of publishing side by side with me for an entire decade. Thank you to the whole team at the Sandra Dijkstra Literary Agency for the additional support, including Andrea Cavallaro, Jennifer Kim, and Nick Van Orden.

Thanks to Sarah Peed, whose boundless enthusiasm guided the development of this book, to my editor, Emily Archbold, whose keen eye shaped the final product, and to Madi Margolis for all the editorial assistance.

A huge thanks to the whole team at Del Rey for their dedication and commitment to my work. Thanks to the publishing team for all their support over the years: Scott Shannon, Keith Clayton, Tricia Narwani, Julie Leung, Alex Larned, and Marcelle Iten Busto. To the marketing team getting this book in people's hands: Tori Henson, Sabrina Shen, and Kay Popple. To Maya Fenter for the social media support. To the publicity team spreading the good word: David Moench, Meghan O'Shaughnessy, and Ada Maduka. And to the good people in production, making sure my i's are dotted and my t's are crossed: Cindy Berman, Paul Gilbert, and Laurie McGee.

Thanks to the art team for putting this book in such a pretty package: Regina Flath for the art direction, Aarushi Menon for the cover design, Sarah Skrutskie for the illustration, and Alexis Flynn for the interiors.

Thank you to my critique partners, Tara Sim and Traci Chee, for their unwavering support as I forged ahead into this new genre and leaned heavily on their expertise as established fantasy authors. Tara, thank you for tolerating my whining over minutiae that I'm told "normal" fantasy writers don't care about. Traci, thank you for all the joyous craft discussions that have helped me cultivate my skill. Old Biddies Whine and Cheese Club forever. Thanks as well to all the writer friends who've cheered and uplifted me on my journey.

This story was inspired in part by a question I always had while watching *The Lord of the Rings: The Return of the King*: "What was it like for the foot soldiers who didn't know Frodo was out there when they marched on the gates of Mordor?" Thank you to J.R.R. Tolkien, Peter Jackson, and all the extras in the Host of the West for making me wonder.

This book owes a great debt to the soundtrack of *Frieren: Beyond Journey's End*, composed by Evan Call, which fueled so much of its drafting that my Spotify Wrapped for 2024 was not at all surprising. It also owes a lot to a video of Rosamund Pike demonstrating how to eat a pineapple without utensils.

Thank you to the Least Baddies and Patrick, because I could

not have written a herbo as magnificent as Kat without four years of practice at the D&D table. Thanks as well to my ever-expanding climbing group, for making it so fun to get up at the crack of dawn and get some jock time in. Thanks to Wop House for the online hangs and in-person vacations, and to the co-workers who make earning my living a joy, even when the hours go long. Thank you to my family—my parents, whose support means the world even if this fantasy book isn't particularly science-minded, and my sister Sarah, whose illustration work was key to visualizing these characters.

Thank you to Mariano for every late-night walk, every little treat, every far-flung adventure, and every way, small and large, you sustained me over the course of writing this book. This one's yours for so many reasons.

Thanks to the members of the book community who have supported me over the years—all the reviewers, librarians, booksellers, bookstagrammers, booktokers, booktubers, book bloggers, and anyone who's ever recommended my work to a friend. I get to keep sharing my books with the world because you share them in turn, and I'll never take it for granted.

And, finally, thank you to you, the reader. Whether you've followed me since the beginning or this is the first book of mine you've read, I'm so thankful you're here. Thank you for spending time in my worlds. I hope I'll get to take you on another adventure soon.

© MARIANO MERCHANTE

EMILY SKRUTSKIE is six feet tall. She lives and works in Los Angeles. Skrutskie is the author of *The Salvation Gambit, Vows of Empire, Oaths of Legacy, Bonds of Brass, Hullmetal Girls, The Abyss Surrounds Us,* and *The Edge of the Abyss.*

skrutskie.com
Instagram: @skrutskie

ABOUT THE TYPE

This book was set in Garamond, a typeface originally designed by the Parisian type cutter Claude Garamond (c. 1500–61). This version of Garamond was modeled on a 1592 specimen sheet from the Egenolff-Berner foundry, which was produced from types assumed to have been brought to Frankfurt by the punch cutter Jacques Sabon (c. 1520–80).

Claude Garamond's distinguished romans and italics first appeared in *Opera Ciceronis* in 1543–44. The Garamond types are clear, open, and elegant.